The
ORPHAN
of GOOD
HOPE

The ORPHAN *of* GOOD HOPE

ROXANE DHAND

BANTAM
SYDNEY AUCKLAND TORONTO NEW YORK LONDON

BANTAM

UK | USA | Canada | Ireland | Australia
India | New Zealand | South Africa | China

Bantam is part of the Penguin Random House group of companies whose
addresses can be found at global.penguinrandomhouse.com

Penguin
Random House
Australia

First published by Bantam in 2020

Cover photographs: woman © Jeff Cottenden; ship deck and mountain
© Depositphotos; background ship and mountains
© The Print Collector/Heritage Images/Alamy
Cover design by Lisa Brewster, The Brewster Project
Typeset in Goudy Old Style by Midland Typesetters, Australia

Printed and bound in Australia by Griffin Press, part of Ovato, an accredited
ISO AS/NZS 14001 Environmental Management Systems printer

A catalogue record for this
book is available from the
NATIONAL LIBRARY OF AUSTRALIA   National Library of Australia

ISBN 978 0 14378 966 6

penguin.com.au

To my sisters, Joanna and Sarah

⁓ PART I ⁓

THE ORPHANAGE

⌒ CHAPTER 1 ⌒

Amsterdam, 1683

TWO BY TWO, THE girls from the *Burgerweeshuis* marched to Divine Service. The smaller girls occupied the front of the column, barely a pace behind the housemother. Johanna Timmerman, in the first row of older girls, was smiling to herself.

'Why do you always look so happy about Divine Service?' asked Malliet, next to her.

Johanna threw her what she hoped was a stern look. 'Shhh. No talking in line.'

Malliet grinned and Johanna felt the corners of her mouth twitch up in reply. Sundays were the best days, despite having to spend three hours standing in the *Nieuwe Kerk* listening to the *predikant*'s dire warnings.

She drew in a breath and said quietly, 'I enjoy Sundays. We're out of doors for the only time in the week, and today the sun is shining. I'm with my friends.' She cast a glance sideways at Malliet to see if she looked sceptical. 'And . . .'

Johanna heard a child's wail, and a disruption in the line

ahead ground their progress to a stop. She craned her neck and saw that one of the little girls had fallen.

Poor little thing. The girl looked to be no more than six or seven years old. Johanna felt an urge to run forward and help her to her feet, but before she could set one foot in front of the other the housemother had gathered the child up, clucking and soothing her.

Johanna felt the swell of her affection for *Moeder*. Her kindness had been a great solace when Johanna herself had been small and lost, after her mother had died. Moeder gave the child one last pat on the head and regained her place at the front of the procession, but her movements looked awkward. As she led them all forward once more, Johanna worried at the hitch in her step.

It was impossible to tell under Moeder's cap and layers of clothing whether her hair had turned grey or her figure changed shape over the years. Only a gathering of lines that crinkled her eyes gave any hint of her age. Yet Johanna fretted at how much frailer the housemother had become recently.

Slowly, the girls continued forward, and she promised herself she'd seek out Moeder after the service. Johanna kept her eyes trained on her back, but as the line snaked towards the main entrance, she lost sight of her.

Johanna had nearly reached the outer doors to the church by now, but Malliet had fallen behind her. She could see the line of boys from the other side of the Burgerweeshuis coiling around the church towards the side entrance. Her heart began to race.

There were only a few seats in the Nieuwe Kerk, reserved for wealthy patrons. The children from the Burgerweeshuis stood in the area below the oak chancel, the entire complement of several hundred girls on the right and a similar number of boys squashed together on the left, unofficially separated by a double

4

line of grave-slabs that ran the length of the central nave. As the girls filed into rows in a single line, Johanna placed herself at the end of a row between the nave and a side aisle, with Malliet wedged to her right.

The congregation settled, and the predikant, robed and bearded, climbed his way to the pulpit, where a large Bible sat on the lectern. He began to turn pages.

Johanna glanced surreptitiously across the nave, her eyes searching for one particular face framed by golden curls and a square-cut fringe. Depending on the light and her imagination, his long-lashed eyes could be green or hazel or brown. She was never close enough to be certain.

'Idleness breeds wickedness,' the minister's voice boomed.

She shifted her gaze to the pulpit and forced herself to concentrate. Heer van der Meer would interrogate them tomorrow on the sermon. It was the height of discourtesy, the schoolmaster said, to ignore the preacher's words, which had taken him all week to write.

The minister always began with a reading from the Bible, which today was Proverbs 31. Next he read out notices and railed against this and that. He condemned the shameful wearing of jewellery and gaudy colours. During his rant about smoking tobacco in public, something Johanna felt she was in no danger of doing, she stole another sideways look and found the blond boy's face. As he was towards the centre of the row behind on the boys' side of the nave, it was impossible to keep her face angled up to God.

Malliet murmured in her ear, 'Face the front or people will notice.'

He must have felt her eyes on him, for he turned and looked straight at her. Her heart began to flutter against her ribs.

5

She forced her attention back to the minister, but the urge to look was too great. When she glanced back to where the boy stood, he gave a broad smile that made her feel sunlight had flooded the nave.

A touch on her elbow nearly made her jump out of her skin. She swung round to see Malliet's face tighten.

'What are you doing?'

Johanna drew in a deep breath and mouthed back, 'Saying my prayers.' As it wouldn't do to lie in church, she lowered her head and began to pray silently, repeating the only words she could think of at that moment. 'The Lord is my shepherd; I shall not want.'

At another touch on her elbow, she glanced up, expecting more censure, but instead Malliet flicked a finger towards the aisle. Johanna peeked round and was surprised to see Moeder moving slowly towards the door.

The girls exchanged a look. Moeder never left church early.

The minister ground on, but Johanna's attention was split. When at last the service concluded, the girls filed out to walk back to the orphanage. In the housemother's absence, the older girls bracketed the younger ones, making sure no one got lost on the way.

Johanna, walking at the back of the group with Malliet, was spared from answering her friend's questions by their mutual concern over Moeder. Up ahead, a girl turned and waved to them.

'Femke!' Johanna waved back.

The girl came hurrying towards them, frowning. 'Why do you think Moeder left the service early?'

Johanna held a finger to her lips, indicating the smaller girls with her chin. 'I'm sure it's nothing to worry about, Femke,' she said brightly, hoping the little ones would be reassured. 'We all know Moeder has so much to do.' She shrugged at the girl and mouthed, 'I'll find out.'

By now they had reached the entrance to the Burgerwees-huis, which lay concealed inside a narrow alley. They filed through the enormous columned entryway. The door had been left open, and to one side a sturdy young woman stood guard, her hair covered by a dark, floppy cap with starched points that fell to her shoulders. Over her green dress she wore an apron the colour of a cloudy sky. She watched on while the trail of girls walked past her, ushering them inside with a wave of her hand.

Johanna paused by her. 'Why did Moeder leave Divine Service early, Hilletje? Should we be worried?'

The maid shook her head. 'Darned if I know.'

'Do you know where she is?'

'She's gone to her rooms, most likely.'

'I'll drop in on her,' Johanna said, then turned to Malliet. 'I'll see you later in the refectory for the midday meal. Could you keep me a place?'

⁓

The light was dim in the housemother's parlour, and it was cold too – a mean peat fire struggled against the chill, the turf hissing like a snake. Moeder was still layered up, seated behind a table in a comfortable-looking leather chair, her winter-white forehead ruffled into a crease under her snowy cap. She had both hands wrapped around a porcelain mug that sat on her desk. As far as Johanna could see, it was empty.

'Are you warm enough, Moeder?'

The old lady pulled her hands from the mug and placed them

in her lap. 'Yes, I am, thank you. I'm never much bothered by the cold.'

'Would you like me to refill your drink?'

'That would be very kind.'

Johanna poured more coffee into the mug and was alarmed to see that Moeder had trouble lifting it up, her hand shaky with the effort. After she'd finally managed to bring the china to her lips, she shook her head and sighed. She looked tired out.

Moeder pointed to a wooden stool and told Johanna to sit. She did so, resting her fingers on the edge of the table.

'It's always lovely to see you, dear. Is there something you needed?'

Johanna took a breath. 'Forgive me, Moeder. I hope I am not out of place in asking.' The old lady smiled and she smiled back, acknowledging the unspoken joke between them about her constant questioning. 'I could not help but notice that you left Divine Service early. Is everything all right?' As she spoke, she noticed a letter on the writing desk. The seal was broken and the ends of the letter roll were weighted down to keep them flat on the desk.

'The predikant believes that the weekly cleansing of one's soul is not to be hurried. Today I could not face it.'

Anxiety knotted Johanna's stomach. 'Is there anything that I can do for you? Shall we send for the physician?'

'No, child, I do not need medical assistance.' A thoughtful look crossed the old lady's face. 'But there is something I would ask you.' She touched the letter roll. 'We have another little one joining us soon, and I would like you to assume responsibility for her induction.'

'Is Hilletje no longer to have that task?'

Moeder inclined her head towards the door. 'Hilletje is keen to move on with her life. She is twenty-three now, and feels that she is denying herself the chance to find a husband if she remains in an all-female establishment. I have given her my blessing to find another position.' Silence descended for a moment before Moeder went on. 'Of all my girls, you are the one I most trust to be kind and ease the transition from the life outside to our particular existence here. I know you felt it keenly when you first arrived.'

'Of course, Moeder.' Johanna smiled and then glanced at the desk. She cleared her throat, thinking that now was as good a time as any to ask a question that had long been on her mind. 'Do you remember the day I arrived here?'

The housemother's mottled white hand hovered by her heart. 'You were very little.'

Johanna looked down at her feet; now the moment had come, she fumbled for the words. 'I sat on your knee. In this room. You told me that my father wished for me to be here, but I have no memories of him. Do you remember anything at all from the notary's letter?'

'It was so long ago. But he must have had money to sponsor you. I have a vague impression that he was some sort of—' She broke off, a look of dismay crossing her face. 'No, no, surely that can't be right. Ask me later, dear. I'll see if I can recall the detail.'

⇜ CHAPTER 2 ⇝

T HE FOG ROLLED IN thick and chill off the Singelgracht. The numerous cargo barges appeared as though they were floating on clouds. Claes van Loon hurried alongside the canal towards his first day as regent at the Burgerweeshuis, an honour he'd not expected but one of which he intended to make good use.

By the time he passed through the huis's main gate, the church bells were striking nine, and nerves at his lateness churned his stomach. He hurried along the corridor to the boardroom, pausing only to cuff the sweat from his brow before entering through the richly carved door.

At the far end of the room, a man sat bent over a stack of papers, the long curls of his blond wig trailing over his shoulders. As Claes moved towards the table, apologies for his tardiness already on his lips, the man straightened in his seat.

'Terribly sorry,' Claes began. 'It's icy out and . . .' He trailed off in horror as he recognised the gentleman.

'Ah, Van Loon, I've been looking forward to meeting you.' The man rose from his chair and came around the table towards him. 'I'm Erick de Witt.'

Panic rooted Claes to the spot. What was De Witt doing there? This did not bode well. 'I know who you are, sheriff. My apologies for being slightly late. As I said—'

The sheriff had crossed the remaining distance and now engulfed Claes's hand in his own, pumping it several times before releasing it. 'No need. It's perfectly understandable. First day, inclement weather. Please. Do let me take your coat.'

He extended his open hand and Claes shrugged off his heavy cloak, handed it over and smoothed the lace at his throat and wrists.

'Take a seat,' the sheriff said, turning towards the table.

Claes followed him to the back of the room, unbuckled his sword and looked around for a place to set it down.

The sheriff waved a hand, indicating the back wall. 'Any-where along here. The corner, if that suits.'

Claes propped his sword against the wall near De Witt's own and tried to make his next words sound casual. 'I admit to being surprised to see you here, sheriff.'

'No need to be so formal, Claes. My first name will do very well when we are in the huis.' The sheriff took a seat and gestured for him to take the chair to his right. 'Make yourself comfortable and I'll talk you through the paperwork.'

He cleared his throat and sat down. 'Thank you. *Erick.*' He considered the documents piled high on the table before him and let his thoughts settle.

The sheriff turned to face him. He was perhaps forty. A tuft of grey beard beneath his lower lip revealed the likely colour of his natural hair. 'It's no surprise that I'm here, Claes. It was at my insistence that you were approached about becoming regent.'

Oh? Claes narrowed his eyes. 'Was it indeed?'

'Of course. Your reputation as a shrewd investor is firm in certain circles. I felt it would be of great benefit to the Burgerweeshuis to have you here.'

Suspicion prickled in Claes's chest, and he barked out a laugh. 'Surely you're joking now, sheriff.'

'Not at all. And it's Erick, remember.' The sheriff laced his fingers together and lowered them to the table. 'Permit me to explain. When a child is admitted to the huis, they are generally too young to have any knowledge of what inheritance they might be due. The assayer makes a tally of the estate before admittance. Our task is to invest that money to cover the cost of their stay.'

Erick paused a moment and shifted in his chair. 'Would you like some wine? I find it's a long, thirsty day at this table, and I'm sure you will soon feel the same.' He pulled a stoneware jug and two glasses from the cabinet in the corner and poured wine into both. He slid one of them towards Claes.

Raising his glass in an informal salute, Claes said, 'Of course, some children will be better furnished than others.'

Erick nodded. 'The luck of the draw. We are barely solvent, and we are to find ways of increasing our investible funds. This, Van Loon, is where I hoped you could use your skill and resources to help.'

Claes felt his stomach clench. 'Are they suggesting we contribute personally? I am not well placed enough—'

The sheriff held up a hand. 'Not at all.' His voice took on a different tone, low and conspiratorial. 'I am proposing you find ways to swell the orphanage's profit line. I thought this task might be of particular appeal to you.'

Taking a larger drink of wine gave Claes a moment to consider his next words. 'I recognise the prestige of being a regent. However, as this position is without direct remuneration, I'm not sure it's in my interest to solicit my personal contacts on behalf of the Burgerweeshuis when I may well need their assistance myself at some future point.'

After a moment, Erick nodded to himself. 'May I speak frankly, knowing that what I'm about to say will go no further than this room?' He narrowed his eyes.

Claes swallowed. *This is it. He knows.* 'But of course.' He could feel his pulse tapping in his throat.

'A clever man might perhaps find that the right course of action would lead not merely to profit for the huis, but for himself as well.' The sheriff stroked the patch of hair on his chin. 'So the only question you need to ask yourself, Van Loon, is: are you a clever man?'

Claes left his glass sitting on the table for a long moment before taking another sip, and then another. *Mustn't let the sheriff see my nerves.* He pushed the wine away and, careful to keep his expression neutral, folded his arms across his chest. 'I'll need some time and detailed information about assets and so forth. Are there records I may borrow?'

'You may take these ledgers home with you.' He gestured at a stack of folders on the table. 'Return them next week when you come back in. We keep a number of copies for just this purpose; that is to say, when we must source additional funding for the orphanage.' He gave a curt nod. 'I believe this will turn out very well for all involved.'

Claes straightened in his chair and picked up the ledgers, taking note of the labels on each. 'What about existing investments? How am I to know whether an idea is already in use?' He stacked the ledgers neatly on the table in front of him.

De Witt raised an eyebrow. 'Bring your ideas to me, and I'll let you know.'

Was that the sheriff's plan? To steal his ideas? Claes twisted his hands together in his lap. 'Very well. If you don't need my assistance with anything else today, I'll take my leave. I have a lot of thinking to do.'

'Of course. Give my regards to your lovely wife. Floriane Peronneau, isn't it?'

He wondered how the sheriff knew his wife's name, and what else he knew about his personal life. Aloud, Claes said, 'Are you acquainted with her family?'

'By reputation only,' said De Witt. 'Your wife's beauty is – I hope you won't take this amiss – a subject of much discussion in certain circles.'

Claes chewed the inside of his lip. 'I assure you I don't take it amiss. Floriane's loveliness is impossible to ignore. And speaking of my wife, we have it on good authority that the regents have a box at the Schouwburg Theatre, which we may now use. Is this indeed the case? Floriane thought to go there this evening, as the current play is one she's been hoping to see.'

The sheriff smiled. 'It's very much the case. Do you plan on accompanying her?'

'Sadly, no. I will be at home, working on ideas for the benefit of the huis.' He managed to keep the sarcasm out of his voice. 'Besides, I am no fan of the theatre. That's her purview.'

Erick nodded solemnly.

Claes stood up and buckled on his sword, threw his cloak around his shoulders and scooped up the stack of ledgers. 'With your permission, I'll be on my way, and see you in a week's time.'

'Until Tuesday next,' the sheriff agreed.

⟫ CHAPTER 3 ⟪

THERE WERE FEW SPARE seats in the Schouwburg Theatre, and Floriane was relieved to be sitting aloft in a private tiered box. Claes's appointment with the Burgerweeshuis had its privileges, it transpired.

She leaned over the edge for a closer look at the stalls. Women were passing along the rows selling beer while programme sellers cried out their wares. The audience was shouting, cracking nuts, spitting; dogs were barking. The din was almost beyond bearing.

The deep apron stage was set for action, and the four-part orchestra was already in position at its foot. She couldn't be completely certain, but by their number and attire, they could well have been the same musicians who had performed at her marriage feast eight years ago.

Behind her, the box's door opened, stirring the air. The candles flickered in the wall sconce and hairs rose on the back of her neck.

'Mevrouw van Loon?' The voice was male, and unfamiliar to her.

Floriane looked round. She recognised the man who had entered the box; his face was well known in Amsterdam.

15

Sheriff Erick de Witt stood in front of the closed door. His elegant red brocade justacorps showed off his neck linen and cuffs, immaculate in their starched whiteness. His eyes were strangely bright in the shadows.

'Might I join you in the box?' He took small steps across the floor.

She half rose from her chair. 'Forgive me. I understood I might use the theatre box without my husband in attendance?'

He took the chair beside her. 'You are perfectly entitled to be here as the wife of Regent van Loon.'

Sheriff de Witt had lines at the corners of his eyes, and his skin was slightly pitted with past illness, but it was the blond wig and greying beard tuft that aged him. As she looked more closely, however, she decided he could not have been more than two or three years Claes's elder.

He hesitated, and she sensed that he was making judgements, decisions. 'There's something I want to tell you about your husband.'

Floriane sat up and smiled. 'Is he doing well at the orphanage so far? He brought work home this evening. He was already immersed in it when I left for the theatre. It is his dearest wish to make his mark.'

'Before I tell you my purpose in joining you here . . .' Sheriff de Witt leaned forward and drew the curtain across the front of the box.

She felt her heartbeat quicken uncomfortably. 'What are you doing?'

'I don't want our encounter witnessed. It is imperative your husband does not learn of it.'

'I am happily married and do not favour your advances,' she said, hearing the fear in her voice.

He gave a puff of laughter through his nose. 'I have closed the curtains to protect your reputation, *mevrouw*, not to hide my actions. My purpose here is to tell you the unhappy news that your husband is a thief.' His voice was matter-of-fact.

She felt her mouth drop open and forced it shut. 'Really, sheriff, my husband has told me of your fondness for jokes, but this is too much. We've only just met.'

Fixing his gaze on the curtains, he said, 'Some weeks ago, a gentleman of my acquaintance was hosting a game of cards. Your husband was in attendance. A collection of jewels disappeared during the event, and my acquaintance has asked me to recover them in my capacity as sheriff. He has presented me with evidence that it was Claes van Loon who took them. It was only chance that revealed they were even missing.'

Floriane shook her head. 'You're serious? No. That is not possible.' This was all a misunderstanding she could smooth over. 'I can assure you that my husband does not make a habit of gambling, much less of stealing jewels. He's a good man. Hardworking. Honest.' She stopped to catch her breath.

'I should like nothing better than if that were the case, Mevrouw van Loon.'

'Peronneau. I did not take his name.'

'Mevrouw Peronneau. I wish I had better news, but the facts do not lie.'

'Claes is a godly man. He reads his Bible every evening. "Thou shalt not steal." It is one of his own very dear commandments.'

Erick de Witt glanced at her. 'I'd much rather it were otherwise.'

'You are wrong.' Confused, she stood up, then sat heavily as her legs gave way. Feeling light-headed, she covered her face with her hands and then dropped them into her lap as her shock turned to anger. 'Why are you telling me this? How did you know I would be here? Was your purpose to ruin my evening in casting doubt on my husband's integrity?'

'Your husband told me this morning that you would be here. I understand that you must be—'

'What?'

'Upset.'

She stifled the impulse to shout. 'Upset? You have accused my husband of thieving. You think I might be upset?'

He held up his hand. 'I'm very sorry to be the bearer of such disturbing news, but I'm here to ask for your help.'

Floriane inhaled deeply. 'No. I am not helping you put a noose around his neck. You will have to find your proof – if indeed there is any – from another source. I will not betray my husband.'

He gave a conciliatory smile. 'The rumours of your beauty do not do you justice.'

She bristled at the compliment. 'Don't think that flattery will change my mind.'

'I am merely wondering how you countenance your husband's infidelities, mevrouw.'

Her hands began to tingle. Applause rang out in the theatre, marking the start of the play. The distraction gave her an excuse to stand up again. 'I don't understand,' she said. 'Any of what you have told me.'

'Claes's *amours* are both widespread and well known.'

She felt her mouth go dry.

'Surely by now you have your own suspicions?'

There was a long silence.

Erick de Witt put his hand inside his coat and withdrew a rectangle of card. 'My trade card,' he said, holding it out. 'If ever you decide to help me catch a thief, my address is on the back.'

In the auditorium below, the pounding of hands continued.

She ran her palm over the back of the chair and snatched the proffered card. In three strides she crossed the room and looked back from the doorway. 'Just because you have told me where you live, please don't imagine that I will help you.'

Gripping the handle, she flung the door open, and, without closing it behind her, went down the stairs and out into the street. She told herself that if she kept breathing in and out, her pulse would stop racing.

The play had barely begun and it was still light. She chose to walk home, hurrying along the tree-lined canals, stopping every now and then to glance behind and check the sheriff was not following. Absorbed in disbelief, she soon found herself in front of the narrow townhouse she shared with her husband.

It was impossible that Claes was either a thief or unfaithful. When could he have found the opportunity, or the time? Were there clues she had failed to recognise? She didn't think so.

And yet.

She shook her head. Erick de Witt was a gossipmonger, trying to panic her into helping him. Claes was not a womaniser.

Floriane let herself into the hall and removed her shoes. She picked up her slippers from their place beside the door but, for a reason she could not explain, did not put them on. The house was silent. She imagined Claes bent over his desk, at work still.

And then she heard a girl's laugh and felt within her the uneasy sense that the sheriff's assertions might not be without foundation.

She tiptoed across the tiles and crept down the steep, dark staircase. Through the cracks, between the knots and splinters of the flimsy kitchen door, she saw her husband busy with the maid. The girl's face was bright with anticipation.

This is not the first time he has paid her a visit.

19

He pulled the maid towards him, patting her bottom with his hand. His hat fell over his eyes and perched on his nose, which made the girl clap a large hand to her mouth, to hold back her laughter. Claes had removed his breeches but still wore his stockings, which bagged at the ankles. With scrabbling hands, pale as the underside of a louse, he reached up under her shift and threw himself upon her. With each thrust of his hips, the maid cried out, her legs splayed on either side of his body.

Floriane tiptoed up the stairs, leaned her back against the front door and slid down its solid length. She bent her face to her knees and told herself to breathe. Nausea burned in her stomach as though she had eaten something vile.

Muffled laughter drifted up the stairwell.

She felt herself replaying what she had seen again and again, her mind protesting all the while. Had she made a mistake?

She thought she heard footsteps.

I have to get out of the house. Claes mustn't know I've been home.

Fingers clammy with perspiration, she stretched up for the doorknob as if towards a hand that might save her. It slipped from her gasp. She rolled onto her knees and pushed up to her feet, the fabric of her skirts slowing her progress. Heart beating wildly, she snatched up her shoes and let herself out of the house.

Outside, the light was fading. She stumbled to the canal then followed its edge towards the Nieuwe Kerk, but had no intention to pray.

The maid's face flashed again before her. Could there be some other explanation?

On the Keizersgracht, she paused before her parents' house, toying with idea of telling them, then she shook her head and crossed over the little humped bridge to the far side of the canal. It was the route Claes took to the orphanage every Tuesday, where he had just begun to work with De Witt, who had just accused him of adultery and theft.

Floriane walked on and on. She passed Dam Square then turned right along the Rokin canal until eventually she found somewhere to sit. Sick and exhausted, she twisted her betrothal ring round and round her index finger, trying to order her thoughts. However much she spun De Witt's words, she had seen what she had seen. There was no other possible explanation.

What an odd coincidence it seemed that she should find Claes thus engaged immediately after Sheriff de Witt had accused him. She asked herself if it could have been set up for her to find him. Perhaps it was the first and only occasion.

No. She could not stop herself thinking of all the times something in his behaviour towards one of their succession of maids had made her uneasy, or when one of his late absences seemed beyond the explanation he gave. Of course, the only time she had questioned it, he had sworn on everything he held dear that she was all that mattered to him in the world.

Unhesitatingly, she had believed him.

With a dry sob, she pulled the ring from her finger and tossed it into the canal. It hit the water with a little plop and disappeared out of sight.

She was still staring at the spot when an old woman carrying a wooden shopping bucket stopped in front of her and asked, 'Are you lost? It's late for a lady to be out here by herself.'

Floriane forced a smile. 'I know precisely where I am.'

'You should go home,' the woman said. 'It's getting cold.'

Floriane watched her go, Erick de Witt's words still swirling in her thoughts. She slipped a hand into her pocket to feel for his trade card. Its long, sharp edge stabbed at her fingers, and she curled her hand into a fist.

⌒ CHAPTER 4 ⌒

JOHANNA SPREAD OUT THE fabric for the boy's shirt she was making on the workshop table and smoothed it with her hand.

Caught up in daydreams, she said, 'What do you think it feels like to kiss a boy?'

Malliet straightened up from her sweeping and rested long fingers over the top of the broom handle. 'You're not going to find out, are you, unless one drops out of the sky and lands in your lap.'

Johanna heard the playfulness in her friend's tone. She stood up and stared through the window. A goldfinch hopped along the brick-lined ledge and disappeared into an evergreen creeper. Wondering idly if it was building a nest, she lowered her eyes to the courtyard below. The last of the boys from the other side of the orphanage were filing out across the yard. Dozens of them set off daily as apprentices to a trade, yet her gaze searched only for one. When she saw him through the rain-fogged glass, she thought how grown up he looked, with his workbag slung across his chest, the swing of his arm propelling him towards the gate.

Femke raised an unruly eyebrow and squinted at her. 'Which boy do you want to kiss?'

Lieken, beside her, laughed. 'The one Johanna stares at every Sunday all through Divine Service. You can't be that oblivious!'

Johanna looked away from the window, annoyed. 'Will you stop talking as if I wasn't here? I don't know what you're going on about.'

'There's no sense denying it.' Malliet flicked her fingers at Johanna's arm. 'We've all seen you grinning across the nave. It's been weeks now. You may as well tell us who he is.'

Johanna shook her head. She wanted to keep this private, and she definitely didn't want competition for his affections from the others. 'He's just a boy who smiles at me sometimes. I don't even know his name. You should all forget about him. The idea of any of us ever meeting a boy from the other side is about as likely as Heer van der Meer growing a new leg.'

Malliet swished her brush under the tables, in and out of the gaps in the thick wooden furniture. 'For what it's worth, Johanna, it's my hope too that I might meet and marry one of the boys next door, if that is what God has decreed for me. A kind one with a nice face.'

'I don't think God's path will have anything to do with it.' Johanna picked up her scissors and began to cut. 'I'd say it would have more to do with whether the huis can make money out of such an arrangement, and it's unlikely that they'll bother trying to match us up. If you want it to happen, you'll have to make the effort yourself.'

Malliet moved closer to Johanna, still sweeping as she went. In a low voice, she said, 'It's only that at moments you seem to forget you could get in trouble if you're caught. If you're going to stare at him so obviously in a church full of people, you'll be sent to bed without supper. If not for that, I would applaud you.'

They exchanged a glance, and Johanna knew that Malliet was on her side.

When once again the only sounds in the room were the rustle of fabric and clacking of scissors, Johanna eyed a small offcut of fabric, and stole a glance about her. Scraps were supposed to be saved for linings. With a racing pulse and sweating palms, she slid her hand across the table, enclosed the fabric in her hand and stowed it in her apron pocket. A sharpened piece of charcoal already lay waiting under her mattress. As soon as she found herself alone, she was going to draw *his* face on the stolen scrap and hide the evidence inside her Bible, next to the etching of her mother and father. It was the only way she could think of to introduce them to the boy she was determined to marry.

*

On the evening of that same Friday, Floriane was twisting her face into a mask of suffering and dabbing at her forehead with a handkerchief.

In his chair by the fire adjacent to her own, Claes was dressed in sober black with his square white collar stiff as a starched altar cloth. He appeared the embodiment of Calvinist sobriety – a staunch Sunday churchgoer, a part-time officer of the civic guard, a respectable member of her father's wine firm and, since his appointment as regent, a fanatical proponent of the Burgerweeshuis. Yet she now knew that behind the respectable public façade there lurked a shocking private man.

She toyed with the words in her mouth before speaking. 'If I may not assist you with your ledger work, dear one, I might seek my rest. I feel a little feverish, and fear I am sickening with something.'

His eyes strayed from his paperwork towards the kitchen staircase. 'First, you must allow me to instruct the maid to prepare a warming pan to slip beneath the covers. Your health is all that matters in the world to me, and sleeping between chilly sheets will do nothing to facilitate your recovery.'

Claes wet his lips and levered himself up to place a damp kiss on her forehead. He pushed back his chair and scooped his papers into a pile. 'Your forehead is not overly warm, but you are wise to take precautions.' He crossed over to the staircase and went down to the kitchen. Floriane heard the sharp click of the latch on the door, a brief exchange of muted voices and his feet on the narrow treads as he returned to the parlour.

Taking her hand, Claes helped Floriane to her feet and clamped his palm against the small of her back. He steered her towards their bedchamber with the determination of a captain set on berthing his ship, and tugged at the fastenings on his breeches. 'She says she put the pan in the bed two hours since, so the covers will be nicely warmed. That being the case, I think I might also profit from an early night with my wife.'

Floriane stepped out of reach and shook her head. 'No, dearest. Neither do I have the energy nor do I think that wise.' She pulled a handkerchief from her sleeve and coughed several times into the linen square. 'You have business commitments lined up all week and it would not do if you were to succumb to this ague that threatens me.' She coughed once more for good measure and touched her forehead with the back of her hand. 'Better by far that I seek out the physician in the morning and you take your rest in the guest chamber so that you are fit and well for the challenges ahead.'

Claes steepled his hands into their praying position and bowed his head. 'My health is a small thing compared to your own, and I will ask God to smile on your recovery. I will not abandon you in case you have need of me during the night, but I shall wait to join you until you are fully asleep.'

She heard how insincerely he said the words. She felt certain now that Sofi hadn't been the first dimpled maid to tickle his fancy. Did he tell them all when they were engaged into service that part of their duty was to perform *any* task that he might reasonably ask of his wife?

Floriane heard Claes creep into their chamber as the first shaft of daylight pushed under the shutters. He slid beneath the covers and settled on his side, his back curved away from her like the bowl of a spoon.

She lay in the fading dark and waited until his breathing settled into sleep.

Inch by inch, she worked her way to the edge of the bed, then swung her legs over the mattress and stood up. As she padded towards the door, she took care not to step on the floorboard that creaked. After a quick backward glance over her shoulder, she plucked her dressing robe from a hook on the wall.

He had been busy at his desk. He'd set out some money-making scheme or other, and had appended a sheet to his notes that bore a list of numbers laid down in two columns.

So, then, he had finally found something among his ledgers to satisfy Erick de Witt.

In the stillness of the early dawn, Floriane sat at the table and lit a single candle. Her most precious possession, a gift from her parents, sat in the circle of the candle's light.

The front panel of the slope-lidded Bible box was carved with spring flowers, the hinges shaped like butterflies. The three internal drawers had miniature wooden knobs like tiny, dark cherries. She drew the box towards her, turned the key in the lock, released the hidden compartment and extracted her journal. She took up her pen and ran the tip of the feather across her lips. She recorded the date – 1683, May 25th – and Sofi's name, as the recipient of her husband's ardour. When she was certain the ink was dry, she returned the damning record to its secret place.

She sat up and looked again over her shoulder. Reassured no eyes were upon her, she slid a sheet of vellum across the polished wood. Very quickly, in her close, neat script, she copied the list Claes had made from the orphanage ledger, taking care not to transpose the numbers, and locked it away with her journal. She took a second sheet and wrote her message; with every scratch of the nib, the words poured onto the page like water from a breached dam.

An hour later, holding on to the thick rope that served as a handrail, Floriane negotiated the steep, scrubbed stairs down to the kitchen, where the scent of Claes's tobacco was still strong in the air. The servant girl was asleep, snoring loudly behind her box bed curtains. Floriane leaned in and, none too gently, poked her in the side.

Sofi sat up and yawned. Floriane slapped the wax-sealed letter on the covers. 'Take this to the Kalverstraat address shown. Do not stop to gossip, and come straight back. By the time the hourglass is empty of sand, I want you at your pots preparing my husband's herring.'

The girl's lower lip jutted forward. '*Mijnheer* says he don't care for fish.'

'I dare say he doesn't, but swallowing something that is not to one's taste and being a better person for it is a true sign of godliness. Mijnheer is a religious man so will dig deep, eat fish and feed his soul. It will benefit him enormously.'

Sofi stared towards the kitchen sink, where three fish lay on a plate, their dead eyes sightless and milky. 'He says he likes cheese and bread better to start the day.'

Floriane turned her back and stirred the embers in the kitchen fire. She had no interest whatsoever in her husband's dietary preferences. There were far bigger fish to fry.

⁓

The maid laid the letter on the table. 'I'm late back because the gentleman made me wait, and he told me to return this. Said there's no need to reply in writing.'

Floriane stared at her name on the letter roll and checked that the wax seal was intact. She looked up at the girl. 'Not a word to Mijnheer van Loon, or you will lose your position here.'

'What would I tell him, mevrouw, except that you sent for the physician first thing?'

It was a shock to learn that Claes had discussed her with the maid. 'When did my husband say that I was unwell?' Floriane watched the blush stain the young girl's face but turned her back as she broke the seal on the letter. It was not Sofi's fault that Claes was a duplicitous rake. 'Never mind. I'll spare you the need to lie. Get on with my husband's breakfast and make me a jug of coffee, if you wouldn't mind. I barely closed my eyes last night and, as you rightly supposed, I have an appointment with the physician this morning.'

The letter was brief, the handwriting untidy.

Amsterdam, 26 May 1683

Mevrouw Peronneau,
There is to be an adaptation of Tartuffe – a Molière comedy – at
the Schouwburg tomorrow week that I hope you will be interested
to see. Please take this note as a cordial invitation to join us in the
regents' box at seven in the evening.

Your humble servant
Erick de Witt

Floriane was grateful there was nothing in the sheriff's letter to
raise suspicions, but she tossed it in the kitchen fire nonetheless, and watched it burn to ash.

⁀ CHAPTER 5 ⁀

IT WAS AS COLD as a church in the hall where the little girl was sitting on a high-backed tan leather chair, her hands resting on its wooden arms, her feet dangling short of the floor.

In the blink of an eye, Johanna took in the girl's pointed yellow clogs, the red knit stockings and the cut of her mud-splashed cloak. The flare of fear in her eyes was hard to miss.

She crouched down beside the chair. 'Hello. Would you like to tell me your name?'

'Annetje Ribenk.' She fumbled in her basket for a scrap of paper. 'I was told to come here.' She spoke quickly, in gulps, as if she were trying to swallow down something too big for her throat.

'We've been expecting you, and I know you are frightened, sweet pea. Everybody is when they first come here. I remember sitting in that exact same chair. I was shaking so much from the cold I thought about hopping to one end of the hall on only the black tiles and jumping back on the white, just to warm up my feet.'

Annetje brightened a little. 'Did you?'

'No, because just as I was about to begin someone came to fetch me, as I have come for you.' Johanna held out her hand.

The girl shuffled forward on the seat and lowered her feet to the ground. 'Where are we going?'

Johanna put her arm round the girl's shoulders. 'I'm going to show you where you'll be living now you have come to join us, and then we can find you something to eat.'

'All right,' the child said, and allowed herself to be led.

'We have a half-hour before supper. I'm going to find you a uniform like mine, and a bed to sleep in, and then we'll find you some friends your own age to talk to. How would that be?' She picked up the girl's basket and led her upstairs to the main dormitory. It was a large barracks – a bleak, utilitarian rectangle – where she would share one of the beds.

'The older girls are two per bed, but the younger girls are three to a bed. You'll be very glad of the warmth. At the city orphanage, they sleep five or more to a bed, so you're lucky you've a sponsor to let you be here.'

Annetje tipped her head to one side. 'Sponsor? I don't understand.'

Johanna dipped a cloth in a basin of water and ran it over the child's face and hands. 'Let's do this quickly or you will catch a chill. A sponsor is someone who provides the money for you to be here.'

The huis uniform was a vertically divided dress, red on one side and black on the other, over a linen shift and petticoat. The girl pulled the shift over her head then worked her feet into the stockings. 'I don't know who that would be.'

'Have you brought anything with you that you don't want to lose?'

Annetje shook her head.

'What about your necklace?' Johanna touched the beads around the girl's neck. 'You must hide this or it might be taken from you, to sell.' She lowered her voice. 'I suggest you put it under the mattress of your bed, as far in as you can reach.'

Nodding gravely, Annetje pressed her necklace out of sight, then pulled on the uniform. 'I look like I'm split in two. Wait, what are you going to do with that?' Eyes widening, she pointed at the knife that was in Johanna's hand.

'This is the worst bit, and you must be brave.'

Annetje was too shocked to protest as Johanna hacked her hair off at the roots, and then picked over the stubble.

'We have to make sure you've no nits. It's not nice for you as they'll make your head itch, and we don't want an epidemic in the huis. If you bend forward I'll scrub behind your ears and down the nape of your neck, because that's where they like to live.' She picked up the hair and tied the ends with a piece of string. 'The regents sell this hair to the wig-maker.'

'That's silly.'

'Of course it is.' Johanna handed her a cap, the same style as her own. 'Don't worry, sweetling.' She lifted the edge of her own cap and pulled down a long lock of hair, its red colour bright against the black of her uniform. 'This won't happen again. It will grow back soon enough.'

A look of relief appeared on the little girl's face.

Johanna handed her a pair of protective sleeves, which reached from elbow to wrist. 'Those are for the workshop and for house-work. We all take our turn – it's training for the future, when you'll leave here and find work as a maid.' She leaned in a little closer and said very gently, 'It is not so bad here. You must earn your keep, but they are kind and you will have lots of other girls for company.' She patted the girl's cheek. 'Shall I tell you a secret?'

The girl looked up at her, her expression expectant.

'Right at the start, on my first day, I was given a very useful piece of advice, and that was to say I could sew when the lady regents ask you if you have any skills. If you use a needle your hands have to be warm, so the workshop is heated. Now, put your feet in those nice new shoes and let's get you downstairs for supper.'

*

Floriane dressed with care in a lace-trimmed silk dress and brocade evening cloak, that evening less heavy handed with the dark smudges she now perpetually wore under her eyes. She did not lie about where she was going.

'The theatre season is coming to an end, and Erick de Witt has made arrangements to have the theatre box. He has sent a message saying that as he now knows how much I enjoy the theatre, he wonders if I would care to join his party.'

That caught Claes's attention. 'It has turned out to be fortunate that you met him there the other evening. This is too good an opportunity to turn down. Find out if he is pleased with me at the huis, Florrie. Make sure he knows how much time I invest in the orphanage. Try to secure an invitation to play cards with the well-connected people he socialises with or – better still – find out if he is involved in any shady schemes that I might use as leverage against him.'

Her first thought was of the jewel theft, but she said instead, 'Really, Claes, blackmail?'

He nudged her gently in the ribs. 'I wouldn't have used that particular word myself, but whatever dirt you can dig up on him would only help my cause.'

Do as you do, not how you would be done by, she thought bitterly.

33

Within the city walls, Amsterdam was a bewildering maze of interlocking side streets that thronged with life and smelled of open drains. Even though it was past six o'clock in the evening when Floriane left for the theatre, the city was not winding down towards sleep. Dogs were barking, church bells clanging, craftsmen were still hammering in their shops, and children swarmed the streets in unruly packs.

She moved quickly through the back lanes to the three gates on Keizersgracht that were the entrance to the Schouwburg. She was early. There was something she wanted to do before she met Erick de Witt.

A half-hour later, Floriane climbed the stairs to the box. Erick de Witt sat there alone, and she wondered how he had managed it. As on the previous occasion, the curtains were drawn tight. The sheriff was dressed in a long silk coat, knee-length culottes and white stockings. His cuffs and collar were elaborate, his evening wig elegant and well combed.

He rose from his chair as she came to his side and did not take his eyes from her face. 'Good evening, mevrouw. You look ravishing.'

Despite herself, Floriane preened at the compliment as she sat down. 'You are most kind, but I do not think I am here to bathe in your flattery.'

Erick crossed to a side table and poured wine into two glasses. Over his shoulder he said, 'In case Claes asks you, the acting in this Molière play is shockingly bad. The statuesque woman who plays Tartuffe speaks tolerable French, but she is purported to have learned the lines verbatim and doesn't understand much of what she is saying.'

She accepted the glass and took a sip. 'That might pique Claes's interest if ever he bothers to ask. Thank you.'

The sheriff lifted his free hand and let it fall to his side. 'He lacks judgement. I have rarely heard of anyone so prone to fits of impulsivity.'

Floriane swallowed, the shock of his words hard to digest. 'He told me he is looking for your patronage.'

He shook his head. 'That will never happen, obviously.' The noise outside the box was deafening and he paused. 'I presume your note was an acknowledgement that you are prepared to help me?'

Floriane forced a tight smile. 'If you don't mind, I have questions.'

The sheriff inclined his head and took a drink of wine. 'Of course, mevrouw.'

'I have now had time to think about this. If, as you say, Claes stole jewels from your acquaintance, why do you not arrest him? Surely that would be the easiest course to take?' She raised her eyebrows as she watched his face.

'My acquaintance has reasons for not wanting to go about this so publicly,' he said into the silence.

She narrowed her eyes. 'What reasons?'

'I'm afraid there are certain confidences I must not give away.' De Witt gave a curt dip of his chin.

'If you solicit my help, sheriff, you must provide me some reason to give it.'

Again he seemed hesitant, but after a few seconds he turned one palm up in surrender. 'Very well. There is, for example, the matter of security. Should others find out such a prize was so easily had, my acquaintance fears he would be robbed blind within months.'

She folded her arms and said nothing.

De Witt sniffed and took a drink. 'There is also the matter of Claes himself. Should, say, the Dutch East India Company learn of the theft, they would not hesitate to arrest your husband, march him to prison and – there is no delicate way to say this – torture him until he confesses. Believe me, they would not try to find evidence first. I fear he would not survive it, innocent or not.'

She drew in a breath. 'The Dutch East India Company? But why would they become involved?'

He moved his chair closer to hers and in a lowered voice said, 'This must go no further than the two of us, mevrouw.'

She nodded.

'They are indeed involved. It is my hope to find the jewels and return them, thus avoiding the whole ugly business of torture. I have no stomach for it myself.'

It was true that she was very angry with Claes. The betrayal she had witnessed had made her realise she hardly knew him. But torture? 'What is it you would like me to do?'

'We believe that your husband has the jewels still and suppose he will soon try to sell them on. I am asking you to search among his possessions to try to recover them first.'

'That could be a very dangerous occupation.'

He inched his chair towards her. 'Then you must be more cunning than he. We have spies who are watching him, but not in your home. Claes will find it almost impossible to offload the gems here in—'

A knock sounded at the door.

Floriane waved away the sheriff's look of alarm. 'Come in,' she called. To Erick, she said, 'This will be for me.'

A young man swung open the door. He was carrying his coat over his arm and Floriane felt his eyes on her, piercing dark eyes beneath his long, bristling brows.

Erick's gaze flicked from one to the other and back again.

'This gentleman is Heer Slootman. He is an actor. Before joining you here tonight, I engaged his services.'

She watched Erick's eyes narrow as he took in the purple satin coat and breeches, and the colour in Heer Slootman's cheeks – too heightened to look natural on a man.

Slootman handed her a piece of card and placed a pen and ink on the side table. She set the wineglass on the table, dipped the sharpened end of the quill into the pot and wrote down her address.

Handing the writing implements and card back to him, she said, 'Early tomorrow, then.'

The man bowed and backed out of the room.

After a moment of silence, the sheriff said, 'Would you care to explain?'

She held up a hand. 'After the theatre this evening, I will take to my bed and complain of fever and a weakness in my stomach. Tomorrow, Heer Slootman will come to my home before my husband has left for the orphanage and say that he needs to bleed me, and that these bloodlettings will sap me of my strength. I will need complete rest.' She picked up her wine-glass and rolled the stem between her palms. 'The visits will continue until I am fully instructed in the art of theatrical face paint. When the bills for my *physician's* services arrive, I will make sure Claes sees them. As I appear more and more unwell and the physician's visits continue, he will become more frantic for money. If he has the jewels, he will be forced to try to sell them, and that will be his undoing.'

Erick de Witt pulled a snuffbox from his pocket and snapped up the lid. 'You are as clever, mevrouw, as you are beautiful. This makes a fine fallback. I confess, however, that I hope you find the jewels first.'

Floriane stared into her glass as she turned things over in her head. 'As the theatre season is coming to a close, we may find it impossible to meet here for some time. Is there anything else you wish to discuss while we have the opportunity?'

Erick leaned forward, a distant look in his eyes. 'What do you know of the Dutch colony at the Cape of Good Hope?'

⁀ CHAPTER 6 ⁀

THE TIME ALLOTTED TO every task in the orphanage was defined by the regents. To complete a boy's shirt, the girls were allowed seven *schoften*, one and three-quarters work days. There was no time to dawdle. Everyone had their head down, intent on their task.

Malliet nudged Johanna. 'I forgot to tell you. They want you in the boardroom after the midday meal. Hilletje gave me the message. And apparently Moeder is not so well.'

Johanna started and ran the tip of a pin into her finger. Disturbed routines were strange and made her fearful. She sucked the bead of blood welling on her skin. 'What's the matter with her?'

A frown gathered on Malliet's forehead. 'She didn't say.'

'Is it fever?' She straightened.

'I told you I don't know. She's getting old, though. Perhaps she's just tired.'

'Who's looking after her?'

Malliet stared, her brown eyes blank. 'I'm only passing on the message, Jo-Jo.'

'Did Hilletje say why I was wanted, or by whom?'

'They want you to clean, I believe. I'm guessing it's Mijnheer van Loon, since it's a Tuesday.'

Johanna felt a fresh prick of concern. 'There's something about him that unsettles me.'

'In what way?'

'I can't really describe it. He makes me feel uncomfortable if I have to clean the boardroom while he is in there by himself.'

'For me, Sheriff de Witt is a touch more slippery.' Malliet raised her voice an octave and mimed taking a pinch of snuff. '"Put a little backbone into your sweeping, girl. Energy is the bedfellow of productivity."'

Johanna hooted with laughter. 'You should audition at the Schouwburg Theatre. The huis owns a two-thirds share. I can't see how they could turn you down!'

Frowning, Malliet said, 'Oh? How do you know that? Have you been snooping in the journals, Jo-Jo?'

Johanna lowered her face and fidgeted with her sewing. 'Whatever they want in the boardroom, they can whistle for it. I'm going to drop in on Moeder after midday break. Can you say you forgot to give me the message if anyone asks?'

*

In the basement kitchen, Floriane's eyes strayed to the maid's closet-bed, and away again. She turned back to the room. Sofi had settled her broad rump on a stool and was eating her breakfast.

'I want you to get some flowers from the flower market while it's still early and there's plenty of choice. I'd prefer roses if you can find them. The house needs brightening up.'

Her mouth stuffed full, Sofi said nothing.

40

Floriane lifted the plate off her lap. 'I'd go myself but I am not feeling up to an excursion, and the doctor said it is important that I rest. Mijnheer van Loon particularly asked that you might fetch some. He thought a long walk by the canal might be to your liking, and I'd like to give you a few *stuivers* so that you might buy yourself a treat. For the excellent work you have been doing since you joined us.' She shook her palm and rattled the coins.

It was a cheap shot but the maid knew no better. 'Of course,' she said, extending her palm. 'If you've set your heart on roses.' She took off her apron and hung it on a peg by the chimney. 'I'd better be off. The best ones are always quick to sell.'

Floriane crossed the kitchen to the door and drew back the bolt. 'Take your time, there's no need to rush. It will be just you and me for the midday meal, and I see you have already made a good start.' A copper pot hung over the spout of the tap, and vegetables lay cubed on a board.

Sofi nodded and seemed pleased. 'What with your stomach ailment and fever, I thought I'd make soup. Still no meat, though. Better give that a miss for a while, till things settle down in your tummy.'

Floriane produced her brightest wan smile. 'That's thoughtful of you. We are so lucky to have you as part of the family.'

When the kitchen door stood open, Floriane stepped to the side, allowed Sofi to pass and climbed up behind her to street level. It was early still, and shreds of mist rose up from the brown canal water. 'It's a lovely morning for a walk. Mind you make the most of it, and don't hurry back on my account.'

The maid wheeled round but did not reply. The grin on her face said it all.

Floriane closed the door with a quiet click and made sure the bolt was drawn. Both entrances to the house were now sealed, and she had time to search for the first time in days.

Heer Slootman had given an exceptional performance, convincing Claes that her fever and stomach ailments were serious. She must have her own bed. Claes must occupy a spare chamber and not make matrimonial demands on his wife. He must be patient and allow her to make a full recovery. Claes had a morbid fear of sickness and had moved straight away.

With the house now to herself, Floriane stood on the threshold of his dressing room. She surveyed the desk, the opulent rug that draped over his great wooden chest and the framed map on the wall, and felt like a traitor.

Frightened to her core, she crossed the wooden floor to his desk. What if the jewels *were* hidden there? Much as she wanted to disbelieve everything the sheriff had told her, she knew that at least half of what he'd told her was fact. Claes was a philanderer. If she found the missing jewels, it would confirm him as a thief. That possibility was too painful to contemplate.

The slope-fronted desk sat on a stand. It was beautiful, inlaid with ivory and ebony. She lifted the hinged lid, surprised to find it unlocked. There was nothing inside to raise the hackles of suspicion: a stack of quills and quill knife, an inkhorn and sand, ribbons and parchment for correspondence.

With her heart in her mouth, Floriane began to investigate the drawer underneath. Pressing her hands on the piles of paperwork it contained, she confirmed to herself that there was nothing jewel-like secreted beneath.

Papers, letters, there were so many. She pulled one out at random, her hand shaking as she held it up and began to read. A creditor was calling in a debt.

Mijnheer van Loon is requested to settle the debt of— She was shocked by the amount owing. *Mijnheer well knows the punishment for unresolved dues.*

Indeed. Claes would be incarcerated at *Castellenje*, the dire debtor's prison at Den Haag, until someone paid the sum owed. The humiliation would be unbearable.

She shuddered, replaced the letter and pulled out another. *Mijnheer van Loon is kindly requested to settle his account at . . .* A third letter from her father's lawyer was even more serious. It appeared that Claes had met an Englishman by the name of Stanford who had taken a trading ship and was crossing back and forth to the East buying and selling goods, making a fortune. Stanford was looking for a particular investor to buy in to his next expedition. Guileless, Claes had emptied his purse and found himself duped by a professional swindler. The lawyer wrote that there was no loophole through which he could reclaim his money. The amount lost was eye watering.

Tears welled up and blurred her vision, but she dashed them away with her fingers. He'd kept her in the dark regarding so many things. Were the jewels another secret he'd kept hidden? Floriane felt she was being sucked into quicksand. She replaced the letter in the drawer and slid it back into place.

Approaching the chest, she plucked the candlestick from on top of the soft silk rug that Claes had used to protect it. Like the desk, the chest was a beautiful item, its shiny lid inlaid with ivory, its handle apparently gold. When she felt the weight of the handle in her fingers, she was sure it was heavy enough to be real.

She knelt down in front of the flame-red wood and ran her hand over the beautifully painted ivory-framed panels. She got up and lifted the lid. It smelled faintly of spice.

Inside, the box was divided into six rectangles, each with its own hinged door opened by lifting a circlet of gold. One by one, she explored the sections, carefully removing items of clothing and replacing them exactly as she had found them. Among the folds and creases, there was not a jewel to be found. Running along the front edge of the chest was a narrow shelf divided into four equal sections by brass fittings, but again there was nothing on it, not even a hair.

Floriane got to her feet and brushed down the front of her dress. *I hope on the matter of jewels you are wrong, Erick de Witt,* she thought, but she feared that he was not.

⤟ CHAPTER 7 ⤠

His wife sighed and puffed out her cheeks. 'What are you doing night after night with those ledgers, dear one? I am beginning to feel that they are more important to you than I am.'

Claes looked up from his paperwork and cast around for something to say. 'You know that could never be possible, Florrie! The sheriff has asked me to investigate certain transactional possibilities between the Burgerweeshuis and the *Vereenigde Oostindische Compagnie*.' The Dutch East India would be a powerful ally – or enemy.

'The VOC? That sounds very important. Do you think he is taking you seriously at last?'

'I doubt it. He made a suggestion that I did not care to undertake.'

Grey eyes the colour of duck down peered at him. 'Was it dishonest?'

He was glad the room was dim, that she couldn't read his expression. 'I will not bother you with the specifics. It could have been spectacularly profitable, but I felt I would be laying myself open to ruin and dishonour if I was found to be the hand stirring the pot.'

'Did he accuse you of cowardice, like the last time he asked you to line his pockets?'

He examined his hands and picked under the nails, one by one, as he spoke. 'He accused me of lacking entrepreneurial spirit.' Claes looked at his wife, at the pallor of her face and the great purple smudges beneath her eyes. He thumbed some tobacco into his pipe. 'Did the doctor call today?'

Floriane smiled brightly. 'Yes. He came with a new medication, and says he finds me much improved.'

It was a game they played. She claimed that the latest cure was working, and he pretended to believe her. The shadows under her eyes only grew darker, her face paler. The undeniable truth was that Floriane was dying, slowly but absolutely, from something the doctors could only guess at.

He took hold of her hand. 'Are you warm enough, or shall I have Sofi fetch more peat and stoke up the fire?'

She withdrew her fingers and smiled. 'I am completely fine, Claes. I have my foot warmer, and Sofi is the sternest maid I have ever had. She keeps me wrapped up and will not let me do a thing. I feel quite idle and useless, but in recompense I am teaching her to read and write.'

'I thought she had those skills already. And she is not a member of this family, Florrie. I do not want you fraternising with the staff.'

Floriane bit her lip. 'Fraternising with the staff? She has no one else, Claes. It is our Christian duty to help her, and I will not abandon her lessons.' She pulled her shawl close round her shoulders. 'Tell me, what did Erick de Witt suggest you might find in the Burgerweeshuis journals?'

He hesitated. It was vital he find something in them that would bail him out, but he could hardly confess to that. 'The sheriff has indicated that if I can find something in these ledgers that will be attractive to the city fathers, then they will remunerate me for my services.'

'I know how hard it is for you, dear one. Short of selling off the children to childless couples, did the sheriff tell you what that something might be?'

Leaning back in his chair, he stared at the raftered ceiling. 'Not really.'

She lightly touched his arm. 'Would you like me to help you to see if there is anything that might jump out, even to a girl whose brain is so filled with cobwebs she can hardly think straight?'

Claes stood up and kissed the crown of Floriane's head. 'It is getting late, Florrie. Take yourself off to bed, but don't stay awake for me to come in and say goodnight. I'm going to have another trawl through the pages and pray to the Lord above that I find inspiration among them.'

As he watched her progress across the room, he crossed his arms and leaned his weight against the edge of the table. *Selling off the children. No one would buy an orphan, but* . . .

He picked up the logbook that related specifically to the orphans who had signed with the VOC in the past eighteen years. The record was scrupulous and bore the heading: *Notes Regarding Orphans Going to War*. Against the child's personal huis number, it recorded the boy's name, the name of his ship, the date it set sail and the outcome of the voyage. In the case of a fatality, it recorded the value of his estate in guilders, stuivers and pennies.

For a couple of hours, he ran his fingers over the columns, turning pages and peering at the entries, tapping the words with his forefinger as the idea formed in his head. His mouth curved into a smile.

Could it really be that simple?

He slid a sheet of paper across the table and picked up his pen. As the idea grew wings, the quill positively flew across the paper, almost forming his loops and strokes and curls by itself. Finishing his letter with assurances of his humbleness and devotion, and the hope that the honourable Company might allow him the chance of presenting his scheme in person, he shook sand over the parchment, tipped away the excess and touched his fingers to his signature.

The proposal was ingenious. Ensure that the orphans were unaware of their inheritance and not apprise them of the opportunity to claim it.

Surely this time, with the promised support of the sheriff, the Lords Seventeen of the VOC would bless his endeavour and start to pay him the money he deserved.

⮔ CHAPTER 8 ⮕

Beneath the dormitory ceiling, the long hours between waking and worshipping stretched out before her. With no lessons or workroom to fill the time from breakfast until church, Johanna almost counted the minutes as they crawled past, until the moment she would see *him* again.

Malliet pulled on her gloves. 'There is no way this infatuation of yours will turn out well.'

'Could you, for once, not play the prophet of doom?'

'I'm just trying to be realistic. If ever I saw an opportunity, I would try to help, but the boys are trained up and then they're sent away. Just like us. I don't want you to entertain false hope and to end up disappointed.'

She let out a laugh, which even to her own ears sounded shaky. 'I have to keep hold of something.'

Malliet pointed a gloved finger towards the window, which looked out on the boys' courtyard. 'You can't hold on to something you've never possessed. You might as well try to hold a snowflake between your palms.'

'That would be an excellent theme for a sermon.' Johanna

picked up her psalter gratefully as the huis bell rang. 'Time to corral the girls.'

———

Outside the Burgerweeshuis, in the bright July sunshine, it was for once a relief to Johanna that talking on the way to church was forbidden. Even though her head knew the truth of Malliet's words, her heart would not accept it.

Since the Divine Service in May when the boy had smiled at her, the merest glance he cast in her direction had set her pulse racing. Their 'conversation', though, had been limited to what their eyes could convey. She loved him but could not tell him. The distance between them was almost beyond bearing.

As they neared the church, the streets became more and more crowded. All but the infirm attended Divine Service. Trade was suspended. For several hours each Sunday, the bustling city stood still.

As the girls pushed through the doors, the church sexton was standing guard, ready to slide the iron latch into place. Inside, Johanna could hear the scuffling, the banging of clogs on stone, the creaking of wood from the privileged seats.

She rushed to her preferred place to stand, where her view of the boys was uninterrupted, and rested against a smooth, round pillar. She stared across the nave from right to left, slowly breathing out when she saw that he was there, the boy with the golden hair.

She found herself counting; were it not for eight other people, they would be side by side. If the smallest glance from him set her heart galloping, how would it behave if they could touch, if only for a second?

He looked up at that moment, and a silent communication passed between them.

He feels the same, she thought. *I know he does.*

Malliet patted Johanna's arm. 'Stop knitting thoughts in your head. You will drive yourself mad.'

'Is it wrong to dream?' Johanna braced herself for the reply, but the predikant lumbered in from a side door, his vestments ballooning in vast black folds, and wheezed up the wooden treads to the pulpit. At the top of the stairs, where the light was brightest, he held his hands to the roof, as if he was checking the air for rain.

The nave fell quiet of chatter, the church now so silent she could hear the swish of wings as sparrows flew up to the roof.

The minister droned through the first part of his sermon, preaching corpulence as the manifestation of the devil and cautioning against gluttony in the worshippers for whom he was responsible. Johanna wondered what Moeder would make of this when she told her. The man was none too slim himself.

Johanna stole a look across the nave. The sun was glinting in *his* fair hair, his head bent yet tilted to one side, his mouth moving as if he was saying the words of a prayer. The boy next to him leaned in and put a hand on his arm. It was hard to know for certain if words were exchanged, but then *he* nodded and wiggled his fingers to show the direction his prayer should travel.

She wove her fingers together and squeezed her hands tight as, one after another, each boy between her and the boy with golden hair whispered into the ear of the next in line. The prayer moved from lip to lip until it was there, across the nave, waiting to be heard.

'What am I to do?' she whispered to herself, unprepared for the surge of dismay that caught her.

'Drop your psalter on the floor,' Malliet whispered into her ear. 'The boy will pick it up and give you the message.'

Johanna looked at her in alarm. 'Did everyone see them?'

'Only those who were watching. Swap places with me. I'll do it for you before the whole church hears us whispering.' Malliet's face was determined.

'No. If you drop the psalter, everyone *will* hear and you'll be the one who gets in trouble.'

Malliet sighed and pushed between Johanna and the stone column, facing the keeper of the secret, who stood two frustrating flagstones away.

In one quick movement he dipped his head and Malliet sank to her knees, and by some happenstance they met in the middle. With an air of awkwardness, he took her hand and raised her to her feet. She grasped the skirt of her uniform, pulling it out from beneath her as she scrambled up. Whether words had passed between them Johanna couldn't rightly say, but seconds later Malliet was back at her side, a grin splitting her face.

Johanna stood rooted to the spot. 'Well?'

'He wants to meet you by the glass lockers after breakfast tomorrow.'

Johanna craned her head to look across the nave. The fair-haired boy gave her a shy smile and nodded once. The thrill that stirred her insides almost made her giddy.

⌒

The following morning in the workroom, Malliet put her head in her hands and let out a low groan.

The girls were stitching by the greasy light of homemade tallows, which in the early dawn lacked the strength to brighten the workroom to any helpful degree. However they angled their work, their eyes strained to see it.

Johanna lifted a wooden candlestick. Malliet's narrow face was the exact shade of a tailor's chalk. She was playing the part well.

'What is it, Malliet?' She spoke loudly, drawing attention to herself.

Malliet took a breath and whimpered. 'My head feels like it is going to burst.'

With the back of her hand, Johanna checked Malliet's forehead to monitor for fever. She was cool, just as she'd known she would be. 'You're rather hot. Shall I go and tell Moeder that you need to lie down?'

'No. I just need to keep my head still. My vision is blurred, but it will pass. It's not the first time this has happened, but I confess it's never been so bad.' She squinted at her needle.

Johanna clucked her tongue. 'I still think you should go to the sick room.'

Face screwed into a parody of pain, Malliet spoke listlessly, her voice monotonous. 'I need a quiet day, if only that were possible.'

'Just take it easy until you feel better.'

'I can't. It's my day to wash the lockers.' Her hand tightened on the cloth of her dress.

Johanna got up and went to the window, pretending to have a think about what to do. She stood there for a moment, resting her hand on her chin, before turning back to her friend. A sidelong glance reassured her that she had the full attention of the sewing room. 'You are not fit. I'll take your slot. Can everyone tell Heer van der Meer, if he asks, that I made a mistake with my housekeeping duties? When it next falls to me to wash the lockers, I'll just swap back with Malliet.'

The pair looked at each other, and Malliet nodded dramatically.

~

Johanna was in a frenzy of excitement when the breakfast bell rang and they filed down to the dining hall. The rectangular room was dim, lit only by a handful of swaying lanterns hung from the ceiling on linked brass chains. As she sat at one of the long tables, listening to someone read a Psalm, she watched the crinkly skin form on top of the porridge cooling in front of them. Too nervous to eat, she fiddled with her food.

When the bell chimed again and the meal was over, a uniformed army five hundred girls strong rose from their seats and funnelled out of the dining hall using the two doors at either end. Johanna and Malliet simply switched the doors they should normally have taken, one towards the schoolroom and the other towards the hall.

Johanna crossed to the back stairs and went down them towards the scullery, where a pail with a measure of shaved soap inside had been left waiting to be filled with cold water. She ran the tap and swirled the mixture around with her hand. The scullery was adjacent to the back entrance to the huis, so close to the boys' section that the shutters were only opened when the boys were known to be busy elsewhere.

The glass-fronted lockers were set into a wall in the boys' recreation area. Like the boys themselves, they were invisible from the girls' side of the huis. Washing down the square cubicles where the boys stored the tools they used in their apprenticeships was an unpopular task.

Johanna took a long-handled brush from the cupboard, opened the back door and walked into the yard.

It was cool out, the sky the colour of bleached linen, which often presaged rain. Gradually she drew closer, her heart beating fast as she mulled over the wisdom of what she was doing and gave herself a good talking-to.

This is ridiculous. If he's there, he's there, and if not, well . . . No! That doesn't bear thinking about.

There was no one in sight as she reached the lockers. Anxiety clawed at her chest as she dipped the brush in the soapy water and lifted her hand above her head. Somehow, she'd thought he'd already be here.

She set to work scrubbing dirt from the glass. The water ran down her arm and soaked into the cloth of her sleeve. For a few minutes, she scrubbed and scrubbed, as if the very act of scrubbing would erase unwelcome doubts from her mind.

'Hello,' said a voice from behind her.

She could feel his eyes on her, and her heart stopped for a moment. She wondered if he'd been watching her for a while, and began to brush more vigorously.

'Could you let me get into my locker before you scrub the glass away?'

Johanna lowered the brush and turned towards him. He stood two feet from her, looking down. His face was a perfect oval, his eyes the colour of freshly shelled peas and fringed with those long, dark lashes.

'Hello,' he said again. 'We are face to face at long last.'

She trembled at the sound of his voice and the way he looked at her, all the while trying to ignore the shakiness in her legs.

A sudden reserve had caught her, and to cover her awkwardness, she began to babble. 'We need to be careful. I got your message and I really wanted to come, but you are not supposed to be here and I'm not supposed to talk to boys. Moeder says boys can't control themselves so we have to be circumspect.' Had those words really come out of her mouth?

'That's a good word to have in one's dictionary of good words.'

Johanna did not react.

His eyes twinkled at her. 'It has two meanings. One, wary, is sensible, but the second? Where would any of us be if we were not willing to take risks?'

She clasped the broom against her stomach, gathering her nerve. 'I'm taking a risk talking to you, but it is worth it. Whatever the cost.'

'I feel the same,' he said, his voice a little rough. 'But I do need to get into my locker because I told the master I'd forgotten my measuring rod and had to run back to fetch it. I don't have much time.'

'Will you be in trouble with the master if you are late to your work?'

He smiled at her, his eyes amused. 'Yes, but I've waited a long while to talk to you.'

She hugged that information close and felt the pounding of her pulse as if she'd been running. 'Yes,' she said, for want of anything more inspired to say. 'It's been two endless years.'

His green eyes brightened. 'I always look for you. Your lovely face is the highlight of my week.'

It seemed impossible that he was there, that they were standing close, and she wanted to repay him, to give him back at least a portion of the joy he'd just given her. Words crowded into her head and she drew in her breath as she edged a little closer. 'I dream about you. Every night.'

He put his hand to her cheek and she felt the fire of it, branding her as his own. 'What's your name?' He extracted the measuring rod from the locker and clicked the door shut. 'I'm Frans de Jong.'

'Johanna Timmerman.'

He repeated her name. She could tell by the softness of his voice that he liked the way it sounded on his tongue.

Smiling and nodding, they both knew that, whatever was happening between them, time was not on their side. There was no way they could deal with two years of questions in two minutes of conversation.

'What work do you do in the orphanage, Johanna? What are they teaching you to do?'

She looked at the stitching on his shirt, but it was not a sample of her own. Disappointment flared in her chest that he was not wearing something she might have made for him. 'I work in the sewing room. Up there.' She motioned with her hand.

'Of all the things you might learn, that is the greatest skill for any wife. To be able to make her husband's shirts and those of their children.'

She almost swooned that he'd used the word wife.

Frans stowed the measuring rod inside his satchel and thrust a hand in the pocket of his long coat. He took her hand and pushed something into her palm, closing her fingers over it, and half turned towards the gate. 'I made this for you. But now I really have to go.' He took a few steps.

Johanna uncurled her fingers and looked down at the miniature wooden windmill that sat in the flat of her hand.

'Is this the trade you are learning?' she called.

He stopped and swung round on his heel. 'Yes. I'm apprenticed to a master millwright in the Jordaan, but I've almost finished my four years. In a couple of months, I'm sailing to

Good Hope with the Dutch East India's fleet to build windmills in the sun.'

As she dropped the broom in the bucket of suds, Johanna reflected that she hadn't any idea where Good Hope was in the world. But one thing was sure: if she could find a way to get there, she'd seize it with both hands.

She raised her eyes from the windmill. 'But when are you going from here? Will I see you at Divine Service next Sunday?'

There was no answer. Frans de Jong had disappeared from view.

⌐ CHAPTER 9 ⌐

T HE INVITATION THAT HAD brought Floriane to the Speel-
mans' house for tea had been signed by Clara Speelman,
but the handwriting on the outside of the letter roll was that
of Erick de Witt. Afternoon tea was all the rage in Amsterdam,
and the notion of Floriane's having met Mevrouw Speelman
at the theatre was plausible. Claes had accepted the scenario
unquestioningly.

The house on Herengracht was an imposing six storeys
high with a façade of sandstone, the outer wall of its basement
embossed with foliated cups. She knocked and a young girl
opened the heavy green door. As Floriane crossed the threshold, an odd feeling of complicity washed over her. Even though
Claes had brought it upon himself, at times she still felt uneasy
about her deceit.

The girl showed her across a spotless, black-and-white-tiled
hall into a richly furnished anteroom whose walls were covered
in paintings, mostly portraits.

A statuesque woman with dark-gold hair curled about her
face nodded to the girl, who slipped silently from the room.

There was a fine tremor in the woman's fingers as she held out her hand. 'Mevrouw Peronneau, it's a pleasure to meet you. I'm Clara Speelman.'

'The pleasure is mine, mevrouw,' she replied, with a smile.

'Please, sit and have a cup of tea.' Clara Speelman indicated a long, low table around which three chairs had been placed. 'You know Sheriff de Witt, of course.'

Erick set his cup down and raised himself to his feet. 'We are very pleased that you were able to join us, Mevrouw Peronneau.'

Floriane tilted her head in acknowledgement. 'Sheriff de Witt and I began a discussion about certain possibilities a few weeks ago. I can only assume your invitation relates to that conversation.' She sat in one of the leather chairs and accepted the proffered cup, which looked to be an exquisite import from Japan.

The sheriff nodded. 'Indeed it does, mevrouw. I received your note concerning the fruitlessness of your search.'

Floriane's thoughts flashed to the stack of debt letters and wondered if the sheriff's knowledge extended to Claes's gambling debts.

'And so I have spoken with Clara – Mevrouw Speelman – hoping to devise a new plan.'

Floriane wondered how much he had told her. She felt a flush of humiliation creep across her cheeks.

The sheriff's eyes rested momentarily on her face and she knew he had noticed her discomfort, for he said, 'We are all allies here and may speak freely.' He stirred his tea. 'We have a proposal to make to your husband. Mevrouw Speelman's husband is the commander at Good Hope. She receives letters from him whenever a ship returns to Amsterdam from the Cape.'

He exchanged looks with Clara Speelman, who took over.

'There are two possibilities that I believe can be made use of,' she said. 'Arent – my husband – has written that he is in need of a man to run security on the Cape, to deal with a number of recent incidents. Indeed, he has said as much to the VOC. Sheriff de Witt tells me that your husband is an officer with the Civic Guard?'

Floriane took a sip of her tea, acknowledging the fact with a dip of her head. She let her gaze roam around the room, studying the portraits. *Why is she not at the Cape with her husband?* She turned back to Mevrouw Speelman. 'The other possibility?'

'The VOC hopes to send marriageable girls to the Cape, in response to a request from Arent. These girls will be recruited from the Burgerweeshuis. To deal with the associated administrative tasks, an Orphan Chamber will be set up at the Cape and its running will require someone familiar with the way the existing system works.'

Floriane nodded. 'Claes would be a good candidate for this as well.'

'We can propose that he combine both within a single position,' Clara said. 'As regentess, I will bring the proposal to the orphan girls. Assuming you plan to go to Good Hope with your husband, perhaps you could assist with the recruitment and chaperone them during the voyage?' She picked up a small phial from a shelf beside her chair and emptied it into her cup.

'Am I to understand that there's a shortage of women in the Cape colony?' Floriane said.

'Indeed. The lack of marriageable women is the root of much unrest among the male inhabitants of Good Hope.'

That did not make the Cape any more attractive.

Floriane had been contemplating the benefits versus the trials of moving so far away from home since the sheriff had mentioned the possibility to her at the theatre. She was not fond of the idea of leaving her parents – whom she saw nearly every day – for who knew how long. But perhaps what troubled her most was something Erick had told her at the theatre. In the Cape, the VOC was the law. As angry as she was with Claes, as much as she wanted him punished, did he really deserve the kind of judgement the Dutch East India Company was likely to mete out if he were caught in some corrupt scheme?

Yet, in spite of these concerns, she felt she must see it through. She had to know. 'I would, of course, go with him. The difficult task, it seems to me, will be to convince Claes.'

'We are dangling a sizeable carrot,' the sheriff said. 'He will be offered the position of fiscal at the Cape. He would be third in rank after the commander and his secunde, his powers extensive. Theoretically he would report to the Lords Seventeen, but he would have free rein.'

Free rein? Floriane narrowed her eyes and, taking a deep breath, said, 'My search through my husband's things was not entirely fruitless. He owes money to a great many creditors in Amsterdam and was duped into giving a small fortune to a swindler.' She looked directly at Erick, reading his expression. 'But I see you were already aware?'

The sheriff nodded. 'I confess I know of his debts, as well as his substantial losses at the gaming tables.'

'Yet you said nothing.' Floriane raised an eyebrow.

'There is only so much unpleasantness one feels one may impart to a lady without appearing something of a scoundrel oneself.'

Floriane tapped a nail against her cup. 'I suppose that's fair.' She looked down at her lap. 'Forgive me, sheriff, but I can't help but wonder that you would offer my husband such a position knowing of both his thievery and his debts. Surely this is not the best way to keep him out of trouble with the VOC.'

'Believe me, Mevrouw Peronneau, I do understand your concern. If there were a better way, I would take it. But Claes is not going to return the jewels of his own accord.'

'I agree that is exceedingly unlikely.'

'So then, to catch a fox, one must build a clever trap. One he would never expect.'

As Floriane mulled this over, Clara lifted a small silver bell and shook her wrist. A servant girl, different from the one who'd answered the door, appeared at the doorway carrying a heavy tray. 'Shall I clear the tea things, mevrouw?'

Clara shook her head. 'The phial is finished. Have it refilled, if you would be so kind?'

The maid barely disturbed the air as she wafted into the room, removed the glass container and retreated.

As she replaced her teacup on the side table, Floriane thought of her own stout, lumbering maid and inwardly cringed. She looked across the table at Clara. 'I am curious as to why *you* did not join your husband on his very great adventure.'

Mevrouw Speelman's stare was still and unsettling. 'My health is delicate, and besides, I have no intention of going to the ends of the earth and giving up my life here.'

Floriane nodded and reached for her cup again. 'How would we progress this plan?'

Sheriff de Witt acknowledged the question with a bend of his head. 'I will allow your husband to believe that there will be opportunities to enrich himself in the Company's employ. You will help sell the idea to him when he tells you about the offer. And for Clara's part . . .' He broke off and turned to Mevrouw Speelman.

In that moment, Floriane wondered whether Clara Speelman's reason for helping in this endeavour might not be an attachment to Erick de Witt himself.

The lady straightened in her chair. 'In hoping that you would agree, I have already laid the groundwork and sent a letter to my husband, ensuring he is on side with our plan. Between Erick and myself, we can make sure the VOC is prepared to sign your husband to the position of fiscal and I shall arrange a visit to the orphanage to recruit marriage maids. I will let you know the details by letter, so that you may join me there.'

⌒ CHAPTER 10 ⌒

B Y LATE JULY, CLAES had given up the pretence of maintaining a clear head on his Tuesdays at the huis. It was still morning when he finished his second glass of the rather good red wine that Erick de Witt kept flowing. From time to time he thought he ought to be suspicious of the sheriff's intentions but it was, as Erick had once said, a long, thirsty day at that table, and he could only drink his gratitude.

They sat side by side, poring over stacks of documents, checking and cross-checking numbers. These periods of silence calmed Claes's nerves. They were working towards a shared goal, and that goal was to find a solution for his financial woes, though the sheriff was thankfully unaware of this.

Claes lifted his head at the habitual sound of Erick snorting snuff. The sheriff coughed politely into the curl of his hand and glanced over at him. 'How are you getting on? Need a refill?'

'Thank you.' Claes pushed his glass in the sheriff's direction.

He poured a generous measure for them both. 'I've had a thought, Van Loon. What do you know of the Cape of Good Hope, on the southern tip of Africa?'

Cradling his glass, Claes leaned back in his chair, thinking. 'I've read about the colony there in the *Haarlem Courant*. It seems a shocking sort of place.'

'The *Haarlem Courant* tends to focus on the more scandalous stories. I have a less biased source, as a member of the VOC's board of directors. But if that is your view, I don't suppose you'd be interested in what I was going to propose. A pity. I thought it might be a solution to your problems.' Erick took a mouthful of wine and leant over the table again, scratching furiously with his pen.

Claes cleared his throat. Looking at the table in front of him, he said, 'It was not my intention to turn away your suggestion, Erick. You know how much I value your assistance, though I'm not certain what particular problem you're aiming to solve.' He lifted the glass to his lips and drank deeply.

The sheriff continued to write for a moment, before setting down the quill and turning towards him. 'I don't wish to poke about in your personal affairs, but as you must be aware, rumours abound, and where there are rumours there must surely lie some truth.'

'What have you heard?'

'I'll not insult you with the details. Surely you know your own affairs better than any gossipmonger. I will say that, should you find yourself in need of funds, I have been asked to recommend qualified candidates for a position with the VOC. I would be happy to put your name forward if you—'

'By position, do you mean to say a *job*?'

Erick gave a little huff of laughter. 'I'm certainly not proposing you become a manual labourer. The man in this position would sit on the council of policy at the Cape and have certain responsibilities making him privy to – let's say – helpful information.

Although the VOC would pay your salary, it is the opportunities afforded away from prying eyes that I believe might particularly appeal to you.'

'I appreciate your consideration, Erick, but my father-in-law has cautioned against the Dutch East India Company. He says that no one but the shareholders make money, and that no private trade is sanctioned by the Lords Seventeen.' He looked into his glass and found it was nearly empty. 'May I trouble you for more wine?'

The sheriff bent forward to recharge the glass. 'I mean no disrespect to Seigneur Peronneau, but do you really believe that the Lords Seventeen, who reside to a man here in the Netherlands, can be aware of everything taking place on the Cape some five months' voyage away?' He widened his eyes.

'Perhaps not. But the more serious problem is that my wife is too unwell to make a long sea journey. I doubt she would agree to it.' But still, perhaps there was some merit to the idea. Distancing himself from his debts might well outweigh the inconvenience of moving his life to the Cape. 'When do you have to propose your nominees?'

*

Johanna stood at the window, watching the leaves stir in the breeze. She found the gentle movement soothing. Behind her she heard someone calling her name, but she didn't turn.

'Oh, there you are.'

She recognised Malliet's voice but continued to stare out of the window.

'It's no use,' Femke said. 'She's sulking about Frans's departure.'

Johanna sighed. 'I can hear you, you know.'

'It's rude to ignore us, then,' said Femke.

'Yes, quite rude,' Malliet agreed.

Johanna turned around to see Femke with her hands on her hips, and Malliet with her arms folded. She sighed. 'I know. I'm sorry. I'm just really let down he went off without telling me. I spent weeks hoping to see him at church on Sunday. Even now I . . .' She could almost read Malliet's thoughts on her face. 'And please don't say you told me so. That won't help at all.'

Malliet came forward and put an arm around Johanna's shoulders. 'I would never say that, Jo-Jo.'

She returned Malliet's hug. 'What time is it? I need to pop in on Moeder.' She started towards the door, stopping on her way to drop a kiss on Femke's head. 'See you in a while.'

Her feet carried her to Moeder's rooms almost without her thinking. She did not stop to knock and went in, making her way through the parlour to the bedroom.

Moeder lay sunken against the pillows, her large worn face worryingly pale in the sunless room. The ties of her cap were drawn tight beneath her chin, and made her skin look even paler than the last time she'd seen her. Eight years ago, when she'd arrived at the huis, Johanna had sat on the woman's motherly knee, hugged in tight against her ample bosom. Now the house-mother was thin and frail-looking, and exuded the sour smell of the very old. It broke her heart to see her so diminished, so helpless.

Johanna perched on the edge of the bed. 'It's Little Red, Moeder,' she said softly.

Moeder's brow furrowed, and Johanna cupped her hand behind the old woman's head. '*Hier is je kleine roodhoofje, Moeder,*' she said again, this time a little louder. 'Try to sit up. The regents

68

say you must eat something or you will have to go to the infirmary, and I will not be able to visit you there.'

Moeder's frown deepened. 'Why not?'

Fear that the housemother had lost her mind washed over her. 'Do you not remember? The building is separate. Only the nursing staff there will be able to look after you.'

The old lady shut her eyes.

She put her hand on the housemother's forehead. Her skin was hot and tinder dry. 'Do you have a pain?'

The old woman shook her head. 'No pain.'

Johanna leaned over, gathered Moeder's pillows to prop her up, and dipped a spoon in a mug of water. She held it to Moeder's lips. 'You must take some liquid to show the doctor you can. Otherwise he will take you away from your room and they will force you to drink. Please. You must try.'

Deep within the huis, a bell announced another shift. A flicker of recognition passed across the housemother's face. '*Haast je.*'

Johanna let out her breath, barely aware that she had been holding it in. 'No need to rush. We have time yet.'

The housemother lifted her head a little and swallowed the spoonful of water. Her mind seemed at last to focus.

'Study bell. You must hurry to your lessons.'

'It's not time for afternoon lessons quite yet.'

'But you must be somewhere. The bell means you must be somewhere.'

Johanna looked at her pinched face. 'I am somewhere, Moeder. That's all that matters.'

'We have a new little one due tomorrow and you must induct her, Roodhoofje. And on Sunday, you must lead the procession to church, as I fear I cannot last.'

The horror of the possibility that Moeder might not live to the weekend knocked the breath from Johanna's body. 'You need to rest, and soon you will be well.'

The old woman's hands clutched at the blanket. When she spoke, her voice was a reedy whisper. 'Hurry and pay the *uytkoop*, or you will lose everything.' She gripped the girl's wrist. 'I heard them, Little Red.'

Pay the payment? Johanna had not the first idea what her housemother meant.

∽ CHAPTER 11 ∽

A T BREAKFAST ON THE last day of July, Floriane watched Claes
as she stirred her coffee with a tiny silver spoon. 'You are
pale as a corpse, dearest. Are you quite well?'

He made a theatrical gesture across the front of his brow.
'My head is a little sore, that's all. This strong coffee is proving
of infinite benefit.'

There was a loud knock at the front door that made him
wince.

She glanced at him and then called, 'Sofi? Could you answer
the door, please?'

The maid stumbled up the kitchen stairs, rubbing her eyes.

'If they ask,' Claes said quickly, 'I am not at home, and you
don't know when I'll return.'

'Yes, mijnheer.' The girl disappeared into the outer room. She
was back in a moment with a letter roll, which she offered to
Claes. 'The gentleman wanted to wait, but I discouraged him.'

He stretched out a hand for the letter, then flicked his eyes
down at the address and mumbled something about time. When
a second knock sounded a minute later, Claes turned his eyes

nervously towards the front of the house. 'I'm still not at home, Sofi, no matter who it is. If I don't leave for the huis shortly, I'm going to be late.' He rose and went to gather his things.

Floriane clamped her teeth together. The way he was avoiding visitors made her suspect his creditors were threatening violence. She tried to listen as Sofi spoke to someone at the door.

After a minute or so, the girl returned. 'A letter for you, mevrouw.' She held out the letter roll. 'It was the same girl who came another time that brought it.'

The writing was Erick de Witt's. 'Clara Speelman's maid, I believe,' she said. 'You may set about your work, but stay near the door. The doctor said he would be here before nine.'

As soon as Sofi left the room, Floriane broke the seal and read:

My dearest Mevrouw Peronneau,
I'm writing to let you know that we have an appointment to present our case to the orphan girls at the Burgerweeshuis tomorrow week, on 8th August, at three in the afternoon.

Erick de Witt has told me that your husband is worried about your health. If you need to cancel, please let me know by letter.

Clara and Erick both knew that she wasn't ill. She considered what message she might be supposed to understand from this. She was deep in thought when Heer Slootman, carrying a physician's bag, followed the maid into the parlour.

'*Dokter!* I didn't hear you come in.' She levered herself out of the chair. 'Sofi, please go and tell my husband that the doctor is here. I'm sure he will not want to leave for the huis until the doctor has examined me.'

72

The actor followed Floriane to what was now her private bedroom and, under his tutelage, she applied purple smudges beneath her eyes and whitened her face with powder. She sat while he applied what looked like a small bruise in the crook of her arm.

As he worked, she murmured, 'Will you tell my husband that you fear for my life unless I have a change of climate? Tell him I need more sun and fresh air, that life in the city, in the grey Dutch climate, is only making me worse. You might also say that I refuse to heed your warnings because I don't want to cause him any difficulty.'

Footsteps sounded in the corridor and the actor smiled, complicit. Adopting his doctor's voice, he said loudly enough to be heard through the door, 'My dear mevrouw, I know it is not your preference, but you really must follow my advice or I can make no promises about . . .' He paused for a moment and then in a low whisper said, 'Do I have the gist of it?'

Floriane pressed her palms together and dipped her chin. 'Thank you,' she mouthed.

She sat on the edge of the bed as Heer Slootman left the room and closed the door behind him. A moment later, she heard the actor's muted tones and Claes's muffled response.

Heer Slootman's voice drifted past the door. 'She's resting now, but you must know her condition is grave.'

She heard Claes thank him as the two men walked across the floorboards. She stretched out on the bed, not bothering to turn down the covers, and a short time later Claes's heavy tread returned. She blinked her eyes shut and tried to slow her breathing.

The door creaked open.

'Florrie?' Claes's voice was barely louder than a whisper.

Opening her eyes, she took a deep breath. 'Oh, Claes.'

He came to the side of the bed and put his hand on her forehead. 'How do you do, my beautiful bride?' He almost sounded sincere.

A cloying burst of guilt surged up, and she blinked, concealing it with the pretence of fatigue. *Does he feel as badly as I did the day I saw him with the maid?* She coughed behind her hand. 'I'm well, Claes. The bloodletting takes a toll for a little, but it's all in my best interest.' She spoke softly, forcing him to stoop.

'You'll have to speak a little louder, you poor pet,' he said. 'Your voice is too weak to be heard.'

He sat down on the chair by the bed, saying nothing for a while. 'The doctor has told me he fears you will not get better unless you have a change of climate. He recommends sun and clean air.'

She shook her head and tried to smile. 'He said the same to me, but it is hardly possible, dear one. Things have only begun to look up since your appointment to the board of the Burgerweeshuis.'

He licked his lips and looked past her to the window, but she'd seen the glint in his eyes.

*

In the regents' boardroom, a fire blazed beneath the grey marble mantel. Claes was sprawled on a chair in front of it, a glass of claret in his hand, attempting to dry his clothes. The walk had left him drenched. His thoughts swirled from Floriane to the most recent creditor's letter to Erick's suggestion of opportunity the previous week. He had questions.

At the work table, Erick de Witt flopped back in his chair and pushed the tip of a quill up underneath his wig. He had a lively poke at his scalp and dislodged a spritz of dust – at least, Claes hoped it was dust.

Claes stood, picked up the chair from in front of the fire, and carried it back to the table. 'We should talk again about the Dutch East India,' he said, and took a steadying sip of claret. 'You said last week that you were prepared to put my name forward for this position. Fiscal, was it?'

Erick scratched at the tuft of beard on his chin. 'Are you reconsidering?'

'Is it too late?' He took another hefty swallow from his glass.

'No, not yet. I've been stalling in case you came back to me about the post, but I can't wait much longer. And yes, fiscal. You would be in charge of the new Orphan Chamber and would also oversee security at the Cape.'

'You mentioned *personal* opportunities. I'd like to hear your thoughts on what that might mean for me.'

Erick's forehead wrinkled. 'There are several avenues to explore. All the things you've uncovered here could work as well there, and you would be under a great deal less scrutiny. You'd need to be creative, though.'

Claes narrowed his eyes, thinking. 'What's the climate like?'

'The climate?'

'Yes, the climate. Floriane's physician informed me this morning that if ever she is to get better, she must have sunshine and fresh air.'

'Ah, I see. Southern Africa has both of those. Long, sunny days. Cool nights. Far from the large cities of Europe, so the air is clean.' Erick went back to the document in front of him. 'Is that your reason for reconsidering?'

'It's only one of several,' Claes said. 'Just how likely is it, do you think, that the VOC would actually offer me this position? If I wanted it, that is to say.'

'If you are serious about it, Van Loon, I will not propose another candidate. I'll extol your virtues, and your relevant experience in all the applicable areas. Your wife would also be an asset. You know, I assume, that she's agreed to help Clara Speelman recruit marriageable girls from the Burgerweeshuis to send to the Cape?'

Claes turned this around in his head. 'I believe she mentioned it.' Truthfully, he hardly recalled. He'd been rather distracted in recent weeks with Sofi. Perhaps he hadn't paid sufficient attention to his wife, but she hadn't complained of neglect.

'It would help your case enormously if you could secure her agreement to accompany you to the Cape.'

A long sea voyage might be too taxing for her frail health, but her physician had been adamant she needed a change of climate. It seemed there was some risk to her health, whether she went to the Cape or not.

'I will speak to her this very evening,' he promised. 'And let you know what she says.'

⌐ CHAPTER 12 ⌐

AFTER LUNCH, AT THREE o'clock, the huis bell rang three times. The only other time Johanna could remember it ringing more than once was when one of the regents had died.

In the refectory, Regentess Speelman stood on the raised platform wearing a yellow jacket trimmed with white fur, and pearls at her neck and ears. Accompanying her was another great lady in a low-fronted lilac dress with a magnificent head of pale, powdered curls covered only by a small, flat cap.

Involuntarily, Johanna's hand flew to her own headwrap.

Malliet was by her side. 'I know,' she said. 'I, too, dream of showing my glossy mane off one day and wearing a string of pearls in my bun.'

'That's not likely to happen in your lifetime,' Johanna retorted softly, hiding a laugh behind her hand. 'Why do you think they are here?'

'Hilletje said they're on a recruitment drive.'

'Recruitment? For what purpose?'

Malliet shook her head. 'I think we're about to find out.'

Regentess Speelman placed a stack of paper on the lectern

used for the evening Bible reading. Rather than speak freely, she began to read from her notes. 'Thank you for attending, girls.'

'Not as if we had a choice,' Malliet whispered.

Johanna kicked her ankle to shush her.

'I know that some of you – particularly in the sewing room – will be anxious for your output. We have decided to credit you with an extra *schoft* so that you will not be inconvenienced.'

'At least we won't have to creep out in the middle of the night to catch up,' Johanna muttered. There had been quite a lot of that since Moeder's illness had taken firm hold.

'I would rather stay up late working than be sent to bed without supper,' Malliet whispered.

The woman looked up from her paperwork but almost instantly looked back down. 'I am sure you are all wondering at the nature of this meeting. We have a most exciting proposal to put to you all on behalf of the huis and the Dutch East India Company.' She paused for a moment as if she was expecting a round of applause. When she was met with silence, she coughed twice and cleared her throat. 'This is an unprecedented opportunity that you are being offered, young ladies. Skilled workers are required as . . .' She seemed to lose her place, but then rallied. 'As wives for many of the company's servants. Women such as yourselves, who understand the meaning of hard work.'

Johanna wondered if someone else had written her words. She seemed disproportionately nervous for someone simply reading from a page.

The other lady touched her arm. They exchanged places and the regentess took a seat on a heavily padded stool.

'Good afternoon, everyone. My name is Floriane Peronneau. I am the wife of your regent Claes van Loon, and it's my pleasure to explain this extraordinary offer. I am sure that many of you will have heard of the Dutch East India Company. Perhaps some of you even have brothers in their employ?' Her eyes flashed round the room.

Johanna turned her head to look as well, but there was only a sea of blank faces.

'Briefly, then, the Dutch East India Company is the most powerful trading company in the world, with a vast fleet of ships that sail between Texel to our north and Batavia in the Far East, primarily to trade for spices. Halfway between the two is the cape of southern Africa. The Dutch East India have established a colony called Good Hope there, where the fleet put in and reprovision.'

Johanna drew in a breath and straightened in her seat. Frans's words rang in her head. *In a couple of months, I'm sailing to Good Hope with the Dutch East India's fleet . . .*

Malliet shuffled closer on the bench and muttered, 'Why are we being lectured on the trading habits of the Dutch East India Company?'

Mevrouw Peronneau looked directly at them. 'Is there a question?'

Malliet looked down. 'No, mevrouw.'

The lady continued. 'I am merely giving you some background. The Company is looking for volunteers to sail to the Cape, and is offering free passage to any girl from the Burgerweeshuis who is brave enough to make the journey.'

Free passage? It seemed too good to be true.

The room was very quiet, a hundred or so girls waiting for the lady to go on.

'There are a lot of gentlemen at Good Hope whose dearest wish is to marry, but there are not enough women to go around. The Dutch East India Company is very much hoping that some of you older girls will find the prospect of offering yourselves as marriage maids to the colony's more affluent free burghers too tempting an opportunity to pass up.'

A lot of gentlemen, Johanna thought. *But not Frans. Surely it's too soon for him to be there.*

Malliet raised her hand to catch the lady's attention. 'May I ask a question now, Mevrouw Peronneau?'

'Of course, dear.'

Malliet stood up. 'The schoolmaster says that the Cape colony is populated by savages who steal from the settlers, and even kill and eat them, because the original settlers stole their land.'

Floriane Peronneau stared at the page as if trying to focus on writing that was too small to read. 'Um. Oh. That may once have been the case. But—' She turned her head to Clara Speelman and an awkward look passed between them. 'I am sure that the heathen tribes have long since converted to Christianity.'

'What I am wondering is, did the early settlers steal from them?' Malliet folded her arms tight across her stomach.

The woman looked confused. She opened her mouth then shut it before mustering a response. 'I am not sure, but I think the point is that there is so much land in Africa the Dutch East India Company is giving it away to those men who pledge to work hard in Good Hope. Those men need wives, which is why we are having this discussion.'

Johanna jumped up and dropped a restraining hand on Malliet's sleeve. 'May anyone apply to go?'

'We have only forty-eight places to offer, so the sooner you make up your minds, the less likely you are to be disappointed.'

'What are the requirements?' Johanna said pointedly.

Mevrouw Peronneau looked at Regentess Speelman, who said, 'You must be at least seventeen, have been trained in a useful skill, and be healthy enough to safely make the five-month sea voyage.'

Johanna nodded and sat down.

Mevrouw Peronneau smiled at her audience. 'Does anyone else wish to speak?' She waited a moment, her eyes scanning the room, before adding, 'We will come back in a week to take names for the list, and if you decide that you would like to go, we will talk to you each individually so that you know precisely what you are committing yourself to.'

⌐∘

Two days later, on 10 August 1683, Moeder was laid to rest in the cemetery surrounding the Nieuwe Kerk. The summer rains returned, lashing down and soaking the hems of the girls' skirts as they huddled at the graveside. Their grief was a terrible sound.

The predikant sloshed back and forth in his sober robes, oozing self-importance, as if he might turn the rain into wine. He read a few brief verses before the coffin lid was screwed down tight, yet Johanna barely heard his words. They held no meaning and gave her no comfort. She looked at his flabby, white face and watched his lips move but understood nothing.

How could she absorb the loss of the woman who had become her beloved second mother and go back to her life as if nothing had changed? They'd had more in common than she could have imagined – the only child of an only child, father some unknown spectre. As she stood in the rain, Johanna berated herself that she'd not learned more about the housemother when there had still been time.

Her jaw clamped tight, she was consumed with misery. Tears poured down her cheeks and dripped from her chin to her cloak as Mevrouw Visser was lowered into the sodden ground and the earth piled up on the coffin.

One by one, the mourners turned away.

'Goodbye,' she whispered, her throat aching. 'I will never forget you, and the pain in my heart is almost beyond bearing. I hope you know how much we loved you,' she sniffed. 'That you saw your family of faithful girls whose heads sagged to their chests with the weight of their sorrow. We will never again hear your voice or gain comfort from your words. What will we do without you?' she tried to ask, but her throat was too tight to allow the words out. 'You are gone to God and we must somehow learn to bear it. Goodbye, dear Moeder. Amen.'

The August sun spilled onto the polished dormitory floor in pools of golden light. Johanna's eyes stung with all the tears she'd shed in the past two days. She leaned out of the window and swung the shutters in. It was stifling, but they needed some privacy to talk.

Malliet kicked off her shoes and lay down on the bed, hands behind her head, her feet raised against the pillows. Her eyelids, too, were red and puffy. 'So what do we think about the Dutch East India Company business?'

Hilletje stood over a pail of water and rolled her apron in her fingers. 'I'm going to go.'

'Have you decided already?' Johanna preferred to remain standing. She pulled off her cap and felt instantly cooler.

'Why not?' Hilletje shrugged. 'I've been looking for a new position for a while now, and if a wealthy old bugger is prepared to marry me, why should I care where in the world that is? It's almost too good to be true.'

'Frans is going to the Cape.' Johanna lifted her hair off her neck and wound it round her fingers.

Femke blinked at her. 'How do you know?'

'He told me when he gave me the windmill. He's sailing with the Dutch East India fleet.'

Hilletje splashed her hands in the bucket and patted her face. 'You have got to put him out of your head. If we sign their papers and agree to go, we are saying we are happy to marry a rich burgher when we get there – not some orphan boy.'

'He's not some orphan boy. I'm going to marry Frans. I'll work out how to make it happen when I get there.'

Femke wrapped her skinny arms around Johanna's waist. 'What if they won't let you?'

Johanna shook her head. 'There will be a way. There's bound to be.' She stole a glance at her friends. 'I'm thinking I'm also going to sign.'

'I don't think any of us has properly thought this through,' Malliet said.

Tears started rolling down Femke's face. 'I know you'll all go, and I'll get left behind because I'm too young.'

Johanna hugged her close. 'Don't cry, sweet pea. There will be other opportunities, and once we get there, the Dutch East India will realise what a good plan they've hatched and they will want more girls. You can come out then and join us.'

Femke looked at the others. 'Do you all think so?'

'Of course they do, and anyway, I have a huge favour to ask you, and there is no one else I would trust with this except you.'

'What favour?'

Johanna crouched down until their eyes were level. 'To look after Annetje Ribenk. She's still finding her feet and needs a best friend.'

'Like you and Malliet?'

'Yes. Like me and Malliet.'

Malliet let out a sigh of resignation. 'I guess that means I'm going to the Cape.'

⟿ CHAPTER 13 ⟾

A WEEK LATER, FLORIANE returned to the Burgerweeshuis. She followed Clara Speelman past a short line of girls waiting at the door to the boardroom. Inside, the table was laid out with paper, ink and pen.

Clara stood at the door, looking at each girl. 'Is this the full complement?' she asked, her eyes wide with disbelief.

A girl with a broad face gave a polite nod of her head. 'Yes, mevrouw.' Floriane recognised her from the earlier visit.

Another girl Floriane recalled, a pretty girl with a spray of fine freckles, said that only eight were willing to travel. 'We've all spent a great deal of time talking about it over the past week. Many have brothers and sisters in the huis and do not want to leave them. Those of us here now are totally on our own. We are making the voyage because we have the courage to hope we might do better there than in Amsterdam. Our dearest Moeder taught us that fortune favours the brave.'

Floriane touched her palm to her heart. 'I am sorry for your recent loss. I understand that Mevrouw Visser was very well loved.'

The girl's eyes welled up and she looked away.

Tears also stung Floriane's eyes. She was so close to her own mother that the thought of her dying one day was almost too painful to bear. Pushing aside the thought, she clapped her hands together, then said with forced brightness, 'Who would like to be first?'

The freckled girl stepped forward. 'I will,' she said, looking back over her shoulder at the other girls. There were nods from them all.

Floriane led the girl into the boardroom and pointed to a chair opposite her own. Clara Speelman sat down next to Floriane.

'Your name is . . .?' She studied the girl's face. Enormous hazel eyes looked back, the girl's tiny freckles like a smattering of gold dust across her cheeks.

'Johanna Timmerman,' the girl replied evenly.

Floriane wrote it in the ledger. 'How old are you, Johanna?'

'Seventeen. I'll be eighteen next month.'

Adding this detail to the book, Floriane set down her pen. 'Can you tell me why you've decided to take up this offer?'

The girl looked away, as if thinking. 'I have nothing to keep me here now.'

'I see.' Floriane recalled the tears in the girl's eyes earlier: she must have been close to the housemother. 'Are you aware that it's a five-month journey by sea?'

'I've been told that, yes.'

'Have you ever been on a sailing ship?'

'Only on the barge from Haarlem when I first came to the Burgerweeshuis.'

Floriane nodded. 'And how do you think you will occupy yourself on such a long journey?'

'I hadn't really thought about that.' Johanna blinked. 'My friends will be with me. I'm sure we'll find ways to pass the time.'

'Do you have anything you like to do in your free time?'

'To be honest, mevrouw, we do not have free time. Just work, lessons, eating and sleeping. Divine Service on Sunday.'

'Of course.' Floriane tried a different approach. 'On the ship, though, you'll have nothing but time. I am also making this long journey because I believe Good Hope will live up to its name. I will be bringing a few books to read as well as some knitting. My husband, Regent van Loon, will no doubt be engaged with his work.'

The hint of a dark look flashed briefly in the girl's eyes, which set Floriane wondering for a moment.

'The only book I have to read is the Bible.' She drew in a sharp breath then added quickly, 'Of course, the copy I use belongs to the huis.'

'Let me be more plain. We are hoping to bring along items to keep you all occupied.' Floriane smiled. 'Do you have any preference for what we might bring for you?'

The girl thought again and then, looking up from under thick lashes, said, 'I used to make sketches when I was little, when I could find something to draw on.'

Floriane nodded and made another note. 'And now we come to the matter of the contract.' She glanced down at the document in front of her. 'Putting your name on the list will require you to sign a bond that binds you to the Cape for five years, where you will be expected to marry. After that time, if you wish to return to the United Provinces of the Netherlands, you may do so, your passage paid in full by the Dutch East India Company. Is there anything you'd like to ask before you finally decide?'

'Yes.' The girl clasped her hands and rested them on the edge of the table. 'Will I have any say in who I am to marry?' She had a rather determined look on her face.

Floriane looked over at Clara, who said, 'That will be up to the officers at Good Hope. Perhaps the new fiscal will have some say in the matter.'

A vague sense of dread stirred in the pit of Floriane's stomach. 'You may certainly come to me and I will have a word with Regent van Loon on your behalf.'

The girl nodded once. 'Five years. Criminals spend longer in the House of Correction,' she quipped, as she dipped the nib in the inkwell and signed her name.

Floriane put the page to one side. 'I am sure you will not regret your decision. I shall see you on board the ship. Might you ask the next girl to come in on your way out?'

When the girl was gone from the room, Floriane said, 'How do you think that went?'

'Very well,' said Clara. 'A lovely girl, that one. Very promising.'

'Yes,' Floriane said. *I'm going to have my hands full keeping Claes away from her on board that ship.*

⤝ CHAPTER 14 ⤞

IT WAS A DARK October pre-dawn when Johanna left the orphanage.

She hugged Femke. 'Remember you promised to look after Annetje for me.'

'I haven't forgotten.'

'And I will write to you as soon as we have news to share. I'll tell you everything there is to know about the Cape, so you will know what to expect when you come.'

Bottom lip trembling, Femke stumbled over her words. 'I hope you find Frans and that he knows how lucky he is to have you, and that you find a way to get married.'

Johanna felt the tears pool in her eyes. She stepped back and pushed out a smile. 'You have become the dearest little sister I could ever have hoped for, and I will miss you with all my heart. But the others are waiting and I have to go, otherwise they will leave without me.'

Femke held on to her arm, misery stamped on her face. 'How will you find your way to the harbour?'

'We have been told where to go.' Johanna disengaged Femke's

hand, pulled her cap down over her ears and squared her shoulders. 'I'm sure we'll manage.' Her heart was leaden as she turned away.

A bundle of clothes in one hand, and the Bible box Moeder had bequeathed her in the other, she walked out through the enormous columned gateway into Wijde Kapelsteeg, the narrow alley that connected the orphanage to Kalverstraat. There she paused and looked back.

Malliet came to her side. 'We need to be off.'

Johanna nodded. 'I know. I was just thinking of the day I arrived at the huis.' She pointed at a shiny brass tube. 'I was so little I couldn't reach the bell pull. I banged on the front door with my clog until Hilletje came and opened it, and now we're sailing away to the far side of the earth.'

'And if we are to do that, we need to go. Passenger boats set off at first light and the barge to Texel follows an exact schedule. It will depart without us if we are not on time.' Her voice sounded panicked.

'What's the matter?' Her concern made Johanna uneasy.

'It's a big day, that's all. I'm just trying to get my head around it, and I've no idea where we are going.' She turned to the others and spread her hands.

Hilletje sucked in her cheeks and appeared to be thinking. 'We walk down to the Dam, cross over it to the quayside and take the barge at Herring Merchant's Gate.'

Malliet let out a low whistle. 'That's impressive!'

'I memorised the instructions they gave us but finding the place itself might be more of a challenge, and eight people do not walk as fast as one. We go at the speed of the slowest, and so we need to hurry, right now.'

Almost eight years ago, Johanna had made this journey in reverse, but her memories were no help now. She followed behind as they turned right on Kalverstraat, crossed over Dam Square with its town hall and weighing house, and traipsed across a humped bridge to where people, crowds of them, shouted and jostled on the greasy cobbles. Elbowing their way through the throng, eventually they reached the quayside, where a brisk trade in fish was in progress. Sailors and bargemen, trousers billowing, dumped baskets of herring on the cobbles, where women slit their undersides from head to tail and pulled out twists of bloodied guts. The stench made Johanna's eyes smart.

A pipe-smoking fishwife shook a herring in her oily fingers. 'Want one?'

Johanna darted Malliet a look and tried not to betray her anxiety when she spoke. 'No, thank you very much, but is this where we catch the barge to Texel?'

'Yes,' the woman said, and lopped the head off the herring. 'Over there, but it's almost full by the look of it.'

The eight girls turned towards the water and began to run. When they arrived, however, the skipper was adamant there was only room for seven passengers.

Malliet fluttered her eyelashes. 'We can all squeeze up.'

He planted his feet. 'Seven only. One of you will have to wait for the next barge.' The man turned his face away. 'An hour at most.'

Johanna felt her chest tighten, but she saw the two-masted sailing boat was indeed laden. 'I'll take the next one and meet you all on the quay at Texel.'

Seven pairs of eyes swivelled in her direction. 'Go on,' Johanna urged them. 'I'm first in the queue for the next one.'

Malliet kissed her cheek. 'See you in Texel,' she said breezily. 'I can't wait to see our cabin.'

Johanna watched them go, Malliet and Hilletje in front, facing her, and the other five girls standing behind them. Karin, a pretty brunette with enormous dark eyes, was laughing with Lisje. Elke, who had slept in the bed next to hers and Malliet's, poked her head around Malliet's shoulder to wave. Lotte and Brigitta were out of sight behind the group.

Happiness flooded through her. *I'm so glad they decided to come. We are all going to have such a good time together on the ship.*

⁓

Alone with her belongings, Johanna stood on the quay and watched. Oars dipped into the water and the barge grew smaller until she could no longer see it. It had begun to drizzle, and the breeze coming off the sea made her shiver. She pulled her hood up over her head and passed time watching the bounce of the rain on the water.

When the skipper extended a callused hand to help her aboard the next barge, she felt frozen stiff. She lifted her things and embarked.

As she sailed out of Amsterdam, she turned and looked at the city behind her. The first part of the journey hugged the shoreline of the bay called Het IJ, which stretched far inland. The Dutch were of the sea, she'd always been told. They were a trading nation, and that history had made the Dutch Republic great. Fitting, therefore, that the skyline was a forest of masts, flags and towers. Windmills lined up on the walls like an army of guardsmen, dipping their arms towards the filth-clogged water.

She tried hard not to breathe through her nose, opening her mouth just a little to allow a tiny breath in and out, and yet still the smell coming off the water caught in her throat and made her retch.

Johanna thought of Frans, and was warmed by a familiar thrill.

A coot bobbed on the water's surface. It kept pace with the gliding boat, weaving among the floating rubbish. Her mother had known her birds and had taught Johanna to recognise them too. *Coots are water birds whose heads look bald. That's not to say they have no feathers on their heads. They just look like that because of their white markings.*

Rats glided through the water, first two, then three, giving chase. The coot moved its head backwards and forwards as it swam, and she felt herself copying the movement, urging it on.

Are you frightened, little coot, and will fear keep you protected?

For a moment the coot seemed to stall and then it disappeared from view behind another boat. She clenched her teeth and found herself praying that it was safe. A moment later she saw it again, pattering across the water on its yellow-green legs, flapping furiously until it was airborne and free.

She could not have said precisely how long the trip lasted, but it seemed like hours before the barge hit the jetty in front of the landing stage with a solid thump.

Johanna stood up. It was bitterly cold, and the iron-grey sea was rough as she stepped from the barge onto the island of Texel. Hundreds of ships from the VOC fleet lay at anchor off the island, huge black shapes that rocked wildly on their moorings.

In the flat afternoon light, she wondered which of the gilded ships of the *Kerstvloot* – the Christmas fleet – would be her home for the next half-year. Clutching the Bible box and her bundle of clothes, she joined a small huddle of shivering souls on the pier who seemed to be leaning against each other for support.

She scanned the crowd in front of her, looking for her seven friends. She could see only a handful of women, and they weren't grouped together.

A sense of unease growing in her stomach, she decided to ask. She walked up to the woman nearest to her, who was standing with a gentleman.

'Excuse me, mevrouw. I'm looking for—' She broke off when the woman turned and she saw her face. 'Mevrouw Peronneau! I'm so glad to see you here.'

'Johanna. We've been waiting for you. I was beginning to get worried.'

As she spoke, the man standing with her turned, and Johanna saw that it was Regent van Loon.

'I'm sorry,' Johanna said. 'There was no room on the first barge, and I had to wait for the next one. They told me it would be no longer than an hour, but I would swear it was twice that. Where are Malliet and the others?'

'They've gone ahead in the yawl and have already boarded ship,' said the regent.

Johanna frowned. 'Will they come back now to get us?'

Floriane Peronneau glanced at her husband. 'I'm afraid that although we'll be travelling with the same fleet, we cannot all fit on the same ship. We've been told to wait here. Our ship does not have accommodation for all of us. The other girls have been taken to the *Middelburg*.'

Johanna looked from one to the other. 'But surely they must have known our numbers. How could this have happened?'

The regent scowled. 'Twenty-eight Huguenot refugees from Provence have been offered free passage to travel at the last minute, because they possess skills that are much needed at the Cape. Everything and everyone has to be shifted around.

94

Some people are changing ships they already boarded. We are told that if we wish to sail, then we must wait.' He shook his head, irritation twisting his expression.

Johanna felt the sting of tears in her eyes. She turned away and stared at the water, willing the yawl's speedy return.

Another half-hour passed before the boat came back. As two seamen rowed the small crowd of passengers across the harbour, Floriane Peronneau gave her a small nod. 'It will be all right, Johanna. We'll make sure you're looked after.'

'It shall be my mission.' Mijnheer van Loon fixed her intently with piercing blue eyes.

Instead of answering, she turned and faced the sea.

The oarsmen drew them alongside the *Borssenburg*, a newly painted East Indiaman. Above the furled grey-white linen sails, the red, white and blue stripes and proud V of the Dutch East India Company flag flapped wildly on the mainmast.

Johanna craned her neck to stare up at the figurehead. Backed by a row of gilded caryatids, a carved roaring lion reared up on its hindquarters. Its golden paws draped over the prow, and its white teeth gleamed. She hoped it was an auspicious omen that the ship, bearing a fearless beast, would carry her safely across the turbulent seas. She made the sign of the cross on her chest and gathered up her belongings once more.

I'm on my way, Frans, she thought. *There's no turning back now.*

~ PART II ~

THE SHIP

☞ CHAPTER 15 ☜

CAPTAIN BIERENS WAS A thick-set man with a waxed, gingery moustache. He scanned the group of awaiting passengers, an unhappy expression on his face. Johanna could feel the weight of his stare as it passed over her.

'I will brook no complaints regarding the accommodation you've been assigned. We've more than three hundred souls on board, and the ship is packed as tight as a barrel of herrings. Some of you have canvas berths midships. Be grateful you're not lashed to the hull.'

The first mate, talking in a lowered voice, asked her to identify her luggage, and apologised for the captain's blunt tongue. 'I hear you've had some bad luck today. I've a daughter myself and I wouldn't want her travelling alone. I've found you a cot in the carpenter's workshop, where you can at least lock the door. It's not much more than a box with a bed, but the carpenter is resigned to give it over and, in truth, it's the only private spot we have left. So, if you'll show me what you've brought with you, I'll carry it down and settle you in.'

'I have no luggage other than my box and clothing bundle.'

Panic bubbled up in her chest. 'Is there no way at all I can rejoin my friends? If not today, tomorrow?'

He began to walk away then turned his head, and she saw a raw line on his face where he must have cut himself shaving. 'With all the delays, we missed today's tide. I wish it were otherwise, but you really must come along with me.'

She threw a desperate look at the masts leaving the bay. 'But they are there now. There must still be time. It wouldn't take long to row me across.'

A blast of cold wind seemed to rob him of his reply. He hung his head and said nothing.

Another wave of acute anxiety swept over Johanna, leaving her perilously close to tears.

Floriane Peronneau stepped forward and said a quiet word to the first mate, who bowed from the neck and turned away to assist another passenger.

Mevrouw Peronneau turned to Johanna, wrapping a gentle arm around her shoulder. 'Wait here a moment. I need to speak with the captain.'

Johanna wiped her cheek with the back of her hand and nodded. She stood watching as Mevrouw Peronneau and the captain took themselves across the deck. Their voices came to her faintly, but she could not make out their words.

She shivered. Surely Malliet would try from her ship to get them all together. There had to be some solution.

Mevrouw Peronneau touched the captain's arm, an earnest look on her face. The captain puffed out his cheeks and then, to Johanna's surprise, he laughed.

After a good deal of nodding, Floriane Peronneau dropped her hand and turned away. It looked to Johanna as if a smile had formed on her lips.

'Come along, dear,' the mevrouw said as she returned to where Johanna stood. 'Do you have all your things?'

Johanna picked up her bundle where she'd set it on the deck. 'What's happening?' she asked. She looked back over her shoulder for the captain but couldn't see him anywhere. It occurred to her that Mijnheer van Loon was no longer with them. She'd been too distracted to notice he'd gone.

'Everything will turn out for the best, Johanna. Come, let's see if we can find our accommodation.'

*

Standing inside the open door, Floriane took stock of the large, opulent cabin, which was situated beneath the poop deck at the back of the ship, and marvelled at the furniture they had managed to cram in. She had to hand it to Clara Speelman. The great lady had provided her with a detailed list of what they would need for the five-month voyage. In addition to the beds and a washstand, a bureau, a couch and even a harp they had in their living space, in the hold they carried a houseful of furnishings, crockery and other goods difficult to come by on the Cape.

That she had managed to both protect Johanna from Claes and rid herself of him for the duration of the voyage in a moment of quick thinking was nothing short of a prayer answered by God. It would have been challenging to maintain the illusion of being ill if she'd had to spend the entire voyage in one room with him. Only the fact that they no longer shared a bedroom made it possible at home. At any rate, she had set her mind to the task of keeping him away from Johanna; this was one young girl he would not be allowed to seduce.

Behind her Johanna wavered, seemingly hesitant to cross the threshold.

'Do come in out of the cold.' She motioned to her, and after a moment Johanna followed her into the cabin.

'What happened? What did you say to him?'

Floriane tucked a stray curl behind her ear. 'I suggested to him that it would be a better arrangement if you were to stay here with me, as I am not keeping good health and will likely need your assistance. My husband must therefore occupy the carpenter's cabin and the captain has agreed to speak to him.'

The girl sniffed loudly. 'But surely Mijnheer van Loon is not going to be happy to change places with me. And how will you manage without your husband to offer you protection for the next few months?'

'I am certain he will make a fuss, but it is unthinkable that you should find yourself without companionship in the bowels of the ship. And he is not banned from this cabin – he can come and go as he pleases. It is just that for the purposes of taking his rest he must lay his head elsewhere.'

'I shouldn't like to make him angry with me.' The girl sounded nervous.

'Do not worry, Johanna. I know you were expecting to travel with your friends from the orphanage, but that doesn't appear to be possible just at the moment.' Floriane was careful to make her voice soft. 'I hope that this arrangement does not inconvenience you too much, and I am looking forward to sharing your company. So, do bring in your things and let me settle you in.'

Johanna took a few steps into the cabin. 'I have two changes of clothes, and the Bible box Mevrouw Visser bequeathed me when she died. Nothing else.'

The paucity of the girl's belongings gave Floriane a slight shock. She indicated a small table by the bow window. 'Why not put your box on there for now. We can accommodate your clothes in one of the drawers in the bureau.'

Johanna seemed surprised and moved unsteadily despite the gentle movement of the ship, but placed her box on the table as she was asked. 'I hope that will not be in your way, mevrouw.'

'It will not in the least be in my way.' She studied the box. 'It looks remarkably like my own, though, so we shall have to ensure we don't confuse them.' She sank into a chair, smiling to reassure Johanna. 'Please, sit down.' She indicated the couch.

The girl swayed a little as she surveyed the cabin but sat bolt upright, perched on the edge of the couch. 'Where is yours?'

'I'm not sure, to tell the truth. As a surprise, my parents sent their servants ahead to arrange the cabin for us and secure the furniture, so it will not slide about when the winds take hold. Right at this moment, though, where things are exactly is as much of a mystery to me as to you.'

Johanna crossed her legs and looked at her with eyes that were wide with unease. Everything about her deportment betrayed her discomfort.

'And which of the two beds would you like?'

The girl pressed her knees together and seemed to have momentary difficulty finding her voice. 'I've not slept by myself in a bed for more than eight years. I am not sure that I will be able to anymore.'

Floriane gave a small laugh. 'I'm not sure that either of us will fare very well to start with, particularly if the ship begins to pitch and roll, but we will make the best of it and watch out for each other.'

Johanna looked around the cabin, her eyes settling on the bed with a green cover. 'May I then take that one?'

'By all means.'

The girl took off her cloak, her face nearly as pale as the linen collar of her dowdy blue dress. 'Thank you for your kindness, Mevrouw Peronneau. I don't know how I would have managed without you today.'

'I think we are lucky to have found each other, and that will be our mutual salvation for the next few months.' She sat down and touched the seat of the chair next to her. 'Please sit down here for a moment. I should like to talk to you.'

Johanna got up at once, changed her seat and stared at her feet.

Floriane kept her expression serious. 'As far as I know, we are the only two women on board this ship now. We are likely to come to rely on one another as the voyage progresses. I know this will not be usual for you, but I seek to have you with me as a companion, more than a maid or a nurse.'

She watched the girl's face, which had closed up with confusion. 'You are going to the Cape to marry a wealthy burgher. It will raise up your social standing in a way that likely would not have been possible in Amsterdam. You will be out in society and should be prepared.'

'I hadn't thought of it that way, mevrouw, but I suppose it's true.' The girl fell silent in apparent thought.

Floriane played with the bracelet on her wrist. 'It is my intention to ask the captain if you might join us at his table for meals. How would you feel about this?'

Johanna's head jerked up. 'At the captain's table, mevrouw? But I-I . . .' She buried her hands in the cloth of her skirt. 'I wouldn't know how to conduct myself, and I do not have suitable clothes.'

'We are of similar proportions. I will lend you something to wear.'

'But, mevrouw, I would feel so—'

'Johanna.' She pressed her arm. 'I must confess that it is not only for your benefit that I wish to do this. It is a very alienating experience for a woman to be alone in a room full of men. It will be much more comfortable for me if I have you for support.'

She could not tell if the girl truly understood the implication of her words, but after a while, she said, 'Of course, mevrouw. Thank you.'

*

As the first day closed in, Claes, fortified by a glass or two of brandy wine, stamped his foot. 'A carpenter's cabin is hardly fitting accommodation for a company official of my rank.'

The captain stood at the whipstaff, his face reddened by the wind. 'I am sorry, mijnheer, but it's all we've got to spare. The carpenter has offered to give up his workspace and sling his hammock on the gun deck to give you privacy. I cannot, in good conscience, consign a young girl to sleep among the rough and tumble that goes on below decks. I've spoken to your wife and she is happy to have the girl stay with her. All things considered, you have done well for yourself. I'm sorry to be the bearer of news you do not wish to hear, but that is where you are to lodge for the duration of the voyage.'

'The cabin is minuscule, and even though I am not a tall man, I cannot stand to my full height. You must find me an alternative.'

The wind had got up, and the captain spread his feet on the wildly swaying deck. 'I'm sorry that you are not pleased, but there is no other solution to be found.'

Claes's hand sat on the hilt of his sword. 'We could share the cuddy, you and I, if you were of a mind.'

105

The captain shrugged, lifting his palms like a Frenchman. Claes recognised the gesture all too well, and it sent a fizz of fury through his veins. It took all of his willpower not to draw his blade. 'That is not possible. On one side I have my stateroom, and the other serves as our dining room. You are most welcome, at any time, to partake of the great cabin if you require space and privacy in which to work but, in case you were about to propose it, the accommodation is taken by my officers. Now . . .'

The ship's bell sounded and the second officer appeared at the captain's shoulder.

'I am needed. I'll leave you to return to your accommodation, until it's time to eat.' He bowed, low and formal, and set off down the deck – doubtless heading to the comfort of the great cabin, Claes thought bitterly.

Navigating the narrow passageways on a swaying ship was not an easy task. It took him several minutes to reach the companionway that led down to the lower deck. Even placing his feet with care on the worn, shallow treads and bracing himself with his hands, he lurched along the creaking, dark corridor until he arrived at his berth.

He pushed open the door and kicked it shut behind him with the heel of his boot. Twice already, he had stubbed his foot on the base of the cannon with which he shared the tiny space. Above the cannon, a shallow wooden tray housing the carpenter's mattress hung suspended from the roof. There was a chair to its side. He had no idea how he would clamber into bed when the ship was in full tilt.

The red-headed girl was agonisingly out of reach in the roundhouse cabin two decks above him, but Claes comforted himself with the thought that when she succumbed, he would have somewhere private to bring her.

106

Floriane did not close her eyes that first night. With the light of dawn she gave up trying to rest, and while Johanna slept on, she made sense of her luggage. Once she had found the things she would need often, she arranged them in the bureau, concealing her face paints beneath them. There were two framed pictures, which she hung as quietly as she could on the cabin wall – one a landscape showing a small glade of trees, and the other a portrait of her parents laughing, her mother holding a fan and her father a bulb-shaped flask of wine. Floriane stared at their faces, wallowing in melancholy thoughts.

'I really like that portrait.'

Pulled from her introspection, Floriane jumped slightly. 'Goodness, you startled me.' She turned to see the girl looking at her from bed. 'Did you sleep well?'

'I did, thank you. I hope I have not caused offence. I have rarely seen a posed picture where people look happy. The pictures in the boardroom at the orphanage are all very grave.'

Floriane smiled to herself, thinking of her mother and father. 'My parents are both great jokers. The levity of this portrait would particularly annoy Claes. He thinks all art should be deathly serious.'

'It is a shame that so many paintings are solemn. Where I lived with my mother in Haarlem, there was an artist who painted with a lively style. Frans Hals. I saw some of his paintings when I was small. I remember because they made me happy.'

Floriane nodded. 'I've brought along the drawing materials I promised to help you pass the time.' She pointed to the table adjacent to the couch, where she'd placed a notebook and some sharpened charcoal in a small wooden box. 'I have all sorts for the other girls in the hold. Such a shame they'll not have them.'

'You were supposed to travel with us all, weren't you?'

'Yes. It was part of his agreement with the Honourable Company that Claes – my husband – was to act as escort, and I would stand in as a sort of housemother cum chaperone.'

'Where did you meet your husband?' Johanna swung her legs out of bed and sat up.

'In fact, it was in Haarlem.'

The girl smiled. 'Do you recall how it happened?'

'It was a chance meeting. I'd taken the horse-drawn barge from Amsterdam with my mother to visit a lace factory run by one of her friends.'

'What was Mijnheer van Loon doing in Haarlem?'

Floriane thought back, bittersweet memories filling her head. 'He had just finished a business meeting. My mother and I were strolling through the marketplace admiring the *Groote Kerk* when a merchant started pestering us. Claes came to our rescue and my mother was beside herself with gratitude.'

'Was it a chance meeting or did he know you by reputation, do you think?'

'I don't think he knew who we were, no. He started to huff and puff about how he would advise the city fathers that they should do something about defenceless women being at the mercies of predatory salesmen. My mother gave him my father's trade card and asked him to call on us in Amsterdam because she wanted Papa to thank him for his intervention on our behalf.' She smiled wryly.

'What happened when he came to call on you in Amsterdam?'

'Quite simply, he set about wooing me. He was so charming, so at ease with my parents and in company, so deeply understanding of my needs and considerate of trying to please me. He dressed well and spoke knowledgeably about the arts and humanities.' She paused, biting back her sense of betrayal. 'I did everything I could to make myself look beautiful, to cultivate an interest in his interests, to make him fall in love with me. It was all I thought about for months.'

'Did he visit you every day?'

Floriane shook her head. 'Goodness, you ask a lot of questions! In the early days, our courtship was conducted largely by letter. He wrote me the most beautiful prose saying how much he loved me, that he existed only for me. So when he proposed, I was powerless. There was no way on earth I was going to turn him down. So there you have it. The story of our beginnings.' She bit the inside of her cheek. Every time she thought about it, she reproached herself at how easily she had fallen for his flattery. *I will see that you pay your debts, Claes van Loon, and they will take more from you than money.*

Johanna shifted in her bed, her elbows resting on her knees, and Floriane realised she had been watching her for some time. 'What are you thinking?'

The girl didn't answer at once. 'You look better today.'

Floriane shook her head slightly. 'Say again?'

'I don't mean to cause offence,' Johanna looked at her, as if testing her reaction.

Floriane laughed at the idea. 'I took no offence, but neither did I take your meaning.'

'It's just that yesterday, you were . . .' She motioned to her own face. 'Paler?'

The girl was far too sharp to be tricked by her ruse for long. She was going to have to bring her in on it, but not quite yet. 'Was I?' Floriane said. 'Perhaps the sea is already working its magic.'

～ CHAPTER 16 ～

Time on board ship passed slowly but, still, days eventually turned into weeks, and there were even moments when time got away from Johanna. One afternoon some three weeks after they'd set sail from Texel, she found herself late for the captain's noontime dinner, tardiness being one of the man's great bugbears. When she reached the narrow steps down to the cuddy, she picked up the hem of the dress Floriane had loaned her and cannoned down them, almost landing headlong on the deck below.

She burst through the dining-room door, an apology ready on her lips. 'I am so sorry, captain, for my late arrival. Mevrouw Peronneau is unwell, and I felt I could not abandon her until I knew she was comfortable.'

In the middle of the room a long rectangular table was set for five. A lantern on a linked metal chain hung over its centre. The room was windowless and its walls were lined with paintings, mainly oils of ships engaged in war. The scenes were a little overpowering, but at least they broke up the ugly reddish brown of the walls – a VOC standard for cuddies, the captain had told her, to help hide bloodstains made during battle.

Captain Bierens rose from his chair and gave a polite bow. 'You are not the last to arrive, Johanna. We shall miss Mevrouw Peronneau at table. Please pass on our sympathies, as seasickness can be a most tenacious companion.'

Johanna was struck yet again by how much the captain's behaviour had softened towards her since their blunt introduction the day they set sail.

'She is merely a little under the weather, and hopes that the malady is a temporary thing, but she did want me to say that she very much appreciated your kind invitation to dine.'

The first officer gestured for her to sit. She slithered into the chair he indicated, which, like the rest of the furniture on board, was nailed to the deck.

The captain poured some wine into a glass and passed it to her. He must have seen her eyeing the walls, for he said, 'They're gruesome enough, but rest assured that we are in no danger of conflict on this trip.'

'Danger of conflict?' a voice asked behind her.

Johanna twisted in her seat and saw Mijnheer van Loon, his body framed by the dining-room doorway as he strolled in. He was smaller than the captain, and his face bore its habitual contemptuous expression, which made her hackles rise.

'You are late, Van Loon.' The Captain's voice was cold as he made a show of studying his pocket watch. 'You are fortunate we have not yet begun to eat. Otherwise I would have sent you packing.'

'I looked in on my wife earlier, captain, and for that I will not apologise. I had hoped to escort her to dinner but found her unwell.'

Johanna wondered at which point of the morning he had popped in to the cabin. Certainly not in the past half-hour.

A servant entered the great cabin carrying an oval platter of salted pork, the first of the three courses. The first officer indicated where he should put it down and all four of them eyed it with varying degrees of distaste. After just three weeks, fresh food was already running low, and the cooks were struggling to render the preserved food palatable with vinegar and spices.

They made polite small talk while they ate. After the third course, there was a lull in the conversation.

'And how is my wife's health holding up?' Claes van Loon asked, as he played with the fork by his plate.

The captain frowned at him. 'Did you not see her less than an hour since, Van Loon?'

'Indeed. I meant generally, of course, not just the current sickness that confines her to her bed. Compared to other passengers you have carried.' He must have partaken copiously of drink before his arrival, as the odour of alcohol wafted strongly when he spoke. He recharged his glass and moved as if to refill Johanna's, even though it was untouched.

She placed her hand over it. 'I think Mevrouw Peronneau is not so badly afflicted. She has asked me to prepare her a tray. She will dine in the cabin when I return to the roundhouse.'

The captain got to his feet and passed around the table, filling a plate. 'Of course. I shall have a servant deliver this to her door so that it will still be warm, and so you will not be troubled with its transport up the companionway.'

'If you will forgive me.' She rose from her seat. 'You are most thoughtful, captain, and I thank you for the invitation to dinner, but would not wish to overstay my welcome. I will take a short turn about the deck before returning to convey your best wishes to Mevrouw Peronneau, who I am confident will be up and about in no time.'

*

The first officer proposed a toast to Prins Willem, and as Claes drained his glass, his head was full of the pretty redhead. On the quay at Texel, his eye had settled on her, and at the thought of her now he literally swelled with desire. He flung the napkin onto his lap.

It had cost him just a coin to get seven of the orphan girls sent to another ship. At the time, he hadn't been bothered as to which one remained, but now he found his thoughts returning to Johanna again and again.

He set his glass on the table and rose to his feet. 'If you will excuse me, gentlemen. As the rain has let up, I too will take a stroll outside.'

Once on the quarterdeck, Claes leaned heavily against the bulwark. The sky was slate grey, an improvement from the black clouds earlier. He withdrew his mariner's glass from his coat and raised it to his eye, focusing the telescope on the delicious red-headed vision moving his way.

As she neared, he lowered the eyeglass and swept off his hat, making a formal bow. The girl's brow furrowed, and she veered away towards the companionway that led up to the poop deck. He strode after her, charting his course across the deck as a helmsman might fix on a landmark. He called her name to halt her and she stood still, slowly turning her head.

'Mijnheer van Loon?'

He kept his voice solemn, with a church-like quiet. 'Did you enjoy your dinner?'

Guileless, she looked at him with her huge hazel eyes. 'I did very much, mijnheer, but I was sorry that your wife was not fit to join us. I know she was very much looking forward to the occasion.'

He let a smile linger on his lips. 'I recognise that frock as belonging to her. It suits you.'

'That's very kind of you to say. I thank you, but I fear it's far too grand a garment for me. It's on loan for today only.'

He held out his arm. 'Would you care to take a turn around the deck, while the rain holds off? I confess that, with my wife so often unwell, I feel deprived of female chatter.'

She drew a startled breath. 'Oh! I have already walked the length of the deck, and thought to spend a few moments aloft before returning to the roundhouse.'

A small pause that he could have filled with myriad compliments followed, but for now he held back. She pulled away from him and climbed the steps to the upper deck.

He darted after her. 'Perhaps I might show you the marvels of my telescope, if ever you were interested?'

She seemed uneasy and lowered her eyes. 'I confess to feeling somewhat confused, mijnheer, at your sudden interest in spending time with me.'

He took a step back. 'I am sorry if I have made you ill at ease, dear Johanna. It was never my intention to do anything more than extend the hand of friendship towards you. I apologise if I have overstepped the mark.'

The tension slipped from her face. 'When she has recovered her health, I am certain your wife will appreciate your company,' she said. 'I could not aspire to such lofty heights. Nor, as you know, am I permitted to engage in unsupervised discourse with a male passenger. It was clearly set out in the Dutch East India's paperwork.'

Once more Claes swept off his hat and bowed low from his waist, laying on all the charm he could muster. 'I do hope to reassure you that you may consider me more equal than superior, now we are no longer constrained by orphanage regulations.'

Johanna dropped a curtsy and turned in the direction of her cabin.

He lingered on the deck, playing with his telescope, until it started to rain. For the moment he might have lost her, but he knew as he gave the tip of his eyeglass a little twist that he had her firmly in his sights.

*

When Johanna returned to the roundhouse, Floriane Peronneau had finished her dinner. The empty dishes were scraped clean and stacked neatly on a tray inside the door. She lay stretched out on the couch, looking up at the ceiling, seemingly mesmerised by the lamp that swung on its brass chain, back and forth with the rolling of the ship.

Johanna crouched by her side. 'Are you quite well? Do you need me to fetch you the ship's surgeon?'

Mevrouw Peronneau seemed surprised to see her and sat up very straight. 'I am perfectly well, thank you. My mind was engaged elsewhere. How was the dinner?'

'You were missed. The captain sends his regards for your speedy recovery.'

'Sit down, Johanna. Here, close to me.' She pointed to a high-backed green chair at the side of the couch and sank against the cushions. 'What excuse did you give Claes, so I know what to say if it comes up in conversation?'

The question was unexpected, and Johanna stumbled over her words. 'I didn't go into details. There was no need. I told the captain merely that you were unwell, and Mijnheer van Loon said you were confined to your bed.'

She stared into space. 'How would he know that?'

'Mijnheer van Loon was late for the meal and the captain almost refused him entry, but your husband said he had visited you because you were suffering from a nasty bout of seasickness. He wanted to see you settled in your bed, or some such—'

Heavy footsteps on the stair and a knock at the door broke off their conversation.

'Who is it?' Floriane Peronneau called.

Claes van Loon strode in, leaving the door ajar, cheeks red with wine and legs a trifle unstable. Even from where she sat Johanna could smell the alcohol, yet his wife smiled and held out her hand, accepting the kiss he placed upon it.

'How did you spend your morning, dear one, to make you late for the captain's dinner?'

He looked at Johanna, his eyes flashing. 'I was in the great cabin working on my papers, and lost track of time.' He eyed the decanter on the table by the window, and walked towards it.

'The captain understood from you that I was indisposed.'

Johanna saw the clench of his fist pressed tight against his thigh. *Ah, he was lying.*

'You are always unwell. If you had been well, you would have come to dinner.' His tone was almost simpering.

Floriane frowned. 'But you told the captain you had visited me this morning and found me suffering from seasickness.'

He turned to face his wife. 'Did Johanna tell you that?'

Johanna steeled herself, but he didn't even glance in her direction.

'I asked her a direct question, and she is not untruthful.'

He began to pace the room, slapping his hands against his thighs. 'You cannot expect a child to recall a grown-up conversation. He put an idea in her head and that is what she has remembered.'

Humiliation washed over Johanna. She watched him, fearful of what he might say next.

Mevrouw Peronneau pulled her skirt tight around her legs. 'There's a cold draught from the open door, Claes. Either shut it and come in, or go back to the cuddy.'

He lurched towards the door. 'I may as well take my leave. I came to see if my wife had need of my services, but I see you are perfectly well set up in here with the girl. I'll pass by again tomorrow in the hope your mood has improved, and I will mention you in my prayers.'

As the door closed, Johanna reflected on the coldness between man and wife. She shivered, despite her utmost effort to disguise it.

Floriane Peronneau held out her hand. 'Have you caught a chill?'

Johanna took it between hers. 'No, but thank you. I do not understand why your husband would say those things about me just now.'

'Is that why you shuddered?'

She withdrew her fingers and looked down at her hand. 'It was a blatant lie.'

Mevrouw Peronneau's tone hardened. 'I know.'

The resignation in her voice was a surprise, and it gave Johanna the incentive to continue. 'I hope you will not hate me for what I'm going to tell you, but at the orphanage, he was always trying to catch one of us alone. Since we boarded, I've had the uncomfortable feeling he's been watching me whenever I go out on deck.' Had she said too much? Surely Mevrouw Peronneau would hear her heart pounding loudly in her chest.

'Why would I hate you for speaking the truth?' The woman got up from the couch and wandered round the cabin, minutely adjusting her already perfectly aligned possessions.

It occurred to Johanna then, watching her warily, that Floriane Peronneau was herself trapped, a prisoner among a cabinful of props. She stopped in front of the bureau and stood there a little, perhaps deciding what she was going to say.

'I think the time has come to confide in you.' Mevrouw Peronneau sank into a vacant chair. 'I told you when first we began sharing this cabin that I had ill health and have purposely given people to believe this, even my husband.' She looked down for a moment, then drew in a breath. 'Let me say that I have my reasons for projecting an image of myself that might not be the exact truth.'

Johanna rubbed her arm absently and said evenly, 'I am not surprised to learn this. I nursed a sick lady for a long time, and you seem in remarkably good order.'

'I persuaded the captain that Claes be induced to exchange cabins with you for two specific reasons. One, because I could not have borne being cooped up in this cabin with him for the duration of the voyage. The other, to remove you from Claes's orbit. He will not leave you be while we are on this ship.' Mevrouw Peronneau spoke in a rush, as though she didn't want to be interrupted.

Johanna got up from her seat and went to the window. The glass was streaked with rainwater and she could see nothing beyond the blue-grey of the water. Without turning, she said, 'I have sensed that all was not well between you.' She swung round then and looked back at Mevrouw Peronneau.

The woman sighed deeply. 'Claes has been repeatedly unfaithful to me since our wedding night.'

'Your wedding night?' Johanna straightened.

'I can't say for sure that his infidelity started then, but I know for certain that in recent months, he has fornicated with our maid in Amsterdam, nearly every night. So naturally I am vexed with myself for all the signs I at first ignored. But since I've known for certain that he is adulterous, I've kept a comprehensive record and have avoided marital intimacy with him.'

'Is that why you have no children?'

Floriane took a deep breath and blew it out. 'We were never blessed and perhaps now it's just as well.'

'Why did you stay with him if you knew what he was? Could you not have divorced him?'

Floriane Peronneau stared at her, lips pressed together. 'The law is not on the side of women, Johanna. If I am to extract myself from an unhappy marriage, I have to find other means to accomplish it. But I believe fate has sent you to help me, and I want to ask you something that you must promise will remain between us if I do.'

'You have my word that any confidence we share will never be spoken of outside this cabin. What would you like me to do?'

'You said that you felt Claes was engineering ways for your paths to cross on the ship.'

'I do feel he is watching me.'

'So, what I'm about to ask you may be unpalatable.'

Johanna stopped by the harp and ran her nails along the strings, the sharp notes echoing the tense feeling in the room. She watched the strings until the sound was mute and said, with feeling, 'Are you asking me to seek out his company?'

'Don't worry. I know you are destined to marry a wealthy man in the Cape, and your reputation will not be compromised. But now you know what he is, you will understand that he will try every trick to get you on your own. You must never let him. He can't force you to do anything in broad daylight, but he will be desperate to relieve his carnal cravings.' She paused, steepling her fingers. 'We are hopeful that he will eventually slip up.'

'We?'

'I am not the only one seeking to expose my husband. The Honourable Company has dangled the position at the Cape in front of him as a tempting bait they hope will eventually ensnare him.'

Johanna raised her eyebrows. 'Do you suspect him of more than infidelity?'

Floriane Peronneau did not answer, and Johanna took the silence to indicate her tacit accord.

Nodding, she said, 'Very well. I'll keep my wits about me and see what I can find out.'

⌒ CHAPTER 17 ⌒

A SLIVER OF MOONLIGHT crept through the roundhouse window, painting the wooden planking with its ghostly glow. Floriane had taken a draught and was fast asleep, but Johanna could not drop off. She punched the cushion behind her head and wondered how Malliet and the others were faring.

She pushed herself up on her elbow to gain a better view through the window. The moon was ringed with a phantom rainbow, a sure sign that another storm was coming. As if on cue, the ship rolled so far to port that she fell from her berth.

She scrambled to her feet and clambered back into bed, clinging to the frame with both hands. As the vessel lurched, she could hear the timbers grinding against each other, and voices shouted to lash tarpaulins across hatches to keep the lower decks dry. She tossed in the bunk, envying Floriane her sleeping draught. Eventually Johanna could bear it no longer. She jumped out of bed and into her clothes and left the cabin, thinking that it would calm her nerves to see for herself what was going on outside.

It took her several minutes to negotiate the companionway's slippery treads, given the pitching of the ship. When she stepped down to the deck, she was almost swept off her feet by a fury of freezing wind.

Rain lashed down, and a fresh roll of the ship sent her running across the tilting deck towards the rail. She shrieked with delight at the raging weather. As she'd scarcely set foot out of doors for nearly eight years, the full force of the storm was exhilarating.

'Do you think we are to perish like drowned rats?' A man was hidden behind the mainmast, his arms hugging the wood as the ship pitched through the churning water.

Johanna pursed her lips. 'Rats can swim if you give them something to cling to. Have you not seen them in the canals? They are great survivors.'

He relinquished his grip on the mast. 'Then we must consider ourselves rats and, in the absence of anything more solid, cling to each other.'

He stepped out so that she could see him clearly. His face knocked the breath from her lungs. She had seen it before, many, many times, from her place in church on Sundays. She had drawn his likeness on a piece of stolen cloth and had it still, tucked next to her parents between the pages of her Bible.

'Frans de Jong.'

He pulled a strand of hair from his mouth and grinned like a lunatic. 'Johanna Timmerman.'

'What on earth are you doing here?'

'Sailing to the Cape. Do you not remember?'

'I remember every word we exchanged, but I never expected to find you on this exact ship. I thought you'd left for the Cape last summer.'

He gave her a quizzical look. 'It must have been meant in the great scheme of things that we should be together. Call it fate.'

She didn't dare to hope. 'Do you think so?'

'There is no other possible explanation. But I am curious to find you on any ship to the Cape, when the last time I saw you you were scrubbing lockers at the huis.'

'Me?' The words didn't come to her in the clever way she would have liked. She waved a vague hand. 'I signed a paper, and I too am taking my skills to the Cape. Unlike you, though, I have no fancy apprenticeship behind me, so I shall do what I have been trained to do, and sew and clean.' She found herself unable to tell him about the marriage contract, though it gave her a twinge of guilt. *Later. I will tell him later.*

He pushed the thick fringe of dripping hair from his face. 'You sound cross.'

'Do I?'

'Yes, you do. Peeved, almost.'

That I am destined to marry a man at the Cape when I want to marry you? 'Peeved' *doesn't remotely describe what I feel.* Tears pricked her eyes, and she was aware that her voice was scratchy. 'I never saw you in church after that time by the lockers.'

'My master, the millwright Willem Cornelis, kept me with him until my passage on this ship. I was unable to say goodbye, even though I wanted to very much.'

Johanna swallowed. 'Oh.'

'So here we both are. Off to the Cape.'

The ship rolled again and upset her balance. She stumbled, reaching for the rigging. Before she could grab hold, the ship lurched in the other direction, casting her against the rail, her flailing fingers clinging to his arm. Frans placed one hand either side of her, caging her against the ship's side with his body. Eyes locked on hers, he leaned in, his breath a puff of white against the dark night sky.

123

She felt the muscles in her neck tighten, her heart pounding in her ears as he pulled her close with one arm, the other cradling the back of her head.

Suddenly shy, she laughed, too loud. 'We should turn in now, don't you think? Before we get caught out.'

His stare did not waver. 'I think they have lashed the hatches.'

'The hatch by the great cabin is never secured, so the watch can go up and down.'

'Where's your berth?'

She pulled out of his embrace, still shy. 'I am with Floriane Peronneau in the roundhouse, serving as her maid. Her husband is in the carpenter's cabin.'

He nodded but didn't pass comment.

It was only when she was back in her cabin, collapsed in her cot and replaying the meeting a hundred times, that she thought about how she would make her dream of marrying Frans come true. *I will tell him about the contract when I know how I can get out of it.*

*

With the dawn, the wind dropped as suddenly as it had blown up, and the ship's paint shone green, gold and red against a calm aquamarine sea. Claes fixed his eyeglass on the girl and for the hundredth time told himself that what he was doing was entirely innocent.

Normally he watched from a distance, but today she was close by, standing between two cannons, leaning against the bulwarks. She appeared to be enjoying the warm sea air. He continued staring at her, his excitement rising. There was no point in denying himself. He enjoyed the company of women. What on earth was the harm in that? He collapsed his telescope and stowed it in his pocket, then crossed the distance between them before she had time to retreat.

He held both hands out in front of him, inviting her to join him. 'May I offer you my arm and promenade you around the deck?'

Her lips parted in a smile. 'Thank you, mijnheer, but I am happy just to stand here and enjoy the sunshine after the stormy weather these past few days.'

He trailed a nonchalant finger along the rail and edged a little closer. Keeping his tone light, he said, 'You must know that I greatly admire you, Johanna.'

'You are very kind to say so, but I am not exceptional. There are seven others just like me travelling on a boat somewhere out there at sea who are every bit as deserving of your admiration as me.' She turned, and her lovely green-brown eyes fixed on the water. 'It's been some days since I saw another mast, though.'

Time now to launch his idea. 'Perhaps if I were to instruct you in the use of my telescope, we might be able to make them out.'

She tilted her head a little, revealing a soft curl of reddish hair on her milk-white neck. 'Do you think that might be possible?'

He straightened up and nodded solemnly. 'Indeed. The telescope's very purpose is to make out objects clearly that you cannot see with the naked eye. What's more, it was invented by a Dutchman. It will reassure you that the fleet is still in touch with our ship and that your friends are safe.' He knew with certainty that they would not find the other ships. They hadn't been visible for days.

'In that case, I would be very glad to learn how it works, mijnheer.'

'Shall we move a little this way so that we may stand side by side?' He motioned her to the left and she came forward.

'Here, do you think?' she asked, looking back over her shoulder at him.

'Perfect.' He took the telescope out of his coat. 'Now, if you would turn this way so I may show you how it works.'

He held out the collapsed telescope and opened it, showing her how it unfolded and locked.

The girl gave a delighted gasp. 'Where shall we look first?'

'Let us try first with something we are certain of. Look up there. Do you see that gull overhead?'

Johanna raised a hand to protect her eyes from the sun, then pointed with the other. 'Oh, yes. There.'

'Now, I'm going to put the telescope into your hands, but you must be careful with it. It's a delicate instrument.' He reached for her right hand. 'May I?'

She nodded and he took her hand, placing it on the base of the mariner's glass. The contact was distracting but he didn't want to frighten her. He forced himself to focus on the lesson. 'Now, your other hand will go around the eyepiece, so . . .' He placed her left hand on the eyepiece and folded his hand around it. 'And now you'll hold it up to your eye and look up at the bird.' He released her hand and took a step back.

The girl tilted her head back and looked at the sky. 'Oh! I think it's gone.'

'What?' Claes frowned at her.

'The seagull. It's flown off.'

He squinted at where she pointed in the sky. 'So it has. Let us look up at the pennant, then. There, atop the mainmast.' He pointed and, when she didn't immediately respond, took the opportunity to put a hand on her waist to guide her around. 'See there.'

She took a small step away from him, dislodging his hand, and turned her face up, the telescope to her eye. 'Oh my. It's so close. I feel I could touch it.'

He fought to keep a smirk off his face. 'Now you have some idea of the advantage it gives you, let us begin our search.' Again, he put his hand on her waist and turned her towards the railing. 'Look out at the horizon. We can see everything on the larboard side of the ship from here.'

The girl raised the telescope to her eye once more and moved it slowly along the horizon from left to right.

'Do you see it?'

'No. Just water and a scattering of clouds.' She sounded disappointed.

He leaned in close, his hand trembling on the rail. 'I suspected as much. They're almost certainly on the port side of the ship. As it happens, I have a window on that side in my cabin and just yesterday sighted the other ships through it.'

Johanna nodded and started off down the deck. Claes followed behind her, feeling an overwhelming urge to sing. But then she turned sharply to the left and paused at the steps to the roundhouse. 'I would like to invite Mevrouw Peronneau, as I know she would enjoy it every bit as much as I would.' She threw the words over her shoulder to him.

He felt his heart sink. 'My wife is rarely well enough to get out of bed. I'm certain this would be of no interest to her.'

'But it would be courteous to ask nonetheless, do you not think?'

He considered his next move carefully. 'It is easier to show one person than two. It really is a very tiny cabin.'

'Without wanting to seem ungrateful, mijnheer, I am not free to spend time alone in the company of male passengers, however much I might like to see my friends' ship.' She said this casually, without even glancing his way, but he understood quite clearly she was turning him down.

'Indeed you are not, and yet you have been fraternising with the windmill boy.'

She twisted her fingers in the folds of her cloak, her posture suddenly rigid. 'Fraternising, mijnheer?'

'The windmill boy is off limits. As your chaperone and a high-ranking member of the VOC, it is well within the scope of my position to prevent you speaking to the boy.'

'I'm sorry?' she said politely.

'You were seen, in the middle of night, cavorting on deck.'

'I know Frans from the orphanage and have spoken to him twice only in my entire life. Here is your telescope, mijnheer.' She held it out to him.

He took it with one hand and settled his other hand on the hilt of his sword, ensuring that she could see. 'I am not a man to be trifled with, and will give you but one warning. You are not to speak with him. If you see him on deck you are to walk the other way. Remove yourself from his company. If I find you have not, I will do it for you.'

She said nothing. She did not need to. With a narrowing of her eyes, and a tightening of her mouth, the flicker of trust he had so carefully ignited had been snuffed out.

The bitter taste of rejection rose in his throat. He swallowed it down, but the feeling was far from forgotten.

*

Johanna sat close to Frans, sheltered by a piece of sailcloth in the waist of the ship. Since the night of the storm, it had become their secret meeting place. Already they had met there a dozen times. A borrowed oil lamp swung overhead, leaving sooty smudges on the planking above their heads.

Where his leg pressed against her she was aware of the shape and heat of it. He still wore his own hair, not the expensive curled peruke that the finer gentlemen favoured, and it fell to his shoulders in a mass of outrageous, unruly waves. His dark lashes lay thick and heavy above his cheeks.

Joy rose up in her chest such as she had never known. He leaned towards her and put a hand on her face. His touch sent a jolt of longing through her, yet with pretended sternness, she pushed him away.

'Do you think you were seen?' she said, glancing at the sailcloth.

'It's grog time. The crew are all pie-eyed.' Her concern made him laugh.

She dropped her voice to a whisper. 'It's not funny. We have to be careful. Mijnheer van Loon was particularly vexed about the lack of entertainment today. He'll likely be prowling the ship in search of something to do.'

'I don't think we need to worry about him just now. He'll be in the great cabin, drinking himself under the table. But you are quite right – we need to be watchful.'

She knew he was trying to reassure her with his words, so laid her hand on top of his. 'I don't think watchful is enough, Frans. Already we are playing a game of cat and mouse behind his back, and I don't trust him one little bit. What do you suppose he will do if he catches us?'

Frans shook his head. 'He won't. I'd rather talk about something else.' He gave her an apologetic smile. 'It's just that I used to think about you so often at the huis, and now that we find ourselves together, I don't want to waste the time speaking about someone so unworthy.'

She didn't want to talk about him either and said, 'I used to wonder about you all the time – about what you were doing and who you were with, about whether you ate the same food for breakfast as I did, and what happened to your family, and how old you were when you went to the huis. I wanted to know everything.'

He leaned his elbows against the ship's side. 'My mother died when I was small. My father went to fight the English and did not return. When we went to the huis, I was eight and my brother was eleven. How about you?'

'I was ten. My mother had died a few weeks before and our maid, Lisbet, was looking after me. She put me on a tow boat from Haarlem to Amsterdam on my own.' She flinched at the memory and changed direction. 'What is your brother doing now?'

Frans didn't reply straight away. 'He died, on apprenticeship to the Honourable Company. The housemother called me into her room after work one day and told me she had received word.'

'How did he die?'

'An accident at sea during a storm.'

She felt the sadness beneath his words and struggled to find something to say. At last she settled on, 'You must have been very close.'

'Yes, we were. I wanted to see how an accident might happen on an East Indiaman, so I could try to understand what had befallen him.'

'It is a terrible thing. Already we have lost two ship's boys, and they can't have been more than ten years old.'

'Nobody said what happened to them.'

Johanna thought of the two small bodies lying on deck, wrapped together in their shroud as the captain committed them to the deep. 'They were unlucky, just as your brother was unlucky.'

He spread his arms wide, as if to indicate his emptiness. 'Do you have brothers or sisters?'

Johanna shook her head. 'No. Just me.'

'Do you remember your parents?'

'My mother, yes, very vividly. I don't recall my father. I used to make up stories about him when I was small so that he would seem exciting – or real, perhaps. I remember telling the house-mother that he sailed off one day on a slave ship, and I knew she didn't believe me. But he existed, because I have his picture and my mother's as well.'

His eyes sparkled. 'Could I see?'

'Not this instant. I keep them in my Bible box in the cabin. When Moeder died, she bequeathed me the box. I think she knew I had hidden my Bible under my mattress. It's where we all hid our precious things – at least those of us who had them.' Johanna felt the sting of tears in her throat as she conjured Moeder's face in her mind. All at once, she recalled what the housemother had said to her. 'When she was ill, she told me to make sure I paid the uytkoop. I never did find out what that was. Have you any idea?'

He shook his head. 'I've never heard of it.'

'No matter.' Johanna gave him a small smile. 'I will show you my parents' picture later if I remember.' She glanced up at him. 'I have a picture of you, too. I drew it from memory when we were back at the huis.' She looked down, embarrassed.

He lifted her hand and kissed it. His hand was broad and callused, but his nails were neatly trimmed. 'Who taught you to draw?'

She shrugged. 'Not my mother.'

131

'Maybe your father, in that case.'

'I don't know enough about him to say one way or the other, but I don't really like drawing people. I'm more comfortable with birds.'

He cocked his head. 'Really? How do you get them to stay still?'

'It's easy if you watch through a window, but looking at the birds is not at all the same as seeing them.'

'I know what you mean. I can draw a windmill because I understand every single detail about it.'

'Do you start with a sketch?'

'Yes, as an exploration into how it might work.'

She clapped her hands together. 'Doodling with direction!'

'Is that how you begin to sketch a bird?'

'Absolutely. I start with the bill and build it up from there, a framework for what comes after.'

He brushed a tendril of hair from her cheek and hooked it behind her ear. 'Do you have one you could show me?'

She turned away, regretful. 'We were told that we could only bring what we could carry. None of us had anything besides a change of clothes and whatever we had first sneaked into the huis.'

He let his fingers rest on her hand. 'What did you hide?'

'The coral beads my mother gave me, which will go to my own daughter one day if I have one, and the Bible I was telling you about. Oh! And a miniature windmill I was given by someone. I can't think who.' She tapped her forehead, pretending to think.

He laughed and so did she.

The ship's bell clanged above them, calling the watch.

Frans jumped up and thrust a hand into the pocket of his long coat. He was tall enough to need to stoop under the beams of their shelter. 'I have to go before someone commandeers my hammock for the night, but I want you to have this. It was my mother's and, like you, I hid it under my mattress when I entered the huis.'

Johanna looked up into his handsome face and felt her knees weaken. In the palm of her hand rested a dainty ring of gold, set with glimmering stones – in the shape of a tiny heart.

~ CHAPTER 18 ~

FLORIANE LAID A FINGER between the book's pages to mark her place and looked up to where Johanna was pacing in front of the windows. 'Please stop fidgeting. You're making me nervous.'

Johanna stopped where she was, twisting her hands together in front of her. 'I'm sorry. I'm used to being occupied at every moment. I find it hard to just sit still. Truthfully, I don't know how you're able to stay in the cabin.'

Floriane took note of the page number and closed the book, setting it aside. 'Perhaps you could sketch something.'

'I suppose so.' The girl crossed the room and lowered herself into a chair, picking up her notebook and charcoal from the side table and dropping them in her lap. Rather than open the drawing book, she began to tap her foot.

'Is anything bothering you?' Floriane asked.

The girl leaned back and turned her face up towards the ceiling. She drew in a breath and blew it out. 'It's just that for so long, my life was exactly the same every day and now I'm on a ship and everything is different. My whole life has changed and I . . .' She turned her hands palms up and let them fall by her sides.

'Yes?'

'I suppose my most frequent activity at the huis was conversation with my friends, mevrouw. It's the one thing we could do while we worked. I miss them all terribly. And it's worse now I finally have something interesting to share and no one to share it with.'

'I think we have been companions long enough to drop the formality between us, and for you to use my given name,' Floriane said, her voice gentle.

'I would be pleased to call you F-Floriane.' A slight flush tinted the girl's face.

'Good. And now perhaps you'll feel able to share your news with me.' She widened her eyes encouragingly.

Johanna did not appear completely at ease, but said eventually, 'It's just that I've made a new friend. I met someone on board who I knew slightly at the huis.'

Floriane raised an eyebrow. 'I didn't know there were any other girls on board. Why are you not spending more time with her if it's lack of companionship that's making you restless?'

'Him,' Johanna said softly. She glanced at Floriane, nerves clouding her face. 'His name is Frans de Jong. He's completed his guild training and is sailing to the Cape to build wood-cutting mills.'

I thought the boys and girls at the huis never met. Floriane took care to keep her thoughts off her face. 'I see. And how did you know him at the huis?'

'From church, every Sunday.'

Floriane saw the caution in her eyes. 'I'm glad you've found someone you know.'

'I can even show you.' A smile transformed Johanna's expression as she jumped up and crossed to the corner where her Bible box sat on a small table. She carried it back and sat down. There was a momentary pause while she fumbled with the catch, then lifted the lid and took out a Bible. From inside the back pages, she extracted a slip and closed the book again.

Floriane scratched her forehead. 'Is that your own Bible?'

The girl nodded. 'It is. My mother taught me to read—' She broke off and hugged the book close to her chest. 'I have to confess to an untruth.'

'Concerning the Bible?'

'Yes.' The girl let her gaze drop to the floor. 'I said that the Bible was not mine and belonged to the huis.'

'I recall as much at your interview.'

'I'm so sorry. I didn't want them to take it from me.'

'Why would they do that?'

'I can't really say. It's just that when I arrived at the huis, Hilletje told me that I had to hide anything I wanted to keep, or it would be confiscated and sold. When I was formally admitted, the regentesses seemed keen to have our family Bible. I couldn't bear to part with it, so I've kept it hidden all these years. Are you very angry?'

'Oh no, my dear girl. I'm just thinking how difficult it all sounds. First losing your family and then having to deny any part of your past life.'

'You won't betray me?'

'Never. We shall always keep each other's secrets.'

'You have my word upon it. Would you like to see my parents?' She stepped forward with the open Bible, turning it so that Floriane could see a drawing of a man and woman standing side by side.

Involuntarily, she looked up at the cabin wall at the portrait of her own parents, laughing together at some private joke. She missed them with an intensity she could barely have thought possible, and understood why the Bible would hold such import-ance for Johanna.

Floriane was surprised at the fine tracery of lines and shading, the marks of a skilled artist. 'That's remarkable. They look well suited. Is it a good likeness, do you think?'

'It is, of my mother. I can't say about my father, as I don't remember him.'

'Who drew it?'

The girl glanced down and considered the question. 'My father did, according to my mother.'

'Was there another drawing?'

Johanna's forehead creased to a frown. 'Another?'

'I only ask as you seemed to be offering to show me Frans.'

'Oh, yes. This.' Johanna held out her hand. A scrap of white fabric lay in her palm, and upon it was a portrait of a boy.

'He's very handsome.' Floriane studied it. It was not as skilled as the drawings in the Bible, but it still showed promise. 'You drew this?'

Johanna nodded.

'You have talent.' She wanted more detail about Johanna's friendship with Frans but decided to leave further explanation for now. Some memory niggled at her, but she couldn't quite place it. 'You said those at the huis were keen to have your Bible?'

The girl nodded, curiosity brightening her eyes. 'Do you know why?' she asked.

'I'm not sure, but—' An idea struck Floriane. She got to her feet and went to her own Bible box. Triggering the secret drawer, she pulled out a folded sheet of vellum. 'You must never mention this to a soul,' she whispered, glancing nervously at the cabin door. 'I must ask you to swear.'

The girl nodded solemnly and touched her fingers to her heart. 'On my life.'

Unfolding the paper, Floriane held it out. 'Do these numbers mean anything to you?'

Johanna took the proffered sheet and ran her finger down the columns. 'These are our admittance numbers. At the huis we use them to get our towels and clean laundry, and I'm sure they're identification for other things, although I couldn't say what precisely. But each number is unique to a particular orphan.'

'Can you think of any reason these numbers should be singled out from among all the orphans at the huis?'

Shaking her head, Johanna looked again at the list. 'I have no idea what they might signify but I do recognise one of them at least – my own. And look, it says "No Bible" next to it in the second column.'

Floriane sat back, her mind sifting through what she knew and what she didn't.

Johanna stared at her blankly. 'What is this list? Where did you get it?'

'I copied it down from my husband's work.'

Their eyes met and a look of understanding passed over the girl's face. 'You suspect him of . . .' She shook her head. 'What, exactly?'

Floriane cast a glance towards the door. 'There's something amiss. Some form of villainy. But I don't know the details. Yet.'

The large hazel eyes were thoughtful. 'Do you think my Bible is . . . Should I keep it hidden?'

'Definitely. As long as we're on board ship, my husband might come into this cabin at any moment. Should I be sleeping, he might take an interest in your Bible box. I would not put it past him. Were he to learn of the Bible's existence, he could claim it on behalf of the VOC.'

'But why?' Johanna's voice held a note of frustration.

'That is the question, isn't it?' Floriane closed the book. 'What do you think of this idea, Johanna: what if I were to keep your Bible and hide it where he would never think to look? Then if he opens your Bible box he'll find it empty.'

Wide eyed, the girl sucked in a breath. 'May I know where it's hidden?'

'Of course.'

'Yes, then.' Johanna's jaw tightened. 'Let's find a place to hide it.'

*

Claes stifled a yawn and threw the quill on the chart room's table. He was copying logs into a VOC journal to show himself willing, and his eyes were sore with staring. 'As the Lord is my witness, boredom is a dangerous enemy.'

Captain Bierens raised an unruly ginger eyebrow. 'Many of the men are learning English to help them pass the time. You might consider doing the same.'

'Why on earth would one want to learn that pig of a language? I have tried but – sweet Jesus – the grammar is full of so many complications it is almost beyond learning.'

'Then why not take some air out on deck? The breeze is freshening, and it will be pleasant when the wind picks up and fills the sails.'

Claes emptied his glass and pulled his gold watch from the inside of his coat. Three o'clock.

Every day, in the middle of the afternoon, Johanna took a walk around the deck. It had been three days since he'd last spoken to her, but he'd kept a careful eye on her movements. He sensed she had become restless.

He closed the journal on the desk in front of him and got up from his chair. 'A splendid idea, captain,' he agreed. 'A turn on deck will blow the fog from my brain.'

As he closed the cuddy door behind him, she came past, across the quarterdeck, a smile on her face as bright as moonlight on water.

He picked up his pace and followed after her. 'Johanna, please stop,' he called. 'I'd like to walk with you.'

She turned and stared at his proffered arm. 'You will forgive me, mijnheer, but as your wife is not well she has asked me to be quick about my exercise.'

The words were out before he could catch them. 'That's a feeble excuse if ever I heard one. She ate a hearty enough dinner.'

Johanna stared around her and, blushing crimson, lifted her chin. 'What is it you want?'

He put his hand on her arm and looked at her in a way that would leave his intentions in no doubt. 'You affect to spurn me, Johanna, but your virtue is a sham. I know you've been busy with the windmill boy.'

She took a step away, trying to resist his grip, her lips white as whalebone. 'I have done nothing that you can accuse me of.'

He pulled her towards him. 'We both know that is a lie.' He ran his hand up her arm, underneath her sleeve. 'You will not deny me forever, girl. Now is as good a time as any. I may have the meanest cabin on board this ship, but it will serve.'

Her distress evident, Johanna turned her face to the officer at the whipstaff, but the watch had just changed and the fellow stood at his post, his eyes fixed on the set of his sails, blind to any signal she might have passed him. 'Please let go of me, Mijnheer van Loon. I am flattered by your attentions, but I am promised to another when we get to Good Hope.'

'It's still weeks till we get to the Cape, for God's sake.' Mad with frustration, he had a sudden thought. 'What trinket can I tempt you with? Perhaps a small emerald might be to your liking, or even a ruby? Every girl has her price. Just tell me what yours is and you shall have it.'

Johanna opened her mouth and he thought she might scream. He dropped his hand from her arm, knowing he'd gone too far. He spoke more playfully. 'You are such a lovely little thing, but perhaps we should leave this for another day.'

She bobbed a curtsy and fled.

He wondered briefly whether the girl would tell his wife, then shrugged. Floriane was ignorant of his liaisons, his financial difficulties, and all of the rest. If the girl squeaked and his wife challenged him, he would quite simply deny it.

Reassured, he made four sweeps of the deck, his sword swinging rhythmically at his side, until he heard a scratch of noise – the familiar rattle of dice in a cup. He followed the sound, unable to ignore it. Before the mainmast, a handful of crewmen were absorbed with a pile of coin and the ivory dice lying between them.

There was no afternoon shade on the forecastle deck and the light was blinding. Claes tipped his hat over his eyes, feeling sweat pool on his brow. It was in his mind to turn away until he saw the windmill boy scoop dice into the cup and rattle them in his ear. There was no way now he was going to resist. 'Is there a game in progress?'

Frans de Jong looked up. Perspiration had gathered on his eyelashes and shimmered in the sunlight. 'Novem Cinque.'

Claes nodded. It made sense that sailors would play the simplest game in the book, requiring only two dice and absolutely no brain. He put his hand in his coat and jiggled his loose change. 'What's the stake?'

'Stuiver stake and guilder limit.'

'May I join you?'

A bead of sweat rolled down the boy's nose. 'There's no limit on numbers.'

Feeling the heady rush that always preceded a game, Claes took off his coat, sat down on the scrubbed white planks, tossed in his stuiver, and reached for the leather cup.

His hands were slippery as he shook the dice and rolled them across the deck. Two fours. He breathed a sigh of relief.

The betting went on, shedding any player who threw a nine or a five, until only Claes and Frans remained.

Claes picked up the dice cup, gave it a good rattle, and threw. A four and five. He flashed a glance at the boy and begrudgingly pushed the pile of coins towards him. The brat was a pretender, a would-be usurper, and nowhere near his league. He leaned in even closer to whisper, 'Heed my advice. Stay away from the girl.'

Frans scooped his winnings into his palm and got up from the deck. 'That's me done, gentlemen.' His voice had gone flat.

'Shall we have another wager and play for the girl?'

The boy looked at him, his callow face suddenly pale. 'I said I am done for the day, Mijnheer van Loon.'

Claes got to his feet and in a cold and precise voice said, 'Don't say I didn't warn you.'

He saw the boy tense. 'Warn me of what? You'll have to remind me, mijnheer.'

'Johanna Timmerman is not for you.' He curled his lips into a scowl. 'Of that I will make certain.'

Frans did not blink. 'I cannot take seriously the word of a man so eager to betray his wife.' Pocketing his coins, the boy turned and said more loudly to the group, 'Gentlemen, I thank you very much for the game.' He turned on his heel and ambled his way across the deck.

Claes's hand dropped to the blade at his belt. 'You will regret that remark,' he said through his teeth.

⌒ CHAPTER 19 ⌒

THE LIGHT HAD ALL but gone from the day and, in the tiny space they had claimed as their own, it was dark. Frans curled his hand under Johanna's chin and tilted her mouth towards him.

She shut her eyes, anticipating what they both knew was to come, but sensed him change his mind and pull away. Her heart quickened with fear. 'Is there something wrong?'

He framed her face with his hands and looked deep into her eyes. 'Are you completely sure about this? Because when it's done there's no going back. There will never be a first time ever again. We might make a baby, and you might later wish you had waited for someone else.'

'Is that what you are thinking? That I ought to wait for someone else?'

He squinted in the gloom and she felt, rather than saw, the rising colour in his face.

'So you do think that.' She spoke before she'd had time to think. 'Because you might give me cause to regret it?'

He hung his head and shook it a fraction. 'Of course not. I hope I'm better than that.'

Johanna swallowed, grateful that the light was faint, that he wouldn't see the embarrassment on her face. 'I'm so sorry, Frans. That was an unpardonable thing to say. But remember I have no experience of any of this.'

'I know.' He gathered her to him once more and stroked her cheek, his callused engineer's fingers soothing her as they traversed the contours of her face.

'That's nice,' she murmured, her voice muffled against the cloth of his coat.

With trembling hands, he removed the linen cloth from her head and wove his fingers through her hair. 'You are intoxicating,' he breathed.

She wrapped her arms around him, attempting to squeeze away an unexpected flutter of nerves in her stomach. 'Are we to do this now?'

'I don't think we want to make a spectacle of ourselves just here. If we are set on this, we must try to find a more private place.' He sank down and pulled her with him. Fully clothed, they lay on the deck, their fingers intertwined. He twisted their hands back and forth and after a brief silence said, 'Do you love me, Johanna?'

'How can you doubt it?'

He caressed her cheek again. 'Will you marry me?'

She had hoped for these words for so long but, hearing them, she found herself hesitant. She raised herself up onto one elbow and looked into Frans's face. 'I have imagined this moment for such a long time, but I . . . There's something I haven't told you.' She stalled, unsure how to say it.

He sat up, a frown marring his handsome face. 'What is it?'

'I didn't tell you because I vowed from the start to find a way around the—'

'For heaven's sake, Johanna. A way around what?'

She gave a forced laugh. 'When you said you were going to the Cape, I vowed to myself that I would follow after you if ever there were a chance. But I'm not a boy, and therefore the only opportunity offered for me to go to the Cape was one by which I must cook and clean for some old man who wants a young wife. My bond says I am to marry a wealthy burgher.'

He looked at her, stunned. 'But surely there's a way out of that. Who are you to marry?'

'I don't know. It will be decided after we arrive.'

Frans reached for her hand. 'They can't force you to marry against your will.'

Despair bloomed inside her. 'I am sure that is true, but nonetheless I signed a document and gave my word even though that is the last thing on earth I want. I didn't really think about what the contract would entail, other than I would sail to the Cape, find you, and then . . .' She felt a spike of heat in her face and fixed her gaze on the planking overhead. 'As long as there is breath in his body, Mijnheer van Loon will never allow us to marry.'

'I am certain that is a fact.'

Johanna was taken aback. 'Have you spoken to him?'

'He joined a game of cards on deck the other day and as he was leaving, he warned me against you.'

'It's quite hopeless,' she murmured.

'But you have the ear of his wife, and you say she is very much on your side. I am sure she would help us.'

'She would. But when she came to the huis, she was recruiting on behalf of the VOC, not her husband. She can hardly tear up my contract, and I would never ask her to as she has been so kind to me. Putting her in such a tricky position is unthinkable.'

He squeezed her hand and pulled her to sitting. 'You are too honest for your own good, but if your conscience is pricking then we will pledge ourselves to each other in front of a witness.' He put an arm around her and gave her a little squeeze.

She heard his words, her misgivings almost forgotten. 'Are you sure?'

'No one can stop us, and the deed will be done. We should do it straight away, as it will not be many weeks now before we reach the Cape. If we marry before we leave the ship, there will be no way for the weasel to interfere.'

Johanna snuggled against him. 'Do we need a minister?'

'We do not. I have seen it done. It is sufficient to pledge ourselves to each other. I take your right hand then you take mine, and we say some words in front of a witness.'

'We could ask Floriane to be our witness, but it still puts her in an awkward position.'

His fingers tightened round hers. 'We can only see what she says.'

Johanna's thoughts were running together. 'She told me she was married in a church, so if she agrees, she would know what words to say. Surely there can be no argument at the Cape if I am already married.'

Staring into her face, Frans pulled her into his arms. She laid her head on his chest, listening to the sound of his racing heart, and for a moment her mind slipped away, thinking of her mother and wondering what she would say if she saw them like this. 'I don't want you to be sorry that you married me.'

He straightened his arms and eased away from her. 'Why would you say that?'

'I may turn out to be a disappointment. My father abandoned my mother, so she must have been a—'

His fingers stayed her lips. 'Neither of us can know how things will be. I don't suppose anyone really does when they get married, but I do know this: you will not disappoint me, and you must never entertain a single doubt that you ever could.'

She pressed his arm. 'I feel the same, but—'

Before she could finish her sentence, his elbows had bent and his lips were on hers, soft and insistent. In that moment, nothing else mattered but the rush of love she felt for her man.

⤔ CHAPTER 20 ⤕

FLORIANE WAS STRUGGLING TO read a book about a Dutch ambassador to the Emperor of Japan by the light of a tallow candle. It was hard going, but as she had many nautical miles of time on her hands before they reached the Cape, she was determined to get to the end.

There was a noise at the door, and Johanna rushed into the cabin, her cheeks pink and eyes bright. 'Frans and I are going to be married.'

Floriane unhooked her spectacles. 'I didn't think you knew him that well. When was this all decided?'

A sound of pure joy burst out of the girl. 'Just this minute.'

'Sit down, Johanna.' Floriane smoothed the velvet seat on the adjacent chair. 'And tell me what has happened to excite such happiness.'

Johanna crossed to the chair and perched on the arm. 'I've been seeing him in secret all the time, every day since I met him in the storm, and he asked me just now on deck. We are going to pledge ourselves to each other, and we would like very much if you would agree to be our witness.'

'Goodness. Whose idea was that?'

'Frans thought of it. He said if we are married with a witness, the Honourable Company won't make me marry a burgher at Good Hope.'

'Before you get too carried away with your plans, I must say I think this would be a betrothal ceremony rather than an actual marriage.'

Johanna's face fell. 'Frans said he had seen it done, and that it was deemed binding.'

'I wouldn't have thought that the Dutch East India would consider such an arrangement binding in the least, and I am certain they would not turn a blind eye to a breach of your contract.'

The girl had no ears for a setback. 'So we could hold the ceremony as an indication of our intention to marry, and then . . .' She trailed off, a fretful look on her face.

'I believe that, on a ship at sea, the captain may serve as a minister and officiate a wedding.'

The joy was quick to return. 'We'll ask the captain!'

'You may certainly ask him.' Floriane found it difficult to share Johanna's excitement. 'I can't think that he would have any particular objections to joining two people together if that was their wish, but these are not ordinary circumstances and the captain will know that.'

'Do you think so?'

'Of course. He captains a VOC ship. How you are to settle it with the Dutch East India when you have pledged to marry a Cape burgher might be a little more ticklish than simply saying you've had a change of heart.'

Johanna puffed out her cheeks and slid onto the seat. 'We'll cross that bridge when we get to it.' She looked at Floriane. 'Do you suppose it matters where we perform the betrothal?'

'I am no expert, but the most common tradition is for it to take place in the bride's house.'

'That could be a problem for me.' She pulled the cushion from behind her head and punched at the stuffing. 'And you haven't said whether you will stand as our witness.'

Floriane reached across and took hold of her hand. 'I will stand as your witness, though Lord above, I have no idea what Claes will say when he learns of it, nor what the fallout will be when he tells the Dutch East India. But if you are set upon it, I think for practical purposes you could consider this cabin your home. When I became betrothed, the ceremony happened in my parents' house.'

'What was involved?'

Floriane returned her hand to her lap. 'Looking back now, it was a typical piece of Claes theatre, and I was so in love that I thought it was perfect.'

Johanna peered at Floriane's fingers. 'I've never seen you wearing your ring.'

'No. I took it off when I knew what he was.'

For a few moments, silence fell.

'Mijnheer van Loon will not be happy about me marrying Frans.'

Floriane sat very still. 'I think that goes without saying, but remember you have me now to fight in your corner. I will always want the best for you. If that means helping you to marry your windmill engineer, then we shall hold the betrothal ceremony right here in the cabin and sniff at my husband's disapproval.' She saw tears in Johanna's eyes and did not wait for her to comment. 'We must find something to bind your hands together with Frans's to symbolise that you are joined as one, and then you will vow to be true to each other.'

'When shall we do this?' Johanna took a deep breath and dashed a hand across her cheek.

'First thing in the morning?'

The girl's voice trembled. 'Tomorrow? That seems an eternity away. Can we not do it tonight?'

Floriane got up and moved to the door. 'Go and find your young man and tell him that I'll be happy to stand in as your witness as soon as we can manage it. But I do think, to make sure that this ceremony is properly binding and cannot be questioned by the Dutch East India, that in the morning you should ask the captain to perform a marriage ceremony in his capacity as predikant on this ship.'

Johanna followed her across the floor. 'Thank you so much, Floriane. I shall find Frans and tell him. We'll be bound this very night.' Tossing a bright smile over her shoulder, she let herself out of the cabin.

'Well, then.' Floriane set her book down on the side table and looked up at the ceiling thoughtfully. 'No more reading for me tonight.'

She should not have agreed to witness the ceremony. But those two had so little, not even family. It seemed only right to allow the betrothal, even if it would cause some trouble. Surely this was nothing compared to the things Claes had done – the theft of jewels, the gambling, the debts – for which he had been awarded a higher rank and a comfortable new life.

Leaning back into her chair, she began to consider what she would need for the ceremony.

*

One by one, the captain's evening guests withdrew, but Claes was in no mind to be prudent. The sips of wine had grown to

152

gulps, until he was downing a glass in a single pull. At last he was the only guest remaining, and reluctantly he said his goodbyes and left the great cabin.

As he turned away from the door, the windmill boy came across the quarterdeck in front of him, crossed the waist of the ship and bobbed down behind a filthy tarpaulin. He had a look in his eye like a stoat caught stealing eggs. A hunter's instinct told Claes the girl was in there too. With measured, slow steps, Claes advanced across the deck until he was inches away from their nest.

He stood still and listened as Johanna's voice whispered to the boy. 'I can't believe all this is happening.'

'Nor can I,' said the boy.

Claes heard the sounds of their kisses.

'In the morning, we must go and ask the captain to marry us officially.'

He crept away without interrupting them, but anger was boiling within him. Backed into a recess at the side of the ship, Claes concealed himself in darkness and chewed on his lip till blood seeped into his mouth.

Slipping his hand inside his coat, he fingered his short-bladed dagger in its sheath at his belt. If the only girl directly under his watch married before reaching the Cape, it would not bode well for his future.

*

From the wide roundhouse cabin window, the wake of the ship could be seen making a soft ruffle of foam that lay on the water, blue-white under the moonlight. The striped flag of the Dutch East India Company floated from the stern, its colours muted in the dim light.

153

When a knock sounded on the cabin door, Johanna crossed the room and opened it. She felt nervous as she invited Frans into the cabin and introduced him to Floriane. 'This is Frans de Jong, Mevrouw Peronneau.'

He stood by the door, one hand holding the wrist of the other.

He's perfectly at ease, she thought. *Please let Floriane love him as much as I do.*

Floriane held out her hand to him. 'Come in, Frans, and shut the door behind you, so that interfering souls do not ruin your evening.'

As he shut the door, he swung towards Johanna, his green eyes soft. She could scarcely breathe for excitement.

Floriane touched her hand to the base of her throat. Johanna knew the gesture to be heartfelt. 'Johanna has told me that the two of you have an understanding.'

Frans bowed. 'It is more than that, mevrouw. It is our dearest wish to be married, and Johanna has said you are happy to stand as our witness.'

'I have questioned the wisdom of what you are doing, but for Johanna's sake am prepared to perform that role,' she said, and took a bright ribbon she used in her hair from the table. 'It is my fondest desire to see Johanna happy, and I am prepared to stand witness as the two of you pledge your intentions. But . . .' She put her arm around Johanna's shoulders. 'I did say that, to ensure there are no difficulties with the paperwork when we arrive at the Cape, you should ask the captain to solemnise this ceremony tomorrow.'

Johanna nodded. 'We are going to see him straight after breakfast tomorrow.'

'Let me come with you, in case there are difficulties.' Floriane dropped her hand from Johanna's shoulder. 'As for now, place your right hands together so that your wrists are touching.'

They stood so close together that the cloth of his breeches brushed against her dress.

Floriane turned to Frans. 'You must take Johanna for your wife.'

Frans lifted their hands and kissed Johanna's. 'Will you take me for your husband?'

Johanna felt the warmth of his palm against hers and thought she might die of happiness. 'I will take you for my husband.'

'As your witness, I'll now repeat a verse I have memorised for the binding oath.' She cleared her throat. '"Upon this day your hands entwined, a symbol of your love enshrined. To witness this I hope for thee, your union forever blessed will be."' She nodded at them both in turn.

Johanna nodded back and turned her gaze to Frans, her chest swelling with pride. Although she was tall, her head barely reached his shoulder.

'And now, Johanna, you must take Frans for your husband.'

Frans beamed his encouragement.

'Will you take me for your wife?'

He held their hands against his heart. 'I will take you for my wife.'

Johanna looked at Floriane. Then she turned to Frans. 'Can I now wear your mother's ring?'

Floriane held up a hand, palm towards them in a staying gesture. 'I wouldn't advise that. Save the ring until we arrive at the Cape, where my husband is unlikely to see it on your finger.'

Frans looked at their hands, fingers entwined, and said, 'The ring can wait. Just know I love you with all my heart, Johanna.'

The thrill of his words was dizzying. 'I love you so much, my heart might burst.'

Floriane laughed at their declarations. 'I'm sorry to be the bearer of bad news, but today has been a full day and tomorrow will be equally charged. As my parents did for me after my betrothal to Claes, I must send you away, Frans.'

Johanna looked up into his beautiful face. 'Until tomorrow. We shall meet here just after breakfast.'

'Until tomorrow, my beloved.' Frans bent and gave her the barest peck of a kiss. Then he turned and walked away from her through the cabin door.

The fingers of one hand resting against her lips, she stood in the open doorway and watched him go, his shoes tapping their tune on the decking. Just before he reached the corner, he looked back, his tall form outlined by the light of the moon. He mimed sweeping off his hat, even though he was bareheaded, then rounded the corner and was gone.

She sighed, latched the door and clasped her hands to her heart.

⸙ CHAPTER 21 ⸙

THE SUN HUNG BRIGHT in a clear sky, the wind just enough to fill the sails. To Johanna, it was the most perfect day she had ever seen. She'd scarcely slept a wink, and had found it difficult to sit through breakfast. But now there were only moments until Frans would come to the door and together they'd go to the captain and be joined as man and wife.

She struggled to stand still as Floriane wove a strand of pearls through her hair. Under the corset and numerous petticoats that coaxed her borrowed dress into shape, she could scarcely breathe.

'For heaven's sake, try to stand still for one more second.' Floriane's voice was coloured with humour. 'I've almost finished. There.' She stood back and, studying Johanna's face and hair, picked up a silver-handled mirror and held it up for her to view the results.

The face that looked back at her from the shining circle of glass was aglow with joy. 'I look quite pretty,' Johanna murmured.

'No, you are beautiful,' Floriane said, and patted her arm.

Johanna bent down to embrace her. 'Thank you for everything. You've done so much for me.'

'I said I would help. Now, are you ready? Have you put on your shoes?'

Johanna giggled. 'I don't know.' She pulled up the edge of the skirt and fought the petticoats aside. 'Yes, it appears I have.'

Floriane adjusted the lace on her own collar. 'Then let us sit down and wait.' She motioned to the chairs.

Johanna sat, but immediately sprang up and began to pace. 'Oh, I'm so nervous. I can hardly bear it.'

Floriane frowned and looked unhappy. 'Are you absolutely sure that this is what you want, Johanna?

'I am—'

Floriane held up a hand. 'Let's be clear. Are you certain you are happy to renege on your contract with the Dutch East India? There will be consequences, but I wouldn't care to guess what they might be, and you must be prepared for Claes's wrath.'

Johanna said she had no doubts. 'It's not that I want to break the contract – and I shall stay in the Cape for five years using my skills where needed. It is only the marriage part I must break. I have looked forward to this day for . . .' She let her voice trail off as she recalled the first time she'd seen Frans looking at her across the nave of the Nieuwe Kerk. 'Years. I have the moment captured in my mind. It feels like a sign from the heavens that Frans and I ended up on this ship together, against all likelihood.' She met Floriane's gaze. 'Yes, I'm certain,' she said with feeling.

'So sit down.' Floriane nodded, the crease between her brows less apparent.

They sat in silence for what must have only been minutes, but Johanna began to feel a stab of unease in the pit of her stomach. Shouldn't he have come by now? She took a slow breath in through her nose and tried to still the tremble in her fingers where they rested on her knees. She glanced towards Floriane, who had taken up her book and begun to read.

Tearing her mind from unwelcome thoughts, she re-ran a conversation she'd had with Frans about where she'd like to live when they were married.

'*On a farm. I've often imagined us living on a farm like the one where I grew up. And there will be birds, lots of African birds, so I can learn their names and sketch them.*'

A knock at the cabin door shocked her from her thoughts, her hands braced on the arms of her chair.

Floriane rose from her seat, crossed to the door and opened it. 'Come—' She took a step to the side. 'Claes! Were we expecting you so early?'

'Good morning, Floriane.' Claes stepped inside, pushing the door closed behind him. He looked back and forth between them, his eyes suspicious. 'I didn't realise I had to make an appointment to see my own wife.'

'Naturally not, but we don't normally see you until later in the day.'

He continued to stare, his eyes seeming to search the space around them. 'Have I interrupted something?'

'Nothing at all,' Floriane said, her voice mild. She returned to her seat and picked up the book. 'I was just reading out passages of this fascinating text about Japan to Johanna.'

Johanna played with the coral beads beneath the neckline of her dress.

Claes again looked from one to the other. 'I see. I've come from the captain and wondered if you'd heard the news.'

Shock again ripped through Johanna, as though in response to the booming of a cannon. Her head began to swim, and her heart seemed to stall. She fumbled for something to say but the words would not form.

'What news? We've not left the cabin since breakfast.' Floriane tapped at her book. She sounded impossibly calm.

Claes turned confidential. 'Captain Bierens tells me that if the winds hold, we shall make landfall at Good Hope in a week's time.'

Johanna's heart resumed its painful banging against her ribs. For a moment she felt as if she would pass out and put a hand to her head, her breathing shallow.

'My goodness, Johanna. Are you quite well?' Floriane was beside her in an instant.

'I'm sorry,' she murmured. 'Something I ate this morning has curdled in my stomach.'

Claes van Loon shot her a reproving look and said dryly, 'Perhaps you're coming down with one of my wife's ailments. Goodness knows there are enough to choose from.'

Johanna felt Floriane tense next to her.

'At any rate, I'll not linger if the air in this cabin is tainted.' Claes van Loon swung on his heel and strode off, not bothering to pull the door shut behind him.

Floriane banged it, hard enough for the whole ship to hear, then she folded her arms and stared at the brass latch.

Johanna realised she'd been holding her breath, and let it out. 'I was so fri—'

Spinning to face her, Floriane pressed a finger to her lips then went on speaking about the book. 'Shall we continue where we left off?' She returned to her chair and picked it up, pointing to her mouth and then to Johanna.

'Yes. I'm sure that would restore my spirits.'

Floriane opened the book and began to read, stopping after a paragraph or two. 'I'm sure he's gone now,' she whispered. 'But we should keep our voices low nonetheless.'

Johanna tipped her head back and shut her eyes. She had a terrible sense that something dreadful had happened.

Floriane was next to her again within moments. 'Johanna?'

She opened her eyes. 'Did you not feel it?'

'I'm not sure what you mean?'

'When Mijnheer van Loon came in. He – he was checking to see what we knew. I'm sure the conversation with the captain was a ruse.'

'What are you suggesting?'

'Mijnheer van Loon warned me away from Frans over and over. He confronted Frans about it as well. He said he would take matters into his own hands if I continued to see him.'

'But you said you were discreet. Do you think Claes can have known that you saw him in secret, or indeed that yesterday we held the betrothal in this cabin?'

'I had hoped not.' Despair closed its hand around her. 'But if mijnheer did not know, then where is Frans? I just don't understand why he has not come.'

'It has only been a couple of hours. It might be explained in a dozen ways. Perhaps he misunderstood the time. Perhaps he misunderstood where you were to meet.' Floriane pressed her arm.

Johanna clung to her words. 'You must be right. Perhaps he's waiting for me now in our usual meeting place.' She leapt out of her chair. 'I'll go and look.'

'Wait just a moment.' Floriane motioned her close and draped a scarf over her hair. 'That's better.'

Johanna smiled, but her hands were unsteady. 'I'll be back soon, hopefully with Frans.' Even as she said the words, doubt clutched at her. But she would not give in to it.

She made her way across the deck and down to the secret place. The piece of sailcloth hung in its usual spot and, at the sight of it, she dared hope that he was there or at least that she would find some sign of him. Ducking behind the cloth, she blinked at the change in light.

She moved inside on her knees, fighting her skirts out of the way, and sat. The space was empty, silent. There was nothing there but her memories of the past few months. Frans telling her about his life. Frans listening to her dreams. Frans laughing, the sound of his heartbeat when she rested her head against his chest. The taste of his lips against hers. The hopes of a future spent side by side. It all washed over her.

But he wasn't here, nor was there any sign that he'd been here today. The tears she'd been holding back for the past few hours triumphed over her defences and spilled down her face. She let herself crumple onto the decking, her hand pressed over her mouth so that no passer-by would hear her sobs.

⁓

At eight o'clock the next morning, the bell signalling the change of watch called the passengers to breakfast.

Johanna rolled over onto her side. 'I can't go down this morning.'

At the mirror, Floriane was busy, lacing a gold ribbon through her hair. 'I understand you're upset, but you know the captain frowns on breakfasting in the cabin. You must put your clothes on and come down to the dining room, even if you eat nothing.'

'Could you please make my excuses this once? The mere thought of that rancid butter and stale ship's biscuit turns my stomach.'

Floriane lingered a moment by the door. 'It's only been a day, Johanna. Frans will come, I'm certain of it. But I will tell the captain that you were fitful last night and that I have given you permission to sleep in.' She left the cabin, closing the door behind her.

Her blanket wound around her like a shroud, Johanna lay on the cot, Frans's voice echoing in her mind. *Will you marry me?* She lifted her head off the pillow and shifted onto her back. With only the ship's bells and the sea's endless symphony for company, she felt misery spreading through her body, stretching out its tentacles and strangling the hope inside her.

Caught up in her thoughts, she had no idea of the time when the cabin door opened and Floriane squelched in.

'It's raining, just a mist really, but it makes for a damp crossing.' She took off her scarf and, looking up, saw Johanna under the covers. 'Are you still in bed?' She crossed the room to her side. 'I'm sure there's no cause to fret so. Perhaps he's unwell. The *mal de mer* can strike at any time.'

Johanna considered. 'Wouldn't we have heard if that was the case?'

Floriane stared at her, her expression brooking no argument. 'We shall search for him.'

'But I've already looked in the only place I'm certain he goes.' Johanna turned her face away, pressing it against the pillow.

'But if he's unwell, he'll be in his cot.'

'He told me he slung his hammock wherever there was room, but I don't know where that might be.'

Floriane came around the bed, crouching down so that their faces were close. 'I'll come with you and we'll look. It will be safer if there are two of us. But you must get out of bed and get dressed.'

A short while later, they climbed down the companionway to the depths of the ship and wandered through the lower decks, where sailors lounged, or lay idling away the time between watches. Eyes around them exchanged glances, some made lewd gestures, but no one approached them.

'Do you think they know something?' Johanna whispered.

'I don't know,' Floriane replied, stumbling over a supine form. 'But we must be quick, I think. I do not feel that this was the wisest of plans to root about down here.'

Together, they searched for a sign of him, anything to give them a clue – an item of clothing, a sketch of a windmill, a strand of golden hair on a rat-nibbled blanket. But there was nothing. It was as though Frans had climbed into one of the ship's flatboats and rowed clean away.

The next morning, Johanna pulled herself from her torpor. Before the breakfast bell sounded, she swung herself out of the cot and inched her way across the cabin floor, still dressed in yesterday's clothes. Her hand trembled on the latch as she pulled open the door, checking as she left that Floriane was still asleep. So that she wouldn't lose her nerve, she strode towards the companionway and gathered up her skirts before climbing down the ladder to the deck. Keeping her eyes trained on the sun-bleached planking to avoid catching an unwelcome eye, she crossed the passageway, raised her hand and knocked on the captain's door.

'Come in.' Captain Bierens was alone in the stateroom he used during the day as a study. He sat behind his desk, no hint of welcome on his face, and pointed at a chair to the side of the desk. 'What brings you here at this early hour?'

Johanna had not thought how she was going to tell him her fears. She breathed in and out, dizzy with nerves, until the words rushed out by themselves. 'Forgive the intrusion, captain, but I am beside myself with worry. My friend Frans de Jong has disappeared from this ship and, after two days of frantic waiting, I fear for the worst.'

He clasped his big hands together. 'What do you mean, your friend has disappeared?'

'The windmill engineer who is going to the Cape with the Dutch East India is missing. We were meeting in the mornings and evenings and spent time together on deck, yet he was supposed to meet me two days ago and didn't appear. I have neither seen nor heard from him since.'

The captain gave her a sharp look. 'I am not a man to condone improper relations.'

Instinct had Johanna keep the betrothal to herself. 'There has been no impropriety between us. I know Frans from the orphanage, and we have become friends.'

The captain appeared mystified. 'I cannot place this person, but there are more than three hundred souls on this ship so that gives me no cause for alarm.' He leaned across the desk and patted her hand. 'I'm sure he'll turn up sooner or later. Try not to fret.'

Patronising manner aside, Johanna could read in his expression that he did not share her anxiety; that she might as well have been reporting a pair of gloves she'd mislaid rather than a missing passenger. 'You must have a record of him in the ship's passenger list, if you would only—'

'His name will be there, as our record-keeping is scrupulous. When was the last time this windmill engineer was seen, that you know of? By anyone other than yourself?'

'In the last two days Mijnheer van Loon has certainly seen him, as has his wife.'

'In that case, I confess myself bemused as to why those esteemed passengers have not also reported him missing.'

Johanna's heart thumped in her chest, but she did not pause to weigh her words. 'Perhaps he was set upon by Mijnheer van Loon.'

The captain drew back. His expression was one of disbelief, as if he had caught her stealing money from the church's collection plate. 'That is a damning accusation, and I would caution you to guard your tongue.'

'He threatened me, captain.'

The man scratched at a spot on his chin. 'You must expand that statement so that I understand exactly of what you accuse a senior Company official.'

Something made her hold back. In her heart of hearts, she suspected that the captain would never have married her to Frans. As Floriane had told her, he would have known she was under contract to the Dutch East India, for whom he sailed his ship, and that he would never have quizzed a high-ranking colleague. These men closed ranks when under threat, like battleships at war.

A tear slid down her cheek. 'I'm sorry, captain. I did not sleep well last night, and fantasies grow large in the dark. I seem to have magnified the situation in my mind, so please forgive my intrusion on your time.'

He pulled open a drawer and held out a square of cloth. 'Mop your eyes and do not distress yourself. I shall ask the ship's mate to enquire as to the whereabouts of the engineer Frans de Jong. He'll be here or thereabouts on the ship, and someone will know where to find him.'

Johanna dried her eyes. 'I know it is not my place to ask this, but will you also ask Mijnheer van Loon what he knows?'

He mumbled something indistinct, then said more clearly, 'Mijnheer van Loon is already up and about and is in the chart room penning letters, so I will go directly and ascertain what light he can shed.' He stood up and indicated that she should do the same.

'I will excuse you from breakfast, so go back to your cabin and take some rest.' The captain walked her to the door. 'Ask Mevrouw Peronneau to administer a calmative, or perhaps a little gin or brandy, if you are unable to settle.' He nodded, as much to himself as to her. 'Yes, I feel that would be the most beneficial course for you just now, as you are, in your own words, somewhat overwrought.'

As he ushered her out of his domain, Johanna felt she might as well have told her fears to Daisy the cow for all the good it had done her. The captain had said all the right words to console her, but she didn't believe for one minute he'd seen her as anything more than a sleep-deprived child.

It was up to her alone, she now realised, to discover what had happened to Frans – and why, in the space of forty-eight hours, he'd completely vanished from view.

⚍ CHAPTER 22 ⚎

FLORIANE SAT IN HER chair by the window, her knitting poles clacking together at a speed she wasn't sure she'd known herself to keep before. Worry propelled her hands. Since Frans's disappearance, the girl had not been herself, and Floriane couldn't help but be concerned about what she might do.

The cabin door rattled. She set the knitting in her lap and looked up as the door opened and the girl came in. She seemed out of breath and hurried across the cabin to where her Bible box sat, opened it up and took something out from between its pages.

'Where have you been?' Floriane knew she sounded cross.

The girl jumped and spun towards her. 'You nearly frightened me out of my wits. I thought you'd be at breakfast.'

'I was worried about you. I decided not to go to breakfast and will have to accept Captain Bierens' lecture.'

'He's given me permission to miss the meal, and told me to ask you to administer some gin or brandy if I couldn't be still. It gives you an acceptable excuse.'

'You've been to see the captain? What on earth for?'

'I went to report that Frans is missing and to ask for his help.'

Floriane sat up straight. 'He will consider that an impertinence. Why didn't you talk to me first?'

'You were asleep.'

'I thought I'd made it clear that the captain would need careful handling over Frans.'

'You don't need to worry, as he wasn't interested in the least and couldn't get me out of his cabin fast enough.' Johanna rubbed her mouth with her hand. 'He said he didn't know who Frans was personally. He agreed to make enquiries about him but I don't imagine he will. I came back here to get the sketch of Frans and the little windmill he gave me. It might help jog his memory.'

Floriane weighed up the captain's response. 'It would be a very poor shepherd who mislaid one of his sheep.'

Johanna blinked at her. 'What do you mean by that?'

'I am thinking the captain knows more than he's let on, and that we should both go and see why he said otherwise.'

⸺

From their vantage point on the poop deck, Floriane looked on as Captain Bierens relieved the helmsman on the upper deck. She touched Johanna's shoulder, encouraging her to turn. 'I think this is as good an opportunity as we shall find. Let's go down and see him.' She made sure the girl realised she was serious, and said with some heat in her voice, 'You are to say nothing. I will speak for you. Is that understood?' She saw that Johanna was upset at her tone, but this was not the moment for an apology.

Holding on to the handrail, they descended the wooden stairs and joined him on the main deck.

'Captain, do please forgive us, but we wonder if we might beg five minutes of your time?'

The captain looked startled. 'Mevrouw Peronneau. This is a pleasurable disruption.'

'Our visit concerns the windmill engineer who we fear has had an accident on your ship.' Floriane searched his eyes, looking for clues. When he did not immediately respond, she motioned with her head towards the sea. *Guess wrong to guess right* was an old maxim of her father's. 'We have come to think he must have fallen overboard in a storm, as there has been no burial at sea.'

A smile, if somewhat lacking in sincerity, appeared on the captain's face. 'We have been fortunate to have had no deaths in recent weeks.'

'And yet Johanna felt that you might not have taken her quite seriously when she came to see you this morning.'

'And you promised to ask—' Johanna began.

'Stop.' Floriane cut over her. 'I told you I would speak.'

With an irritated gesture, the captain flapped his hand at the girl. 'That was barely two hours since, and it's not a five-minute task to quiz every person on board a ship of this size.'

'Captain Bierens, I beg your forgiveness, but know I must provide an eyewitness's testimony. I have seen Frans de Jong with my own eyes not two days since, and have stood as close to him as you are now standing to me.'

The captain ran his hand along the tiller. 'I'm not disputing that.'

Floriane knew she had his full attention now. 'Frans has quite unexpectedly disappeared at a time when it seems very unlikely he would do so of his own volition. If you do not recall his face, Johanna can show you his portrait if that would help to jog your memory.'

The captain stood at his post, stiff and straight. 'I'm at a loss as to what you expect me to do beyond what I have already promised. Two deputations in one morning will not speed up the process.' Their eyes met, his challenging, hers cold.

'I am certain it is not your intention to treat an enquiry after the wellbeing of someone I know as unwelcome.' She stared straight at the captain as she spoke.

He dropped his eyes to the deck, a dark flush staining his cheeks, but when he looked up his face was drawn. He moved slightly, slackening his grip on the whipstaff, and flexed his fingers, scanned the deck to ensure they could not be overheard then said behind his hand, 'We should continue this conversation in the privacy of my stateroom. If you will permit me five minutes to secure the services of the first mate, I will join you both there.'

Captain Bierens held the door to his stateroom open for them, closed it behind them, and remained on his feet while they occupied the two chairs that flanked his desk. Floriane could not help but notice it was a handsome room, lined with rich panelling. A pair of gilt-framed mirrors hung from two silver sconces, and an immense carved chest not dissimilar to the one Claes owned sat in one corner. The windows were thrown open, and a warm breeze fluttered the embroidered curtains that framed the captain's canopied bed.

He walked up and down, seemingly reluctant to begin, then dropped into a wide wooden chair and drew a leather-bound journal towards him. Taking a bunch of keys from the purse he wore on his belt, he unlocked the clasp and searched for an entry. 'I must present my most sincere apologies, ladies,' he said, 'that I was not honest with you from the start.'

171

Floriane watched his face but chose not to speak.

He rested his chin on his tented hands, then lifted his head. 'I have struggled with this matter since it first came to light, and perhaps it is a good thing that you have forced my hand. Perhaps.' With one of his elbows propped on the desk, he momentarily rested his forehead on his hand, his eyes unfocused, then he sat up and said, 'At least I can share what I know to be the truth concerning the windmill engineer.'

Johanna jerked upright in her chair and opened her mouth to speak.

Floriane shook her head and placed a finger against her lips. 'Wait for the captain to tell us what he knows.'

'Three days ago – I have the time recorded as "gone midnight" on the twenty-fifth of February 1684 – the second mate found Frans de Jong on the lower deck, and dragged him under a tarpaulin while he searched out the ship's surgeon.'

The colour drained from Johanna's face. 'Is Frans dead?'

He breathed deeply and Floriane saw that he was composing his words. 'You must understand that coming across a bloodied man is not unusual on board a long-distance ship. Boredom, cheating at cards, a perceived insult . . . Sailors are renowned for settling scores with their knives, more often than not ending in death.'

'So he *is* dead.' Johanna fell back in her seat.

Floriane trained her eyes on his face. 'Captain?'

He stared at the roof, as if checking the night sky for stars. 'No. Frans had lost consciousness. Between them, the surgeon and second mate got him to a hammock in our makeshift sick bay. As usual at this late stage of the voyage, it is full to brimming with those suffering from scurvy, and so they were able to conceal him quite easily.'

Johanna jumped up. 'I must go to him.'

The captain looked at her and stroked his moustache. 'Please sit down. There is no question of you seeing him.' He reached for the decanter on his desk and poured a measure of port wine into a glass. 'Drink this and gather yourself. You have forced a response from me, and you *will* oblige me by remaining calm and listening to what I have to tell you. Frans had been knifed twice in the chest, with a piece of the knife left behind in one of the wounds. A very grave matter. But for the surgeon's skill, he would be lying on the ocean floor providing sustenance to the sharks.'

With a stricken look, Johanna gulped at the wine.

'For reasons you might guess at, I chose to keep the matter to myself. With no explanation for what provoked the attack, I felt the boy was safer stowed away with no attention drawn to it.'

The next question filled Floriane with foreboding. But she asked it anyway. 'Did anyone see who made the assault?'

A troubled look crossed his face. 'There were no witnesses except the boy himself. I think you know what I am going to say.'

She cradled her cheek in her palm. 'Johanna told me that Claes warned her to have nothing to do with the boy. But they fell in love, and being together was all they wanted in the world. They were on the point of asking you to marry them.'

'Mijnheer van Loon said that if I didn't put an end to our friendship, he would do it for me.' Johanna's face filled with bitterness.

The smile the captain produced was tight. 'Frans is alive, and the surgeon is optimistic he will survive. We will drop anchor in Table Bay within the next few days, if the winds remain as favourable as they have recently. As soon as we have secured the ship, we'll have him removed to the hospital. But it is vital to keep his survival secret. You will understand, I am sure, why I did not want to broadcast this to the ship's complement.' He paused while Floriane waited for the inevitable.

'The attack on the boy was murderous in intent. If I have misjudged the wisdom of my telling you this, Frans de Jong will not survive the last days till Good Hope.'

Back in the cabin, the bolt drawn against intrusion, Floriane sat beside Johanna on the bed, stroked her hair, and listened to the outpourings of her grief. The girl clung to her hand, her eyes closed against the pain, quiet sobs shaking her shoulders.

Floriane blinked tears from her own eyes, and in a soft, unsteady voice, said, 'Shh, Johanna. You have to try to calm yourself.'

The girl's face glistened with tears. 'I love him more than I ever thought it possible to love another person, and your husband tried to destroy it.'

Floriane wanted to reassure her that all would be well, but hearing the words out loud somehow made the horror of it too true. The captain had not named Claes, but in her heart, she knew that Claes had done this vile deed. 'Don't cry, Johanna. I cannot bear your heartache. The captain says Frans is alive, and we have to hold on to that.'

'If the captain suspects it was Mijnheer van Loon who did this thing, why has he done nothing? Thieves are hung for less.'

Floriane stared into Johanna's red-rimmed eyes. 'The captain may suspect, but suspicion is not enough to bring a man of Claes's influence to justice.' She paused to consider her words. 'Claes was the man who had captured my heart, who would father my children, with whom I would grow old. It took a stranger to point out to me Claes's sins. In the wink of an eye, he can transform himself from the most tender and loving companion to the craftiest, most deceitful gambling philanderer one might conjure in one's imagination.'

Johanna sat up a bit straighter, twisting her hands in her lap.

Floriane leaned towards her. 'I do know how it feels to be in love,' she said. 'And I also know what it is like when the feeling has gone. I thought I had learned not to care what Claes does, but now, the need to fight back and have him suffer is beyond ignoring.'

The girl had stopped crying, but her expression still conveyed her misery. 'What are you going to do?'

'As women, we are not empowered to act for ourselves. I believe I told you that in matters of the law I cannot divorce him, and so I have to find other means of manipulating events.'

Johanna didn't answer at once and when she did, she asked another question. 'As you can't divorce him, are you looking to other ways of ridding yourself of him?'

'I am, and there are others involved. We are working together to expose him for what he is: greedy, impetuous and of poor judgement. If he is given enough rope, he will eventually knot the noose that will hang him. I promise he will pay for what he has done to Frans, but you will need to be patient.'

Johanna rolled off the bed and went to Floriane's Bible box. 'May I borrow your Bible?'

Floriane nodded, broken beneath the weight of her anger. Had she been wise to explain so much? Probably so, she told herself. There was more to tell even still – the theft of the jewels, Erick de Witt's involvement. It would have to wait its moment, though.

The girl lifted the lid of the Bible box and, taking Floriane's Bible in her right hand, she said, 'I promise that I will help you in any way I can. I will do anything and everything to make sure Claes van Loon is held to account for what he has done.'

*

A week after he had removed Frans de Jong, Claes mounted the companionway to the dining room, taking the steps two at a time.

Luck was on his side, and he found a spare seat next to Johanna at the breakfast table. He gave her his most beguiling smile, keeping his face slightly averted so that Floriane would not see. Heaven only knew how little diversion there had been aboard this ship in the past five months. A little dalliance with the girl to 'console' her in her loss would be just the thing in the last days of the voyage.

This morning her face looked different: paler, more vulnerable, in need of an experienced man's closest attention. Claes's fingers tingled where they lay on the table, inches from her own, craving a touch of that milky white skin.

The captain rose and passed round to the head of the table. He looked unkempt, as though he had spent the night at the card table and come away the poorer. His eyes were heavy lidded, and a few wiry strands of grey hair poked out from under his wig. His moustache was unwaxed and drooped at the sides of his mouth, dragging the corners downwards and making him look grim. Claes touched his own neat, waxed tips.

Floriane also looked pale, with dark smudges beneath her eyes, preoccupied almost. She poured some tea into a delftware cup and slid it across the table. 'Are you quite well, captain? You look completely done in.'

The captain did not blink. 'I apologise for my poor appearance this morning, but I have not slept and have sad news to relate. Last evening a member of the crew succumbed to knife wounds. We stitched him into a canvas shroud, and in the early hours committed him to the deep. We must all ask for God's blessing on his soul.'

Claes forced his jaw to drop and pressed his hat to his breast. 'Knife wounds! But that's appalling news. Was there not a witness to this dreadful crime?'

Johanna clutched at her throat. 'How terrible for him.'

'Who can know what it was about or what provoked it? The attack – and these happen more than you might imagine – was unwitnessed. Of course, we have our suspicions as to who was responsible.' The captain's gaze ranged around the table.

For the briefest moment, Claes found the man's eyes directly on his face. He felt his heart quicken. He'd been certain that no one had seen him cross the deck and bide his time in the shadows.

The captain continued, 'The fellow is a notorious brawler, however, particularly when he loses at dice.'

Glad of the explanation, Claes pushed the doubt aside. The captain's eye was clearly elsewhere. 'Will you string him up on the yardarm, or haul him under the keel, as a salutary lesson to the others?'

The captain raised a finger. 'No. The Dutch are not barbarians like the English. He is confined on the lower deck but will have a fair trial when we reach the Cape.'

Claes recoiled a little from the reprimand and reached for his tobacco pouch and pipe. He turned to Johanna. 'I haven't seen you much on deck recently.'

Floriane glanced at the girl and almost imperceptibly shook her head.

'Is there something I should know, dear wife?' Claes narrowed his eyes.

Johanna looked across at him as if considering her reply then looked down at her plate, her voice thick with emotion. 'I've not been well and have been keeping out of Frans's way, as you told us we must.'

'Van Loon.' The captain's eyes met his. 'Is this a discussion I should be aware of?'

Claes felt a vague sense of unease rise inside him and puffed slowly at his pipe. 'I've not exchanged two words with the lad since we set sail, and barely know what he looks like. If you want to know anything about him, you should ask Johanna. Isn't that right?'

Johanna stood up from the table. 'Please excuse me, mijnheer, captain. I'm still not completely myself.'

Floriane also got to her feet. 'I think you have said enough, Claes.'

Shocked that his wife had rounded on him, Claes fell silent. When breakfast was over, he was slow to leave. Even though he knew the windmill boy was dead, his mood was not quite so buoyant as when he'd sat down to eat.

⮜ CHAPTER 23 ⮞

FIVE MONTHS AFTER SETTING sail from Texel, the *Borssenburg* floated into Table Bay on a fading breeze that barely ruffled Johanna's hair. It was a March morning and the sea was smooth, the waves flat as a millstone, the sky a brilliant blue.

'So this is Africa,' she said to herself, leaning over the poop-deck rail. Her heart was still heavy with sadness, but she calmed herself with the knowledge that Frans would be safe now that they'd reached the Cape.

She gazed at the triptych of immense mountains before her. The central one was as flat as a table. Flanking its right was a sleeping lion, and on its left, a peak. Even from the ship, she could see the lower slopes were rich with trees and grey-green plants; on the beach, dark-skinned people gathered brushwood from the sand. To the right, her eye was caught by a great stone fort, its bell tower rising tall, the flag of the great Dutch East India Company drooping lifeless from its pole.

As they drew nearer to the quay, a gentle hand dropped on her shoulder and she turned to see Floriane, who was shielding her head with a brightly coloured parasol. 'You look deep in thought,' she said.

'I was wondering where the hospital might be.'

'You should not hold out hope that you will be able to visit straight away. The captain will want to make sure that Frans is safe before he risks exposing his whereabouts.'

They stood together in companionable silence. Before long, with a loud rattle that shook every plank on the ship, the anchors were let down in the bay. Shading her eyes with the flat of her hand, Johanna strained to look at the great cliff of grey rock at whose foot lay the little township in which she was to live for the next five years.

From behind them, the first officer said, 'You are fortunate indeed to see the Cape for the first time when the weather is calm.' He pointed towards the shoreline, beads of perspiration filming his face. 'Disembarking in a swell is no picnic, believe me, not with the ship pitching from left to right.'

Johanna took a step away, pinching the tip of her nose between her fingers. The sailor smelled appalling, for there had been no water on board for days other than for drinking, and even that had been in poor supply. 'Will we be able to get off quickly?'

'That depends on a number of things. Certainly not until after dinner. We must wait here until the commander sends a message aboard, inviting us to come ashore. Let's hope the lookout on Signal Hill saw us some days back and passed on that we were approaching.' He jerked a thumb over his shoulder. 'The usual protocol is for the sick to disembark first. You should even prepare yourselves for the possibility that we might still be on board tomorrow evening.'

The morning wore on. Johanna could not tell how many times she had heard the helmsman call the hour by the sandglass, yet no word came from the shore. Grey mullet swam in shoals in the clear blue water, darting among fronds of brown seaweed, and gulls and other birds she did not recognise soared overhead, diving now and then like a plumbline to the depths. She should by rights have been happy, thrilled even, to have made it to their destination, but her heart was heavy with thoughts of Frans.

Floriane looked at Johanna, then at the water, and sighed. 'I am delighted we are here at last, but I shall miss your company when we go our separate ways.'

'Will I not see you at the Cape?' Johanna felt a stab of alarm.

'I would most certainly hope so, but it won't be quite the same, will it? As we won't be sharing accommodation, I mean.'

'What do you think will happen to me?'

'Truthfully, I don't know. A great deal depends on Frans's recovery and whether we can persuade the commander to sanction what has happened between you on board this ship. But I promise you, Johanna, I will do my utmost to see the two of you married and settled in a home of your own.'

⁓

By three o'clock in the afternoon, the air in the dining room was sour with the smell of sweat. Johanna sat with Floriane to her right. The first officer was busy securing the ship, and six of the others in the cabin were the Company's scribes – unshaven, unwashed, their clothes filthy and neglected.

Claes van Loon was at the far end of the table, at the captain's elbow. Johanna tried not to look at him, but his presence filled her with a sense of dread. At moments, she thought she could feel his eyes on her. It was at those times in particular that she focused all her attention on eating; putting tiny bites of meat and bread into her mouth and counting to a hundred as she chewed.

Floriane must have been aware of her discomfort, for she leaned close and muttered under her breath, 'Don't catch his eye, because he cannot suspect we know.'

Johanna lifted her glass, which shook in her hand, the contents splashing over her wrist. *If only I had never caught his eye*, she thought.

The captain rose from his seat and banged his knife against the table. 'This will be our last meal together, and I thank you for your company over the past few months. We are safely arrived in Table Bay and, thanks be to God, have sighted the rest of our fleet already at anchor.'

Johanna felt a sharp pang of guilt that she hadn't thought of her friends in weeks. Since the night of the storm when she had clung to the mast with Frans, their love had been all-consuming.

The captain went on with his commentary. 'We have sent a signal to shore to say that the sick are to be first off the ship. They will be transferred directly to the hospital, and we beg the Lord they will rally quickly.'

'God's truth, I say. Amen to that.' Claes began to heap cheese on his plate. 'But as high-ranking officials of the Dutch East India Company, I think I must insist my wife and I disembark first. The Cape commander will be eager to extend the hand of welcome, and I am sure he is impatient for us to meet.'

'I am sure he will be able to contain his enthusiasm for one more day,' the captain said dryly.

'I repeat,' Claes said, banging a fist on the table, 'I must insist.'

The captain's face was as dark as a storm cloud. In a flash of temper, he flung out, 'The sick will be removed first, Van Loon. I do acknowledge your senior status with the Honourable

Company, and that your quarters have been less than ideal.' Full of apologies at the inconveniences that Claes had undergone, the captain changed tack. 'I know it is vexing that we are forced to wait, but might I ask you to accept my personal invitation to pass the remaining time on board in the comfort of my stateroom. We will have your baggage brought up from the lower deck, and you can relax and avail yourself of anything from my personal cellar until it is time for you to leave.'

Claes van Loon regained his seat with a soft grunt. 'My wife and Johanna as well?'

He was staring at her too intently. Johanna gripped the chair arms so hard her hands hurt. She fixed her gaze on the captain, widening her eyes and beseeching him with a look that even a half-blind man could not mistake.

With profound relief, she heard him say, 'I believe the ladies are not yet finished with their preparations in the roundhouse cabin.'

'Are you not ready to disembark, Floriane?' Claes van Loon glanced at his wife and then at Johanna, his expression surprised and annoyed.

'You know how I am, Claes. Never quite ready when I should be – even after all these months on the ship.' Floriane's laugh came out as an uncertain squawk.

Johanna could not laugh, and turned her face away from him, pressing her lips together to hold back her words. There'd been no way to ask how Frans was faring, and her fears had begun to mount. She would find out though, somehow or other, before she left the ship.

'I've had enough of waiting about,' Claes van Loon said eventually, his foot tapping irritably on the floorboards. 'I'll take you up on your offer, captain, and repair to the cuddy.'

'I'll join you in a short while, Van Loon,' the captain said.

With a huff, Claes van Loon rose from his chair and moved around the table to the door of the cuddy. As he passed, Johanna kept her eyes trained on the table. When he'd gone, Johanna could not contain her impatience.

Touching her fingers to her temples, she slipped off her chair and tilted her head towards the door. 'If you would excuse me, captain, I find the dining room a touch too stuffy now that we are no longer at sea.'

Floriane was quick to her rescue. 'I too am finding the air somewhat stale, captain. Before we complete our packing, might I ask that we take a turn on deck if we are not in the way? Perhaps we might tempt you to join us as well?'

The captain seemed at last to understand the purpose of the walk and stood. He nodded briefly. 'As the anchor is down and the whipstaff lashed, I believe I have time for a short promenade before we start to offload the ship.'

From the dining room, Johanna trailed behind the captain and Floriane across the quarterdeck and up the ladder to the poop. They sat down on the poultry coops, long since empty of their fowl, and waited for the captain to light up his pipe.

Johanna felt tears well in her eyes. 'Pardon me, Captain Bierens, but I am frantic for news of Frans.'

He placed his hand on her arm and nodded, but his face was grim. 'I expected as much. I fear my news will not be what you'd hoped. The surgeon reports that Frans de Jong is far from well. This morning he lay in his bunk, feverish and in pain, too ill to recognise his physician and unable to swallow his ale.'

She opened her mouth, but tears rendered her unable to speak.

Floriane turned to the captain. 'You will transfer him to the hospital as soon as you can?'

'He will be the very first to leave the ship. I will keep your husband in my stateroom – under lock and key if necessary – until the young man is safely away.'

'And then he will get well,' Johanna said, her voice faint with dread.

He looked at them frankly. 'You must pray for him, dear ladies, as only God will grant that he lives. I am cautioning you to prepare yourselves for the worst. The truth is that we fear very greatly for his life.'

PART III

THE CAPE OF GOOD HOPE

⪩ CHAPTER 24 ⪨

I T WAS LATE AFTERNOON by the time Johanna and the ship's passengers were lowered, one by one, into longboats. The wind had picked up and the oarsmen struggled as they rowed them through the surf. Half an hour later, the stink of rotting seaweed sharp on the air, she climbed the rough stone steps to the jetty, feeling unstable on sea-accustomed legs.

She saw her new home through eyes blurred by tears. Only wariness brought Claes van Loon into focus ahead of her. He'd changed his clothes since noontime dinner. The dazzling white of his square-edged collar seemed absurd next to the creased and dirty clothing of the other passengers, whom he was elbowing out of the way. Floriane had been watching her, concern etched on her face.

When they came to a halt, Johanna steadied herself with one hand on the handrail and looked up. Claes was face to face with a short, rotund man who stood in the midst of a military escort. From the orange sash tied around his waist and the heavy medallion that swung from his neck, she supposed this was the commander.

Claes touched the brim of his hat. 'May I present my compliments on behalf of the Honourable Company, Your Excellency. Claes van Loon at your service, and may I introduce my wife, Floriane Peronneau, who is delighted to make your acquaintance.'

The commander stepped forward and offered his hand. 'Welcome, welcome. We'd begun to worry that something had befallen your ship. It's happy news to see you've all survived the voyage.'

'We are grateful and relieved to have Dutch soil once again beneath our feet.'

'And will you introduce me to the young lady?'

Holding her breath, Johanna dug her nails into her palms.

'She is no one of note.' Claes van Loon almost spat the words. 'One of the orphan girls whom we have chaperoned from the Netherlands.'

Floriane stepped in front of her husband. 'Johanna has been my dearest and closest companion for the duration of the voyage.'

'Sweet heavens, she looks distressed. Is she quite all right?'

Shaking her head, Floriane said quietly, 'The poor thing has just said goodbye to Captain Bierens and is grief-stricken by the thought she might never see him again.'

How Floriane had conjured the lie so readily, Johanna could not think, but she was grateful nonetheless.

The Cape commander took a step towards her, removed his wide-brimmed hat, and placed it over his heart. 'Five months on a ship will often forge a close companionship and I, of course, understand the pain of separation from dear friends. But,' he said, placing his hand on Johanna's shoulder and speaking alone now to her, 'your friends from the

Burgerweeshuis have been anxious for your safe arrival and will be delighted to have you among them once more. I hope this might in some small way lessen the wrench of leaving the captain behind.'

Clutching a wad of damp cloth in her hand, Johanna gave a polite bow of her head. 'Thank you, Your Excellency,' she murmured, her voice quavering slightly.

*

Floriane touched Johanna's arm in what she hoped was a comforting gesture as, bowing and smiling, Commander Speelman indicated the man on his left. Tall and thin, the man had a pleasant face, with high cheekbones and a strong jaw. 'May I present my secunde, Merkel Rosenmüller.'

The secunde came forward and, bowing, swung his plumed hat with a certain elegance. 'It is my honour to welcome you to the Cape and to escort you to the Castle. Generally, we proceed on foot, and I thus could give you a brief tour of the *vlek*. However, if the ladies are too fatigued, there is the option of taking a carriage.'

Floriane glanced towards Claes and saw that he and the commander were in conversation a few steps away. She squinted into the distance. 'Is the Castle far away?'

The secunde followed her eyes and for a moment seemed confused. 'No. It's right there, where you are looking.'

His voice held a slight accent but Floriane couldn't place it at first. Rosenmüller – German? She put a hand to her forehead, shielding her eyes from the glare of the sun. 'But surely that's a fort? It has bastions at each of its corners.'

'Yes, it is a fortification, but it is such an upgrade on its predecessor that it is known locally as the Castle.'

'Ah. I see.' She turned to Johanna. The girl looked wretched, her face even paler than usual, her eyes red and swollen with crying. A walk should have been a relief after being cooped up on the ship for so long, but Johanna looked as if she might collapse at any moment. 'I'm afraid I'm in no state to walk anywhere. May I reserve the offer of a tour for another time?' She gave Johanna's hand a squeeze, which the girl returned.

'But of course, mevrouw. I am at your service. Please allow me a second to confer with Commander Speelman.' He gave a slight bow and turned to where the commander and Claes were conversing.

She linked her arm with Johanna's and felt the girl sag against her. She wanted to tell her that everything would be all right, to promise her that Frans would live, that they would be allowed to marry. That justice would be served. But none of those things were within her power to promise, so she said nothing, instead keeping her eyes trained on the three men. They were such different specimens.

The commander's voice rose to a level where she could hear him.

'Nonsense, Rosenmüller. The new fiscal and I can walk to the Castle. It will give us time to discuss his role and allow him to see the vlek. Isn't that right, Van Loon?'

Claes's thin lips tightened, but he acceded to the commander's suggestion.

The secunde backed away and returned to where she and Johanna stood. 'Mijn dames, the conveyance awaits.' He indicated the enclosed carriage, drawn by four black horses and bearing the stylised gilt initials of the Dutch East India Company on its side. The driver sitting on the padded bench at the front was dark skinned, but what particularly caught Floriane's eye was that he wore no shoes.

She looked back at Claes, but he was fully engrossed and paying them no attention at all. She waved in his direction, her jaw tightening.

'Mevrouw?'

She turned to Merkel Rosenmüller, their eyes meeting briefly. For the barest instant, she saw surprise in his expression, but then a veneer of politeness returned to his face. He gestured to the carriage's attached metal step, which now protruded below the carriage door, and offered her his hand.

'If you don't mind, let's get Johanna into the carriage first,' she said. It occurred to her that the girl might never have ridden in a horse-drawn conveyance. 'Come,' she said to Johanna, who came forward mutely and, fumbling with her skirts, tried to mount the step. Between them, she and Mijnheer Rosenmüller managed to usher her onto the carriage's leather seat. She scooted across the bench seat, clutching her Bible box awkwardly, and settled herself in the corner.

The secunde again offered Floriane his hand and this time she took it. He smiled then, transforming his face from merely pleasant to handsome. She could see from the trio of lines that formed on either side of his mouth that he smiled often. Gathering her skirts in her other hand, she stepped up, sliding into the seat next to Johanna. The secunde followed her, swinging himself up with practised ease to sit in the opposite seat.

'Ready?' he asked.

When she nodded, he banged on the carriage ceiling and said, 'The Castle, Doman.'

As they trotted off, she caught sight of Claes and the commander, who were walking in the opposite direction. Claes looked up as they passed, but she stared straight ahead and pretended not to see him.

Secunde Rosenmüller angled his head. 'It appears the commander is taking Mijnheer van Loon through the town. We will most likely reach the Castle some while before they do.'

Floriane folded her gloved hands in her lap and said, 'That will give us time to get our bearings and make ourselves presentable. It's been quite some months since we've had the luxury of lingering over our toilette.'

They drove past a noisy throng of spectators who had gathered on the quay.

Rosenmüller pointed at the window. 'With every ship that docks, people flock to inspect the new arrivals. You can imagine in a settlement such as this, with so few ladies among us, that any woman stepping ashore provokes great interest. They will have dressed in their Sunday best. They will be thrilled if you might wave to them.'

Floriane leaned closer to Johanna and waggled her fingers at the crowd. She tapped Johanna on the back of the hand and the girl gave a half-hearted wave as well. Some of the spectators who were closest to the coach smiled or laughed, and one young bespectacled man merely gawped.

'Are we to like Cape Town, Mijnheer Rosenmüller, do you think?' Floriane asked, settling back in her seat.

'It will be much to your liking, I am certain. The vlek stretches a little over two miles front to back and side to side, so there is much to appreciate.'

'Vlek? Is that how it's referred to locally, as a hamlet?' She tried to get a better view out the window. From what little she had seen so far, Floriane thought it likely to be a bitter disappointment.

Rosenmüller acknowledged her comment with a nod. 'It's true that it's a bit larger than a hamlet, but it's by tradition, I believe, that it's called the vlek. The founding colonists called it the "spot", and we still use the term.'

It was a bustling port, of that there was no doubt – the noise and activity of the vlek rang out across the wharf – but the settlement was tiny in comparison to Amsterdam. The account of Cape Town that Clara Speelman had given had vastly over-flattered the place. As they navigated a rutted square, the carriage clattering over the uneven ground, she saw a gallows and a pillory. The knot of misgiving twisted taut in her stomach.

'Is crime so very rife in the Cape that these punishments are deemed necessary?' She recalled Captain Bierens' words that morning. *The Dutch are not barbarians like the English. He will have a fair trial.*

'These measures preceded Commander Speelman's stationing here. He opted to keep them, since a remote territory such as the Cape can tempt visiting sailors to misbehave. The presence of these reminders helps maintain law and order.'

Floriane could not help but wonder whether one of these constructions would provide the backdrop against which Claes's fate would play out.

The coach lurched over a particularly deep rut, and the movement seemed to re-energise Johanna. She lifted her head and peered through the glass. 'Might you tell us where the hospital is?'

The secunde tapped the window and waved his index finger at a building some distance away. 'It's there – the cross-shaped one.'

It looked a bit decrepit, Floriane thought. But perhaps inside it was in better repair.

She looked out at the town they were passing through. There were no avenues that she could see, no trees to give shade, no leafy squares, merely rows of whitewashed houses with flat, tiled roofs. Behind the Castle, a great, flat-topped grey mountain rose up. At least the view of that was impressive.

Driving through the Castle's entrance, the coach came to a standstill in a dusty courtyard and the secunde climbed down first to help the two of them out. Floriane again took Johanna's arm and, murmuring her appreciation to Merkel Rosenmüller, followed him to where he said the other seven girls were waiting.

'Here we are, Johanna,' the secunde said, motioning to a doorway. 'I hope you will feel better once you have had a chance to put the voyage behind you.'

Johanna thanked him for his concern, her voice a shaky whisper.

Floriane put a restraining hand on her arm and took her to one side. 'May I have a word before you go?'

The girl's fevered eyes widened but she nodded, once.

When they were out of earshot, in low tones Floriane said, 'Remember what we spoke about. You must pretend that all is well. Claes thinks he has won for now, and your ability to appear unaffected by Frans's disappearance will be the difference between him living and being condemned to certain death. Claes will ensure he does not fail a second time. Your acting skills must be your salvation, as they are mine. Say nothing of this to anyone. Not even your closest friends.'

The concern still on her face, Johanna asked softly, 'How am I to know of his progress?'

She patted the girl's cheek and murmured, 'I will see what I can learn of his whereabouts and how he is recovering. I will bring you word as soon as I know.'

Johanna bit her lip but seemed to accept this.

'Now, in we go.' Floriane took Johanna's elbow and steered her towards the door. To the secunde she said, 'Do you mind waiting just a moment so that you might show me to where I will be staying?'

'Of course, mevrouw.' Rosenmüller graced her with another of his brilliant smiles.

Inside the room, the flow of conversation was brisk. 'Good afternoon, ladies,' Floriane announced.

From where they were seated at a long table, the girls looked up, followed instantly by a chorus of exclamations. One of the girls, a broad-faced girl whom Floriane remembered from the interviews, leapt to her feet with a cry of 'Jo-Jo!'

Johanna pulled her hand free and ran into the blonde girl's arms.

'Please look after her,' Floriane told them. 'And I will see you all at the dinner that is planned for us later on.' The chatter from the young women became deafening as she left the room.

Feeling some relief, she returned to where the secunde was waiting. 'Thank you for your patience, Mijnheer Rosenmüller.'

He led her a short distance along a narrow corridor and indicated an iron-studded door. 'Here is the apartment we propose for your husband and yourself.'

She peered inside. The rooms were clean and well furnished, but one item of furniture – a large bed which bore two pillows – unnerved her. She had not slept with Claes for months, and the thought that she might have to almost gave her palpitations. She sank down on the nearest chair.

Mijnheer Rosenmüller voiced his concern. 'Is there something I can do?'

She kept her eyes lowered, hoping he would not see her panic. 'May I ask a favour, mijnheer?'

'But of course. Anything.'

She half glanced towards the door. 'It will require your discretion, and I am sorry to put you in this position.'

'You may trust me absolutely. What do you require?' He spoke quietly, like a physician.

'I wonder if I might ask for a second bed. Perhaps not immediately next to the other.' She felt heat flood her cheeks. 'I have spent the voyage being unwell and—'

His eyes as they rested on her were full of understanding. 'There is no need for explanation, mevrouw. It is a perfectly reasonable request. I will have another bed set up. At the far end of the room.' He straightened up and offered her his hand. 'Hopefully before Mijnheer van Loon arrives with the commander.'

Floriane allowed him to pull her from the chair and felt her burden lighten. 'Thank you, Mijnheer Rosenmüller. I am in your debt.'

He nodded solemnly, and she imagined she could see questions in his dark eyes, yet he said only, 'As I have said, I am at your service, mevrouw. I shall go and organise matters, and will hope to see you at the reception dinner this evening.'

⌐ CHAPTER 25 ⌐

JOHANNA BREATHED OUT A long sigh, murmuring into Malliet's ear, 'I've missed you so much.' The other girls were on their feet, clustering round and enfolding her in a group embrace. There were greetings all around, the familiar voices reassuring in spite of the heaviness in her heart. She attempted to pull away but found herself still surrounded. 'Let go, all of you. I can hardly breathe!'

Soft laughter filled the room as they all took a step back. Johanna twirled around slowly, taking them in.

'When did you get here?' Malliet asked.

Johanna swung back to her. 'This morning. It took hours to disembark. There were . . .' She felt tears stinging behind her eyes again. 'Many of the sailors had come down with scurvy and the captain wanted to get them to the hospital first.'

Hilletje gave Johanna a long look and then said, 'We should sit down. Johanna looks like she's done in.'

Malliet squinted at her. 'It's true. Why do you look like you've been chopping onions?'

As the girls made their way back to their seats, Johanna

considered her words. Malliet took a chair and then patted the seat of the one next to her. Johanna lowered herself into it and set her Bible box down on the table in front of her. 'It was a difficult journey. I'm sure yours was as well, but in particular, I was cooped up with Mijnheer van Loon.'

A chorus of sympathy sounded from around the table.

Lisje, the pretty blonde, shook her head knowingly. 'Whatever did you do to keep out of his way? He was bad enough in the Burgerweeshuis.'

Nods and sighs of agreement rose up around the table.

Johanna bit the inside of her cheek to stop herself from saying too much. 'I don't know how I would have managed if it weren't for Floriane.'

'Floriane!' Hilletje cried out, inciting another flurry of comment. 'You mean the regent's wife?'

'Mevrouw Peronneau, yes. We spent the entire voyage sharing a cabin and she gave me permission to use her given name. She's been a good friend.'

Karin shook her head slightly, her dark curls tumbling over her shoulders. 'Captain de Vries told us you'd been kept back to help look after the regent's wife because she was ill, but she looked well enough when she brought you in just now.'

It was Johanna's turn to exclaim. 'He said what?'

Malliet exchanged glances with Karin and then said, 'He told us Claes van Loon had asked that one of us be kept back to tend to his sick wife.'

Johanna grimaced. He'd intended all along to get one of them alone. 'He did not ask for any specific one of us?'

'Not that Captain de Vries said.'

It *was* fate, then. But Johanna would not give that hateful man credit for her spending the voyage with Frans. She was

200

suddenly overcome with the memory of their first meeting on board the ship, the storm swirling around them. *Are we to drown like rats?* As her vision blurred again, she prayed silently to herself. *Oh, Frans, you have to be all right.*

Malliet gasped. 'Oh, Jo-Jo, what on earth has happened?'

'Nothing. Nothing at all.' She pressed her palms to her eyes to hold back the tears before they fell, and then let her hands fall to her lap. 'I'm just very tired. I haven't slept properly in days.' With a sigh, she cast a glance around the table and took in the sewing projects at each station. She swallowed the lump in her throat and, sounding more cheerful than she felt, said, 'I'm very glad to finally be with you all again. What has been happening here? What are you making?'

'Our wedding dresses.' Brigitta lifted up what was clearly the bodice of a dress to show Johanna what she was doing.

Lotte sat up then, holding up a skirt in pale-blue fabric. 'The VOC gave us two bolts of fabric each to make our dresses and some other new clothes. We chose the fabric ourselves. I'm sure they will take you to the warehouse for yours.'

Another girl spoke now. 'How will you catch up in time for the wedding? You're two weeks behind as it is.'

Staring towards the windows, Johanna struggled to remember the girl's name.

'I'm in no hurry, Elke.' She didn't tell them she wouldn't be getting married with the rest of them.

They went around the table then, showing off their projects. Johanna praised their efforts, allowing her eyes to move to each of them in turn, but she was only half listening. Her thoughts were elsewhere.

Captain Bierens had said she mustn't see Frans, but the man would soon be gone. There must be a way to sneak out to the hospital. Who would stop her? Was it a danger to Frans, though? She thought about the perpetual disdain plastered on Claes van Loon's face. There was no doubt in her mind that she would find a way to outwit him. She had to.

Johanna thought she heard her name a great distance away. She glanced around and saw seven pairs of eyes glued to her face.

She bit her lip, feeling uncertain. 'What?'

Malliet gave her a strange look. 'Did you not hear the call to supper?'

Johanna stood up. 'I'm afraid not. I can barely hold my head up. Can one of you show me where I am to sleep? I'm so tired I will end up with my face in the soup if I am made to sit at the supper table.'

The silence that followed was too long, and Johanna knew Malliet would seize on it. They looked at each other until Malliet stood up and held out her hand. 'You and I will share a bed as we did at the Burgerweeshuis,' she said as she began to edge towards the door. 'Karin, do you think you might bring us a plate of food? I'll stay with Jo-Jo while the rest of you go down to eat.'

'You should go to supper, Malliet,' Johanna said gently. 'I'm afraid you'll be bored and hungry for no reason if you come with me, as I'll be asleep as soon as I lay my head down.' She didn't trust herself to keep her secret from Malliet. When the girl had made her mind up about something, nothing in the world would push her off her chosen course.

Malliet kissed her cheek. 'I won't be bored. You can take a nap now and then you'll have an appetite for supper. We can eat it together.'

'I will make your excuses,' Karin said, nodding. 'They will know how it feels coming straight off the ship.'

The girls tidied their sewing and began to disperse.

Hilletje moved closer to them as she left the room. 'Between the six of us, I'm sure we can manage to bring food for you both.'

Malliet put a hand on Johanna's shoulder and steered her to the end of the corridor then gently guided her through a doorway, inside which a number of beds had been set up. At the back of the room, spare mattresses were stacked to the ceiling. Johanna remembered that they'd wanted up to forty-eight girls.

Malliet led her to one of the beds. 'Here we are. I've slept here by myself for the past two weeks. It's most peculiar having so much room to oneself.'

For the first time in days, Johanna laughed. 'Yes, for me as well. I have to say I'm looking forward to sleeping in a bed that's not being shaken like a milk churn.'

She flopped onto the bed with Malliet beside her.

'I missed you, Malliet.' She swallowed hard to mask the catch in her voice.

'Not as much as I missed you.' Malliet tilted her head so that it rested lightly against Johanna's. They lay quietly for a moment, both looking up at the ceiling.

'So,' Malliet sat up and straightened her cap. 'Truth time. Tell me in three words. How was the voyage?'

Johanna stared at the rafters. 'Fine. Uneventful. Dull.' She looked at Malliet from the corner of her eye and knew she was not taken in.

'Don't lie, Jo-Jo. It's been stamped across your face since you arrived. Something's up, and you know you will tell me what it is eventually, so you may as well do it now and save yourself some anguish.'

Johanna cast her mind back to all the things that bound them together, that made her love Malliet. Finding comfort in small routines; their silent communications; Malliet's willingness to accompany her to the Cape. There was no way on God's earth she could keep a secret from her.

Her fingers sprang up as she counted the words. 'I. Met. Frans.'

Malliet's eyes were huge. 'Where? Here at the Cape?'

She shook her head vigorously. 'I met him on the ship. Where we fell in love.'

'I thought he was just a girlish crush to help you pass the time at the huis.'

'I thought you of all people would know I really meant it.' She pressed her lips together and then said, 'The captain was going to marry us.'

At first Malliet found no words to answer that, the silence only punctuated by the insistent whining of a mosquito. 'And yet you look like death,' she said eventually. 'All puffy and blotchy, as if you've been blubbing for a month.'

Gripped by a spasm of grief, Johanna curled over, her hands clutched to her stomach, and pressed her misery down.

Malliet took hold of her hand. 'Do you remember that time at the huis when you stole a scrap of cloth and thought no one had seen? I never told a soul, so whatever it is that you are holding on to, you can tell me without fear of disclosure.'

She took several deep breaths before she could trust her voice not to break. 'He's going to die, and I don't think I can bear it.'

Malliet brought Johanna's hand to her lips and kissed her fingers. 'Start at the beginning and tell me everything.'

Her story spilled out, finishing with the betrothal ceremony and what Claes van Loon had done. 'Frans's life is now hanging by a thread. He's in the hospital and we don't know whether he will live.' Johanna watched the information register.

'Why wasn't Mijnheer van Loon apprehended?'

'There were no witnesses except Frans, and he . . .'

'No witnesses? Then there's no evidence that Mijnheer van Loon is the one who stabbed him? I don't understand. How . . .?' Malliet looked at her. 'There's more you haven't said, isn't there?'

'Please, Malliet, don't make it any harder for me than it already is,' she said. 'I promise I will tell you everything eventually, but for now it's not safe. I can't risk putting anyone else in danger, and what I don't tell you may keep you alive.'

⊸ CHAPTER 26 ⊸

Seated next to Commander Speelman, Claes let his eye travel the length of the enormous teakwood dining table. Floriane sat on his left and the orphan girls – six of them, at least – occupied the whole of one end. The wretched redhead had not appeared. Across the table from him, hollow eyed and gaunt, sat the secunde, Merkel Rosenmüller.

The commander had changed from his uniform to elaborate dinner attire. His coat was made of exceedingly fine, heavy silk, though the style was less fashionable than Claes's own. The dining room, painted a light pea green with gold beading lining the walls, was elegance itself.

The commander cleared his throat and lifted his wineglass. 'Tonight we drink to the safe arrival of all of you who have travelled these last months from Amsterdam to be here with us. We give thanks to God above, and we pray that your new lives here will be everything you have hoped for.'

'Amen to that,' Claes said, lifting his glass to take a sip of the smooth Batavian wine. He observed the others, in particular the girls at the other end of the table. He had definitely had the prettiest of the lot on his ship, though two or three of these would do very nicely. And they were almost certainly more obliging.

Next to him Floriane said, 'Where is Johanna? And we are short of one other.'

The girls exchanged looks. One of them, a pretty blonde, leaned forward. 'She was too tired to come down, so Malliet stayed to keep her company.'

'Of course, of course.' Commander Speelman nodded politely. 'When I last saw the girl, she was beset by tears. I'm sure a night's rest will do her a world of good.'

Floriane spoke in the voice she used with her parents at lunch on Sundays. 'The lamb is delicious.'

'And the cabbages are a credit to your garden.' Claes took another nip of his wine.

His wife continued in that same tone. 'Perhaps, commander, you would allow the girls to take some supper back to the two of them. After the last weeks of rations, I'm certain it can only be good for them to have a decent meal.'

Claes could not for the life of him understand why Floriane insisted on fraternising with orphan girls who were leagues from her in standing.

'Yes, indeed. We shall make sure they are fed with the best the Cape can offer.'

A girl across the table, strands of dark hair escaping from her cap, smiled in his direction. He had noticed her at the Burgerweeshuis. What was her name? Karina? Karla? Tonight, she was wearing a deep collar over a navy dress that flattered her curves and dainty wrists and long, slender fingers. He almost grinned before realising her interest was directed at his wife.

'I will take a plate up to them as soon as we've finished. Perhaps Johanna will feel more like food by then,' the brunette said.

The commander nodded and turned his attention to Floriane. 'How have you found the vlek so far?'

'Truthfully, I've hardly seen it, Your Excellency, but I expect there will be an opportunity to look around before too long. Speaking of which, did you and my husband have a good tour this afternoon?'

A dark-skinned man in the same kind of robe and red turban Claes had seen on other male slaves on his tour of the Castle entered the dining room on silent feet and with a burning taper lit several candles in wall sconces. The action was well timed. Only now did Claes notice that the light had begun to fade. He wanted to ask about the slaves, how one acquired their services, but decided it was something better addressed when he had the commander's private ear.

Speelman glanced over his shoulder at the man. 'Thank you, Fortune.'

The slave bowed low and slipped noiselessly from the room.

The commander returned his attention to the table. 'To answer your question, mevrouw, my focus was more on a discussion of the fiscal's new position than on thoroughly acquainting him with the layout of the vlek. There will be plenty of time for that in due course.'

'I too am looking forward to it,' Floriane said, then turned her side plate to see the markings on the underside. 'These plates are too beautiful.'

'They were imported from Japan,' the secunde said, with undisguised pride.

The man was irritating, Claes decided. He would see what he could do to be rid of him. He too inspected the dinner service, with its elaborate blue-and-gold pattern, and did not pass comment. Turning to his wife, he smiled perfunctorily and then, looking at the far end of the table at the girls, said, 'I learned this afternoon that I will be selecting your future husbands, *mejuffrouwen*.'

Speelman nodded. 'Indeed, the new fiscal has informed me he knows a great deal about each of you, and it will therefore be a simple matter to decide on the best matches. That was a very great relief for me to hear, as I know it will be done well.'

The girls exchanged looks, and two of them whispered behind their hands.

Claes could not resist. 'Is there something pertinent you wanted to add?'

'I do.' The remark came from his immediate left.

'Yes?' He spoke to his wife in a louder voice than he'd intended.

'I had just been thinking that although I met and interviewed all of these girls at the Burgerweeshuis, some of their names escape me. Such a dreadful thing, but it has been months. Perhaps this will afford you an opportunity to display your knowledge and introduce them all?'

An immediate sense of horror arose in his chest, but before he could open his mouth to protest, the commander joined in. 'What an excellent idea, Mevrouw Peronneau. It will serve both as post-supper entertainment and as an opportunity for Fiscal van Loon to show us why the Dutch East India holds him in such high esteem.' The commander sat back, wineglass in hand, making it clear he expected a show.

'I'd be only too pleased,' Claes said, and prayed for some insight to save him. Two of the girls laughed, prompting him to send his hand to his glass. 'I should start by saying that it

209

has been half a year since I had any interaction with the young ladies, and I haven't looked at my notes recently to remind myself of their details.'

The commander raised one eyebrow.

Claes studied the candles for a moment, then the toes of his shoes, and threw back the contents of his glass. He signalled a slave to fill it. 'But I'm sure I shall be able to name the majority.'

'Good, good.' Speelman took a sip of his wine. 'Whenever you'd like to begin.'

Looking again around the table, Claes let his gaze rest on each girl's face in turn. Yes, he recalled most of them. He had certainly seen their faces, but their names were slower to return to him.

He glanced at his wife, but she seemed busy with her napkin and determined to maintain her silence. Just then, as if she had felt his eyes on her, Floriane turned to him and gave him the sweetest smile he'd seen on her face for some months. 'Like you, dear one, I was testing my memory. It seems only fair, don't you agree?'

With every eye in the room turned in his direction, it was difficult to think. He picked up his glass and took another substantial slug. 'I will say that there is one girl here whose name I don't believe I know. Perhaps we did not meet in my time at the huis, though your face is somewhat familiar.' He said this last with a nod in the girl's direction, and saw a faint look of acknowledgement on her face.

'Which of them would that be, Van Loon?' asked the commander.

'The girl next to my wife,' Claes said, gesturing in her direction. 'I do apologise, *mejuffrouw*, for my ignorance. I can't think why I don't know you.'

The girl pulled a chunk of meat from her knife and set it on her plate. 'I am the only one among us who you would not have seen as an orphan. I have been a maid on the girls' side of the huis for eight years. It is understandable, mijnheer, that my name might not be on the very tip of your tongue.'

'It is inexcusable that we don't know your name,' Floriane said, touching the girl's arm.

'Hilletje Lampbrecht.'

'Oh, yes.' Floriane nodded. 'I remember you from the interviews. Johanna spoke of you on the voyage.'

'Good things, I hope.' The girl popped the square of meat into her mouth and began to chew.

'She mentioned you were a good friend.'

Before a reply was forthcoming, the commander cleared his throat. 'One out of six, Van Loon. Do carry on.'

Claes noticed how expectant they all looked. The two prettiest ones – surely he could remember those at the very least.

He smiled to himself. *Karin! The dark-haired one is called Karin.*

'Well as I said, I haven't looked at my ledgers, and today has been exhausting—'

'It would appear you don't know them quite as well as you've implied?' The commander smirked at him. Was the secunde gloating as well?

'I was about to say that the girl third from Hilletje is called Karin.'

The girl gave a single nod of her head, her face unreadable.

'And her surname?' the commander pressed.

Just then footsteps sounded from the corridor and a slave led in another girl, blonde and square-faced. Ha! This one he knew. Malliet something.

211

'Malliet?' Hilletje asked. 'Is Johanna not with you?'

Standing uneasily, the girl glanced about the table, a deep frown creasing her brow. 'I was hoping she was here. We were talking and we both fell asleep. When I woke up, she was gone. I went back to the sewing room but she's not there, so then I thought she might have come down to have supper. She must be lost somewhere.'

A sense of relief at the interruption surged through Claes, but before he could say a word, his wife stood up from the table.

'We should go and look for her right away. She was quite disoriented earlier, and I am concerned for her safety. She could have gone anywhere.'

Claes stood up as well. 'Agreed. This name game will have to wait until the girl is found.'

To his surprise, the secunde also got to his feet. He wiped his mouth and threw his napkin on his chair. 'If Johanna has wandered beyond the Castle walls, she is likely in grave danger. After dark, wild animals roam in the vlek, even lions, to say nothing of—' he dropped his gaze for a moment, as if considering his next words carefully '—the dangers of sailors who have been too long at sea.'

In the way his wife turned and walked briskly to the door, Claes felt the extent of her alarm. 'Malliet,' she called to the girl, 'can you show me exactly where you were before you lost track of her?'

'Of course.'

The secunde moved towards them. 'I will come with you. I have the full layout of the Castle at my fingertips. If I may be excused, commander?'

'Yes, yes, Rosenmüller. I agree the girl must be found. I will remain here as chaperone to the rest.'

Quick to sense an opportunity, Claes said, 'I beg leave to assist in the search, Excellency.'

The commander seemed unconcerned. 'The girl can't have gone far. We won't clear supper until we hear that she's found.'

The blonde girl had linked arms with his wife, and with the secunde in tow, they were already through the door and hurrying towards the corridor. Claes gave Speelman a notional bow. 'I fear this may take some time, Excellency. Please do continue your meal, and if some misfortune keeps us late, let us reconvene in the morning as we have planned.'

*

As they hurried along the corridor, Floriane touched Malliet on the shoulder and glanced back towards the two men. Merkel Rosenmüller was a step behind them, a grim but determined expression on his face. A few steps further back, she saw her husband had also joined the search. She barely prevented herself from rolling her eyes as she noticed the jaunty cadence of his steps.

He is rather pleased with himself for avoiding exposure as a braggart. She sighed. 'Is there anything you can think of that might help us find her, Malliet?'

The girl seemed hesitant to say. 'She wouldn't tell me everything. But she did tell me . . .' A slight tilt of the head and a squint of one eye gave Floriane to understand she was indicating someone behind them. 'What happened on the ship.'

Floriane gave the barest shake of her head. *I should have known she wouldn't be able to keep the entire story to herself.*

They came to the head of the stairs and waited for the two men to catch up.

'Malliet and I will search from here to the front doors, as I am sure I know where those are. Might you, *mijnheeren*, try the opposite direction?'

Claes moved close to her and gave a puff of protest. 'I can easily show you where things are. As you know, I have an unerring sense of direction, and I walked the whole place earlier with the commander.'

Floriane withheld the sarcasm from her tone. 'You are indeed a marvel, Claes. And all the more reason why you ought to go with Secunde Rosenmüller. That way, if you need to split up for some reason, you'll have no trouble finding your way back.'

The secunde agreed. 'I believe Mevrouw Peronneau has the right of it, mijnheer. Shall we take the north side of the building and the inner courtyard?'

Claes did not look pleased, and Floriane thought he might refuse, but after a few seconds he let out a sigh and they all went down the stairs, Claes taking the lead.

They paused on the ground floor, allowing the secunde to indicate where the front and the back of the building lay. The men went off, leaving Floriane and Malliet on their own. The corridors would have been pitch black if not for a series of lanterns hanging from hooks set along the wall. Their flickering lights threw wavering shadows across the stonework but left the corners dark.

Malliet made no attempt to disguise her agitation. 'I'm worried half to death about Johanna. Do you have any idea where she might have gone, mevrouw?'

Floriane sniffed, considering. 'I believe I may have.' She caught Malliet's elbow and gently urged her forward. 'This afternoon, when we were in the coach travelling from the quay to the Castle, Johanna asked Secunde Rosenmüller to point out the hospital. I suspect she may have gone off to find it.'

'Oh dear.'

'Exactly. And as the only way she knows into or out of the Castle is through the main gateway, common sense tells us she will have gone this way.'

They hurried in the direction of the guardhouse, their footsteps and the rustling of their skirts too loud in the oppressive stillness. The wall-mounted lanterns bathed the corridors in saffron light and as they raced past one it went out, tainting the air with the faint scent of smoke. Gooseflesh prickled Floriane's skin; she knew Malliet was also spooked, for the girl put a nervous hand on her arm.

As the door to the main archway appeared some little way ahead, Floriane started at a fearsome sound in the distance – a low-pitched guttural rumbling far too deep to have been made by a man. She had never heard such a noise, but she thought on the secunde's words – *wild animals roam in the vlek, even lions* – and knew immediately what it must be.

Just then, in the shadowy corner where the door out to the main gateway stood ajar, a flicker of movement caught her eye.

Frozen to the spot, they peered into the gloom. 'Don't make a sound,' she whispered. 'Until we know what's there.'

After a moment, their eyes adjusted and they made out the form of a girl, seated on the floor, her skirts tucked around her legs, which she hugged against her chest.

'Jo-Jo?' Malliet whispered.

Out of the shadows came Johanna's voice. 'I'm here.'

Floriane crouched down beside her. 'What are you doing sitting by yourself in the dark? We've been worried to death.'

Johanna looked woebegone. 'I've just been thinking about when I first arrived at the Burgerweeshuis and I used to imagine I would run away. The doors were never locked. I discovered that early on. But in time I grew used to it, came to feel it was my home even. I thought this place would be like that. But since Frans . . .' She went quiet as the lion outside let out another spine-chilling roar. Slowly, she picked up the thread of her sentence. 'I am not sure what will happen, but running away is not as straightforward as I thought.'

She pressed her cheeks with both hands, as if trying to squeeze out the words. As they waited for her to say more, footsteps rattled down the corridor towards them.

'Mevrouwen?' The secunde's voice sounded hollowly down the empty passageway. A moment later he appeared, breathing heavily as if he'd run from a long way off. 'We heard the lion.' He looked back. 'Mijnheer van Loon sought to reassure you.'

Claes appeared from around the corner, cursing under his breath.

'It's all right,' Johanna said. She had got up and stepped into the light. 'I'm sorry I caused so much bother.'

Floriane broke in, hoping to stay the inevitable inquisition. 'There's nothing to worry about. She lost her way, that's all.'

Claes, his voice tinged with impatience, said, 'What a nuisance you've made of yourself, and you've only been here five minutes.'

The secunde seemed pleased that the lost sheep had returned to the fold. 'Ladies, I am relieved that all is well, but I must ask you to promise that you will never go out on your own after dark unless you are accompanied by a person you trust – by preference, someone carrying a musket.'

216

Claes looked at them but did not smile. 'Do heed the secunde's advice, because I do not intend to chase after anyone like this again. I could have done without this interruption on my first night with the commander.'

The secunde motioned them towards the stairs. 'I believe, mijnheer, that all of our accommodations lie in the same direction, if you would allow me to show you?'

'Come, Floriane. You've had quite enough excitement for one evening.' Claes placed a hand at the small of her back and propelled her towards the stairwell, Secunde Rosenmüller falling a step behind as they climbed.

Halfway up, Floriane stole a backward glance at the commander's right-hand man and was sure he gave her a wink.

⥈ CHAPTER 27 ⥈

FLORIANE WAS ALONE WHEN she woke up. Claes was already at work on his interviews with the line-up of hopeful suitors. As she lay in the bed, she was glad she did not have to start her day with him in full view and could think on her own, knowing that her decision to stand witness at Johanna's betrothal ceremony had been ill-advised.

After the incident with Johanna the previous night, they'd returned to their apartment and Floriane had seen the glitter of excitement in Claes's eyes. How she'd managed to climb into the additional bed Secunde Rosenmüller had organised for her, with Claes milling about in the darkness, she couldn't rightly recall, but when he had come near and whispered her name she'd managed to put him off.

She dressed with her usual care and, having decided to delay the application of face paint until she returned, climbed the stairs to the flat rooftop. From there, she looked down across the vlek and out to sea. The breeze had cleared the clouds. It was a fine autumn day, sunny but cool, and when she looked in the opposite direction she could see the full extent of the colony and beyond into the countryside. For a moment she felt that if her eyes had been strong enough, she'd have been able to see back the way they'd come, all the way to patria.

Now that they had arrived and begun to settle in, she felt a profound hollowness inside her. In Amsterdam she'd seen her mother and father every day. Somehow, although rationally she had known otherwise, she'd felt that when she arrived at the Cape, she would finish what she'd set out to do and return home right away. She shook her head, still shocked at the attack on Frans; it seemed impossible that Claes could have escalated his wickedness in the five months at sea.

A breeze swirled about her, tugging blonde curls from their pins. After pushing them back into place, she straightened the cap on her head. As Clara Speelman had promised, the Cape was bright with sunlight, the air crisp and fresh. If what ailed her could be cured by such things, she would soon be rid of it. Sadly, that was not the case.

Betrayal. Humiliation. It will take more than pure air to purge me of those.

She looked down at the vlek again, thinking that she should see if Johanna was feeling brighter with the new day. Perhaps it was too early to disturb her. A good night's sleep certainly wouldn't have hurt the poor thing. Floriane was worried about her, worried about the trouble she might bring upon herself if the windmill engineer succumbed to his injuries.

Beyond the Castle walls, she noticed a figure striding across the parade ground towards the building. As he drew closer, she could see his long, dark hair lifting in the breeze and swirling around his head. The uniform he wore was familiar. She felt the corners of her mouth soften and when he looked up at her, she broke into a full smile.

The secunde stopped on the spot and raised his arm, extending a hand towards her. 'Hello!' he called.

She waved back to him. 'Hello.'

He cupped both hands around his mouth and shouted, 'What are you doing up there?'

After a few seconds, she made a gesture with two fingers of one hand, imitating walking, and then pointed to her eyes.

'I'm not sure I understand,' he shouted back, laughing.

'I'm taking a tour of the vlek with my eyes,' she called.

He said nothing for a moment, and then, 'Would mevrouw's feet care to join the tour?'

'Only my feet?' She tucked her chin, trying not to laugh back.

He gave her another bright smile. 'I would certainly hope not, mevrouw.'

'I'll come down.' From the rooftop, the entire conversation had seemed safe enough, but at the thought of coming face to face with the secunde, she felt a twist of nerves. She told herself not to be foolish. A tour of the vlek was the only way she would find her way around the town.

She walked quickly across the flat roof, but slowed when she reached the stairs, straightening her spine and reminding herself she was the wife of the new fiscal. When she reached the bottom of the first flight of stairs and turned to gauge the next one, she saw the secunde was standing at the bottom, hand held towards her. 'Shall I come up?'

'Stay where you are,' she called, and took a deep breath.

He stood aside and, to her great relief, turned so that he wasn't looking directly up at her. The last thing she wanted was to catch a heel in her hem and fall while he looked on. By the time she reached the bottom of the stairs, she had taken control of her nerves. Conquering the smile that threatened to overtake her took somewhat more of an effort.

'Mijnheer Rosenmüller, I must thank you for your assistance last night. I was a poor chaperone in an unfamiliar place, and you came to my rescue.'

'Is the young lady in better spirits?'

'I haven't seen her yet today. I was thinking of visiting her when you came into view.'

Another smile, though brief, displayed the three lines at the corners of his mouth. 'Would it be more convenient to take our tour on another occasion?'

'No, no. This is a perfect time. I shall pop in on her when we return. That is, if you are free from your duties just now.'

He gestured that they should walk. 'This, in truth, is part of my current duty – the orientation of our most recently arrived colonists.'

She hesitated. 'I wonder if I might return to something you said last night. You implied it was safe enough to walk around in the vlek during the day, but is it only at night we should be mindful of the lions?'

'I have never known of a lion to come into the vlek by day. In fact, they rarely come into the vlek at all. They are wary of people, although they do steal sheep from farms if they are starving. If that animal is still in the vicinity this evening, we will run him off or someone will shoot him for his skin. I don't think you need to concern yourself unduly.'

'That is good to hear.'

They crossed the cobbled path over the Castle's moat, which gave off such an unpleasant odour that it forced them to walk in silence. As they reached solid ground again, Floriane stole a look at the secunde. She had not thought him handsome when they'd first been introduced, but after the carriage ride to the Castle that had changed absolutely, and she could see him no other way. She wondered about his age. Mid-thirties, at a guess, though there seemed to be a seriousness about him that few of his peers carried.

Perhaps he'd felt her eyes on him, for he looked over at her then, their eyes meeting briefly before he gestured to the right.

'You'll see that we have four large streets that run on a slight incline. Not that it is so difficult to find your way around, as you can always use Table Mountain and the ocean to orient yourself should you lose your way.'

Unpaved and uneven, the streets were lined with a jumble of freeburghers' houses and Company buildings. A long cart drawn by a span of six oxen rattled towards them. The secunde put a cautionary hand on her arm and stood in front of her as it passed, receiving the splatters of muck it sent up.

Floriane gasped. 'Oh, mijnheer! Your clothes!'

He brushed at the dirt with his fingers. 'Do not concern yourself, mevrouw. I assure you it is nothing.' He seemed genuinely unconcerned.

She shook her head slightly, then let out a deep sigh despite herself. 'I must confess, life at the Cape is not what I was led to expect.'

A frown creased his brow. 'By whom?'

'The commander's wife and a business acquaintance of my husband's.'

'I believe some deception was necessary to attract the marriage maids to come. To make the Cape more than what it is in reality. Experience has taught us to be more—' he seemed to search for the correct word '—boastful.'

'Does the deception not bother you?'

He looked down for a moment before replying. 'The vlek has its appeals, but these may not at first be obvious to someone used to European city life. Remember that this colony is scarcely three decades old. A city like Amsterdam has had hundreds of years to grow, and tens or perhaps hundreds of thousands of people to help build it. This place will also grow and flourish, but only if people come.'

She nodded. 'I suppose I hadn't thought of it that way.'

'Shall we?' He put out a hand to show their intended direction. When they had rounded the corner, he continued. 'I thought we should start with a walk in the Company garden, where the produce that supplies the Dutch East India's passing fleets is grown.'

The road they followed led them down Eerstestraat, and past the great tank of the freshwater station. Sweet water from the mountains was piped to it, the secunde told her, so that any ship could replenish its barrels. When they arrived at the garden's entrance on Jordaanstraat, he halted. 'The head gardener's house is within, but he is tolerant of polite European visitors.'

Floriane smiled at him. 'That reminds me – I wonder whether we have passed the house that is meant for us or, indeed, if it is in sight.'

'One of the options under discussion for your residence is on Thuynstraat, across the Square of Arms we passed yesterday. If we save the delights of the garden for a later occasion, we could go and look at it now. The walk will help fix the street plan in your head.' He gave an expansive wave of his hand, as if the layout of the town was his personal creation.

'I'd like that very much.'

As they walked, the high doorsteps of several houses made straight passage impossible. At either end of these stone *stoeps*, people sat drawing on long-stemmed pipes, women as well as men. Floriane shuddered at the regret that she fancied she saw on every face.

'Watch where you step.'

She managed to avoid a steaming pile of manure. Sheep, goats, and cattle roamed free on the street and dropped their calling cards wherever they hitched up their tails. 'Thank you for the warning.'

They finally came to a brick house with steps rising from the street to a stoep lined with red tiles. It had two storeys with unadorned gables, roofed in dark, shining reed rather than the Company's tiles. Floriane surveyed the front of the house and wrinkled her brow. 'Are we not to be given a Company-owned property?'

'Well, this is but one option. But wherever you are placed, I fear it will be your husband's responsibility to maintain it.'

Floriane's spirits sank. Rust pitted the doorhandle, and the glass was covered in water stains and dust. 'I wasn't expecting it to need so much . . .' She broke off and glanced over at the secunde.

He hurried to fill her silence. 'This might not be the actual house, and if it is, slaves will clean it for you. Don't worry until you absolutely have to. Hope for the best yet accept the worst. That's always been my motto.'

She smiled. 'Is that why you came to the Cape initially? To hope for the best?'

'In a way,' he said. 'But I also had a lifetime of gratitude to repay to the commander and his wife. He needed help, and I gave him mine.'

'That's a response that requires some explanation.'

He pressed his lips together and then said, 'We must save

that for later, so we will have something to talk about when I take you out to look at the Company garden.'

She kept her eyes focused on the road ahead. 'Of course.' When they had walked a little further, she said, 'I was just thinking of the young ladies. Do you know when they are to be married?'

'It will be soon. The commander is keen to see the girls wed.'

'I see.' Floriane was mute for a few steps but felt him watching. Pulse throbbing in her throat, she said, 'You must have a wife somewhere. Shall I meet her soon, or is she back in Amsterdam like Mevrouw Speelman?' The secunde did not immediately answer, and Floriane silently cursed herself. 'I fear I have been indiscreet.'

'No, no. Not at all. It's merely that I have no wife, mevrouw.'

A few more paces brought them to the wooden jetty. She felt the awkward moment stretching between them. She swallowed and said the first thing that came to mind. 'Look, they're still unloading our ship.'

The secunde nodded. 'Yes, it usually takes some days.'

Floriane watched the sailors working at the crane and windlass as they brought wooden cases ashore and lowered them into a bright green wagon.

She could feel his eyes on her and looked over at him. 'Please accept my apologies for my appalling curiosity about your personal life. It is certainly not—' She saw her husband standing on the jetty, animatedly directing the delivery of what looked to be furniture. Remembering that she had not made up her face, she turned quickly, worried that Claes would see her. Why was he out there instead of interviewing suitors as he said he would be?

The secunde shook his head. 'Please, there is no need to apologise. You have shared some private information with me, when all is said and done.'

At first she was unsure what he meant, but then it occurred to her that he must be referring to her request for a second bed in the apartment she and Claes shared. Drawing in a breath, she said, 'I appreciate your discretion. And . . .' She turned slightly to catch Claes in her sights and saw that he had not seen them.

When she turned back, Mijnheer Rosenmüller was also looking out at the quay.

'I wonder if we shouldn't head back to the Castle now. The time's ticking by.' She realised as she said it that it was close to mid-morning. 'I'm anxious to visit Johanna. I heard her weeping during the night and hardly know what to do to relieve her anguish.' It was true, yet a dishonest excuse to cut short her time with the secunde.

He bowed his head in acknowledgement, but the smile had slipped from his face.

⮜ CHAPTER 28 ⮞

CLAES SAT AT HIS office desk, arranging a new set of ivory chessmen on their chequered sandstone board. One of the Cape's wealthiest burghers had sent it as a magnificent thank-you gift for confirmation of the wide-hipped Dutch maid soon to be his bride.

Across the desk sat the nephew of Cristoffel Mulder, one of the most prominent merchant burghers. Claes fingered the beautifully carved pieces as the blond buffoon set forth his plans for the future. 'So in conclusion, it is my dearest wish to marry the red-headed orphan, Johanna Timmerman.'

'Let's not rush things,' Claes said. 'There is a great deal to be discussed before we can think about finding you a wife.'

Pieter Mulder pulled a leather-bound book from his coat and released the clasp. 'I have thought of no one else since she stepped onto the quay. I have written several odes to her beauty, if Your Honour would care to hear a few verses.'

Claes tossed his quill on the desk and failed to smother an impatient sigh. 'I am sure that they are fine lines, but they are for her ears alone. You are free to marry, I assume?'

The boy's voice shook with emotion. 'Oh, mijnheer, of course. I have been waiting my entire life for that lovely creature.'

'Forgive me for asking, but have you kept yourself away from the taverns and the lures of female flesh? Perhaps you have visited the slave lodge and sampled the treasures in that pleasure house?'

The young man reddened and looked down at his hands. 'I have yet to sample the delights of the female body, mijnheer. I walk "not in orgies and drunkenness, not in sexual immorality and sensuality, not in quarrelling and jealousy".'

'I see you know your Bible. Romans, I believe.'

Pieter's eyes were round, like the frames of his spectacles. 'Romans thirteen, verse thirteen. I attend Divine Service each Sunday.'

The boy said it with such a sense of delight that Claes almost laughed out loud. 'On a more delicate matter, do you have the funds to support a wife, and have a homestead in which to house her?'

Some of the glow left Pieter's face. 'I have fine prospects, but for the present am dependent on my uncle as I cannot subsist on my salary. I have a room at the Castle, where I am employed as scribe to the Honourable Company, but I have also a modest dwelling upon my uncle's land. As a marriage gift, he promises he will give me some morgen of land to farm near the Eerste River, where he has his own country estate. He says that I will make a fair farmer if I take the advice of those with more experience, and he is most willing to instruct me in agriculture and cattle-breeding.'

As Claes let the boy indulge himself, he raised his eyebrows several times in mock admiration. 'You are indeed fortunate. Had I a farm on such land as your uncle owns, I too would experiment, but in wine-growing. The current quality of the Cape's wine is so dire that even a modest contribution could do nothing but benefit us all.' He took a deep breath and waited.

A more worldly man would have seen the rocks ahead and steered to avoid a collision. Pieter took a giant leap towards them. 'I am certain that my uncle would happily part with a parcel of land for that purpose. He believes every man should own a farm where he might relax away from the cares of Castle administration.'

'I understand that your uncle has also the finest mason in the colony in his service.'

'Indeed, and his wood-carving is superior to his masonry, according to my uncle.'

Claes glanced at the boy's unsuspecting face and rose from his seat. He walked around the table and settled a hand on Pieter's shoulder. 'Then I am sure that the maid Johanna will find in you the most perfect of marriage partners. But now we must press on. The evening is drawing in, and I think it were well we conclude our interview and think of our supper. I have a few papers for you to sign before I am able to contemplate issuing your marriage certificate.'

Claes returned to his chair and rested his hands palm to palm on the table. 'On a more delicate matter, I fear I must relieve you of a handful of guilders to cover the young lady's passage from patria on the Company's behalf.' He pushed a stack of papers towards the youth. 'Three separate documents require your moniker. I have marked the places where you are to sign. When that is done, we will drink a toast to your future happiness from the VOC's very own loving cup.'

As the boy scratched away with his pen, Claes poured a generous measure of red wine into a goblet that bore the

Company's ship and monogram. He held it out to Pieter. '*Proost*, mijnheer. I wish you health and happiness.'

Grinning from ear to ear, Pieter accepted the glass and drained every last drop. 'Will you preside at the marriage ceremony?'

'Of course. You may depend upon it.'

When the door closed behind the boy, Claes turned to the chessboard and studied the pieces.

Almost immediately he heard shuffling footsteps along the corridor and was surprised to see the door shudder at the force of the knocks that rained impatiently on the wood. He played a little game with himself: *who might now be about to present his suit? An older man,* he thought, *with sufficient gravitas to know he'd not be denied.*

'Come in. Come in,' Claes called, and as the battered door swung open, he settled back in his chair, giving himself a moment to consider the elderly colonist before him. He gave him an encouraging smile. 'Greetings, mijnheer. You have the floor for five minutes to run through the details of your personal finances. Our dear girls must be sure of their security, and I will require some evidence.'

The man reached into his pocket and extracted a jingling bag, which he opened, spilling the contents – gold florins – onto the desk.

And so, for the umpteenth time that afternoon, Claes sat back and pricked up his ears.

⌐ CHAPTER 29 ⌐

THE FIRST TIME HER husband went off on an excursion away from the vlek, Floriane called on Commander Speelman in his private chamber. They sat side by side on the stinkwood bench to drink coffee from delftware cups.

Arent Speelman gave her an apologetic look. 'These settees are never comfortable, are they? However I settle myself, I feel the rawhide strips digging through my clothes.'

'There is one in our apartment too. It is on my mind to stitch a cushion or two to soften the effect, but I haven't yet found the time.'

The commander shivered slightly. A barefooted slave noticed and hurried to the door to call for a fresh shovelful of burning charcoal for the stove. A few moments later, another slave arrived and fulfilled the request, then they both bowed to the commander.

'You wish for something more, Excellency?' the first slave asked in accented Dutch.

'Bring us a plate of *zoetekoekies*.' He turned to Floriane. 'I find I can't drink this filthy coffee without something sweet to help it down.'

Still working up the nerve to broach the topic she'd come to discuss, she let her eyes rest on the portrait that hung on the wall of the chamber. In it, the commander was wearing full armour, mace in hand, his periwig falling on his polished breastplate. 'Your wife told me decent portraiture in the Cape is a rare thing, but that image is very fine.'

'It is a gift from Clara, immortalising a younger version of myself. It is very flattering that she should think of me thus.'

The slave returned with the sweet cakes and placed them at the commander's elbow. Wiping an invisible smear from the blue-and-white china plate, Arent Speelman appeared to weigh his words. 'I am aware that your husband is riding out with Merkel this morning to view a potential home near Signal Hill. Is there something particular you wanted to ask me that profits from his absence?'

She touched a finger to her lip and set her cup on its saucer. 'You are indeed perceptive, commander.'

He had picked up a cake but now set it down, uneaten, on the plate. 'Not so very much, mevrouw. I am in receipt of a series of letters both from my wife and a close acquaintance of hers – Erick de Witt.'

She tried to keep her face neutral. 'Ah.'

'Clara has written that she had you both to tea.'

'Yes,' she began carefully. 'I had that honour. It was a privilege to see your lovely home in Amsterdam.'

He took another sip of coffee. 'She also writes that you gave them both great assistance in recruiting the marriage maids, for which she is most grateful.'

'I did very little in that respect.'

'Please, tell me what it is that you have come to ask.' He folded his hands in his lap.

She looked down at her cup, frowning into it. 'It concerns the windmill engineer, Frans de Jong.'

His hesitation only lasted a second, but she heard it, nonetheless. 'I wondered when that topic might come up for discussion.'

'How is he? Do you have word of him from the hospital?' She hardly dared breathe, fearing what he might tell her.

'I know only that he lies gravely ill in an isolated room in the hospital.'

So he still lives. 'I see. Did Captain Bierens speak to you about what occurred?'

'He did. When he came ashore with the dispatches and paperwork for the Castle, he told me what he knew. With no explanation for what had provoked the attack, he felt the boy was safer stowed away with no attention drawn to him.'

'The captain said the attack was not witnessed.'

A troubled look crossed the commander's face. 'Do you know something different?'

She cradled her cup in both hands. 'This is a delicate matter and, in discussing it with you, I will invite your censure. No loyal wife should speak ill of her husband.'

'Then you must tread carefully.'

'Or keep what I suspect to myself.'

The commander rubbed his chin. 'There are certain – ahem – traits to your husband's character that are not the most praiseworthy, so I think, provided you hold to the facts, I can allow you to continue.'

Floriane took a sip of coffee. 'Johanna and I shared a cabin. Frans and Johanna became close on the ship. She talked about him incessantly and even though she'd only known him for a matter of months, she loved him with an intensity I envied. She told me that Claes had been pursuing her, and that he had told both her and the boy to have nothing to do with each other or he would *intervene*. Putting two and two together, I feel the aggressor had to have been Claes. Nothing else makes sense.'

He stared at the stove and massaged his hands. At last he said, 'Only Frans can say for certain. We must hope he will soon regain consciousness.'

'And that brings me to what I came to speak to you abou—'

'Let me guess. You would like the girl to care for him? I would not be happy with that arrangement.'

'Not Johanna – that would be madness. I myself would like to volunteer. However, there is one obstacle. I fear Claes would never agree to it unless you put it to him as your own idea.'

He smiled weakly, appearing relieved. 'I confess that would be a great help, if it would comfort Mejuffrouw Timmerman. I have not properly slept since the first night after your ship arrived. I am awakened at all hours by the sound of weeping through the walls.'

His words stirred her resolve. 'Yes, I too have heard it. The young lady fears greatly for the boy's life.'

He twisted the waxed tip of his moustache, perhaps considering the best course of action. 'Given the many cases of scurvy in our hospital, I propose that we should call you an outside matron, to allow you to make your visits in an official capacity. I will speak to your husband about the matter. Should he question you, you might also say to him that while at the hospital you will be able to seek the advice of the resident physician, which will save him considerable fees in attending to your *health problems*.'

Floriane felt he said the last two words a touch too meaningfully. She simply stared at him, trying not to betray how stunned she felt.

'I am not a fool, mevrouw. My wife is an invalid. You, whatever your reasons for the pretence, are not *souffrante*.'

Hoping to shift the conversation away from the state of her health, she said, 'You know French, Your Excellency?'

He let his gaze remain on her a second longer and then said, 'The colony is overrun with French Huguenots. The language has rubbed off.'

She smiled politely. *'Dès que vous aurez le temps, nous devrions continuer cette conversation en français.'*

'On espère que ce sera possible.' He looked quite pleased with himself.

She thought to seize on the moment. 'Indeed, I'm certain we shall find the occasion, but I have been meaning to ask. Regarding the windmill engineer, what will happen when he is well? What am I to tell her?'

Concern touched his eyes. 'I too envy their devotion, but she is obligated by the contract she signed to marry a burgher.'

Her fingers closed around the handle of her cup. 'You allowed me a certain licence earlier when speaking of Claes. I wonder if it might again prevail?'

'If you are brief.' He spoke without heat, but she felt that his patience was thin.

'There is more to this story, Your Excellency, and if you were aware of the details, I believe you might change your opinion both in the matter of Johanna Timmerman's relationship with the windmill engineer and with respect to allowing my husband free rein.' She pushed back her hair, giving him time to think.

'I am uncertain what details you think I am ignorant of, but in the matter of Johanna we must be resolute. I will not allow her contact with the boy at the hospital. As for your husband, against my better judgement, I have been persuaded by the commissioner to give him every possible leeway at the Cape so he may decide whether the man might be fit for a higher rank in time. It is my intention to leave this posting eventually, and I have requested a transfer . . .' He toyed with the little cake on his plate, pushing it back and forth. 'If indeed he stabbed a man and left him for dead, it reinforces my impression that your husband is not fit. But this will be up to the commissioner in the end.'

Floriane poured more coffee into their cups. Claes's theft of jewels would have been a most persuasive argument, but Erick de Witt had made clear to her that the entire plan rested on keeping the jewel theft away from the notice of the VOC. Even the commander was not to know of it. She felt uneasy, but chose to maintain her silence in this one regard.

'My husband believes that in putting thousands of miles between his creditors in Amsterdam and himself, the slate is now wiped clean. He thinks the boy is dead so, on that front at least, he will do no more harm.' She stared at him, hardly able to believe her boldness. 'But I must warn you, Commander Speelman, that he is wily and unpredictable. I can make no assurances about what he might do. As for Johanna, on promises from the Honourable Company of far better prospects than she would have had in Amsterdam, she has come to the Cape in good faith.' She managed a smile. 'You must remember what it is like to fall in love? By chance, she met a boy. If she keeps her contract in every other respect, must the Company insist she marry a burgher in particular?' She allowed her deference to colour her tone.

'The Dutch East India is judge and jury at the Cape and I cannot be seen to show favouritism. I am weary of it but my hands are tied.'

Floriane cradled her cheek, thinking how else she might petition for the young couple, but the commander rose from his chair. 'Forgive me. I must return to my duties, mevrouw. I believe that your husband has all but completed his match-making interviews and the weddings will be conducted three days from now. Eight marriages for eight maids.'

Floriane blinked at him. 'Three days?'

'We have been waiting years for the VOC to agree to send us girls. Now they are here, I see no reason to delay whatsoever.'

She eased herself up from the chair and draped her cloak around her shoulders, trying to hide her surprise. 'Thank you for the coffee and your confidence. Given the speed with which the girls will be married, I should apprise them of the good news.'

◄ CHAPTER 30 ►

JOHANNA BENT SLIGHTLY FORWARD as she laced Malliet into her new bodice. Around her the sewing room was filled with excited chatter. In a few hours, they would all be married. She felt numb, distant, so she focused all of her attention on the task of feeding laces through small eyelets.

Since Floriane had come to the sewing room to tell them the news three days ago, she'd been unable to think of anything else. She had told herself again and again that there was a way out of the VOC's contract, but as yet she had no idea what it might be.

I'm thankful we've all made it here alive, Floriane had said on her brief visit. Even though she'd addressed her comments to them all, Johanna had read the message in her eyes. Frans was still living.

She finished the lacing. 'There, now. What's next? Have you sleeves?'

Malliet tucked the ends of the laces into her bodice. 'Yes, I'll fetch them.' She nudged Johanna with her elbow and darted across the room.

The other six girls stood about in their new clothes, resembling a scattering of vibrant flowers in an otherwise bleak field. They seemed excited.

A familiar voice cut through the giddy chatter. She glanced over her shoulder as Floriane Peronneau crossed the threshold.

'Good morning, everyone. Are you almost ready?'

A volley of affirmations sounded, followed by an eruption of laughter. Malliet reappeared with her sleeves, which she handed to Johanna.

Floriane took a step towards them. 'How are you getting on?'

Johanna shrugged and looked at her blankly.

'We're almost finished. Sleeves, cap. We'll be ready in no time,' Malliet said.

'Can I do anything?' Floriane asked.

Johanna handed her one of the sleeves and they each began to tie theirs to the bodice.

'And what about you, Johanna? No finery for your big day?' Floriane kept her eyes fixed on her hands as they worked.

Johanna concentrated on the sleeve. 'There was no time for me to make a new dress, so I'll just be wearing what I have on.' Johanna tied the last knot and tucked in the ends. 'There you are, Malliet. Just your cap and you'll be a perfect bride.'

Malliet looked between the two of them. 'I told Jo-Jo she looks like she's just come in from mucking out the stables, but she can't be persuaded to make more of an effort. Perhaps you'll have more luck in convincing her that first impressions count.' She dropped a curtsy and turned.

As she walked away, Johanna stepped closer to Floriane and whispered, 'You have news?'

'None that you will want to hear, I'm sorry.'

Johanna knew what that meant. The commander was still insisting that she marry a burgher. 'You know I cannot marry anyone while . . .' *While Frans lies in the hospital, his life hanging by a thread.*

Floriane fiddled with the lace at her neck. 'I understand, Johanna. But I cannot see how you are going to avoid it.'

Johanna straightened her shoulders. 'At the moment I don't know either, but I must trust in providence. I cannot believe that we were brought together on the ship by mistake; therefore, there must be some grand plan. Perhaps this is a test of my loyalty.'

Floriane produced a thin smile. 'I'm sure you will pass any test of loyalty. Are you certain you would not like to borrow a dress?'

Johanna could not return the smile. 'I am very grateful for the offer, but I won't be needing it today. I will ask this favour, though. As I've been forbidden to visit myself, is there any way you can send me word of him? If not daily, as often as possible?' Her voice broke and it took a concerted effort to find it again. 'I fear that if he slipped away, I would be no wiser.'

'The commander has given me leave to care for Frans at the hospital and I give you my word, insofar as I can manage it, that you shall know his daily condition.'

Just then, the sonorous ringing from the clock tower tolled the hour, and Johanna felt as if all the moisture had been wicked from her mouth. She ran her tongue around her lips and willed herself calm.

'Very well, then.' Floriane moved away towards the others. 'It's time, ladies. We should make our way to the Council Chamber.' She turned back to Johanna and in the softest whisper, said, 'Providence.' Then she crossed the room to the door. 'Follow me, please. It would be an ill omen to be late to your own weddings.'

Malliet appeared by Johanna's side, her cap now on her head, a bright scarf fastened around her shoulders. 'Come along.' She punched Johanna's arm. 'Best foot forward. We're about to meet the men who will change our lives!'

Johanna could not help but smile at her best friend's enthusiasm.

Together, they made their way through the Castle to the Council Chamber. As they went in, Johanna saw the commander, decked in his ribbons and badge of office, his wig tied back with a narrow white ribbon edged with gold.

Malliet lowered her head and clasped her hands together then filed into the room to find her allocated seat, but Johanna remained where she stood. As if drawn by some defensive instinct, her eyes sought out Claes van Loon where he sat behind the long, central table, a towering pile of parchment before him. His arms crossed over his chest, a heavy glass at his elbow, he looked smugly satisfied. Involuntarily, she ground her teeth together and looked away.

From a cloth-draped table to his right, Company slaves were offering wine. For a fleeting moment, as a wave of panic washed over her, Johanna was tempted to throw back a glass.

Providence, she reminded herself.

The secretary was a tall man in a brown velvet coat and plain buff breeches fastened at the knee. He noticed her hesitation and waved an impatient hand at a seat bedecked with ivy and flowers. 'I'm about to get started with proceedings. Perhaps you might take your place so that I can begin? Save the wine for later, when you truly have something to celebrate.'

Chastened, Johanna perched on the edge of the woven-seated chair alongside her seven fellow orphans. Floriane stood in the corner behind the girls but her face was impossible to read. Wishing for all the world that her mother would rise from the dead and whisk her away, Johanna scanned the room, her heart beginning to gallop.

Half the colony had been herded into the Council Chamber. The promise of free wine and food and a glimpse of the girls had flushed the outlying colonists from their homes. Soldiers who'd become farmers and Frenchmen who'd become Dutch and Dutchmen who'd grown fat in their adopted land had turned out in their droves.

Next to her, Malliet gripped her hand. Across the room, a group of eight men stood. Johanna wondered whether they already knew which of the girls they would wed. She tried to swallow, but her mouth was still too dry.

As a cohort, the grooms ranged from middle-aged to grand-fatherly. One seemed particularly frail. Another, though, was far younger than the rest, hardly old enough to be thinking of marrying. There was something naggingly familiar about him. As she combed through her memory, she felt his eyes on her and watched his face as his jaw dropped. Then she remembered. From the carriage, the first day at the Cape, he'd given her the exact same look, staring at her, open-mouthed from his place on the quay, like a guppy in a pond. As the memory grew wings, she almost laughed out loud.

Johanna tapped Malliet's arm. 'Help me out here. Who's the boy who looks like an owl – over there with the spectacles?'

Malliet narrowed her eyes. 'Oh! That's Pieter. He works as a scribe here. I know him only because he was the one who took us to the warehouse to pick out fabric.'

'I think I saw him when I first arrived, but how can a Company scribe be one of the suitors?'

'I don't know.' Malliet studied the group of men. 'I wager I'll get the old one.'

'Young ladies!' the secretary snapped. 'We will have quiet in the chamber now.'

Johanna exchanged looks with Malliet as the secretary began with an elaborate and lengthy discourse on their future responsibilities as Cape brides. As he ground relentlessly on, Johanna offered up a prayer, asking God to show her the way out of this. She bent her face to her knees, consciously trying to breathe. An odd sense of calm came over her and she felt almost as if she were watching the whole spectacle from a distance. Something Frans had said came back to her. *They can't force you to marry against your will.*

The knot of wig-wearing husbands-to-be stretched their necks to get a better look at the girls. Johanna coughed to clear the lump in her throat and turned her head to look at Hilletje. She looked pretty in her green-and-red dress. Johanna smiled in spite of herself as she recalled why Hilletje had come to the Cape. *I'm going to marry a bigwig, Roodhoofje, and have a maid of mine own one day.*

The young woman registered her look. 'I don't think we've much longer to wait,' she murmured.

Claes van Loon lumbered to his feet. His sword swung out from his belt, and he steadied the swaying blade with his hand. He shuffled his papers and brought one page to the top. It looked to her like he was enjoying his power.

He cleared his throat. 'Malliet Wagenaar.'

Malliet cast a glance at them over her shoulder and hopped to her feet. The fiscal called on the frail old man, who took his place at Malliet's side. Diamond buckles twinkled on his shoes, and his eyes sparkled with pleasure. She glanced back at Johanna with an expression of resignation on her face.

The fiscal pushed the page towards the couple and, when they had signed against their names, declared them married in the eyes of God.

The fiscal consulted his list. 'Elke Zuidmeer,' he read out.

Elke was coupled with a short man running slightly to flesh, with a powdered peruke that was a bit askew, yet his face was kind. He swept off his hat in an exaggerated bow.

'Well done,' Johanna whispered. 'He looks really nice.'

One by one, she watched as the girls she had known for eight years were married up as the Honourable Company had promised, with the wealthiest bachelor freeburghers at Good Hope.

Eventually, only two of them were left. Johanna's heart raced so fast she felt breathless. She caught Floriane's eye and the woman nodded her encouragement.

'Hilletje Lampbrecht.' The fiscal gave the girl a slight bow when she looked at him.

She was pledged to a raw-boned giant with a weathered complexion. In spite of his impressive moustache, his grin was so wide it seemed to overtake the lower half of his face.

Johanna was impressed. 'Good for you,' she whispered. 'He looks thrilled to bits.'

She turned her gaze back to where the group of suitors had stood. One remained – the bespectacled scribe.

Claes van Loon read from the last document, his voice a bored drone. 'Tall, red hair, pale, penniless peasant. Henceforth to be known as the property of Pieter Mulder.'

The crowd in the room let out a collective gasp. Johanna narrowed her eyes at the fiscal, biting back furious words before turning to eye the boy as he advanced from across the room.

Pieter Mulder pulled his face into an earnest smile and dropped to one knee. He grabbed her hand and clutched it to his chest. 'I have written a sonnet to you in honour of the occasion.'

She could feel her chest tighten and the blood pound in her temples. He dropped her hand and, pulling a leather-bound book from his coat, placed his finger on the open page and traced the words as he read them out. 'On bended knee, I plea to thee, that you'll say yes and marry me. For me you are the perfect wife—'

'Wait,' she blurted out.

The boy looked confused, and returned his poetry book to his coat as he scrambled to his feet.

Claes van Loon appeared by her side. Although she couldn't be absolutely certain, she thought she heard him snicker.

Thinking she must buy herself some time, against the possibility the boy would change his mind, very quietly, with unmasked directness, she turned to address Claes van Loon. 'The Honourable Company led me to expect an older, established man.'

The fiscal leaned in close, his breath hot on her cheek. 'Having seen your tastes, I knew you'd like a fresh young whelp in your bed. I warned you it would end in tears.'

Johanna did not flinch. 'You should have kept a better eye on me on board ship than just peeping at me through the lens of your telescope.' She turned to Pieter Mulder and said, in a voice loud enough to be heard by all, 'I'm sorry, mijnheer, but I cannot marry you, for I am already joined to another.'

Commander Speelman picked up his glass and threw it at the fireplace in his private chamber.

'What manner of nonsense is this, Van Loon? Before this morning, the girls were all unmarried. You assured me that you knew the most minute details about them. How is it then *possible*—' his voice seemed to slip away from him as he finished his sentence '—that Johanna Timmerman is not free to wed?'

Claes bit his lip. 'It is *not* possible, Excellency. The girl is lying.'

'But she declares she is already wed.'

'Even if there had been a marriage, which there has not, the boy is . . .' Claes caught himself just in time. 'A phantom. Where is this person to whom she says she has been conjoined? He is not here at the Cape.'

The commander flung himself into a chair. 'This embarrassment is on your head, not mine, and will be recorded as such in my journal. The girl has contracted to marry one of our burghers and I am not releasing her from that obligation. And whatever were you thinking, trying to join her to that blond scribbler? The girls came to the Cape on the promise of being married to wealthy burghers, an opportunity they would likely not have had in patria. The outlandishness of your pairing makes her rebellion almost excusable. The Honourable Company has outlaid a considerable sum of money in bringing her to the Cape – not to mention the cost of her board and lodging since she arrived – so that she might marry well. I will confine her to the Castle until you find a solution to this . . .' He waved his hand about his ear. 'This *mess*.'

Claes's eyes stung as the sweat from his brow seeped into them. 'We could send her back to her orphanage in Holland

246

in disgrace. That would show her this little game has been for nothing.'

'Are you an imbecile, man? We need women to *come* to the Cape, and you only managed to bring me a pitiful few as it is. Do you suppose for a moment that I am going to sanction her return when there are so many men anxious to wed?'

'Is she not to be punished?' Claes scowled.

For a long moment the commander stared at the shattered glass by the fireplace, unblinking, before he made his pronouncement. 'Get back to the wedding banquet and toast the happiness of those who *have* wed. I want you there in full view of the colony, so they will remember who is at fault here.'

⌒

Claes lingered in the Council Chamber after the last of the wedding guests had departed, draining bumper after bumper of the commander's fine red wine. When the light began to fade, he made his way across the cobbled courtyard towards the Castle's entrance and watched as the lamps of the vlek lit up.

Blood throbbed at his temples, and behind his eyes sharp needles seemed to pierce his brain. He'd been made to look a fool. Did the commander think he would overlook such a public humiliation? Smirking at the thought of revenge, he managed a spring in his step as he approached the slave lodge. His passage was blocked by the slack-wit Pieter Mulder and a sour-faced man he assumed was his uncle.

He inclined his head in a polite bow. 'Mijnheeren.'

'My uncle would like a word, Mijnheer van Loon.' Pieter took two steps forward.

Claes looked at the heavy wooden door and considered the physical delights that lay within. 'Can't it wait until tomorrow?'

'It cannot,' the sour man said.

'And you are?'

'Cristoffel Mulder, Pieter's uncle.'

Claes slapped on a smile to soften the effect of his words. 'I assure you the girl is not married. This matter will be settled in due course. The girl will be proven a liar.'

Glowering, Mulder said, 'We will settle this right now, inside.'

The short walk from the Castle gates to the Council Chamber seemed to take forever. Seated at one end of the wide, wooden table, Mulder looked Claes up and down, tapping the arm of his chair with the heavy ring on his finger. 'You have taken a monumental payment from me for something you have not delivered, and you have reneged on a promise to my nephew.'

The boy picked at the frayed cuff on his coat and whined, 'You said it was perfectly acceptable for me to have the girl, but everyone gasped when you read out our names. Then they sniggered at me. It was very shaming, and I feel I am due some recompense.'

Claes found his fingers itching to take the boy by the collar. 'It is a temporary setback. The girl has signed a contract. Just as soon as we unpick her claim, she will be yours. You have my word.' Clamping his jaw tightly shut, he reached for his inkhorn and made an elaborate show of dipping his quill. 'I am making a note to myself to sort this out first thing tomorrow morning.'

Mulder rounded on him, his cavernous nostrils flaring. 'That is not good enough. I gave you forty morgen of prime farming land to make this happen for Pieter. While he waits for the girl, I suggest you promote him to clerk of the Orphan Chamber and double his salary, backdated to the start of this year.'

Claes quirked his upper lip in a sneer, but his breathing would not steady. 'I do not care to be told my business.'

'If you play with fire, you'll find yourself burned. Loose tongues will wag in the vlek if the Company's most recent vulture is revealed to be rotten and stinking.'

The heat rose in Claes's face. 'I have no idea to what you're alluding.'

The man folded his arms across his chest, a slight sneer on his face. 'I applaud your pretence at portraying an honest soul, but I have spies everywhere. While you may think you covered your spoor well, my contacts reach way beyond the vlek. I still know exactly what goes on in Amsterdam. A word from me to the commander would blow your cover in a heartbeat. And there is a long list of creditors who would be happy to know of your current location.'

'What more are you after, Mulder?'

He pulled a paper from the inside pocket of his jacket. 'A mere three things, in exchange for my silence. To start with—' he held up his index finger '—they have strengthened the guard on the barrel room. You are to see it removed.' A second finger sprang up. 'When the commander places wine, meat or grain licences on the agenda at the Council of Policy, I want foreknowledge of his thinking.'

Claes folded his arms. 'And the third?'

'I want Pieter wed to the redhead by the end of the week.'

⤳ CHAPTER 31 ⤳

WIDE AWAKE, JOHANNA LAY in her bed in the solid dark. The stillness of the room, now that all her friends had gone off to their new lives, did not help. She had opened the window, but she took no comfort in the eerie noises that came from this strange land – the whispering of the wind, the cries of unfamiliar birds and animals. Her mind kept replaying what had happened in the Council Chamber. She had no idea how she had dared to announce that she was married. The words had simply flown out of her mouth. In her heart, she believed them. She was married to Frans; she had pledged herself to him without the slightest hesitation and he had done the same in return.

Malliet's eyes had been full of questions, but she'd had to turn and take her new husband's arm. Hilletje had actually covered her eyes with her hands, as if to deny Johanna's outburst had happened. Only Floriane's face had shown understanding and acceptance of what she had done.

After another half-hour, she sat up and pummelled her fist against her pillow, turned it to the cool side, and tried again.

She closed her eyes and tried to quieten her thoughts, yet sleep would not oblige her. It was barely light when she got up, still dressed from the day before. She took care ascending the stairs to the flat roof of the Castle, gripping the iron handrail as she trod, aware of the slick stone underfoot. The hairs on the back of her neck prickled as she caught a movement in the shadows.

'Who's there?' she breathed.

'Did you really expect that I would be able to sleep?' The distress in Floriane's voice was hard for her to hear. 'You are in very deep water, Johanna, and I do not know how to pull you out.'

'I know. But I couldn't marry Pieter Mulder while Frans . . .' She shrank from the hint of reproach and began again. 'I had to come up with a plan, and it was the only thing I could think of to gain myself some time.'

'Your friends are bewildered, and Pieter Mulder was humiliated in front of his family. But at least Claes was embarrassed in front of the commander and the entire vlek. What exactly did he say to you?'

'He said he'd warned me that it would end in tears. I do not know whether he meant my friendship with Frans, or my refusal to sleep with him. What do you think they will do to me?'

'I've no idea.'

Johanna's mind was racing. 'What about the betrothal ceremony? That has to count for something.'

'I have asked the commander if we can meet him later this morning.' She reached out an arm and hugged Johanna to her side. 'I think I've found a loophole.'

Feeling like a naughty child, Johanna stood with her back against the wall as she watched Floriane pace backwards and forwards in front of Commander Speelman's desk.

'You see, commander,' she said, wagging her finger, 'the problem is the banns were never read out for Johanna, nor for any of the girls.'

The commander tilted his head to one side, inviting her to go on.

'The colony is Dutch. The law is Dutch. Everything you do to run the vlek is based on Dutch tradition. When the pairings were announced at the marriage ceremony, legally three successive announcements should have been made before the official ceremony could take place.'

The commander did not hesitate. 'I dispensed with the necessity for publishing banns given the exceptional circumstances. We deemed it sufficient to have these "announcements" recorded on the paperwork on three successive pages. The marriages were thus properly registered by the hand of your husband at the Orphan Chamber.'

Floriane's mouth tightened. She cast Johanna a sidelong glance and went on. 'On board ship, we conducted a formal betrothal ceremony between Johanna and Frans. I witnessed this, so at the very least my word is proof of their engagement. As you know, engagements are binding in Dutch law, and breaking one off is a legal offence in the Netherlands.'

He stared at his journal and frowned, eventually saying, 'We cling to many of patria's better legal niceties at the Cape, but this is not one of them.' He looked straight at Johanna. 'You signed a contract with the Dutch East India, and you are to honour it. However much you plead or beg, I will not be flexible in your case.'

Johanna bowed her head and asked in a quiet voice, 'And am I to marry Pieter Mulder? He is a scribe and barely solvent, and my contract said that I was to marry an established, wealthy man. I cannot see how that is honouring my contract?'

The commander rose from his seat and crossed to the window. He stared out through the glass for a moment or two, but Johanna could not see what had caught his eye. He turned just enough so that his words would be clear. 'I will take my time deciding which of my burghers will derive the greatest benefit from a marriage with you. In the meantime, you are to remain here at the Castle under house arrest.'

Johanna stepped closer to his desk. 'I don't understand.'

'You will remain within the Castle walls and may not leave for any reason whatsoever. You are not legally married, and I will not tolerate dishonesty from anyone – male, female, old or young.'

Floriane flashed her a look of alarm. At last she said, 'Your wife says that you are a fair man, Your Excellency, so I am wondering how you would react if one of your children told an untruth? Would you correct it with repeated beatings, or would you leave the lie for what it was – an inexperienced person's clumsy attempt to save themselves from a mistake? Might you not allow Johanna to leave the Castle with me as a chaperone, so that she can open the door of her cage from time to time?'

The muscles in his jaw clenched and unclenched. When he spoke again, his voice carried the bitter tone of resignation. 'Johanna is fortunate to have you as her champion, Mevrouw Peronneau, and you to have my wife as yours. I will agree to the chaperone—'

Johanna let out a small gasp. 'Thank you so very much, Your Excellency. You—'

'But—' He raised a finger in her direction. 'She may not, at any time, visit Frans de Jong in hospital. Is that understood?'

Floriane nodded once.

He continued in a grim tone. 'While we have no proof that your husband made the attempt on the boy's life, we cannot risk him taking notice until we are certain that he is not the guilty party.'

Or that he is, Johanna added to herself.

The confinement scarcely affected Johanna until a few days later, when Floriane, the last of her companions, stood at the door out to the main gateway, bags packed and ready for removal to her house in the vlek.

'I shall not be far away.' Floriane put on a reassuring smile, but Johanna knew her well enough now to read her underlying concern. 'It's a few minutes' walk, and I will be visiting you regularly. Remember you have all the nooks and crannies of the Castle to explore, and the inner courtyard where you might sketch. And perhaps the commander will give you something meaningful to do.'

Johanna nodded, her throat tight. Floriane held her arms open and Johanna stepped into the hug. 'I shall miss you, mevrouw.'

'And I you. But we shall see each other all the time, and I shall bring you word from the hospital soon.'

She tried to look hopeful for Floriane as she turned and went out through the gateway that Johanna was now forbidden to use. On a whim, she turned and walked quickly to the stairs and up to the roof. From there she watched her friend heading into the vlek and down the streets that ran between houses, until she vanished from sight.

⋘ CHAPTER 32 ⋙

As Claes crashed about the house throwing items into a holdall, Floriane let her knitting drop onto her lap. Loneliness pressed in on her. Through the window she watched the oily, black waves roll in from the north-west, breaking in noisy fury on the wooden jetty. He burst into the room, slapping his riding stick against his thigh, flung his hat and gloves onto a chair and in three long strides reached the window. 'When will this damnable weather let up?'

Floriane shook her head and picked up her knitting poles. 'I wish I had the answer, dear one, but the commander says this weather is unseasonal.' She puckered her lips. Somewhere along the row, she had dropped a stitch.

He jabbed at her with his crop. 'Stop making that French face.'

'I beg your pardon?'

'That face you do with the pouty lips. You were keen enough to join me. I told you to stay at home but, oh no, you had to come too. I'm fed up of your sniping, miserable comments.'

She looked up from her knitting and locked her fingers tightly together. 'Why are you so waspish this morning, Claes?

I confess that I do not know what I have said to make you so disagreeable.'

The riding stick snapped in his grasp and he threw it to the floor. 'I have matters to attend to but I cannot get to them, and my patience is sorely tried. I care not for the Castle's workforce. These men at the Cape work so ponderously that a tortoise could move quicker. I have told you that a score of times, yet still you fail to listen. Small wonder my fuse is short if my own wife is too deaf to hear my words.'

She sank back in her chair. 'What business do you have that cannot be conducted from the Castle?'

He waved his hand vaguely. 'I am setting up an Orphan Chamber in Stellenbosch and have meetings with the magistrate. The Khoi are stealing cattle again. A commando raid would sort the lot of them out, but I have to deliver the order to muster myself, it seems.'

Floriane stowed her knitting in the bag at the side of her chair and faced her husband. 'I am sure they are very glad of your wise counsel, dear one, and that is why they have summoned you in person. But Stellenbosch is seven hours away, and that troubles me.'

Claes ran his fingers through his new blond wig in an almost boyish gesture of contrition. 'I am a selfish brute to burden you with my discontent, Florrie. May I beg you to forgive me? The weather tries and impedes us both. Are you visiting the hospital this morning?'

She hardly flinched at the change in his mood. Since the upset with Johanna's wedding, his behaviour had become impossible to predict. That he had shown a flutter of interest in her visits to the hospital was little short of astounding.

'Yes, the hospital is overwhelmed. Scurvy has taken a heavy

toll on the ships newly arrived from Batavia. Despite the weather, the less urgent cases are in tents in the *kraals*.'

'The cattle enclosures? Hopefully not near Stellenbosch, where—'

Floriane saw the thought gather on his brow that they might be where he was building, and seized the opportunity to cut across him. 'The surgeon says that there is nowhere else for the poor souls to go, and is asking that those with private homes at the vlek take in some of the less affected men. Commander Speelman is urging further work on the new hospital, but the weather impedes its progress as well as yours.'

He jerked his head back towards the window, his momentary bonhomie abandoned. 'You distress me greatly, spending so much time in intimate conversation with the Cape commander. I do not want you bringing diseased men into this house.' His expression hardened. 'Do not volunteer our home under any circumstance.' He raised an eyebrow at her. 'Are we in agreement?'

Half turning towards the window so that he wouldn't see her face, she said in a meek tone, 'Of course, dear one. Of course.'

'As soon as the rain lessens, I intend to ride to the country and install myself at the Mulders' farm for the next few weeks. I need to supervise the start of work on the land he gifted me.'

Floriane widened her eyes. 'I am surprised that they will offer you hospitality after their disappointment with Pieter.'

'The delay in marriage is a temporary inconvenience, that's all.'

'I think it is a little more than that if Johanna is *actually* already married to the windmill engineer.'

'So produce the boy and let him corroborate her statement.'

Floriane stood up and crossed the polished floorboards. She threw back the upper part of the heavy front door and leaned into the space. 'Claes, the rain has stopped at last! You can send for your horse, and I can be on my way to visit the poor devils at the hospital.'

Claes frowned. 'It seems to me that you have a lot on your plate and could use assistance with household chores. When I get back from the country, I intend to buy a couple of female slaves. They are ten a penny, and their help will ease your workload while you are busy at the hospital.'

Floriane sucked in her cheeks. *You must think I came down with the last shower,* she thought. *I know exactly what you'll be up to while I tend to the sick.* But she said only, 'When might I expect your return?'

Claes gave an airy wave of his hand. 'Two weeks, give or take.'

The hospital was a short walk across a water-logged parade ground. The dilapidated building was gabled and lime-white, in the shape of a cross. It stood on the seashore close to Zeestraat, not far from the meat store. There were a cluster of outhouses behind it, and two or three taverns lined the path to the beach.

The wards were communal, apart from one room that housed a poor soul who, it was rumoured, had lost his wits and had to be segregated. Otherwise, irrespective of their maladies, the sick were thrown in together, black and white nursed on equal footing and on adjacent grass-stuffed mattresses. At least they all ate generously – that is, those who still had teeth and could chew.

In the room assigned to the 'poor soul', Floriane stood beside Frans's bed and looked him over. His hair was matted, his eyes were closed, and he was making small sounds as if in pain.

'Frans. It's Floriane Peronneau.'

His lips moved but no words came forth.

Even from a distance, she could feel the heat coming off him despite his shivers. She skimmed his face with her hand. His hair stuck limply to his head, and he was now muttering to himself, restless.

Gently, she lifted his head and placed a pillow beneath his neck. She pulled up the blanket to cover him and pushed it round his body as a mother might tuck up a child. She brought a chair next to the pallet and sat by his shoulder, watching the rise and fall of his chest, a flair of fear in her own. *I don't have the skills to deal with this*, she thought. *But there is no one else to help him.*

Night fell and dawn came. Another day passed, and then another, yet Frans hung on to life. She left his room only to get fresh water and other supplies, and to eat a small amount of food herself.

It was late in the afternoon on the fifth day, the light fading to dusk, when Frans opened his eyes. Floriane held her breath, watching him as his eyes moved around the room until they found her face.

She sat on the bed and took his hand. 'Frans?'

For a while he did not speak and then, with what seemed a great effort, said, 'Mevrouw.'

'Do you know me?'

He closed his eyes for two heartbeats then blinked them open. This she took to mean he did. She watched his throat move as he tried to swallow then she picked up a cup of water, holding it to his lips while he took small sips. She wiped a stray drip from his chin and sat back, willing him to speak. Eventually, he muttered something she could not make out, then seemed to motion to her with two fingers. She leaned in closer and put her ear near his lips.

'How,' he said, his voice faltering.

'Go on,' she urged.

'Johanna?'

Floriane pulled back slightly, feeling the corners of her mouth lift. 'She is well.'

He gave the same slow blink. 'Free to marry—' he licked his parched lips '—me?'

⁓

Floriane emerged from Frans's room. Dazed with exhaustion, she stumbled down the unlit hospital corridor. In the dim distance, she heard the commander's voice, but did not see to whom he was talking. 'Merkel is too thin, and his face has taken on a waxen pallor that concerns me greatly. I fear that his heart, weakened by his privations in Germany, might give out at any moment.'

When Speelman caught sight of her, a gleam of hope seemed to lighten his face. As she drew near, his brow furrowed and he gave a tiny shake of his head. 'You look dreadful, mevrouw. Are you too in need of the surgeon?'

'Thank you for your concern, Your Excellency. I am well but have spent the past days with the patient we spoke of. He will, I now believe, recover.'

'You are indeed a matron of great skill. We all feared the worst, but now I must ask for your help with another patient. Merkel has been two days in the hospital and is already starting to fade.'

Fatigue was making her slightly unsteady on her feet. 'Then we must concentrate on getting him well. If you would escort me to my house, Your Excellency, so that I may wash and change my clothes, I'll come back and see how best I can help him.'

⮚ CHAPTER 33 ⮘

OUTSIDE IN THE CASTLE'S inner courtyard, Johanna strolled past the coach-house, the grass fringed with late blooms. With the autumn sunshine warm on her face, she settled on the tiled rim of a circular pond, in the middle of which a tiny fountain tinkled. A school of sleek, glittering fish darted between the blue water lilies. She watched a scarlet-breasted sugarbird dive among the flowers, plunging its long-pointed bill into each of their hearts to rob them of their nectar, and began to draw its beak.

'Can you stop what you're doing and catch up with your old friends?'

Malliet and Hilletje stood in the Castle garden, dressed in smart new clothes, looking scrubbed and in the best of health.

Johanna jumped up, tossing her sketching paper to the ground. 'Oh, my goodness! Does this mean you received my letters?'

Malliet enfolded her in a hug. 'We were both distressed to hear you'd been confined to the Castle. We sent each other a note and – voilà – here we are. We came up last evening and stayed at my husband's townhouse in Herengracht.'

'You have a house at the vlek?'

'HH – Husband Henning – has it for practical reasons. Travelling back and forth in the space of a day is too much for him.'

Johanna nodded but declined to comment.

'Jo-Jo, I'm worried for you. You're not your usual self. In your letters you've been practically taciturn, and you definitely used to smile more.'

Johanna felt her shoulders sag. 'I'm sorry.' Trying to coax a smile to her lips, she said brightly, 'Being by myself at the Castle, I seem to have lost the art of easy conversation. So, tell me, I want to hear all about your country houses. Are they grand?'

Hilletje held up her hand. 'First, I want a full account of what happened after the fiscal marched you away from the ceremony.'

'No,' Johanna blurted out. 'I will tell you all about it in a moment, but right now I'm starved of your news. Please tell me something, as I'm stuck here and haven't even had a proper look at the vlek yet.'

Hilletje settled herself on the edge of the pond and dipped her fingers in the water. 'After the wedding feast, I set off with my husband, Kief Eksteen—'

'So you're now Hilletje Eksteen?' Johanna broke in, grinning.

Hilletje nodded, her face aglow.

'And yours?' Johanna turned to Malliet.

'Van Wyk.' A dimple showed in Malliet's cheek when she said it.

They all laughed and after a minute, Johanna said, 'Apologies, Hilletje. I had to know your new names. Please continue your story.'

'So. We set off in a covered wagon with a lamp at the front and back to guide us. Before long, the road from the Castle vanished into the bush. Our Khoi driver, Johnny, pushed the horses into a full gallop through the night, over rocks and rough terrain. I'd never been so frightened in my entire life – not even during those storms on the ship!' She adjusted her position on the stone rim. 'And that's all I'll say until you answer my question.' A smirk appearing on her face, she went quiet.

Laughing, Johanna sat next to her and said, 'Very well, then. Claes van Loon locked me in my room while you were all enjoying the banquet and dancing. I learned afterwards that he himself was then hauled over the coals by the commander. Floriane came with me the following morning to see the commander, to try to argue my case.'

Hilletje nudged her in the ribs. 'Are you really married, or did you just say that to get out of marrying Pieter?'

'I didn't lie.'

'Who did you marry?' Hilletje turned to Malliet. 'Did you know about this?'

Johanna shook her head. 'It's not safe to talk about yet. Floriane is helping me to sort things out and I, in turn, am helping her. The look of shock on your faces at the ceremony weighed heavy on my heart, but there is more to this than you might imagine.'

'Such as what?'

'That is a secret, Hilletje, and one that is not mine to tell.'

For a moment they sat in silence and stared at the fountain. 'Do you think they will force you to marry Pieter?' Hilletje asked.

'Since being cooped up here I have had plenty of time to think. The fiscal would have to prove that I am not married, and to do that he would have to confess to something he did. In the meantime, I am trying to keep out of Pieter's way so as to not upset him any more than I already have. If the worst comes to the worst, I'll stay here under guard for five years – probably as someone's maid – and then the Honourable Company has to return me to the Netherlands.'

'How are you passing the time?'

Johanna picked up the sketch paper. 'I've started drawing again. I'm learning how to cook the commander's favourite food, and I lend a hand in the kitchen most days. I've spent some time with the Castle folk. It's interesting to hear their stories, but also desperately sad.' She stared out across the courtyard. The commander's Khoi translator had only that morning explained how the Castle was built on the land of her people, and how some twenty years earlier the Dutch had killed them and taken it for themselves.

Malliet cleared her throat. 'There you go again, taciturn Timmerman.'

Johanna looked back at Malliet's reassuringly familiar face. 'Sorry. I was just thinking. What else has been happening? Floriane pops in from time to time and has given me wool to knit, and I've been feeling guilty I haven't written to Femke.'

Malliet turned towards the bay. 'The return fleet sails at the end of next week, so you had better get on with it. I haven't written yet because I didn't know how much it was safe to tell her.'

'I confess to being lazy on that score too,' Hilletje put in.

'Well, I promised her I'd send full details of life at Good Hope,' Johanna said. 'The problem is that I have no experience of day-to-day life in the colony because of this incarceration. I don't even know what happened to you both after the wedding beyond what Hilletje just hinted at.'

'Shall I go on, or would you like to hear from Malliet next?' Hilletje looked from one to the other of them.

'Go ahead,' Malliet said. 'I want to hear the rest of your story, too.'

Looking into the middle distance, Hilletje said, 'Where was I? Oh, yes. When we got there, candles were lit about the place and it was obvious that someone else lived there with him.'

'Children?'

'No. Slaves. Three work in the house, and sixteen more on the wine farm.'

Johanna glanced over at Fortune, who stood a deferential ten paces from where they sat. He had been assigned to her as a sentry. He was wearing a white tunic, his hair tied up in a red cloth twisted around his head in the style of a turban. She frowned, wondering how much he could hear of their conversation. 'I don't understand how you can be so casual. Forcing someone to work for you against their will is wrong. The commander wonders why so many run away, but the answer is obvious.'

Malliet crossed her ankles. 'We have a lot of folk, but we are not like that. HH grows corn on a large estate to the west of here. It's like a little village in itself, with granaries, workshops and stables. Our folk have their own lodge where they live, but Henning has insisted they are all taught a trade. When he does not need them on the farm, he hires them out on a daily or weekly basis. They are allowed to keep a proportion of what they earn because he wants them to be able to buy their freedom.'

Johanna bit her lip and stilled an urge to exchange a look with Fortune.

'On his death he will manumit every last one, but they don't know that of course.'

Hilletje waggled her eyebrows at Malliet in a suggestive manner. 'What about – you know what?'

'Henning wanted a wife for companionship because he was lonely after his first wife died. All of his children died in infancy, so he is not interested in having more. And what about you?' Malliet threw back at her.

'Kief has been a long time deprived. Night is as busy as—'

Johanna gasped and kept her voice down. 'Tell us everything. Did it hurt the first time?'

Hilletje settled her hands on her stomach. 'In hindsight, it only hurt a little. Not at all now. It's something to look forward to.' She blushed crimson and grew quiet.

Johanna searched for a new direction for the conversation. 'I forgot to ask, Hilletje, where is home?'

'We have a wine farm at Groot Drakenstein.'

Johanna spread her hands in a gesture of incomprehension. 'Where's that?'

'About ten miles from here – to the east.'

'I see,' Johanna said. 'And do you not find that your hands itch from inactivity?'

Malliet shook her head. 'Not for a minute. Our folk wear the worst shirts in the colony, and I have made it my personal mission to turn that about.'

Johanna wondered how slaves who were truly valued could still wear the worst shirts in the colony, but she held her tongue, instead saying, 'And you, Hilletje, who dreamed of wearing fine clothes and aspired to a position in which you could direct a maid?'

'My huis habits also die hard. I cannot stop myself from sweeping!'

The Castle bell tolled the hour. Johanna stood up and smoothed down her skirt. 'I have to present myself to the Captain of the Guard so he can see I am still here, so you will have to excuse me a moment. Before I forget to mention it, though, there is one thing I have been thinking about that I cannot seem to reconcile in my mind.'

They both regarded her and Malliet said, 'Go on.'

'I heard there were nearly fifty suitors who asked to be considered as husbands. That is why Mevrouw Peronneau said at the recruitment that they wanted up to forty-eight of us. Do you remember?'

Malliet and Hilletje both nodded.

Johanna clasped her hands behind her back. 'I've been turning over in my head on what basis everyone was chosen. Do either of you have any idea?'

Hilletje exchanged a puzzled look with Malliet. 'Darned if I know the answer to that, but it's a simple question to ask.'

*

It was midday, and Merkel lay on his bed, in the area reserved for those who had been ill for some time. Patients were close together and the stale air reeked.

Floriane dipped a spoon in the copper bowl. 'As I told you when the commander brought me here last night, mijnheer, you must try to take some soup. The smell in this hospital is more likely to kill you than any malady from which you are suffering, but the surgeon will not let you out unless he has seen you eat.'

He held up his hand. 'I cannot. I am sorry.'

'It's my understanding that it has been a good many days since food passed your lips. That is how you ended up here in the first place. The donkey died when it gave up eating.'

He gave a short laugh. 'That's a turn of phrase I do not know.'

She replaced the spoon in the bowl and laughed. 'My mother used to say it, when I was over-particular with my meals.

Somehow the vision of a starving donkey did the trick and made me pick up my food.'

'I am beyond such pictures. I would prefer quite simply to have your company and your ear, if you can lend them both to me for a while.'

'I shall stay until your tongue is still and your eyelids begin to droop.'

Merkel lay his long, white fingers on her arm. 'Will you stay in the Cape when your husband is finished here?'

She was stunned by the question.

He raised an eyebrow. 'Is that a yes or a no?'

'Do you mean when my husband moves on elsewhere? Or will I move on when my husband is dismissed?'

Merkel looked at her, his face grave. 'Tongue-waggers in the vlek say that in the Netherlands your husband helped himself to money that was not his, and that he has embarked upon a similar path once more.'

She was frozen to the spot. 'Should you be saying these things to me, mijnheer?'

After some time, he steepled his fingers and held them to his lips. 'I am dying, Mevrouw Peronneau. It matters very little to me what I say and to whom I say it. There is never smoke without fire, and I think too highly of you to see you burned.'

'Has the commander placed you in his confidence?'

Merkel gave a faint nod of his head. 'The commander is on his guard, but as yet we have no proof of any wrongdoing at the Cape. He is also bothered by the red-haired girl's protestations, but seems to have no inclination to help her.'

Floriane's heart dropped. 'He's said as much to me. I wish she had not declared herself so publicly.'

Merkel elbowed his way up the pillow, and she saw how

much the effort cost him. He lowered his voice to a whisper. 'That is not to what I was referring. She says your husband tried to murder Frans de Jong.'

Floriane knew he was watching her, waiting for a rebuttal. She tightened her grip on the chair arms and leaned forward. 'Yes, and I believe her.'

He lowered himself back down and lay still for a while, eyes seemingly focused on the wall opposite. Floriane assumed he had lost his train of thought until he said, 'Let us hope the boy can confirm the identity of his attacker, and we can bring the fiscal to justice, for that at least.'

All she could do was agree.

Later, on her way home, she stopped in at the Castle to visit Johanna. The girl was sitting in her room, which had been rearranged, and was absorbed with her knitting. When Floriane knocked on the door, she started as if she'd been caught doing something illegal.

Johanna threw the kitting poles on the table beside her and jumped up to embrace her.

When they separated, Floriane reached into her bag and handed her the writing paper she had brought.

'How did you know I'd run out?' Johanna frowned at it.

'I did not. Frans is awake. If you wish to help his recovery, you must write to him as often as you can. I will pass the letters to him and if he is unable to read them for himself, I will read them out to him.'

The girl put a hand over her mouth to muffle her excited cry before she threw her arms around Floriane's neck. 'You are my angel of mercy. I cannot thank you enough.'

It was late afternoon and Floriane had only just returned home when a pair of slender, golden-skinned girls with huge, dark eyes and straight black hair arrived at the house.

Floriane stood in the doorway. 'Is there something I can do for you?' She looked at the young women who now stood at the bottom of the stoep, their bundles at their feet.

'I am Rosa of Bengal and this is Angela of Madagascar,' one of them said. 'Mijnheer van Loon has purchased us at auction.'

❦ CHAPTER 34 ❦

THE CAPE COMMANDER SAT at his office table, drumming his fingers. A slave stood behind him and flapped at the air with an ostrich feather, trying valiantly to stir the air. Sitting opposite him on a plump leather chair, Johanna waited for the commander to speak. She stared at a pair of stinkwood wall cabinets set on either side of a marble fireplace and concentrated on the tick and whirr of the wall-mounted clock. Apprehension left her mouth dry.

She had been incarcerated now in the Castle for many weeks, and the commander still had not ruled on her case. Floriane had set up this interview on her behalf, telling the commander that Johanna was desperate to learn *something*, but that morning he was not in an expansive mood. She ran her tongue around the inside of her mouth. 'Your Excellency?'

He dabbed at his face with a handkerchief. 'The air is very heavy.' He rose from his chair and lumbered across the gleaming floorboards to throw back a weighty teak shutter.

Winter sunshine flooded the chamber and made her squint.

'Come over here where I can see you, girl.'

Taking the windowseat he indicated, Johanna locked her hands together to still the shaking in her fingers.

'Tell me why you came to the Cape?'

Johanna saw no point in masking the truth. 'I came because Frans de Jong told me he had accepted a position as a windmill engineer at Good Hope, and I wanted to be with him.'

'Are you saying that even when you signed your contract you had no intention of marrying a burgher?'

She rolled the hem of her sleeve between her thumb and forefinger. 'Is an engineer so different to a burgher? Both are men of the Cape.'

Commander Speelman flared his cavernous nostrils. 'There is no need to be flippant. What of the poor boy who was shamed in front of the colony? He is also a man of the Cape.'

Johanna gulped down the lump in her throat. 'I repent that I embarrassed him, but how is it that I am not allowed to marry Frans because he is not a burgher, but Mijnheer van Loon is allowed to marry me to a penniless poet who is also not a burgher, just because I refused the man's repeated – and, may I add, disgusting and immoral – advances on board the ship?'

He fiddled with the catch on the shutter. 'Pieter *is* a burgher's heir. But setting aside suitability, the fiscal had no idea that you considered yourself married to the windmill boy.'

She couldn't help herself. 'That is only true because he believed he had widowed me with his blade. When Frans is well enough to confront him, he will name Mijnheer van Loon as the man who almost killed him.'

'You are very certain of that fact.'

'Yes.'

'If this was a matter that had originated here, I would have full authority to pass judgement on your situation. Your contract, however, was generated in Amsterdam by the Lords Seventeen. We must wait for the arrival of the commissioner to decide how you should be dealt with.'

'When will that be?' She sensed it wouldn't be soon.

He gave her a sharp look. 'He is sailing, and the vagary of the winds is in the hands of no one but God. You must learn patience, Johanna. It is said to be a virtue.'

'Must I be locked up till then? Even slaves can free themselves, if they find the way.'

'You have broken your contract, and still insist you will not honour it. I am not confining you for the pleasure of your company. You must think long and hard about what to say to the commissioner when he gets around to judging your case. If, say, you were to find evidence of the fiscal's wrongdoing, perhaps he might consider that sufficient service to the Company to allow you out of your contractual requirement to marry, specifically, a burgher.'

*

When Merkel had fallen asleep, Floriane knocked on the door to the isolation room in the pattern she and Frans had devised.

'I'm here,' Frans called.

She let herself in. 'You look much better today. You've a lot more colour in your cheeks.'

'The surgeon is pleased with my progress.'

Floriane pulled out a chair and sat down, placing some coins on the blanket so that he could buy food from the cart. 'Eating better food has had its effect, it's plain to see. I wish I could persuade the secunde to do likewise.'

'Whatever the surgeon says, I know that it is you who has restored me to health, and I thank you for the money to buy that food. How is the secunde getting on?'

273

'It's difficult to say, because I am not certain what ails him.' She pulled a letter from her pocket and put it in Frans's hand. 'I am concerned for Johanna. She is not in a good place, whatever she writes to the contrary. Her case for breaking her contract to marry you is legally weak, and I fear the Company will prosecute her. The commander has suggested that evidence against Claes might help when the commissioner adjudicates her case in a few months' time, but it all looks rather bleak.'

Concern flared in his eyes. 'I have spent all my waking hours trying to recall the moment clearly since you first asked, but I cannot lie. It happened so quickly, in the dark of night . . . If I saw anything of the man who stabbed me, it is lost to me now.'

This was not what she'd wanted to hear. 'I had hoped to bring her more comforting news. She must not know this. I'm not sure she could survive it.'

'If I could reassure her that my feelings for her have never wavered, I know it would give her comfort.'

'I will take your letter to her, but perhaps . . .' Floriane studied her hands where they lay in her lap. 'Perhaps there is something else we can do. Not today, but soon.'

*

It was barely two minutes into Floriane's visit when she delved into her bag and held out a letter to Johanna. 'From Frans. His wounds have almost completely healed. He is now able to sit up in bed and is taking his meals at the prescribed times.'

'Did you write it for him again?'

Floriane stood, her back to the fire. 'He wrote it himself, but as I said at the start of your correspondence, names must be omitted in case it fell into the wrong—'

Johanna could not contain her impatience. 'May I read my letter first, before you tell me the rest?'

'Of course. Take your time.'

There was no wax seal to break, only a page, folded twice. She sat down by the fire and began to read.

Beloved,

At long last, I am able to say what is in my heart without fear of embarrassment. I am hopeful that I will now live thanks to the ministrations of our angel. I know how worried you have been, and that you have feared so many times you might lose me. I've heard of your prayers and the things you must endure in these cruel circumstances, but which you bear so stoically. I have no doubts that your deep love has kept me alive. I love you, my heart, and cannot wait for you to be properly my wife.

Johanna hugged the letter to her chest and thought she might die of happiness. 'Do you know what's in the letter?'

Floriane seemed surprised by the question. 'As I said, I am now merely the messenger.'

'He says he loves me.'

'Of that I'm certain.'

'And that you saved his life.'

Floriane smiled. 'Probably I could take a little credit for that.'

'Thank you for all you have done for us. I don't know how we will ever repay you.'

'Friendship carries no cost,' Floriane said. She walked to the window and looked down on the inner courtyard. 'I have been thinking about how you might convince the commissioner to let you out of your contract.'

Johanna sighed. 'I fear he will be as angry as Commander Speelman seems to be that I never intended to marry a burgher.'

Floriane turned back to the room. She did not immediately catch Johanna's eye but when she did, she seemed uneasy. 'We must step up our efforts to expose Claes, I believe. He has now taken up residence in the countryside, where he is spending a fortune on this property he is building. So, for the time being, the coast is clear. He has to be up to his old tricks again, but before we can condemn him to the commissioner, we need to get clear proof to try him.'

⤧ CHAPTER 35 ⤦

JOHANNA LEANED IN THROUGH the doorway to the office of the Orphan Chamber. Pieter was sitting alone on a backless bench in front of his desk, peering at his work. She'd avoided even going past his office until now, for fear he would see her.

She knocked as quietly as she could and stepped into the room, a bowl of stew in her hand. 'Pieter?'

'Ten thousand thunders!' he cried out in surprise as he knocked over his inkhorn. The tide of blue-black slush spread across the polished teak, dripping through where heat had shrunk the joints. He jumped up and scooped the ledger off the desk, then mopped ineffectually at the wood with a scrap of waste paper. 'What are you doing here, Johanna?'

She set the bowl on the table. 'I brought you some stew, but first tell me if there's anything I can do to help with that mess.'

He pressed his fist to his forehead, stamping a circle of black above his spectacles. 'I'll have to re-copy all of today's work when the pages dry and I can cut them free.'

'Does that mean you can stop for a while?'

He looked at her unhappily. 'I don't have time to stop with

the fiscal away, and now I have to redo an entire morning of work. There's only me to reconcile these accounts. He won't have anyone else touch the books.'

'Everyone has to eat.'

He eyed the bowl, his mouth opening and closing, and she could see that he was tempted.

'The commander's housekeeper made it just now.'

'What do you want, Johanna?' He seemed wary, not sure of his ground.

'I came to beg your pardon. I wanted to explain why I said what I said at the marriage ceremony.' She saw the flare of hope in his eyes.

'Mijnheer van Loon says that you are not married, and that when the visiting commissioner arrives at the Cape he will rule in my favour.'

'He cannot make you that promise, and neither can I. On board the ship, I rediscovered someone I have known for a long time in Amsterdam, and I pledged to love him forever. We held a betrothal ceremony, with Floriane Peronneau as our witness. I do, truthfully, consider myself married to him.'

His eyes widened, and his expression fell. 'That story has been the talk of the Castle since the day of the weddings.' He jerked up his chin. 'Where's the lucky man?'

'Please, have your stew while I explain. I am trusting you with this secret, because for all the world I will not hurt you again or lead you to hope that things are other than they are. You must swear you won't tell a soul.'

'I don't see why I should,' he said, and dipped his spoon into the bowl. 'But you might as well talk while I eat.'

Short of divulging Frans's name, Johanna told him every-thing of her own story, from start to finish. She said nothing of

278

Floriane's personal business against her husband. 'So, my best chance is to find evidence to condemn Mijnheer van Loon. But there is limited time.'

The hope was back in his eyes, but he left enough silence for her to understand that he was conflicted in his decision. 'You must not forget that I work with Mijnheer van Loon and my loyalties must lie with him.'

'You will not help me?'

'I did not say that. More that it is not so straightforward to reconcile in my mind.' He spooned up his stew, nodding, as if he was speaking to himself.

Johanna studied his face but could not work out whether he would help her or not.

Eventually he pushed the bowl aside. 'I will not relinquish my hope of your hand in marriage until I am certain it is useless. But what sort of man would I be if I declined to assist the woman I love? I will do all that I can in your aid and trust my heart to providence.'

Johanna stood before him, feeling like a supplicant at the church door. 'I am so sorry that I embarrassed you in front of your family. They cannot think of me kindly.'

Pieter shrugged. 'My uncle is only annoyed at not seeing a return on his investment.'

'What do you mean?'

'Uncle Mulder settled a prime parcel of land on the fiscal in exchange for the promise of your hand. Given that the number of marriage maids was so much lower than that of the many local suitors, it's likely the other free burghers did so too.'

She felt her heart race. 'Do you have proof?'

'I only have proof that they paid sums to the Honourable Company to cover your passages from Texel, as registered in the ledgers. The commissioner will see that the Company has recouped that expense, and will congratulate his fiscal's splendid endeavour.'

'Do you know the amount they paid?'

'I know the passage fees, but not whether that was the full extent of what they paid to Mijnheer van Loon.'

Johanna moved about the room. 'Are you saying that—?'

'Eight men paid the fiscal directly. Given the great value of the land my uncle gifted to him, it seems likely to me that those other men also paid significantly more than the money which found its way to the Company coffers. I also do not know whether the other suitors paid bid gifts.'

'Could you give me a list of the eight, and the amounts they paid for our passage?'

He pulled a stack of parchment towards him and began to scratch with his quill. 'You must also swear you will keep this between us.'

'You have my word.' She watched him transfer names and numbers to the page.

He looked up. 'Of course, this list proves nothing without a written confirmation of the exact amounts the burghers settled on Mijnheer van Loon.'

'I have asked the girls to ask their husbands. But I think I have to find more if I am to really expose him.'

'There is plenty to find if you know where to look.'

'Go on.'

'The fiscal keeps my hands busy, thinking that my eyes will see nothing.'

'What is it that he doesn't want you to see?'

Pieter set the quill down on the desk and pushed the list towards her. 'That he is as corrupt a Company official as it is possible to be.'

☞ CHAPTER 36 ☜

THE CAPE AUTUMN SLIPPED into a cool and tempestuous winter. It was a lonely, shapeless existence for Johanna, framed only by periodic visits from her friends. One afternoon in late August, when the south-easterlies were blowing at full force, she sat knitting in the sewing room, accompanied by her minder, Fortune. Footsteps sounded in the corridor and a young slave appeared at the door. He exchanged words with the man, their voices low, and then the slave went away. Fortune resumed his stance against the wall.

Johanna put down her knitting. 'If you don't mind my asking, what was that language you were speaking just now?' Fortune bowed his head, and she went on. 'It's only curiosity. It's all right if you'd rather not say.'

He looked up. 'Yoruba.'

'Is that your native language?'

He nodded.

'Are you from West Africa?'

'Yes, mevrouw.'

She wanted to ask how he had come to the Cape, but she

knew from other folk she had spoken to that it would not be a happy tale. 'When I first came to the Burgerweeshuis, the orphanage in Amsterdam, they told me I must be called Kleine Roodhoofje – for my hair – instead of my name.' She forced a laugh. 'I don't suppose Fortune is your real name.'

He shook his head and said, 'Olumjimi.'

'Olumjimi,' she repeated. 'Did I say it properly?'

He flashed her a brief smile. 'Yes, mevrouw.'

She took up her knitting from her lap. 'Do you mind me asking you questions?'

He shook his head.

'I'm also wondering what kind of work you did before you came here.'

'I had a farm.'

She pretended to study her stitches. 'If you were freed, would you go back there?'

'No. They would only catch me again and bring me back. If I was free . . .'

'Yes?'

'I would go on a ship to the Netherlands. There is no slavery there.'

She nodded, thinking about how terribly her countrymen had violated their own laws as soon as they left their own borders.

The clock chimed the hour and she looked up. 'Oh, forgive me, I must go and meet Malliet at the door. I know you're not supposed to let me out of your sight but you don't have to come with me, Olumjimi. I'll not be very long.'

He maintained his position and nodded. She hurried to the main entrance, where Malliet was struggling up the Castle steps, holding on to her mass of dove-grey petticoats to keep them from rising about her.

Johanna stood at the top of the steps and pulled the woollen shawl about her shoulders. 'Come inside and warm your bones.'

When Malliet reached the top, Johanna linked arms with her friend and led her to her room. Pointing her to a chair, she added a log to the fire before pulling up another chair.

'You are looking well,' Johanna said when they were sitting side by side in front of a blazing fire.

'I am well.' Malliet seemed less breezy than she once had, as if becoming a wife had calmed her. 'I see you've been busy with your knitting poles.'

Olumjimi had by now perched himself on a stool by the door. He was wrapped up tight in a heavy blanket, his feet encased in brown fluffy stockings against the chill of the tiles on the floor.

Johanna shuffled forward in her seat and leaned towards the warmth. 'I honestly haven't much else to do *but* knit, and everything seems too much of a struggle. I find it hard to get myself motivated to concentrate, and have become adept at putting off today what I tell myself I can do tomorrow. Knitting clothing for Fortune – or Olumjimi, as I now know his real name to be – has been my salvation.'

Malliet rubbed the chill from her arms. 'I have brought you news.'

Johanna frowned, momentarily at a loss, before she saw the letter Malliet pulled from her sleeve. 'Oh!'

A sudden gust rattled the carved salon door and made them both shiver. Johanna called across the room. 'Might you like to stretch your legs for a bit and find us all something hot to drink?'

Olumjimi nodded and removed his stockings, before slipping from the room on bare, noiseless feet.

Johanna took the letter from Malliet and opened it.

Beloved,

I have good news. Our angel declares me well and says that I am soon to leave my dreary abode. I took a long walk in the garden this morning and stared at the wall. How long I stared at it, thinking, what if you were but a hand span away, and that we could touch. How many prayers have I offered that soon we might speak, but our angel says that the devil would spit fire were we found out.

I try to be patient, my heart, but it is not my greatest virtue.

She looked up, her heart thumping wildly. 'How did you get this?'

'Floriane was on her way here when she saw me. She said to tell you she would drop by later on, so that she would not dilute your enjoyment of my visit.'

Johanna couldn't hold back a smile. 'Frans says he is soon to leave the hospital and wants to see me.'

'Then we must think of a plan, but it won't be easy given your current incarceration.'

'I can leave the Castle under supervision, with the commander's permission.'

'Will he give it?'

'Not to see Frans. I am forbidden from any contact with him. I've been talking to Pieter about gathering evidence against Mijnheer van Loon, but so far it's been fairly hopeless. The fiscal is careful to always leave himself a whisker of plausible doubt, and so will be able to justify everything he does when the commissioner comes on his annual visit. I am beginning to despair that I will never be released from that stupid contract I signed.'

'Pieter is very kind to help you.'

'I think he still entertains hopes that we will marry, even though I've told him otherwise.'

'He's a nice boy and if we all put our heads together, we'll think of something. And don't give up on seeing Frans. In the meantime, Hilletje sends her very best wishes, but she is expecting a child and is so sick she can hardly leave her house.'

Johanna gave an excited gasp. 'Expecting a child? Already? That's such wonderful news. I can't wait to speak to her, but I'm not even allowed to see my friends on special occasions like this. It's as if they're trying to wear me down.'

Malliet tutted. 'Don't fret. I am here to fill you in on all their news. Elke has moved about one hundred miles inland and will only come to the vlek for New Year and the commander's birthday celebrations in October. Last month I know you saw Karin with Lisje and Brigitta.' A shadow crossed her brow. 'That was before Karin fell and broke her arm. Poor thing.'

'Oh no. How is she?'

'Trussed up like a chicken, but she's healing.'

Johanna pressed a hand to her chest. 'Goodness, as soon as we separate, they all fall to pieces. And what about Lotte?'

'Honestly, I haven't heard from her in ages.'

'And Femke?'

'It is too soon to have heard again from Amsterdam. She said she would write after receiving news of our weddings, and not enough time has elapsed for our letters to arrive and a reply to come back. Oh, and I have news from Henning about the *suitors*.' Malliet emphasised the word as if it was a species of rare plant that might need a classification of its own.

'What did he say?'

'It's more what he did. HH said the enquiry would be less obvious if he quizzed those men himself, so he has been to see them individually.'

Tears welled in Johanna's eyes. 'I don't know what to say. I am so grateful.'

Her friend sighed. 'He is a fine man with gentle manners, but he is getting on in years and time is not his best friend. He insisted on coming with me to the vlek because he is concerned about you, and says *because* you are my dearest friend that I am to take you to the Company store and buy anything that you might be lacking.'

'Please pass on my thanks, but I actually need nothing. The huis habit of relying only on oneself is keeping me well enough in this existence.'

'Life changes when you get married. You no longer have that independence, not even in the thoughts you are supposed to have. It doesn't stop me thinking them, but—'

'You just don't say them out loud.' Johanna smirked, grimly.

Malliet laughed, but then her face turned serious. 'Henning's experience when Mijnheer van Loon interviewed him mirrored that of the others. He paid the passage price for my journey from Texel to Good Hope, but first he provided a sealed paper with a personal bid for my hand. The bids were apparently quite varied – anything from a contribution of labour to the fiscal's building project, to money, a personal gift, or something else entirely. When he'd selected the eight most attractive bids, those names went on his list.'

'Do you know who gave what?'

'I do, but Henning said it would be hard to prove that this involved wrongdoing. The position of fiscal has considerable latitude attached to it.'

Johanna sighed. 'So taking bribes isn't illegal?'

'It's all in the perception. HH says that there are a thousand opportunities for private gain in Good Hope if a man has a bent for trickery.'

Johanna wanted to yell with frustration. It was the same story that Pieter had told her. As fiscal, every area of Van Loon's work seemed to enjoy a hidden benefit. As long as he put down on paper what the Honourable Company expected to see, the rest could remain safely ignored.

'How am I to ever catch him out if the system itself allows him to be corrupt?'

'A better way might be not to hang your hopes on one particular thing you have discovered him to have done, but to make a comprehensive study of everything he is involved in, and that way unmask him as a rogue.'

Johanna considered. 'Yes, and if we can find out what exactly he wants, perhaps we can put such great temptation in his path that he will expose himself by his own hand.'

At three o'clock that same day, Floriane arrived at the Castle. She got straight to the point with Johanna. 'I know you had a visitor this morning, but I believe a walk in the Company garden before we lose the light will be reviving to us both.'

Johanna got to her feet and, as they made their way out of doors, she asked, 'How have you managed this?'

'The commander said you hadn't stretched your legs for a few days and agreed that you would be glad of the exercise. He is grateful for my help with Merkel. It wasn't hard to persuade him.'

They made their way through the muddy vlek and into the garden. To Johanna's delight, it was as neat and colourful as a tapestry. Its paths were bordered with tall, thick hedges to shield them from the ravages of the south-easterlies. The beds, watered by streams that had been cut into deep channels, ran either side of the central walkway. In the far corner, the head gardener was pointing and waving, instructing a slave in the art of grafting a fruit tree. When he saw them, he whipped off his hat and made a low bow.

Floriane took Johanna's arm. 'Did you have a good visit this morning?'

'It was lovely to see Malliet, but she's concerned for her husband's health.'

'Did she say he was ill?'

Johanna puffed out her cheeks. 'It is not that he is ill so much as just old. Henning has been instrumental, though, in gathering intelligence for our cause. The suitors all handed over large bribes to grease Mijnheer van Loon's palm.'

Floriane rolled her eyes. 'I wish that surprised me.'

'Pieter is also helping us.'

'What have you told him?'

'Nothing to compromise you. Even though it's not in his best interests, he is helping me find evidence to put to the commissioner to release me from my present predicament. What about you? Have you managed to find anything out?'

Floriane pointed to a low bench by the central water channel. 'Let's sit for a while and I'll share what I know.' They settled themselves side by side on the bench and for a moment sat in the silence of the garden.

'Claes is involved in smuggling wine to the garrison, and is using our house in Thuynstraat as a staging post.'

Johanna clapped a hand to her mouth. 'Oh my goodness, Floriane. That is an illegal activity and could get you into trouble. The commander comes down hard on smuggling. Where has the wine come from?'

Floriane shook her head. 'There are no distinguishing marks on the barrels, and I am turning a blind eye for the time being.

288

It is something that potentially could be useful to us, though, and Claes is involving himself in just about anything that will turn him a profit, but—'

'We'll never be able to prove it.' Johanna lowered her voice. 'He offered me a ruby or an emerald on the ship, so he can't be short of funds.'

'You never told me that!'

'It was just another ruse to get me to his cabin. There was nothing unusual about it.'

'Except I didn't tell you that Claes stole jewels from the Honourable Company. Offering you some on the ship strongly suggests he has brought them with him. I searched for them in Amsterdam with no result, but I must hunt for them again when I'm certain he's not going to be at home.'

'Pieter is presenting his monthly report for the Orphan Chamber tomorrow morning, so mijnheer will certainly be out of the house for that.'

Floriane picked at a loose thread on her sleeve and looked around them. 'This garden is beautiful, isn't it?'

Slaves were clearing several of the water channels of debris, and though Johanna wondered at the swift turn in the conversation, she kept her thoughts to herself. 'Pieter told me one hundred slaves work in this garden.'

'Merkel told me the same. He says they need that many as there is so much to be grown to supply the commander's table and the passing ships.'

'It does look more practical than ornamental.'

Floriane waved an airy hand. 'The finer species are at the far end of the garden. Why don't you walk up and take a look?'

Johanna narrowed her eyes towards the pines in the distance. 'Are you not going to come too?'

'Oh, it has been a long time since you were at liberty to walk by yourself.' Floriane stood up from the bench. 'I believe I will take a different direction and return here in an hour.'

Before Johanna could say another word, Floriane had strolled away. Bemused, she followed the woman's instructions. A *bokmakierie* bushshrike caught her eye from its perch on a budding Persian silk tree. Enraptured by its brilliant yellow, green and grey plumage, she lamented the absence of materials to sketch it, and continued her progress past the commander's summer house and the small dwelling where the under-gardener lived.

The door to the under-gardener's house opened and closed behind her, and boots clicked on the stone path. Her heart began to pound, and at first she dared not look round. The footfall was not that of a stranger. It was one she'd strained to hear every day for months on the ship.

She swivelled round and stared at him, too frightened to move. Frans clutched a large, bright-orange flower against his chest and smiled. He was thinner than she remembered, and shadows underscored his green eyes. He took a few steps towards her.

'Am I dreaming?' she whispered.

He held out the bloom. 'Johanna,' he said, his eyes brimming.

She reached for the flower, feeling as if the air had been sucked from her lungs. 'I thought I would never see you again.' She lifted it to her nose.

'There was a time when I thought that too.'

She held out her hand to him and he came to her, folding it in his fingers. 'Floriane made me believe I was being allowed a walk on my own.'

His eyes did not stray from her face. 'She thought it best not to tell you, in case our hopes were dashed. She wasn't sure that she would be able to get you out of the Castle.'

'But here I am.' She took a step closer and gazed up into his eyes.

'We must go inside in case we are seen,' he said and, taking her hand, led her towards the house. 'Floriane bribed the under-gardener to vacate his home for an hour, but he has no idea why.'

Inside, he pushed the door closed with his hip and lowered his forehead so that it rested on hers, his hand warm at the small of her back. After a while, he stepped back, his lips travelling from her temple to her cheek and coming to rest on her mouth. She closed her eyes and felt desire singing through her veins.

When they finally drew apart, he tipped his head to one side. 'We'd better not get carried away. You are in enough trouble as it is with the commander.'

She couldn't leave the question unspoken any longer. 'Will you testify to the commissioner that it was Claes van Loon who stabbed you?'

His smile slipped from his face and he wouldn't meet her gaze. 'In truth, I don't know who it was.'

'What?' She touched his arm so that he looked up. Searching his eyes, she said, 'But it must have been him, do you not think?'

Frans put his arm around her. 'Yes, my love. But that is belief, not knowledge. Floriane has told me about your plan to catch him.'

The weight of his admission overwhelmed her. She bit her lip in an effort to hold back her tears. 'Half of that plan has just gone up in smoke.'

'And what about the other half?'

'Malliet is helping me collate the bribes he took from the burghers. The clerk at the Orphan Chamber is also helping me assemble details of opportunities Mijnheer van Loon has taken to cream off money, but it won't be enough to get me out of my contract. There has to be more, and the days are ticking down to the commissioner's arrival.'

Frans looked out of the window. 'The commander is sending me to Stellenbosch to build a new water mill.'

'So soon?' Johanna felt her hands clench.

Before he could reply, the sound of voices floated to them from the pathway outside. She recognised one of them. *Van Loon!* She gasped and pressed her fingers to Frans's lips. They stood face to face, and as they looked into each other's eyes she saw the moment when he understood her reaction, and moved her hand to his chest.

A loud creak arose from outside. The wooden bench.

'We can talk plainly here without risk of being overheard,' Claes van Loon said.

There was another creak and someone else, a man, said, 'I hear the annual wine licence is still to be auctioned in four parts.'

Who is that? Johanna raised her eyebrows and Frans shook his head.

'That's my understanding, yes.'

'Don't pretend you've forgotten our conversation, Van Loon. You were supposed to inform me as soon as the licence came up for discussion. This is not what we agreed.'

'You have the patience of a hummingbird. It's a complicated process and will take some time. You have not been compromised, you have my word, which—'

'Is worth as little as the Huguenots' grape.'

Claes cleared his throat. 'I advise patience, at least until the commissioner drops anchor in the bay. I am certain he will decide in our favour.'

The sound of gravel crunching made Johanna start. Frans tightened his arm around her, but they both breathed again when the conversation continued.

'And what about the girl?'

Johanna broke eye contact with Frans, shame flooding her face.

'Pieter tells me he has your assurances that all will end well for him.'

Could it be Pieter's uncle?

Frans took gentle hold of her chin and tilted her face up. *I love you,* he mouthed.

Van Loon sounded impatient. 'And if it does not, all the work I'm doing in Hottentots Holland will be for *your* benefit, as the land will revert to you.' There was a brief pause. 'It's beginning to rain. It will bring the gardener this way. We should adjourn.' The bench creaked again.

'Just remember that the matter of the licence is vital. Fail me and I shall make sure the Honourable Company gets wind of . . .' His voice, and the sound of the gravel crunching under their feet, faded as they walked away from the house.

'That conversation smells of corruption,' Johanna whispered. 'It could be just what we are looking for. That must surely have been Pieter's uncle.'

Frans's forehead resting against hers, he said softly, 'I will endeavour to find out for certain.'

'You mustn't, Frans. It's too dangerous. I will speak to Floriane. Surely she can find out the most easily. Promise me you'll do nothing.'

He nodded reluctantly. 'I promise. And now you must go,' he murmured in her ear. 'The gardener must not find us here.'

She stared up at him. 'Not yet,' she said, and pressed herself into his arms.

He held her tightly and she tried to memorise the feel of him against her, his warmth, his breath against her hair. It lasted mere seconds, but she knew it would give her something to cling to until she could free herself from her contract.

⌐ CHAPTER 37 ⌐

C LAES TOOK THE STEPS that led up to the Castle two at a time in an attempt to escape the rain, cursing the Orphan Chamber for dragging him out in such miserable conditions. Even Floriane had cancelled her hospital visit and had opted to spend the morning at home. A second reason to curse: she'd been looking particularly comely of late, the pallor and dark circles had gone from her face, and she'd been far less snippy towards him. She'd even refrained from passing comment when Mulder's barrels arrived at the Thuynstraat house. Despite his initial horror at the idea, he had to acknowledge that working with the sick seemed to suit her.

The change had also reminded him that he was married to a beautiful woman still. If he could get this meeting over with in record time, he'd surprise her at home and see how the land lay in the bedroom department.

The boy was sitting in a high-backed chair at the far end of the audience room, a plate of bread, butter and cheese and a mug of beer before him. When he saw Claes enter the chamber, Pieter Mulder leapt to his feet and bowed with exaggerated deference.

'Mijnheer van Loon. I thought that you would come later, towards midday, but the journals are on my desk ready for your inspection.'

Claes shook the rain from his cloak and tossed it on a chair. 'Have you not yet had your breakfast?'

He dropped his eyes to the plate. 'I was anxious that all was ready for your inspection. I can eat at any time.'

Claes looked at the mountain of paperwork on the desk and felt his heart sink. 'As time is of the essence, is there anything that you wish to draw to my attention?'

'It is very much as last month. Some new deaths, complete with unclaimed salaries from the Company, but the last of the unwilled inventories from the previous month have now been sold. One inheritance to pay out to a carpenter who turned twenty some days ago.'

Claes sat behind the table and pulled a journal towards him. Deaths were useful. The property of orphans dying *ex testamento* on the voyage to the Cape reverted to its Orphan Chamber in the absence of other claimants, and he made certain that he got his fair share. He opened the leather book at random.

Pieter Mathijsz Sparmont from Amsterdam, to the East Indies on de Ridderschap *in 1683, as a ship's boy. Missing since the end of November 1683, his estate worth 131 guilders 4 stuivers and 15 pennies, brought into the orphanage's account.*

He flipped forward to a recent entry.

Frans de Jong from Amsterdam, to the Cape of Good Hope on the ship Borssenburg *in October 1683, as a windmill engineer. Died on 25 February 1684 at sea, his estate worth 244 guilders 4 stuivers 5 pennies, brought into the orphanage's account.*

It all seemed to be in order. Claes clamped his teeth together to hold back a grin.

Pieter coughed politely. 'Our profit line is healthy, mijnheer. I think you will be pleased. But there is one thing I might bring to your attention.'

'Make it quick.' He drummed his fingers on the desk and smothered a sigh.

'There is the small matter of the marriage maids' settlements.'

Claes flicked the back of his hand irritably at the journal. 'We have recuperated the cost of their transport to the Cape. It was recorded months ago.'

'It is not that, mijnheer. The commander has provided the Orphan Chamber with an inventory of assets and property held in the Netherlands for the girls who came over. The value is to be paid out to them in cash upon an order on the Company's Pay Office when the Lords Seventeen are satisfied they are wed. I am wondering how you would like me to record these trans-actions when we receive them.'

There had to be a way to turn that to his advantage. 'I'll have to think upon it, Pieter. I'm not prepared to make a snap judge-ment on so weighty a matter, but you have done well to bring this to my attention. Are we now done?'

Pieter made a peculiar pecking motion with his head that brought an unwelcome image of an undertaker nailing the lid on a coffin to mind. Claes presumed he meant yes, so he levered himself up from the table and turned towards the door. As he did so, his gaze fell on Pieter's blotter, which froze him in his tracks; enclosed in a hand-drawn square were traces of the names of those burghers who had paid him for a wife. 'What is this, Pieter?'

The boy removed his spectacles and polished the glass with his cuff. 'Oh, that. It's nothing. Mejuffrouw Timmerman asked me for the names of the burghers who were conjoined with her friends, as she wanted to write to them and hear of their news.'

'When was this?'

'It was two days ago, the time of that visit.'

'I see. Is she a regular visitor?' He studied the boy. He seemed nervous now.

'Three times so far. She came to apologise that she made such a fuss at the marriage ceremony and suggested we forge a friendship for later on – when the commissioner gives us permission to marry.'

Claes narrowed his eyes. 'What else have you talked about?'

'She asked me how the selection of husbands was made, but I couldn't enlighten her as I was not clerk to this office at the time.'

'Did she say anything else?'

'No. But I think—' He broke off, the pink in his cheeks betraying his discomfort.

Claes dropped an encouraging hand on his shoulder. 'It is my dearest wish to see you both wed, so please don't hold back. Anything you say within these four walls will never be repeated outside them.' He banged his chest for extra emphasis. 'What goes in the vault stays in the vault.'

Lured like a mouse to a trap, the foolish boy continued. 'It's not really for me to say, mijnheer, but when the commissioner arrives at the Cape, I know she's hoping to set forth her case for why she should be allowed out of the marriage aspect of her contract.'

⁓

At home in Thuynstraat, the usual morning clutter had been tidied away and a collection of pipes, tobacco jars and papers removed to his private den.

'Someone's been busy.'

Floriane sucked in a surprised breath as she snapped a drawer closed and swung round to face him. 'Goodness me, Claes, you frightened me half to death. I wasn't expecting you back till dinnertime.'

Claes flopped down in his favourite chair, a large one with an elaborately carved frame, and stretched out his legs. 'How has your day been?'

She gestured at the furniture. 'Angela and I have been cleaning. We've been missing Rosa since you took her to the country.'

'Does cleaning usually include the scouring of the contents of my personal cupboards?'

Floriane straightened, tense as a startled deer. 'Any Dutch housewife would do far more than me, dear one. After the dusting, I have still the doorhandles and candlesticks to rub up, and then there's the berry wax to cut up and blend with spirit so Angela can polish the floors.' She babbled on for a bit, seeming rattled. 'Did you have a successful meeting at the Orphan Chamber?'

'The Mulder boy is doing a reasonable job as clerk. He's a diligent scribbler, although I wonder at his patience with the redhead.'

She sat in a low chair, folding a cloth in her lap. 'I didn't think she was that keen on him.'

'Nor me. She's been in the Orphan Chamber wanting the names of the burghers who married her orphan friends. Is it possible she's trying to stir up trouble?'

For the briefest instant a look passed over her face, as if a shadow had crossed the sun, before she gave him the full force of her smile. 'Johanna's not a mischief-maker. I'd say it's more likely that, cooped up by herself, she's lonely and needs an

299

occupation.' She got up and threw open the door of a wide cabinet with tarnished silver handles, clucking her tongue.

'This is the first time I've seen you bothered with the shine on our woodwork since the day we were wed.'

She bunched the cloth in her hands and spent a moment scrubbing at some invisible stain on the cabinet. 'Commander Speelman surprised me with a visit when you were out at your meeting, to offer you some tobacco. So besides polishing and dusting with a little more pointed urgency than usual, today I am also checking to gauge your supply.'

That was believable enough. The commander made a habit of providing tobacco to anyone who wanted it. He smoothed the lace on his cuff and studied her from the corner of his eye. Something wasn't right. Why was she so unsettled about a visit from the commander when she saw him regularly? And why was she fiddling with the contents of the cabinet? She could simply have waited an hour for him to return and then asked him about the tobacco. He ran his tongue over his upper teeth.

For the first time, it occurred to him that his wife and the girl might be conspiring against him. His passion for Floriane forgotten, he went to his salon and closed himself in with his inklings.

⮒ CHAPTER 38 ⮓

TWO SHEETS OF WRITING paper lay before Johanna on the long table the girls had used for sewing. Both were covered in small, cramped text – the items in her plan. Some had been crossed out, not because she'd managed them, but because they'd been eliminated as possibilities.

More difficulties remained on the list than solutions.

Suitors.

There was at least some evidence there, though insufficient for her purposes.

Witnesses? Confession?

She had uncovered no witnesses to Claes's corruption, and even what she'd overhead in the garden could not be disclosed as she was not supposed to have strayed beyond the Castle walls.

The man in the garden.

Thanks to Floriane, she was now certain of his identity. It was indeed Cristoffel Mulder, Pieter's uncle. She had tried to work up the courage to speak to Pieter about him, but that was yet another hurdle. She let her eyes move to the next item on her list.

Pieter.

He was helping her, but it was easy to see why in the way he looked at her, mooning about in hopes that the commissioner would approve their marriage. She had to find some way to put him off.

Johanna set down the quill with a heavy sigh.

It would only be a matter of weeks before the commissioner's ship dropped anchor in the bay. She was no clearer on how she would present verifiable evidence that she was married than she had been when the girls were wed, more than five months ago.

The days in the Castle were now too short. The hours ticked by too quickly, and weeks rolled over each other in a frightening blur. All the calmness she had felt had disappeared; she was nervous, unsure of herself, panicked into inertia.

She clutched her head in despair and stared down, unseeing, at the notes, and found herself thinking of Malliet. Word had come that Henning van Wyk had passed away unexpectedly two days before. Yesterday the funeral had taken place. Johanna asked to be present to support her friend. Women did not go to funerals in the Cape, it turned out – not even Malliet herself had been allowed to attend.

Her vision blurred as she listened to the sound of the wind whistling against the windows. She felt more trapped and powerless than she had done since the day she'd first arrived at the door of the Burgerweeshuis.

'I won't ask what you are doing in here.' Breathing hard, Malliet paused in the doorway.

Johanna stood and pushed back her chair, crossing to Malliet with her arms extended. 'Oh my goodness, Malliet. How are you, dearest? I was so sorry to hear the terrible news, and was just this moment thinking of you.'

Dressed in black, a peaked hood covering her hair, Malliet put her hand against the wall. 'Give me a moment to get breath in my lungs.'

Johanna wrapped her in a hug and felt a wave of sadness settle over her. For a moment they just stood, two friends seeking solace in each other.

Malliet made a vague motion at the window, beyond which the pennants on the swaying masts at the quayside were just visible. 'I can't believe that a few days ago Henning and I walked along the jetty and watched the sailors bringing supplies ashore. Now he's gone.'

'What will you do?'

Malliet shrugged. 'I have money in the short term. Henning kept a strong box in both his properties.'

'Everyone at the Castle was shocked how sudden it was.'

'He had become frail enough to want to be at the vlek. He felt safer here. The physician is our neighbour.'

Johanna stepped back, leading Malliet to a chair. 'Do you think he had some sort of foreboding?' She seated herself in the chair next to her.

'He told me that since he passed his three score and ten a few years ago, he'd been sorting out his affairs with the Orphan Chamber. He'd hoped to hang on until October, because he said the commander's birthday celebrations are the highlight of the year.'

'I hope his passing was peaceful.'

'He just fell asleep in his chair. I went to wake him up, to tell him it was time for his dinner, but he had already gone.

The coffin was made right away, and yesterday he was taken from the townhouse to be buried.'

'Did you hear how the funeral went? I wish I could have been there to hold your hand.'

'I know you would have been if you could. Even most of what I can tell you is what was passed on to me afterwards.'

Johanna cast back to the funerals she'd attended – her own mother's and the housemother's. The first seemed very long ago, yet she remembered every detail. The other seemed so like yesterday that thinking of it brought tears to her eyes. She wondered how she would have felt if she'd been denied access to either.

'The sexton marshalled the procession. The commander was up near the front. Behind him should have been the fiscal, representing the Orphan Chamber, but he didn't come up from the country.' Malliet's voice was oddly matter-of-fact.

'Forgive me for saying this, but you don't seem very upset that you have just lost your husband.'

'He was a lot older than me, Jo-Jo. He was kind and thoughtful, but he was not any grand passion. Not like you and Frans.' For a moment she seemed to study the floor, adjusting her peaked hood. 'Truthfully, I haven't shed a tear. The notary came this morning and poked about the house, making little jottings as he assessed each room. He said that once he'd completed the full inventory of Henning's estate, the paperwork would be lodged at the Orphan Chamber and administered from there. I haven't the slightest idea how the Chamber enters into it, and I'm scratching my head as to whom I should ask for guidance.'

At last, a way she could help. 'The person who can explain all this to you is Pieter Mulder. I think we should go and have a chat to him and see what he can tell you.'

The Orphan Chamber table was its usual jumble of journals, papers, discarded quills and stumps of candle, but the clerk himself was absent from his chair.

Malliet parked herself in front of the fire and held her palms towards the blaze. 'Do you think it's worth waiting, or should we come back another time?'

Johanna eyed the empty dishes among the clutter. 'Pieter practically lives here. He'll be back soon enough, don't worry.'

As if on cue, Pieter came in, an armful of papers clutched to his chest. He deposited them on the table, adding to the chaos. 'Good Lord! What on earth brings you here?' An expression passed over his face as if he had suddenly remembered a lost fact. 'Oh! By the way, I was sorry to hear of your loss, mevrouw.'

Malliet turned to face him. 'I was hardly married long enough to deserve that honorific, but I thank you for your good wishes. "Malliet" will do, as ever it did when I lived at the Castle.'

Pieter crossed to the fireplace and smiled across at her. 'The funeral was well attended, and your husband's life was celebrated in great style. I know he would have been pleased. In fact, the papers I've just carried in are the accounts for his funeral expenses to go into the records.'

Malliet thought for a minute and crossed to a chair. Johanna imagined she would sit but instead she began to pick bits of fluff from the tapestry seat. 'I know Henning is barely in his grave, but I don't understand why the Orphan Chamber is involved in the winding-up of his estate, and so quickly.'

He threw a log on the fire and gave it a vigorous poke. 'It's to do with registering titles and listing assets so that the estate can be valued and transferred properly to the beneficiary – which is you. You don't have to register his death and his will, because the commander has already done that.'

Something occurred to Johanna. 'Since the Orphan Chamber is involved, does that mean the fiscal will be the one overseeing the inheritance?'

'In this case, no.' Pieter sucked his lips. 'Henning specifically excluded the fiscal as executor so that your interests are protected.'

Clever man, Johanna thought.

He turned back to Malliet, who had rolled the fluff into a little round ball. 'When the notary has completed his inventory and it is lodged with the Orphan Chamber, you will know exactly what you are worth and what is due to you. He has also drawn up and registered Letters of Freedom for the slaves, so that when your husband's affairs are finally wound up, they will become Free Blacks.'

Malliet nodded. 'That was his dearest wish.'

'You will be a prize catch, and all the hopeful fortune-hunters at the colony will be knocking at your door.'

Johanna frowned. 'I don't think you should joke.'

'I am not,' he said, sitting down at his desk. 'Under Dutch Roman law everything Mijnheer van Wyk owned will pass to Malliet, as there are no children with whom to share his estate. Apart from individual bequests, she will receive the lot.'

Silence fell while his words sank in. After a moment, Johanna said, 'Did you know?'

Malliet walked to the fire and tossed in the fluff ball. 'I suppose it makes sense, but Henning never spoke about it to me.' She smoothed the dull broadcloth of her dress. 'If I choose to, how long do I have to wait before I may remarry?' Her voice was almost inaudible.

'There is no fixed period of mourning, but some favour deep mourning for six months and partial mourning for another six. Generally, a spouse may marry again within nine months of their spouse's passing without censure. The commander can overrule that if he chooses to.' He pressed his lips together. 'If I may say, you are far too young to remain a widow and far too attractive – that is . . .' He pulled at his cuffs. 'I mean to say, you will certainly have a lot of flattering offers.'

'Presumably because I have honoured my contract with the Dutch East India, I will be able to choose my own fate?'

Pieter waved aside the query. 'I regret I don't have the answer to that, but I do have a letter Mijnheer van Wyk left for you, to be opened upon his death.' He rose from his chair and went to a cabinet, which he unlocked with a key on his belt. 'Here.' He placed it in Malliet's hand. 'Why not read it now? If there is anything in it that requires explanation, I'd be only too happy to help.'

Johanna allowed herself a small, internal smile at the blush that was spreading across Malliet's face.

Malliet took the letter and cast about for a seat. She dragged the chair she had picked clean next to the fireplace, sat down, broke the red seal, and started to read.

⌒ CHAPTER 39 ⌒

THE HOSPITAL WARD WAS filled to almost bursting with the very ill, with all the inevitable sights, sounds and smells. Floriane was certain that Merkel did not belong there.

'If you remain in this damp, chilly hospital, filled with the reek of wet plaster and festering humanity, you will die,' she informed him. 'If I take you back to your apartments at the Castle and care for you there, the surgeon fancies you will fare much better.'

Merkel settled his slight frame on the edge of the bed. 'I will die either way. I have had lung problems since I was a child. When I came to the Cape, I had no idea that it would rain quite so much.'

'You have a lung congestion that is symptomatic of an ague brought on by the wet. You are feeble because you do not eat. The surgeon insists that if we cure you of the fever, keep you warm, and ensure you take regular sustenance, we have every reason to hope that you will rally. So no argument. You are coming with me.'

He arched an eyebrow. 'I fear your husband will not be over-joyed at that idea.'

Floriane helped him into his coat and gave him her arm. 'Lean on me as we walk. Claes is not at the vlek just at present, and you are not going to die.'

He looked faintly amused. 'You are very certain of that fact.'

'While there is breath in your body, there is hope.'

'Is that another of your mother's sayings?'

She tried to keep her voice level, hoping that he would not hear the catch in her throat. 'There are so many that if placed end to end they would stretch around Good Hope.'

'And you miss her so much you can hardly bear the pain.'

She felt her stomach constrict and bit her lip. Something in the brown of his eyes unravelled her, peeling away layers of the shell that disguised her raw emotion. 'You cannot possibly know the depths. I could not have guessed how much I depended on her company.'

'Never judge a person, Floriane Peronneau, until you have walked in their shoes.' He looked at his feet.

They continued on in silence, Merkel stumbling at times like a drunkard.

Outside, as they climbed into the hospital's cart, the sky was the colour of granite.

Merkel blinked in the daylight. 'I will not see another winter, and that is a relief.'

'Your perspective on life is far too gloomy. Rain is a good thing. The cattle feed on grass, and that needs water to grow. The Dutch have water in their blood and have learned how to tame it.'

'You are no more Dutch than I.'

The cart lurched as it sank into the ruts on the road and flung up dirt in soft, sticky spatters. She scraped at an oozing patch on her skirt. 'So? The colony is. I am proud of my French origins, even if the commander is not keen on his Huguenots.'

'Commander Speelman is a true Dutchman. He is suspicious of them because they are suddenly many. He fears that he will lose control.'

'He or the Honourable Company?'

'They are one and the same. He is a dedicated man.'

'Is that why he has asked for a transfer, so that the responsibility is no longer his?'

'I didn't know that he had—'

Floriane drew in a sharp breath. 'I have been indiscreet and betrayed a confidence that I had no right to share. Please forget what I said.'

'—asked again. He has requested relief from this posting at least ten times, to my knowledge. All correspondence in and out of the Castle is copied into journals recorded for anyone who has a mind to see.'

She nodded, relieved. For a man who considered himself on the very brink of death, he was remarkably sound of mind.

⁓

Floriane watched over Merkel, who lay stretched out in his tiny, boxed-in bed in the Castle, with its red pelmet and velvet curtains. Most of the time he slept, his breathing a shallow rasp.

On the fourth day, he pushed his way up his pillows. Floriane held a glass of watered-down brandy to his lips and encouraged him to drink.

The secunde placed his fingers loosely on her arm. 'I am not much of a drinker.'

'This is medicinal.'

He watched her over the glass's rim. 'I don't know why you waste your efforts. I am all but a dead man.'

Floriane folded her fingers over his hand, the tiny hairs along the back of his knuckles bristly beneath her palm. 'Not if I have anything to do with it.'

'My body endures out of stubbornness, but my mind has reached its own conclusion. You should have left me in the hospital and saved yourself the bother.'

She set the glass down on the bedside table. 'Are you warm and comfortable?'

He toyed with a button that dangled loose on his nightshirt. 'Yes, I am. Thank you.'

'Were you so in the hospital?'

'Not that I recall.'

'Then for that small improvement you can be grateful. And to show that, you may oblige me by eating some food.'

He seemed taken aback by the suggestion. 'What is the point? I am dying, mevrouw, and I would rather it was sooner than later.'

Floriane looked into his hollow-cheeked face and squeezed his fingers. 'You are a godly man, mijnheer, and study your Bible. Think of Psalm seventy-eight.'

His brows knitted together and then he shook his head. 'I think you must remind me.'

Perched on the edge of the bed, she smoothed the matted hair from his eyes, trying to ignore a stirring that had crept into her heart. 'After He had delivered the Israelites from Egypt, led them between walls of water, and destroyed the might of the world's greatest empire, God blessed Israel with water in the desert, gave them manna every day, and everything else they needed for forty years.'

The secunde tapped his fingers together, remembrance apparently dawning. 'And because they believed not in God, and trusted not in His salvation, they invoked His wrath.'

Floriane crossed her arms. 'They did.'

'Am I invoking yours?' The telltale smile lines appeared on the sides of his mouth.

She shook her head but before she had time to articulate a reply, from the courtyard below, a shout and the clattering of hooves rang out. Mijnheer Rosenmüller inclined his head towards the door. 'Does your husband know you're here?'

Floriane followed the direction of his eyes and gave him back the glass. 'Is that relevant?'

'Would he be happy that you are doing this for me? That we are so much in each other's company?'

'Claes says that until the press of work summons him back to the vlek, he will remain in the country to oversee his building project.' She waited for Merkel to comment and when he did not, went on. 'As wife of a company official – according to Commander Speelman, mind – I must fulfil a duty to earn respect from the colonists. He has given me the title of Outside Matron to the hospital, and it is now my job to provide comforts for the sick.' Floriane ran a hand over the quilted cover. 'To my mind, the location of the hospital bed is irrelevant.'

'I think you might find some opposition to that view, were your husband to be at home.'

It was true that Claes came home at irregular intervals, and that he would object if he knew where she was. Any absence from their home he would associate with the hospital, though. At any rate, he could not stop her. 'But he is not, and I find I care very little for what he thinks.'

Surprise spread across Merkel's face and halted the brandy glass halfway to his lips. 'Is there something you wish to unburden, mevrouw?'

The clock on the mantel struck one, the single low-pitched chime sombre in the bedchamber like a call to confession.

'If we are to share secrets you must call me Floriane, so that there can be no formality between us.'

'Then you must call me Merkel.' He glanced again at the door, reached out and touched her hand.

She looked down at his fingers and out of nowhere felt happy.

'Perhaps, Floriane, I might manage a little bread and a small slice of cheese, after which, if I find I retain the food and have the strength, we might talk a little.'

Within a week, Merkel, it seemed, had given up on the idea of dying.

Barely aware of how it happened, little by little, she told him her story: that appalling night at the theatre; the succession of maids; Claes's visits to the taverns; the gaming debts; the theft of the VOC jewels; even why she had taken to daubing her face with theatrical paint.

'It's the only weapon I have against my husband's attentions,' she said. 'He believes I have a disease. The idea disgusts him, and he is keen to keep his distance, but I have been less diligent with the deception of late and he has noticed.'

He took her hand and placed it against his cheek. 'I'm sorry.'

At the tenderness of his gesture, her lip began to tremble. 'You must get well, Merkel,' she said. Her voice sounded strained in her own ears.

He nodded, his eyes holding hers.

She stayed with him until he closed his eyes. When his breathing grew slow and regular, she gently pulled her fingers from his grasp and wandered into the anteroom next door.

She'd not been expecting to find this large, cool space with its shining blue floor tiles. It was like a theatre set, she thought, offering visual clues to the man who had dominated her thoughts for the past few weeks.

Merkel lived as a solid Dutchman, one who toed the Honourable Company's line with more rigour than most. The room was not crowded with furniture like Claes's workspace in Thuynstraat. Almost every item was simple in outline and fit for purpose, its workmanship tasteful and elegant.

There were objects on shelves, maps on walls, Chinese pottery that Delft artisans had learned to copy, a set of shuffle-board disks and cue, and an astrolabe and a globe perched on a dark cupboard with heavy ebony handles.

In a grand cupboard on a stand, Merkel had a curiosity collection of objects from Japan and Bengal – six Japanese dishes, two Bengalese pitchers, and a collection of spittoons, four large and a dozen small. She wondered if the spittoons were his ironic nod at the tobacco-smoking Dutch, as she had never once seen a man – or woman – at the Cape part with a pipeful once it was in a mouth.

A rug from the Orient adorned a wooden table, where she guessed he sat to his work. She closed her eyes, aware that her heart was thumping, and ran her hand over the soft, rich pile, imagining the feel of his hair beneath her fingers.

Stop it! You just came to look around.

In the corner a tall clock struck the quarter-hour, the little painted ship with its wind-filled sails on the dial of the clock rocking backwards and forwards to mark the minutes as they passed.

She pulled a volume from the shelves, tucked it under her arm and returned to Merkel's room, where she regained her seat in the chair next to his bed and began to read. Her mind wandered and she leaned back, her eyes fixed on the ceiling. After Frans had left the hospital, he'd gone to Stellenbosch, to build his windmill. She hadn't become aware until recently that Claes's building project was closer to Stellenbosch than to the vlek by a couple of hours. With Claes spending so much time there, it was almost certain he'd go into Stellenbosch from time to time. She dreaded what would happen if he caught sight of the young man.

The bedclothes stirred, and Merkel's tousled head appeared from beneath them. He must have caught sight of the book in her hand, for he said, 'The Cape is not addicted to reading.' Sleep had turned his voice to a low rumble that she could feel in the bones of her chest.

She turned towards him. 'How did you sleep?'

'Soundly.' He squinted at the book. 'Which did you choose?'

'A depiction of Amsterdam.' She showed him the cover.

'But you do not appear to be reading it.'

She set the book down in her lap. 'You've caught me out. I was thinking about Frans in Stellenbosch, and the chances he might run into Claes.' She let her gaze rest on his face. 'Frans is defenceless against a sword. I suspect he's never even held a weapon. He went to the huis at eight years of age. I was thinking that if Claes should discover him there, everything we've done to protect him will be for nought.'

Merkel wrinkled his forehead. 'I wish there were some way I could help.'

'If only someone could.' She drew in a breath. 'There is something I've been wanting to ask, if you might give me leave. You told me when I first set foot in the Cape that you had come to Good Hope to lend assistance to the commander.'

He kept his eyes fixed on something at the foot of the bed. 'My family fell victim to plague in Germany, yet somehow I was spared. Sleeping rough, I found myself in Amsterdam and took to begging in the streets outside East India House. That's where I met Arent.'

'How awful.' She let him stare for a while as she tried to imagine such a life and found she could not. 'Commander Speelman befriended you?'

Merkel hesitated. For a moment Floriane thought he might simply decline to speak of the matter, but then he said, 'It was more that Clara's unmarried sister, Cornelia, befriended me. She was forever patching up wounded strays.'

'I understand that the commander brought her with him to the Cape.'

He glanced in the direction of the commander's apartments. 'Cornelia was very close to her sister, and she doted on her nephews and niece. She went almost daily to visit them.'

'So he brought her along to care for his children?'

He said that was the truth of it.

'But still, I don't understand why Clara Speelman didn't come herself.' She thought back to the time she'd spent in the lady's parlour. 'She is unwell, I know.'

Sunlight squeezed through the chinks in the shutters and danced patterns on the floorboards. Merkel stared at the golden shapes and frowned. 'It is not my place to talk about such personal details. Perhaps you will meet her again and speak to her about it yourself.'

Floriane felt his reproof and changed tack. 'How did Cornelia fare at the Cape?'

She watched him carefully as Merkel composed his response. 'Well,' he said. 'The children adored her. She was a calming influence on the commander. No one had an unkind word to say about her.'

Floriane closed her eyes, acutely aware of the stillness in the room, her heart tapping in her throat. 'And you?'

His hand tightened on the bed covers. 'I was as smitten as all the rest.'

'And?' Anything more specific felt a violation of his privacy.

'Nothing.'

She let her eyes rest on the side of his face, hoping he would say more.

At last he looked at her and tried to smile, but the laughter lines that softened the edges of his mouth and of which she had grown so fond were nowhere to be seen. 'One day she was well, a brilliant flower that brightened all our lives. The next she took a fever. A few days later she was dead.'

'That is tragic.'

'Yes it is, and—'

She put her hand out to stop him saying more. She could feel his eyes on her and wished she could have prevented him from telling her about Cornelia. 'And has there never been another so esteemed in your affections?'

'No.' His eyes locked on hers. 'Not until quite recently.'

She jumped up, sending the book from her lap to the floor. Flustered, she leaned down and scooped it up with trembling hands. 'I don't know what I was thinking, gabbling on like this, when it's high time I brought you something to eat.'

His face registered amusement. 'Forget the food for now, but while you are on your feet I wonder if you might bring me my journal, from the anteroom. It's been some weeks since I wrote in it and I've a mind to set my thoughts down on paper. I have it tucked away in my cabinet.'

'In the beautiful Coromandel piece? I noticed it when I was looking through your books.'

'That's right, but I'll have to tell you how to find the journal. Like most of these chests it has a hidden drawer inside, and opening it requires a little know-how.'

'Are you sure you want to give me access to such a secret?'

'Let us say I have confidence in your discretion.' He explained in some detail how to work the hidden drawer.

Floriane's thoughts were racing as she crossed into the anteroom and, following Merkel's instructions, was able to release the secret compartment and extract the journal.

Returning to him, she placed it in his hands. 'I hope these hidden drawers are not all the same.' She laughed. 'Otherwise, they would hardly be secure, would they? Once you can open your own, you could open anyone's.'

'I have only seen the workings of one other such cabinet. It was not precisely the same, but once you know how to look, a chest will rarely hold on to its secrets.'

❧ CHAPTER 40 ❧

FLORIANE HAD NEVER FELT more set upon her path. Leaving Merkel's rooms, she rushed to the Thuynstraat house, slowed only by the detritus she had to skirt. She was unsure how much longer Claes would be at his project in Hottentots Holland, so it was vital to strike while she had the chance.

She climbed the steps and burst through the front door.

'Angela!' she called.

The young woman came hurrying into the parlour and dropped a small curtsy. 'Mevrouw?'

'I want you to go to the market on Green Street and pick up some fruit for Secunde Rosenmüller. It doesn't matter what you choose but I want you to take it straight to the Castle and leave it in the kitchen, where I have arranged for you to have your noontime dinner.' She took a deep breath, thinking of the worst that might happen. 'It's unlikely that you will see Mijnheer van Loon, but if you do—' she took a shaky breath '—just tell him I've sent you on an errand.'

A look of bewilderment crossed the young woman's face, but

whatever she might have thought of the unusual request, she kept it to herself. 'What time you want me back?'

Floriane tried to keep the urgency from her voice. 'Oh! Don't worry about the time, as it's just me at home. One o'clock is soon enough, if you've had your meal by then.'

Angela dipped another small curtsy and took off her apron, closing the front door with a soft thud as she left the house.

The tower clock began to ring the hour. The clock in Claes's study echoed its chimes and made her heart lurch. Eleven o'clock. An uneasy feeling made her question the wisdom of doing this now, but the longer she waited, the more likely it would be that Claes would find some other place to conceal the jewels. If, indeed, he had not already done so.

Lifting the hem of her skirt, she crossed the house to Claes's salon, and hesitated by the doorway. It was only guilt that rendered her so jumpy, she told herself as she moved to stand before the chest, a close likeness of the one in Merkel's anteroom. Each of the six sections had its own hinged door that opened by lifting a circle of gold. What Merkel had shown her was that the hiding places were designed to be accessed when the chest was on its side and not when it was upright. She braced herself and, pulling it sideways, lowered it gently to the floor. As she did, its contents made a jangling sound.

After removing two drawers, she reached into the opening and felt for the guide that ran between them. If indeed this chest concealed drawers, these drawer guides would double as handles.

With sweaty palms, she took hold of the nearest and pulled. Nothing happened. She wiped her hands on her skirt and bent down to look into the opening. It was empty. Disappointment mounting in her chest, she replaced the pair of drawers and removed the next set, placing them on the floor while she conducted her search. As she knelt, wrenching open the drawers one by one, the clatter of hooves on the road in front of the house almost stopped her heart. She froze, her hands – surprisingly steady – poised to replace the drawers at the faintest sound of footfall on the stoep. The horse passed the house at speed and, ignoring her near heart attack, she continued with her search.

Reaching into the final opening, she grasped the drawer guide and pulled. To her surprise, it gave way. As the guide slid out of the cabinet, it brought with it a narrow drawer. Exhaling calmly, she examined the drawer's contents. It was filled with gold coins. She combed her fingers through them, searching for anything that might be hidden beneath. When she saw a flash of colour, she pushed the coins aside to reveal the jewel-embellished hilt of a dagger. She recognised it as one Claes used to wear; she had wondered why it had fallen from favour.

Curious, she withdrew the dagger from its sheath. With a gasp she saw the tip of the dagger had broken off.

Captain Bierens' words came back to her. *He was stabbed twice in the chest. The knife broke off, leaving a piece in the wound. If not for the surgeon's skill, he would be feeding the sharks at the bottom of the ocean.* Although in her heart she had always suspected Claes to be the guilty party, the evidence now before her was damning.

Her throat dry and tight, she forced herself back to her search, sped along now by fear.

Apart from those embedded in the hilt of the knife, the drawer was empty of jewels. She left the coins in their hiding place, but after some internal deliberation, held on to the dagger. Its value was irrelevant, but she would not risk it disappearing before she learned if it was the weapon used in the murderous attack on Frans.

Setting the knife on the floor, she restored the secret drawer to its hiding place and put back the two outer drawers. She heaved the chest upright and walked it to its usual home, tight against the wall.

She studied the front of the cabinet, thinking about what Merkel had said. *Once you know how to look, a chest will rarely hold on to its secrets.*

Examining again the narrow shelf that ran along the cabinet's front, she studied the vertical brass spacers that divided it into four equal sections. When she'd searched the chest in Amsterdam, the shelf had been spotless, as if newly dusted, and today was no different.

She ran her tongue over her lower lip, considering, then took hold of one of the spacers. It was rigid, hard to grip between her fingers and in no mood to move. She pulled and pushed, up and down, and waggled it from side to side, but she couldn't get it to budge.

She moved on to the next one, again struggling to get a solid grip and again failing to disturb it. By now she felt nauseated. If the jewels were not in this cabinet, she was out of hope for finding them.

She gripped the third spacer and tried to encourage it to move, this time managing to maintain her hold as she pushed and shoved. It was no use. The spacer simply wouldn't shift. In a flare of frustration, she slammed the heel of her hand into the brass. To her shock, the spacer dropped to the floor with a clatter, and a false front popped free and fell to the floor alongside it.

Stunned, she stared for a moment or two then bent down to pick up the brass fitting and peered inside the dark space its absence had revealed. Poking with her fingers, she closed on something soft and tugged it out. A black velvet pouch, secured with a drawstring, sat snug in her palm; there was no doubt in her mind what was inside. A further investigation into the space revealed two more bulging bags.

After stashing two of them in her pocket, she picked at the knot that held the mouth of the initial bag shut.

Was that a noise? Goose pimples prickled her arms as she glanced at the door, straining to hear.

Seconds passed until she felt reassured that she was still alone in the house, then she bent to the task again. Eventually loosening the knot, she wriggled her fingers into the top of the bag and worked it open.

Astonished, for a moment she let her gaze rest on its contents. No wonder Erick de Witt was trying frantically to recover their loss. The pouch was filled with dozens of glimmering stones.

Struggling with the tangled drawstring, she eventually retied the bag. Her mind was whirling as she carried the bags into her bedroom. She left all three lying on the nightstand then returned to the salon to ensure it was restored to order. She was mulling over what to do next when the unmistakeable sound of the front door scraping against the stone step froze her in her tracks.

She didn't move, the taste of iron filling her mouth as the seconds slipped by.

'Hello! Anyone home?' Claes called from the doorway.

Cursing herself for her carelessness in not locking herself in, she inched her way towards the door. She glanced over her shoulder at the chest. Only the open front of the cabinet revealed what she'd done. A silent prayer of protection on her lips, she tiptoed back to the cabinet and replaced the panel, then refitted the brass divider. It was only then that she noticed the dagger, lying where she'd set it, and with a shock of relief swept it up and tucked it in her waistband.

Claes's spurs clanged on the tiles, and in panic she flattened herself against the wall. A scraping of a chair, the chink of glass against bottle, and she knew he was in the front room, pouring himself a measure.

Her heart banging like a drum, Floriane groped her way along the wall trying to keep her footsteps light. At any minute her theft would be discovered, and she was alone in the house, as vulnerable as an antelope cornered by a lion.

She paused and listened. Claes was on the move again. Floorboards creaked and she knew he had reached the backroom.

Silence. Was he lying in wait?

'Angela?' he called. 'Are you hiding from me, you minx?'

Angela's room was on the opposite side of the house to where Floriane had concealed herself behind the salon door. Using both hands on the latch to lessen the possibility of it squeaking, her fingers clumsy with nerves, she opened the door a few inches, and tiptoed into her bedroom.

The boards creaked again and his voice rang out. 'Show yourself, Angela. I haven't got all day.'

Floriane snatched up the velvet bags, pulled the knife from her waistband and pushed them all under her mattress. Only just in time, she slipped behind the curtains, and hid herself in the box bed, pulling the cover up to her chin.

If he came in she would be ready – a half-baked story of masked men and muskets was forming in her head. Screened only by the curtains, once more she heard his footsteps and huddled beneath the blanket. She closed her eyes and barely dared to breathe.

He was in the salon next door. His sword bumped against the wall and something crashed to the floor; then his footsteps came to a halt.

What if she had missed something? It was only a matter of time before he saw.

The boards squeaked once more. Sweat stung her eyes and trickled down her face. She had no idea where he was in the house and even though she strained to listen, she heard nothing but the sound of her pounding heart.

The silence was unnerving. She waited a long time in the box bed before she parted the curtains and ventured out. She padded to the door and placed her ear against wood. Nothing.

She crept into the backroom. It reeked of the sickly perfume Claes used on his wig, but he wasn't there either.

She turned to the right and faced his salon. The door was wide open, and she cringed as she took in what he would have seen. Though everything was as it should have been at first glance, when she looked again she noticed a speck of colour on the floor. Crossing to it, she saw it was a tiny ruby. She breathed out a sigh of relief that he hadn't found it and stooped to pick up the jewel. Holding it tightly in her fist, she began to cry, tears of fear and betrayal.

A cabinet full of his wickedness, right beneath my nose.

She only lingered in the house until she was certain Claes was gone, then gathered up the evidence and fled.

➢ CHAPTER 41 ➣

THE SHORELINE OF TABLE BAY fluttered with pennants and the streets resonated with the sound of booming drums and guns as the fleet from Texel dropped anchor.

Next to Floriane, Merkel looked out on the shimmering water and up to the clear, unclouded top of Table Mountain. Gulls flapped overhead and screamed at the sky. The parade ground was crowded with spectators, assembled to witness the arrival of the great fleet and its most distinguished passenger.

She took a few steps away from the jetty. 'Are the arrivals of dignitaries always accompanied by all this pomp?' she shouted.

Merkel gave a reply that she could not make out amid the noise. She squinted at him and shook her head. He pointed to the state barge, its approach quietening the crowd. 'Forgive me, but I must be in position before it touches the jetty.' His face had filled out, and he'd even applied scented wax to the points of his moustache.

She smiled at the change in him. She'd seen rather less of him recently, as he had begun to spend a few days a week on some mysterious mission. All she knew about it was that he attended to it on horseback. The exercise had done him a world of good. He removed his broad-rimmed hat and hurried bareheaded to take his place behind the commander.

Within moments, the great man stepped out of the boat and was escorted up the barnacled stone steps with all the ceremony that the commander could muster.

Prosperity was written large on the commissioner's smiling face, and reflected in the polished silver buttons on his expensive velvet suit and the richly plumed hat on his now silver-wigged head. Floriane widened her eyes.

Erick de Witt had hardly changed one bit.

⁓

For the gala dinner that evening, Floriane arrived wearing her finest taffeta dress. Erick offered her a sweeping bow, bending low over her hand to kiss it. 'The Cape must agree with you, Floriane,' he said. 'You look better than ever I saw you in Amsterdam.'

Floriane smiled with all the charm she could muster. 'I'm glad to see you, Erick. Did you have a good voyage?'

'It was a fast crossing, the captain told me, but "good" depends on one's point of view. Foul weather and violent seas had me tortured by seasickness and confined to my cabin for a twenty-three-day stretch. It was terribly monotonous and my fellow travellers dull, but I am safe and sound. My girth is reduced somewhat and that is, to my mind, a positive outcome.'

'It will shock Claes to find you here. I admit to being somewhat surprised myself. I'm sure there's something more to know about how you went from sheriff to commissioner in under a year.'

'I will tell you the story someday, but for now . . .' Erick scanned the room. 'Where *is* your husband? His absence will have aggrieved the commander, and I confess myself not best pleased either.'

It was barely a week since she'd hidden from Claes at their house, and the memory of it set her pulse racing. 'He's rarely here. He spends the majority of his time at the homestead he's building near Stellenbosch. I am, therefore, resident in a guest apartment at the Castle with my maid, Angela.'

'I am sure that suits you admirably.' His eyes were full of amusement.

'Let us say his absences do not inconvenience me. I have plenty to do in Good Hope and have become quite occupied with caring for patients at the new hospital.'

He leaned towards her and emptied the last drops from the cut-glass decanter into her glass. 'May I call on you in the next day or so, when I find a gap in my agenda? I have brought letters for you from your family, and words from Clara Speelman that she particularly asked I deliver to your hands.'

Floriane lifted the heavy cup and took a sip of the sweet Constantia wine. 'Proost, mijnheer. I shall be glad to speak where we can be private for I, too, have some news to impart.'

*

At Johanna's request, they gathered in the sewing room. It was the only place inside the Castle where Claes van Loon was unlikely to interrupt.

Malliet had arrived first, with Pieter on her heels. The three of them sat chatting for some minutes before they heard footsteps along the corridor and Floriane appeared in the doorway.

Pieter got up from his seat and bowed. 'Mevrouw Peronneau.'

Floriane curtsied in return. 'Mijnheer Mulder. Johanna. Malliet. I am sorry to be the last to get here, but I was held up by the arrival of the commissioner.'

'Did you meet him?' Johanna gulped. 'How does he seem?'

'Somewhat surprising.' A smile tugged at her lips.

'In what way?'

'I believe at least two of you have met him.' Floriane glanced from face to face.

Johanna tried to think of when she might have met such a high-ranking VOC official. 'Are you certain? I can't think of . . .' She shrugged her shoulders.

Floriane's tone was amused. 'Commissioner de Witt assures me you have met.'

'Erick de Witt?' Malliet scoffed.

Impossibly, Floriane affirmed it.

Johanna let out a gasp and Malliet a groan.

'The man is ghoulish!' Malliet jumped up and began to pace. 'Surely this cannot bode well for us.'

'You don't seem to find this revelation problematic.' Johanna studied Floriane's face.

'No. In fact, quite the opposite.' She waved the notion away. 'I can't say more just now, but I believe it will work in our favour. So, tell me, what is the plan thus far?'

Johanna took a deep breath. 'Malliet will give her husband's evidence. You, Floriane, will give evidence about . . .'

Floriane nodded.

'There is another part to the plan, but it depends partially on Pieter.' Johanna turned to face him.

Pieter looked confused. 'On me?'

'Yes.' Johanna stood up and walked over to the window. 'I apologise for being the bearer of unwelcome news, Pieter, that involves your Uncle Mulder. This case appears to hinge on a connection between Cristoffel Mulder and Mijnheer van Loon. But out of appreciation for all your help, I feel it would not be right to present evidence against him unless you are agreeable.' Nervous, she waited for his reply.

'What exactly is it that he's done?' Pieter pushed up his spectacles to the bridge of his nose.

'Wine-smuggling,' said Floriane.

Johanna nodded. 'Also, a plot to change the wine licences from four licensees to just one, ensuring that his smuggling business will flourish.'

Pieter rubbed his chin and gave Malliet a sidelong glance. 'I knew he was involved in smuggling wine to the garrison. He's been doing it for years. I didn't know about the wine licences. It makes sense, though, now that I think about it.'

Johanna scratched her cheek. 'Are you saying you don't mind if I tell Commissioner de Witt?'

'He's my uncle, but he's not above the law. Truthfully, having become aware of this information, I feel as if I'm now obligated to come forward with it. Otherwise I might be considered complicit.' He gave his spectacles another shove. 'There is one additional fact I've happened upon that may be of interest. It seems that the forty morgen of land my uncle gifted to Mijnheer van Loon are not his to give. In fact, they are registered to the Dutch East India Company.'

Floriane stood back from the group. 'Are you saying that your uncle bribed my husband with property he has no claim to?'

Pieter nodded his head to confirm it. 'Yes, that's exactly what I'm saying.'

There was silence for a while as they all took this in, then Floriane began to laugh.

The next day, sometime after three, a loud knock at the door of Floriane's Castle apartment pulled her from her afternoon nap. When she opened the door, Erick de Witt touched his hat in greeting.

'I didn't think there was anything to be gained in delaying, Floriane. I knew you would be anxious for your letters, and I am keen to hear what you have for me.'

As she picked up the bell to ring for tea, she could not have said why, but a sense of unease was growing in the pit of her stomach. 'Please, do sit down. Do you want to speak first?'

He nodded and reached into an inside pocket, withdrawing a substantial sealed packet. He held it out. 'From Clara Speelman.'

She took it from him and ran her finger over the wax seal. 'Do you know what is inside?'

'I don't remember specifics. What I do know is that Clara has spent a great deal of time over the list you transcribed from Claes's notes on the orphanage ledgers. She sends her apologies that she was not able to draw conclusions sooner, but what she has to tell you is both concerning and revealing.'

A tap at the door announced the arrival of tea. Floriane got up and cleared a space on a low table to her right. Angela set a bowl of hot coals on the surface and placed the pewter kettle on top.

'Thank you,' Floriane said to the maid's retreating back, then waited for the soft click of the latch. 'How is Clara?'

He waved his arm in a vague gesture. 'Much the same.'

A ribbon of delicious-smelling steam rose from the small cup as Floriane poured the tea. 'Milk?'

Erick peered at the oily yellow globules on the surface of the liquid and flinched. 'No, thank you. I'd rather not spoil the taste.'

'I know Clara does not suffer in the usual sense of the word from, say, a fever or a persistent cough.'

He hunched his shoulders and raised the cup to his mouth. 'What is it that you wish to know?'

'What is the name of the tincture she takes?'

'Bhang.' He took a sip without looking up.

Floriane shook her head and confessed herself to be confused.

He raised his head this time. 'This is between you and me, and if I am ever challenged, I shall deny all knowledge of this conversation.'

'Of course. Who would I tell, in any event? I have no friends here to run to with gossip.'

Erick looked at her searchingly for a little while. 'Clara suffered very badly after the birth of her last child. Arent was beside himself that she would die. Her screams were harrowing. The surgeon told him that he had come across bhang from sailors in the port, and that it might ease her nerves. It is a powdered opiate. She takes it mixed with milk.' He looked down once more and ran his finger round the rim of the cup. 'It's addictive. She needs more and more each day, and eventually it will kill her.'

She saw the pain in his eyes and bowed her head. 'That is truly terrible. I had no idea.'

'There's no reason you should have known.'

Floriane had once entertained the idea that Erick and Clara were perhaps more than just friends, and had remained uncertain about their status. Now she would never ask. 'Tell me. Were the numbers on Claes's list informative?'

'Clara found that they identified the orphans with larger inheritances. Claes singled out children whose parents died with either substantial property or a significant financial legacy, or both.' He paused and allowed Floriane to refill his cup. 'At the huis we send a notary to make an inventory at the time of the parents' death so that the estate can be valued, and decisions as to how it is managed put in place. In the main, the list is of children who have died long since without issue of their own.'

'What happened to their legacies?'

'They came back into the orphanage's account. I am happy that the ends of the circle tie up in these instances, because we are trying very hard to take care of an increasing number of beleaguered children and need money to be able to do it.'

'And those with issue?'

'The legacy passes to the children, if the orphan had paid the uytkoop.'

'What sort of payment?'

'It is the fee for the notary to organise the paperwork for transfer of the estate.' Erick took a sip of his tea.

'Are there any orphans on the list who are still alive?'

'Of present relevance, Johanna Timmerman.'

Floriane narrowed her eyes. 'Interesting.' She remembered from the ship that Johanna had said her number was on the list.

'Yes. Her estate is still officially unsettled. The paperwork from our notary in Haarlem is solid but, try as we might, we couldn't find the family Bible. It is known to certify the family tree and is the key to putting her inheritance beyond any reach of the Crown. However, as Clara discovered, Johanna hadn't paid the uytkoop. Nor had any of the orphans who came with her. Since they are in the Cape now, were they to die without issue – or without paying the uytkoop – their money would come to the Orphan Chamber here. And its fiscal.'

'Was Claes supposed to inform them about the payment when they left the huis?'

Erick studied the tea leaves in his cup.

Floriane studied Erick. There was much about this that still didn't make sense to her. 'This is deliberate, presumably?'

He spread his palms. 'One can only guess.'

Floriane kept her expression purposely blank. 'And if the Bible were to come to light?'

'It might prove beyond doubt that she is the sole claimant, making it certain that her estate would devolve to the Cape's Orphan Chamber in case of her death. If Claes found that out, it would put her in the utmost danger.' He gave Floriane a hard look. 'Yes. One of the many reasons it took Clara over six months to make sense of the list is that he covered his tracks so carefully.'

Floriane flicked her eyes towards her Bible box and felt the chill of sweat snake down her back. 'I understand that you will be adjudicating Johanna's case.'

'Yes. The commander feels that it falls to me to determine whether she has breached her contract with the Dutch East India.'

'Before you decide, you must know there are extenuating circumstances. I'm sure that when you are acquainted with the facts you will come to the right decision.'

'Then tell me.'

She told him the story of Johanna and Frans, and what had happened on board the ship, including what Captain Bierens had told them about Frans's injuries. 'When, the other week, I was searching for the stolen jewels, I found this concealed in Claes's cabinet.' She withdrew the jewel-handled dagger from her knitting bag and passed it to him.

Slowly he nodded and she saw he had understood what she had not said out loud.

'It is my belief these two young people have been through quite enough difficulty to last a lifetime. Do you not think?'

While he took this in, she pressed on. 'Forgive me, because I should have mentioned this right at the start. I have found something you've been seeking for a while.' A second time she reached into her bag of knitting, and this time pulled out the three velvet pouches and placed them on the table. 'They were in Claes's chest all along. Had I known the chest held such damning secrets, I would have been spared the journey to Good Hope.'

He sucked in a sharp breath and with delight in his voice said, 'This is excellent news indeed. You have absolutely made my day.'

What she didn't say was that she also had Johanna's Bible, hidden in her Bible box on a table by the door.

~ CHAPTER 42 ~

S HORTLY AFTER SIX O'CLOCK on the day of the hearing, Johanna
put on the better of her two dresses, the pale-blue one with
a ruffle around the hem. She had hardly slept at all, the nerves
in her stomach keeping her still and stiff. Her dream of marrying
Frans would either be granted or denied forever today. Her mind
dashed forward to a future where she was married to a burgher,
and Frans to someone else – perhaps even to someone she knew.
She tied the strings of her cap extra tight to distract herself from
unwelcome thoughts.

Dressed, she climbed up to the rooftop to watch what might
potentially be the last sunrise of her life as a free woman. *Please,
God . . .* she prayed, but was unsure how to continue. She had
involved herself in such a mess and felt overwhelmed by the
detail. In the end, she decided on a general prayer. *Let everything
work out for the best.* Her very next thought was of how she and
Frans had ended up on the same ship to Good Hope, against all
probability. *Providence.* She nodded, giving silent thanks.

The mere idea of breaking her fast turned her stomach.
She felt cold, rather sick and in no mind to eat. Instead, she

went down to the door to the main gateway and stood uneasily, waiting for Malliet and Floriane to arrive. A half-hour passed before she saw Malliet cross the bridge and, as she watched her friend walk under the portcullis, she felt a light touch on her shoulder and turned to Floriane. They had no need to speak. It was heartening to know that the two people she loved most in the world apart from Frans would be with her on this day of judgement. She tried to push down the sorrow she felt that Frans would not be present, but everyone knew it was not safe for him in the vlek – at least until Mijnheer van Loon's fate had been decided.

As Malliet approached, Johanna thought she looked pale in her widow's black, but there was colour in her cheeks, and encouragement in her eyes. Floriane seemed resolute, but otherwise unreadable. Her two friends flanked Johanna and each took one of her hands as they set off for the hearing.

The route took them past the Orphan Chamber. Johanna poked her head inside and Pieter looked up from his desk.

'Is it time already?' he asked.

'The hearing starts at seven. We have a few minutes still.'

He got to his feet, gathered up his papers and motioned for her to lead. Together the four of them made their way to the great Council Chamber. Three soldiers stood guard outside, one in red uniform and two others in blue, holding muskets with broadswords strapped to their hips. The sergeant eyed them but waved them into the chamber; there was no need for explanation.

Floriane squeezed her hand as they entered the room. It was already darkened against the upcoming heat at midday, yet sunlight snaked its way through the gaps in the shutters, casting shadows on the walls. Behind a long table, seated in a great carved chair, was Erick de Witt and to his right Commander Speelman, each in the uniforms of their respective ranks. Johanna dropped a curtsy and from the corner of her eye saw that Floriane and Malliet did the same.

Erick de Witt did not pass the time of day in idle chat. 'Take your seats, please.' He indicated three chairs on the opposite side of the table.

There was something different about him, and it took a minute for her to realise what had changed; the tuft of beard under his lip had gone. They'd named it 'the dead squirrel' at the Burgerweeshuis and its absence suited him, making him look younger somehow.

Johanna sat, still sandwiched between Floriane and Malliet, with Pieter to Malliet's right.

Slowly, the commissioner looked from one to the other. There was little warmth in his gaze. 'Johanna Timmerman, I know you from the Burgerweeshuis. As I do Mevrouw Peronneau and Malliet Wagenaar.' He glanced down at his notes. 'Now known as Mevrouw van Wyk, having married according to her contract with the Honourable Company.' He raised an eyebrow and let his eyes settle for a moment on Johanna before shifting his gaze to Pieter.

'And you, sir, I am informed, are Pieter Mulder, the young man who ought to have married Mejuffrouw Timmerman.'

Pieter said that he was.

De Witt's eyes sought her out again. 'For what purpose have these good people accompanied you?'

Johanna stood up from her seat in front of the table. 'Each of them comes to corroborate aspects of what I am sworn to tell you. Pieter is scribe, secretary and clerk to the Orphan Chamber and has sole responsibility – in the frequent absences

338

of Mijnheer van Loon – for the recording of its business in the company journals.'

Pieter nodded his encouragement.

'As Malliet was paired with a burgher at the same time that Mijnheer van Loon paired me with Pieter Mulder, she was able to ask her husband, Mijnheer van Wyk, how the pairings were determined, and he subsequently investigated the matter. Tragically, he recently passed away, but left Malliet his notes and she will present that information to you.'

'I am sorry for your loss, Mevrouw van Wyk. I have heard only the very best things about your late husband.'

Malliet produced a thin smile. 'Your Excellency is most kind.'

The commissioner returned to Johanna. 'And Mevrouw Peronneau?'

'She was witness to my betrothal ceremony on board the *Borssenburg* and what happened after.'

Erick de Witt picked at a speck on his sleeve and glanced at the clock, which stood on an intricately sculptured mantel. 'Sit down, Johanna. I have no intention to let this drag on all morning. We'll start with the contract you signed with the Dutch East India. As far as I see it, you are not wed and there-fore are free to marry one of the many petitioners who has asked for a wife.' He looked across at Pieter, a frown cutting a deep furrow between his brows. 'Who is at the front of the queue?'

Johanna felt a coil of fear, slippery as weed in her gut. *All of this and he won't even listen?*

Pieter cleared his throat. 'We wondered if you might be prepared to reconsider your decision in exchange for, let's say, certain facts.'

'I do not understand why you are rolling up your sleeves and going into battle for someone who has made you look a fool.' There was something dark in his voice.

'I do believe that Johanna is married, in *all* but name, and that her heart is taken elsewhere. Mijnheer van Loon picked me for a husband over more senior applicants because he was bribed to do so.'

'That is a heavy allegation.'

Malliet stood up. 'If I may speak, Your Excellency, that is where I can shed light.' She curtsied and sat down again.

Johanna saw a flutter of movement on her left, where Floriane sat. Erick de Witt must have noticed it as well, for he looked in Floriane's direction.

Johanna glanced over at Floriane, who offered her a small smile.

After a moment, the commissioner said, 'I am persuaded that perhaps it might be worthwhile to listen to the testimony of your witnesses before delving into the details of the contract. Please proceed.'

For the next little while, they took it in turns to present their facts. Malliet spoke about the bribes offered by the suitors. Pieter offered the details of the various ways the fiscal had found to turn a personal profit on his work at the Orphan Chamber. When Pieter mentioned the smuggling of wine and the planned change to the wine licence, Commander Speelman could be heard to curse under his breath. Erick de Witt's face, however, remained inscrutable, and Johanna began to lose hope.

At last the commissioner interrupted. 'This is all damning but I've heard no testimony about your marriage.'

Floriane rose from her seat. 'This is where I have information to impart.' When Erick de Witt indicated she might continue, she said, 'I was present when Johanna signed her contract. She did ask whether she might have some say in choosing whom she was to marry. I was unable to answer her question, but I did agree I would speak to the fiscal, should he be the one to determine the matter.' She gave a heavy sigh. 'On board ship, in what still seems to me a serendipitous turn of events, Johanna met a young man whom she had known at the Burgerweeshuis. They began spending time on deck together. I could see that she grew happier as time passed, until the day she announced that he had asked for her hand. As neither of them had parents to facilitate the service, I agreed to hold their betrothal ceremony in the cabin I shared with Johanna. It was decided that the next morning—'

Johanna couldn't help herself. 'The captain was to ratify the ceremony, but circumstances got in the way.' She gave Floriane an apologetic look.

'Circumstances?' the commissioner asked, his eyes darting back and forth between them.

'The young man was stabbed and left for dead the night before Captain Bierens was to solemnise the ceremony,' Floriane said.

'So in truth you are not married?' His face was set hard.

'I do not have an actual marriage certificate but believe myself wed.'

'Assuming the young man recovered, where is he? Why is it that his name is never mentioned?'

Johanna swallowed. *Providence.* 'If I may speak truthfully.'

Erick de Witt spread his hands, exasperated. 'By all means!'

'We continue to fear for his life. It is my belief that it's only by keeping his identity secret that we prevent his would-be murderer from trying again.'

For the first time, Erick de Witt appeared concerned. 'How is that? Surely the guilty party was on board the ship you arrived on and has since been carried away on that same ship.'

'If that were the case, Your Excellency,' Johanna said, 'the past three quarters of a year would have been far easier on all of us.'

De Witt directed his gaze to Commander Speelman. 'Commander? Are you aware of this tale?'

'Yes. Both Johanna and Mevrouw Peronneau have spoken to me about the matter on numerous occasions. But as there is no evidence and no witness, it appears nothing can be done.'

'Who is the suspect?' The commissioner rested his elbows on the table before him and supported his chin on his folded hands.

Johanna took a moment to find her voice. 'It is Claes van Loon.' She looked about the room at the faces of her friends and of Commander Speelman. 'I would also tell you that of late the weapon we believe was used to commit the crime has come to light in a search of Mijnheer van Loon's private belongings.'

'Why did you not present this information at the start?'

'Because the evidence is incomplete. Without Captain Bierens or the ship's surgeon, or at the very least the broken portion of the knife—'

Commander Speelman lumbered to his feet. 'Johanna, are you saying you have acquired the knife used to stab Frans de Jong?'

Johanna stared at him blankly. 'We were not to utter his name. I thought it was understood.'

The Commander shook his head. 'I'm sorry, Johanna, but it's all out in the open now.'

Floriane stood up. 'We have, commander. On the day I fled the Thuynstraat house for the safety of the Castle, it was in part because I found the knife in Claes's Coromandel chest.'

'Good God!' Erick de Witt exclaimed. 'Why in the world would Van Loon not throw the knife overboard? It beggars belief that he would keep it, even if it was hidden away.'

'The handle is jewelled. I believe my husband would not throw away a thing of value, no matter how damning. At any rate, as evidence goes, it is nothing but a knife with a broken blade. It cannot be proven to be the actual weapon used—'

'—unless we had the missing piece,' finished the commander.

'Please,' Johanna broke in. 'If I may add: we have done so much looking. We have uncovered so many offences committed by Mijnheer van Loon. Some he has done on his own. Some with the help of others. Surely the sum total of these crimes is sufficient to convict him and, in so doing, be payment enough to free me—'

'Commissioner de Witt,' Commander Speelman said, 'may I continue?'

The commissioner nodded. 'Go on.'

'When Captain Bierens came ashore, he did give me the broken piece removed from the boy's wounds by the ship's surgeon against a future moment such as this. It should now be a simple matter to match it to the knife in question and prove one way or another whether Fiscal van Loon is indeed the responsible party.'

Johanna felt her throat go dry. She opened her mouth to speak but the words swam round and round.

'If I may, Your Excellency.' Pieter stood up again. When Erick de Witt signalled that he might speak, Pieter said, 'Mijnheer van Loon firmly believes the young man died on board the ship. He has recorded the date in the ledger and the monies attributed to him have been transferred to the VOC. If he is indeed the party responsible, he must know himself to be a murderer.

See for yourself.' He held up one of the Orphan Chamber ledgers, which the commissioner took and began to examine.

The commissioner was on the point of responding when the great Council Chamber door crashed open, flattening a young slave against the wall. There was some sort of kerfuffle in the corridor and the red-uniformed guard marched into the room.

'My apologies, Your Excellencies, but the gentleman will not be deterred.'

Claes van Loon appeared in the doorway, a blue-jacketed guard making a poor effort at restraining him. The fiscal shoved the man away with his elbow, strode into the room and thumped his fist on the table. 'As independent fiscal, I should have been notified that the girl was trying to wriggle out of her obligations.'

Every eye in the room turned to look at him. Johanna clenched her jaw and narrowed her eyes as she glared at him.

Erick de Witt rose from his chair and leaned his weight on the tabletop.

'You are late to the party, mijnheer.' He pointed to a straight-backed chair that stood a little apart from where Johanna was sitting. 'Sit down. You have shown the greatest discourtesy to the commander and the Dutch East India, both in your disgraceful outburst and your contempt for Company protocol. We should have seen you days since, and present at this assembly from the start, as the marriage maids were your responsibility. And if these were the least of your infractions, perhaps you might be forgiven.' The commissioner regained his seat.

Van Loon sauntered to the vacant place. Johanna noticed that he wasn't wearing his sword and wondered if he had given up the habit. He clicked his fingers at a slave, miming with his hand that he wanted a drink. 'I have no idea what you mean by the least of my infractions, and as to my absence, I have business at Stellenbosch and cannot be in two places at once. I have also spent time looking for my wife. I have not seen her for the last two weeks, but Lord above us, I see that she has been here all along.'

The commander shook his head. 'Mevrouw Peronneau is living at the Castle with her maid, Angela. We judged it unsafe for her to stay alone in Thuynstraat after the house had been broken into.'

Claes snatched his wine from the slave, who hovered by his elbow, and downed the lot in two mouthfuls. He signalled for the glass to be refilled. 'Your Excellency, could you not have thought to tell me?'

The commander toyed with the documents in front of him. 'I might have done, Van Loon, but I have seen neither hide nor hair of you since the event occurred. One would think you might have been concerned enough for her welfare to present yourself at the vlek.'

The commissioner drummed his fingers on the table, his voice shrill. 'You are out of order, Van Loon, and ill-qualified to pass judgement on what Commander Speelman does or does not do. Far better, now that you are here, for us to discuss the allegations that have been made against you.'

'What, do tell, are these *allegations*?' Claes van Loon swung around until his eye fell on Johanna and her allies.

Pieter stood and scooped up several sheets of paper from the tabletop, then handed them to the fiscal. 'By all means, read what is written.'

Claes van Loon glanced at the sheets and slammed his fist on the teak surface. 'These amounts are perquisites of the job and perfectly above board. How dare you call my good name into question?'

'I believe the paperwork speaks for itself.' Pieter lifted his chin.

The commissioner motioned that he should sit, and returned his attention to the fiscal. 'What have you to say in response to these allegations, Van Loon?'

Claes van Loon stared at him and laughed. 'The author of this document is deranged. How dare he criticise me, who seeks only to serve his homeland loyally in the Cape and is rewarded with its bitter ingratitude.'

'Sit down, Van Loon. I have not yet finished.'

The fiscal looked towards the door, which remained open, but was now filled with the two blue-jacketed, musket-bearing guards. He gave a grunt of protest and sat.

Erick de Witt fingered the snuffbox on the table in front of him but appeared to decide against a pinch.

Johanna looked between the two men and said a silent prayer.

The fiscal's sneer was possibly more exaggerated than usual. 'I will write to the Lords Seventeen and advise them of this treason that your false accusations have brought to light. There will be a high price to pay, for they will not hesitate to investigate the charges brought against me. When they discover an innocent man, heads will roll for this, Erick. Be very careful indeed that yours is not one of them.'

Commissioner de Witt spoke in cold, measured phrases. 'Address your correspondence to me, Van Loon. I represent the Honourable Company overseas and am authorised to rule as I see fit. As well as testimonies of the Cape's most senior burghers that you have sought to defraud, you have smuggled illicit wine to the garrison – and a large quantity of jewels reported stolen to me in Amsterdam nearly two years ago has been discovered among your possessions.'

Claes van Loon began to protest, but the commissioner silenced him.

'There is no question about the charges that I have already listed. There is, however, another matter that I want to put on the table. Tell me what you know of Frans de Jong, a young man who boarded the *Borssenburg*, the same ship that carried you, your wife and one of the orphan girls you were intended to chaperone, Johanna Timmerman, to the Cape.'

'Very little,' Claes said smoothly. 'Before boarding the ship, I had never seen nor heard tell of him. I became aware of him only as Johanna Timmerman began to fraternise with him. I understand he was a windmill engineer, sent to the Cape, one assumes, to build windmills.'

'I see.' The commissioner stared out of the window, his lips pressed together. 'And what happened to the boy?'

'I only know what Captain Bierens told me – us – the day after the boy's burial at sea. That there had been some sort of argument among sailors and one of them had stabbed him. The captain had a suspect in custody and was holding him until a fair trial could be held.'

'Was anyone here a witness to that conversation?'

'Of course. It occurred at the captain's table. My wife and the girl were both present.'

'Mevrouw Peronneau, Mejuffrouw Timmerman, can you confirm this?'

Commissioner de Witt waved his hand impatiently. Johanna exchanged looks with Floriane, who indicated she should speak.

Johanna again rose from her seat. 'Captain Bierens told us that a sailor had been buried at sea the previous night. He did suggest that there had been a knife fight. No name was mentioned.' She lowered herself into her chair, eyes fastened on the satin bow on the back of Claes van Loon's wig.

'Mevrouw Peronneau, is this what you remember as well?'

'I remember that it was a very distressing day, and while I do not recall exactly what Captain Bierens said, I know that Frans de Jong's name was not mentioned. If it had been, I cannot imagine what sorrow would have been unleashed.'

The room fell silent.

Claes van Loon cleared his throat. 'Is that the extent of your questioning, Erick?'

'It is not. And, further, you may refer to me as Your Excellency going forward.'

'I—'

'Be quiet!' Erick de Witt stroked his lower lip in the manner Johanna recalled seeing him stroke the patch of beard that had once grown there. 'A further question, Fiscal van Loon.'

Johanna could not see the fiscal's face, but his voice did not sound contrite when he spoke. 'What now, Your Excellency?'

'Do, please, explain why the name of Frans de Jong, his date of death and the amount owed to him by the Dutch East India appear in this ledger before me?' The commissioner leaned back in his chair, his elbows resting on the chair's arms, one hand still on his chin.

'The boy is dead, Eri— Your Excellency, or so I believe.'

'Do you? Or do you *know* him to be dead?'

'Yes – no! I was only going on Captain Bierens' word. Surely the testimony of the captain himself is enough.'

'Except, according to your wife and Mejuffrouw Timmerman, the captain did not mention Frans de Jong by name in his statement.'

One of the fiscal's hands clutched the wooden arm of his

348

chair. 'I assure you, if Frans de Jong is alive, he is not in this colony.'

'Have you searched for him?'

'Of course not.'

'Your conviction that he is dead is quite strong. Could this be because the deed was done by your own hand?'

'How dare you! The stench of conspiracy in this chamber is sickening, and I will not pollute my nostrils breathing it in. You have no evidence for your accusations.' Claes van Loon got to his feet, knocking over his glass of wine in the process, and made as if to storm to the door.

'Guards, detain Mijnheer van Loon and remove him to custody.' Erick de Witt rose to his feet, his eyes blazing as he regarded the fiscal. 'As of now, you are to remain under guard until you return to Amsterdam and face charges there. You are removed from your post as independent fiscal. Your property is forfeit, and the land on which you are building is given up.'

Johanna watched the spilt red wine spread across the polished wood floor like an advancing tide of blood as, with a guard on either side of him, Claes van Loon was escorted from the room.

At the last moment, he twisted around to cast a parting look at the group of them. 'You will be sorry for this, the lot of you, my traitorous wife included.'

Johanna turned to Floriane and touched her arm. 'Are you all right?' she whispered.

Floriane's face looked grim, but she said nothing and nodded. Malliet reached across and squeezed Floriane's shoulder.

'Never mind me for now, girls. We have yet to hear the commissioner's ruling.'

As Claes van Loon's ranting faded into the distance, Erick de Witt waved them all back to their seats.

'Having heard your evidence, I am in a position to give my decision regarding the issue of Johanna Timmerman's contractual obligation to marry a burgher.' He steepled his hands on the table and looked down at his notes.

'It is my belief, based on your testimony, that it was never your intention to marry a burgher, wealthy or otherwise. Before leaving Amsterdam, you and Frans de Jong were acquainted with each other. Mijnheer de Jong informed you that he was to travel to the Cape colony to build windmills, and this influenced your decision to travel to the Cape yourself.' He lifted his eyes and looked directly at her.

Johanna felt the heat in her cheeks, hot as fire. Everything the commissioner said was true.

Erick de Witt picked up his quill and slapped it on the table. 'I acknowledge that you have spent time and energy highlighting the crime and corruption of Fiscal van Loon, for which the Dutch East India is grateful.' He paused, again stroking the empty space beneath his lower lip and looking at each of them in turn.

Scarcely breathing, Johanna waited until at last Commissioner de Witt went on.

'It is for that reason my ruling today is made specific to the facts laid before me and specific to your case alone. If circumstances had been even slightly different, I would have been required to make quite a different judgement. In conclusion, I judge that you have earned the right to marry the man to whom you were betrothed on the voyage here, providing this is also his wish.'

'Thank you.' Johanna straightened, tears flooding her eyes. 'Thank you. Thank you,' she repeated.

He put up a hand. 'I have not finished. Please, let us have no weeping just yet.'

She nodded and wiped her eyes with her fingers.

'Given the attempt on Frans de Jong's life and the continued presence of Claes van Loon at the Cape, it is my strong recommendation that you do not attempt to solemnise your vows until after Mijnheer van Loon has been deported back to Amsterdam. As I must continue to Batavia and will take custody of the prisoner on my return, that will be another year.' He produced a clean white handkerchief from his pocket and threw it across the table.

Her eyes blurred and a sob closed her throat. The thought of another entire year spent waiting made her spirits quail, but Frans would be near her. She would endure. In a moment she was surrounded by Floriane and Malliet, who pressed her into an embrace. Over Malliet's shoulder she caught sight of Pieter and blew her nose on Erick de Witt's hanky. 'Thank you,' she mouthed to him, and then out loud, 'I thank all of you, so much.'

She turned to the commissioner. 'Your Excellency, I am so grateful for your ruling. I wonder, am I now free to leave the Castle?'

The commissioner turned to look at Commander Speelman, who raised his shoulders towards his ears.

'I see no reason to detain you any longer. But where will you go?'

Malliet took two steps forward and said, 'With me, Your Excellency. Just like old times.'

⌐ CHAPTER 43 ⌐

EARLY IN THE MORNING the day after Claes's arrest, Floriane returned to the Thuynstraat house with her personal belongings and Angela. Closed up for weeks, the house had become overwhelmingly musty, so she threw open the windows to let in the air. Unprompted, Angela set about dusting and polishing. Floriane took up a broom, but soon found herself standing with her hands crossed over the top of the handle, gazing out across the vlek at the waves that crashed against the shore.

She had done what she'd come to do. Claes was undone. She would certainly return to Amsterdam eventually, but she had responsibilities here, things she had to deal with before she could go home. After Johanna and Frans were wed, though, was there anything to keep her at the Cape?

Almost as if in answer, there was a tapping at the front door. The broom still in her hand, she opened it and found Merkel and Johanna standing at the bottom of the stoep.

'Good morning,' Merkel said, removing his hat and pressing it to his chest. 'We have come to rescue you from whatever it is that you are doing.'

Johanna looked up from the street. 'Sweeping, by the looks of it. Surely after your great efforts these past weeks, an outing is just what you need.'

Floriane narrowed her eyes at them. 'What, at this very moment?' She hoped she didn't sound openly rude. 'Where in the world do you expect me to go at a moment's notice?'

'To a secret destination,' Johanna said, tapping her nose. 'Merkel's purloined the commander's carriage for a couple of days. We'll be gone overnight, so bring whatever you need. Do say you'll come, Floriane. Otherwise I shan't be able to go, as it will not be deemed fitting.'

Floriane looked back and forth between them and let out a little laugh, shaking her head. 'Very well then! I'll need a few moments to get some things together and make certain Angela will be all right here on her own. When shall I tell her we'll be back?'

'Early tomorrow.'

'And where are we to spend the night? Not in the carriage, I hope.'

'You need not worry, mevrouw,' Merkel said. 'Arrangements have been put in place.'

⌒

Floriane shifted around on the carriage seat, seeking to relieve her cramped limbs. 'May I be allowed to have some hint of where we're going? We've been driving for hours, it seems.'

'I've decided to show you what I've been doing these past months when I've been absent from the vlek,' Merkel said.

Seated across from her, Johanna's eyes were wide. 'Are you making this up, Secunde Rosenmüller? I thought—'

He clucked his tongue. 'As we are almost there, let us not ruin the surprise.'

Floriane looked out of the window, her hands folded in her lap. They were lucky that it had not rained in a few days. The roads were dry, and apart from a fine cloud of red dust that rose up through the carriage's open windows, the journey was less burdensome than it might have been.

Merkel followed her gaze and pointed. 'If you look that way, you'll see Parrot Mountain, where the commander's birthday fair will be held in two weeks' time.'

Johanna craned her neck. 'I have heard a great deal about it from Pieter. I am going to ride with him and Malliet on the day.'

'And what about you, Floriane? Do you plan to attend the fair?'

Floriane turned to Merkel and shrugged. 'I hadn't actually given it any thought. You're attending, I presume?'

'Indeed I am, and you would be most welcome to join me.'

'I'd like that. Is that where we are going now? To Stellenbosch?'

Johanna beamed, and Floriane understood at least some of the plan.

To Merkel, Floriane said, 'Were you serious when you said you were going to show me what you've been doing every week?'

'Patience, Mevrouw Peronneau. You are about to find out.'

At last, they came into an area where there were buildings, and a familiar sight that sent a wave of homesickness crashing over her heart – the framework of a windmill under construction, its workforce about to begin the process of nailing together its wooden base.

A tall blond man stepped out from behind it. Floriane knew him at once.

'Frans!' Johanna breathed. She swivelled in her seat and Floriane read instantly the joy in her eyes. 'Oh please! May I get out and speak to him?'

'I don't see why not.' Floriane looked at Merkel. 'We'll give you some privacy.'

'Shall I help you down?' Merkel asked, but before he could slide off his seat, the girl had jumped from the carriage and darted off.

Floriane watched the young couple through the window for a moment or two and smiled fondly.

'The boy looks well.'

'Yes.' He nodded and seemed to be thinking about something.

'Have you seen much of him on your weekly visits?'

He did not reply straight away. 'An acquaintance suggested that something should be done about the young man's vulnerability and so I thought, as I had such a skill to impart, that the something should be lessons with a sword.'

Floriane studied his face and almost kissed the delicious laughter lines around his mouth. 'What a lovely thing to do, Merkel.'

'He has a natural ability, and a long reach. I believe he could now defend himself as well as any modest swordsman. Although now it seems your husband is under lock and key, so the danger has passed and he is no longer at risk.'

Floriane looked back at the blond, sun-tanned giant. 'Let's hope not. But for what it's worth, the exercise appears to have done you both the world of good.'

Outside, Frans raised a hand in their direction. 'Merkel! Mevrouw Peronneau! Please get out of that dusty coach and join us.'

Merkel turned to her. 'Would you care to stretch your legs?'

On the morning of the commander's forty-seventh year, the Castle was at last almost deserted. Time to choose. It was barely light when Claes got up, dressed in the clothes he'd thrown over a chair, and peered out at the dawn through the small panes of his garrison windows. He wrapped his arms across his chest against the chill.

He would settle the score with Floriane and Johanna, by hook or by crook. He smirked as he thought about it.

Eighteen or so months, first in the Castle and then on a ship, would certainly give him ample time to prepare his case of innocence. *I am strong in the justice of my cause. I can confront my accusers and that snake Erick de Witt. The Honourable Company will back me up when they are apprised of the facts.*

He considered their utter ruination for a few delicious moments.

But there was a price to pay, and not just that of time. The gold stashed in Stellenbosch was enough to see him victorious in the Netherlands, but pressing his case would eat into it deeply, and there was a whole world beyond the poxy Cape. *I have the money to hide until a ship is bound for India. There, I'd be a prince. And then they'd be laughing on the other side of their faces.*

Both options were as tempting as ever, but as he breathed in deeply, he could almost smell the tang of spice in the air. *India it is, then!*

Claes took care descending the guardroom stairs to the courtyard, one hand gripping the polished hardwood handrail, the other bracing the wall to lighten his footsteps. Carefully he negotiated the treads, knowing that three of them creaked, and paused on the bottom step for a minute or two, listening for voices. At the bottom, this morning, was only a single guard. The courtyard, usually bustling with guards and civilians, was empty.

He eyed the guard, a young, bored-looking fellow, and decided to pretend ignorance of the day. 'Good morning,' he said conversationally. 'Where has everyone disappeared to?'

'Stellenbosch,' the guard answered, his face rigid.

'Indeed? What is the occasion?'

'His Excellency's birthday, mijnheer. He throws a fair every year. Most everyone in the vlek attends.' He mumbled the words as if he were talking to himself.

Claes flashed him a sympathetic smile. 'Drew the short lot, did you?'

'Yessir.'

'Are you to stand here all day with no relief?' His eyes remained on the boy.

'Aye, mijnheer.' He hitched the musket higher on his shoulder.

'What a shame,' he said heartily. 'That is so unfair. I could tell you a thing or two about unfairness. It's exactly how I ended up here. The commissioner has been planning this since before I left patria. Worse, he was aided by my wife and my scribe.'

'Begging your pardon, mijnheer, but they say you killed a man on board ship.'

'Yet another false allegation. Just as you must miss the fair today by random circumstance, so they have used random circumstance against me. A boy was killed. I was on the ship at the time. They wanted me out of the way. Therefore, they invented a tale about my guilt. Now I shall be sent back to Amsterdam, just as you are now forced to stand here and keep watch.'

For the first time, the guard's stony countenance faltered.

Claes glanced around the guardroom. 'I see your flagon is empty. A pity. I was going to suggest we have a drink together to commiserate, given that we are companions in our solitude.'

The young man rolled his shoulders. 'That is my own doing, mijnheer. I neglected to refill it before I came on duty. On any other day it would be simple enough to fill it up.'

'That at least should still be simple enough, even today.' Claes spread his hands, palms up. 'I would offer to do it myself, but we both know that is not allowed. You could go and be back with a full flagon in less than a quarter of an hour, surely.'

The young man snorted. 'I could do it in five minutes.'

'Well, then, it's decided. I shall stand right here and wait for your return.' Already Claes was plotting his route to the stables, where he had left his horse, a handsome roan gelding, and his sword, tucked into the locker he kept in the horse's stall.

When the guard disappeared into the Castle, Claes counted to ten and took off at a run.

*

Before dawn brightened the velvety black sky, Floriane and Merkel had left the vlek, packing into a green wagon drawn by a span of six oxen. Around three in the morning, the Khoi driver cracked his whip, shook up his reins and set off.

Eight people were wedged together with the tents and baskets of food for the journey to Stellenbosch. Was it madness that Floriane felt such a thrill sitting beside Merkel as they were pulled towards their destination? Eventually, they arrived at the Papegaaiberg, the hill where the annual parrot shoot took place.

Merkel nodded his head towards the hill to his rear. 'I've always felt "Parrot Mountain" far too grand a title for that little mound.'

She turned and squinted at the bump behind them. 'The Dutch are prone to exaggeration, it is true. Are you to be a bystander, or will you participate in the contest?'

'It's not really my sort of thing, firing arrows at a lump of wood.'

They walked on, weaving their way among the clutter of carts and wagons, and for a while, neither of them spoke.

Eventually, Floriane felt it was now or never. Before her courage left her, she began, 'Merkel, I want to speak to you about my plans for the future.'

'I had wanted to talk to you about that as well.' He spoke very low, with an intensity that scared her.

'It cannot be a secret that I miss my family, nor that I prefer city life.'

He appeared to study the soil beneath his feet. 'You're thinking of returning to Amsterdam when your husband goes?'

'Not when he goes, no, but on the next ship after that. I do not care to spend five months on a vessel that also carries him, even if I am guaranteed to never set eyes on him. I am hopeful that once he has had his trial before the VOC, I will be granted a divorce.' She glanced at him and nearly performed a jig when three little lines appeared at the sides of his mouth.

On a hillock a little to the west of the fair, the girls sat on the grass, sharing a meal as they had done so often at the orphanage. One plate, eight spoons; old habits ran deep.

'You all look very fine,' Johanna said, for once regretting her brown woolsey dress. While appropriate enough in the cold Dutch spring, it was out of keeping in southern Africa in the bright October sunshine. She felt dowdy and out of place.

Hilletje ran a jewel-laden hand across her expanding green silk middle. Malliet had given up her deep mourning attire and now wore only weepers, bands on her upper arms, to show that she was recently bereaved.

Johanna swung round to the field, where eighty-eight burghers crammed into blue-and-red uniforms trotted on horseback in front of the commander. 'Are all your husbands also proud defenders of the Dutch flag?'

'That's all for show.' Elke shook her head, fluttering the lace trimmings on her cap. 'They'll be out of those costumes and back among the rest of us as soon as they've finished saluting the commander. It's just like archery practice. Compulsory for men and boys in every parish in the Cape, up to two hours each week after Divine Service, but nobody ever does it unless there's someone senior checking up.'

'That should make the parrot shoot dangerous, if no one has put in the practice.' Johanna rolled her eyes.

Lisje pursed her lips. 'It will be worse still, because His Excellency has given the command a half-legger of wine just for trotting by on their horses.'

'How exactly does the parrot shoot work?' Johanna looked to Malliet, who didn't seem to be paying attention. Following her friend's gaze, Johanna saw why.

Pieter Mulder was crossing to where they sat, and when he arrived Malliet turned pink with pleasure. 'Pieter, might you tell the girls about the parrot shoot?'

Pieter held out his hand and pulled her to standing. 'There are small monetary prizes of a few stuivers each for knocking off the wings, tail and head. If you raise a splinter but do no real damage you receive a single stuiver. The overall winner, who carries the title of King of the Marksmen, receives five ducats in cash from the Honourable Company as well as a commemorative silver arrow.'

'Have you ever taken part?' Johanna asked.

He made a face and straightened his wig. 'Every year it occurs. Last year, the Honourable Company declined to provide prizes or refreshments, so the magistrate cancelled the event.'

Malliet did not hesitate. 'This year they will do no such thing, and you will be splendid and take the title. I shall cheer very loudly when you do.'

He beamed from ear to ear. 'I shall give my very best effort to not let you down.'

Glad that something good had come from her difficulties, Johanna looked on fondly at their obvious delight in each other's company. Pieter was kind, attentive and one day would make Malliet a splendid husband.

As the girls were finishing their picnic, Floriane strolled over. 'Look who we found.' She gestured behind her to where Merkel and Frans were approaching side by side. As the men were wrapped up in their conversation, it gave Johanna a moment to let her thoughts linger on how well Frans had recovered from his injuries, and how well dressed he was, how handsome he looked. When they were close, she held out her hand. 'While everyone is together for once, it's time you met my friends from the huis.'

By now the girls were clearing up, and clustered around the pair of them when they drew near. Johanna jumped in the air, waving her hands. 'Stand back everyone and let me introduce Frans de Jong, the man I'm going to marry.'

Hilletje caught her eye, stroking her stomach, a mischievous glint in her eye. 'Nice work, Jo-Jo. You're going to have fun making one of these!'

Johanna's cheeks felt a little hot, fearing more embarrassment from that quarter, but Malliet pointed at the commander, saying, 'Now the officers have finished their procession, don't you think we should go and wish Commander Speelman a happy birthday?'

Merkel agreed. 'I should think he would be greatly pleased by that.'

Johanna gathered up her cloak and draped it around her shoulders. 'Are you not coming with us?'

'Merkel and I will be along a bit later,' Floriane said. 'Go on with your friends and make a glittering parade of marriage maids.'

Frans held back as well. 'It looks as though there's a queue forming, so I'll give you a head start and follow in ten minutes.' He waved her off with both hands. 'Now go, before you get left behind.'

Johanna gave him a flash of smile and ran after her friends. In spite of the dark clouds gathering in the east, it was still a beautiful day. As she made her way through the crowd, she considered everything around her to be perfect: bees hummed and birds sang, children hopped on the grass, the plants were in glorious springtime blossom and her friends up ahead were like bright blooms in the wilderness.

Afraid she would spoil the effect, she kept to the edge of the crowd, watching her friends queue up, her spirits high. It was liberating to be out in the world, to finally see this new land she was to call her home. And to know that she and Frans were at last to be married.

As she looked on, Lisje, in her finery, was the first to stand before the commander. They spoke at some length, but the noise of the crowd around her drowned out whatever pleasantry they were exchanging. One by one, the girls stepped forward, passing on their best wishes, but Johanna was glad she stood apart, thinking that she had never been so happy, that finally life was taking the direction she had set her heart on for years.

She was so wrapped up in her thoughts that it was a while before she realised the commander was no longer in her sights and the mood around her had sobered. 'Have they started the parrot shoot already?' she said to her neighbour, an older woman whose dated attire suggested she had been a long time at the Cape.

'There's been a message from the Castle that's soured the afternoon.'

'What message?'

The woman frowned. 'They're saying the fiscal has escaped from the guardhouse.'

Alarm overwhelmed Johanna. 'When was this?' Without waiting for a reply, she spun on her heel and began to run through the tide of partygoers, fixing on the spot where she'd last seen Floriane and Merkel, praying that Frans was still with the secunde.

And what about Floriane? Dear Lord, please keep them safe from that terrible man.

As she neared where she'd left her friends, she caught sight of Frans through the crowd. Relieved to see he did not look concerned, she fought her way past the throng of colonists, who jostled and swarmed in the same direction, and had almost reached his side when she stopped dead in her tracks. Frans was in conversation with someone.

'And apparently at your hands,' he said, clearly.

'I will not be tried for the murder of a man who yet walks among the living.' Her blood ran cold at the vainglorious tones of Claes van Loon. 'Take up your sword, boy. I shall make short work of you, followed by the sickly German and that traitor Pieter Mulder.'

A crowd, three colonists deep, surrounded them and prevented her from gaining ground. People were calling, shouting out: spectators at a show.

'But as you can see, mijnheer, I have no sword.' Frans seemed unruffled.

There was a whisper of metal on metal as Van Loon pulled his blade from its sheath. 'I fear this will not dissuade me.'

Trembling from head to foot, Johanna clawed her way to the front of the group. Frans was unarmed, a mere ten feet or so from Claes van Loon's slashing blade.

'Help him, someone!' Johanna shouted.

Merkel pulled the sword from his belt and threw it in an arc towards Frans. Quick as a flash, Frans caught it in his right hand and planted a blow on the ground.

'You lend credence to the idea that you stabbed an unarmed man to death, Mijnheer van Loon. I have no skill with the sword and no wish to fight you.'

Claes hesitated, his eyes fixed on the blade in Frans's hand.

'Ah, I see you prefer to attack the unprepared.' A note of scorn coloured Frans's voice. 'I suppose now you'll run away and hide like the coward I know you are.'

The fiscal clenched his jaw and swore into his moustache. Lunging forward, he turned his palm towards the ground so that the blade lay on its side. Johanna could barely breathe as the sword's tip advanced towards Frans's chest, but before it could strike home, Frans sprang to the side and, with a rasp of steel, knocked the blade away with his own.

Johanna cheered silently, but her fear was quick to return.

Van Loon took a step back and caught his breath. 'You hop like a frightened rabbit, windmill boy,' he said and raised up his sword.

Frans lunged. Van Loon whisked his sword into the air and cut off his attack, then as Frans dropped his sword to his side, he stumbled on a rock and lost control of the blade. The fiscal struck at his head and Frans jumped back, but the long, sharp edge sliced the upper part of his arm, leaving a line of dark red on the sleeve of his coat.

'Dear me. It seems you bleed,' Van Loon crowed.

Frans held his left hand to the gash on his arm. 'Are you satisfied that now you have won?'

Claes van Loon slashed at the air. 'I think not, windmill boy. You are a pitiful opponent, but we fight to the death.'

Johanna waited a moment, rocking on her heels. *I have to do something*, she thought. After steeling herself to re-enter the tide of watchers, she squeezed her way through the onlookers to Merkel's side. 'Frans is going to be killed. You have to find the commander and make him stop the fight.'

Merkel leaned his head towards her but did not take his eyes off the contest. 'Van Loon will lose his concentration, but Frans will not. It's how I taught him to defend himself. Face the danger, and the eye must not wander.'

Frans lifted his blade, sword held out before him. Johanna saw that the stain on his sleeve had widened and that the weapon trembled in his hand.

'Sword too heavy for you?' the fiscal taunted.

Frans bounced on his toes and attempted some sort of counter, driving the fiscal round in a circle.

Van Loon worked his mouth as if he was freeing an olive from its pit. 'Stand still and fight, boy.' He lunged low. 'You are a coward. Contemptible. I should have finished you off on board ship when I had the chance.' He lurched forward and let forth a volley of blows.

'This is appalling.' Floriane appeared at her side and pressed one of Johanna's hands between her own.

'Where have you been?'

Floriane spoke, her eyes trained on the skirmish. 'One of the girls was feeling unwell, so I took her off to find the physician. I am so sorry I have done nothing to help.'

Johanna shook her head. 'This is in no way your doing, but I am frightened beyond bearing. Everyone knows that Van Loon has escaped from the Castle, but why has no one come to arrest him? Even the commander seems to have disappeared.' She cast a pleading glance at the secunde.

'You are quite right,' he said. 'This has gone on long enough. Van Loon has admitted that he made an attempt on Frans's life and is attempting to do so again.' He looked stricken. 'You must excuse me, mevrouwen.'

Floriane held on to his arm. 'Merkel, what are you doing? You're not armed.'

'I am not, but Frans is.'

A chill wind blew across Parrot Mountain as the secunde called out, 'Claes van Loon. You have been remanded to custody by Commissioner Erick de Witt for crimes against the Honourable Company and for the stabbing of Frans de Jong. Under the authority of the Dutch East India Company, I order you to stand down.'

The fiscal sprang back, sweat shining on his brow. 'Where is Erick de Witt, that treacherous bastard? I shall slit his throat as well.'

'Would you indeed, mijnheer? Are you not satisfied that the charges you face are enough?'

Claes van Loon turned his face in the secunde's direction and in that moment, Frans drove his sword straight at his opponent.

Floriane gasped and covered her eyes, but Johanna could not look away. The tip of Frans's blade flew across Van Loon's body, hooking into the basket of his sword. In one smooth movement, Frans leapt forward, shoving Van Loon in the chest with the heel of his hand while throwing up his sword. The fiscal's weapon flew out of his hand, tumbling end over end through the air. Thrown off balance, Van Loon stumbled backwards and fell to the ground. Quick to seize the advantage, Frans towered above him, his sword point pressed to the fiscal's throat.

Johanna put her palms to her face. As much as she loathed Mijnheer van Loon, she had no wish to see him die.

Frans removed the point of his sword from the fiscal's neck. 'You are disarmed. I will not kill you today. I would rather see you stand trial for your crimes. This is over.' He turned, breathing heavily, towards Merkel. 'Thank you for lending me your blade, my friend.' Handle first, he extended it towards the secunde. Before Merkel could reclaim it, a gasp went up from the crowd and Floriane cried out, 'Frans! Behind you!'

Van Loon had snatched up his sword and was charging forward like a bull at a gate, a look of murderous intent in his eyes. He was almost upon Frans when the younger man swivelled around, his sword outstretched.

The fiscal's eyes widened in horror as he saw the sword directly in his path, but he was moving too fast to dodge the tip; it pierced him in the centre of his chest and buried itself nearly to its hilt.

Time seemed to slow to a crawl.

Frans staggered back, the sword loose from his grip. 'Oh God,' he breathed. 'Why did you not . . .?'

Claes looked down in disbelief, the colour draining from his face. 'You—' he gasped and flailed at the tip of the sword protruding from his back '—have run me through.' His legs buckled beneath him and he sank to the ground.

Floriane turned away, her hands covering her face.

As Johanna began to bunch up her cloak and run towards the fiscal, for the first time in her life, she felt pity for Claes van Loon.

*

Nothing moved. Not the air, not a cloud, not a leaf on a tree.

Claes thought to do the same.

The Timmerman girl was the first to arrive. She knelt by his shoulder, wadding her coat into a makeshift pillow and placing it beneath his head. She seemed a long way away.

Floriane appeared by her side. She was speaking, but her words made no sense.

Johanna smoothed the hair back off his face, and he felt her take his hand between her palms. 'Try not to move. You have a nasty wound, but we have sent for the surgeon.'

Claes tried to raise his arms, but his clothes clung stickily to him, binding him in place. There was a pressure on the back of his skull, so he closed his eyes just for a second. He was bored now, sick of lying in the dirt.

Floriane touched his forehead. He wondered about that. Did she still care for him? If only he could turn back the clock to when she was well, and their love was new; before he'd got himself into such a mess.

Sweat tickled his sides, which was odd as it was cold out – he could barely feel his fingers. He angled his head a bit and his breath squeezed out of his lungs and bubbled up in his mouth.

The redhead was on her knees beside him. She'd lost her cap, her hair streaming past her shoulders in a glorious red wave. Shadows had settled under her eyes – or maybe the sun was setting; it was quite hard to see. He lay still and watched her for a while through his eyelids. Her clothes were patched and darned, the fabric pilled. They looked clean. Orphanage clean. The bills for soap were huge. Surely there were ways to cut down on all that incessant washing. Make economies, or the money to pay for it all. Find a way to get some back from the little brats. He opened his eyes properly and saw there was a scattering of freckles on her cheeks. 'You shouldn't work in the sun,' he wanted to say. 'It will ruin your lovely complexion.'

But the words never left his mouth.

∼ CHAPTER 44 ∼

FLORIANE WAS IN THE front room of the house on Thuynstraat two days after her husband's death when Merkel arrived. The morning was all wide, blue African sky and racing white clouds.

She put down her latest foray into the secunde's extensive library. 'Is Claes now laid to rest?'

Merkel frowned as he came into the room, then lowered himself into a chair. 'The commander ordered the carpenter to fashion a cheap, unremarkable coffin, telling the man a story about why he needed it. It was put in the guardroom with Claes inside it, just as he was when he died. He was carted away from the vlek, and at midnight, six soldiers carried the coffin from the cart into the bush. Two officers guided their path by carrying lanterns suspended from a pole. The commander himself read words over the grave, but there is no marker to identify the spot.'

She pushed her spectacles up over her forehead. 'The funeral today was a sham?'

He stretched out his legs and nodded. 'After the real funeral had been performed, the carpenter was instructed to make a

370

second, elaborate coffin and with this, today, the funeral cere-
monies were carried out in the newly built church on the
Herengracht.'

'But there was no body to bury.'

'No. That funeral was purely for reputation. Lavish, ritual-
ised woe with stopped clocks, covered mirrors and professional
wailers singing hymns in sad, broken voices.'

'Claes would have delighted in all that.' Her feelings about
not having been permitted to attend the funeral were a mixture
of guilt and gratitude, but she felt perhaps slightly less bothered
now, knowing that even Claes himself had not been present.

Merkel did not disagree. He took his clay pipe from his jacket
and cradled the bowl in his palm. 'It was attended by a great
many people. His cortege was over two hundred metres long,
and when it passed the guard on duty at the Castle, men presented arms, officers saluted and drums were beaten.'

'Why such theatre?'

He smiled faintly. 'Partly to save face for the Honourable
Company, but the commander was also putting a spectacular
cap on his own time here.'

'His posting has been approved at last?'

He gave an energetic nod. 'He will be going to Batavia with
the next outgoing fleet, in several weeks. The commissioner is
preceding him to pave the way.'

'Who will take over from him here?' Floriane's voice was
tight in her throat.

Merkel looked down. 'He offered me the position.'

She felt panic pulling her in and hoped Merkel would not
read it on her face. 'And what did you say?'

'I have yet to reply,' he murmured, his voice barely audible.
'But I must make my decision soon.'

Floriane turned her head towards the clock. The sun shone bright on its gilded casing and reflected into her eyes. She put up her hand to shield her face from the pain of his words, and to hide the tears coursing down her cheeks. She was not certain she had prevented him from knowing, but if he had seen he had respected her dignity and said nothing.

He took his leave shortly thereafter. She stood at the window for some time, watching him walk away, her heart filled with longing and confusion.

Knowing what she did then about Merkel's future and what she planned for her own, time moved like a slow river that flowed heartbreakingly away. She knew it must end. Yet the first weeks of November still came to pass, as they must. Merkel came for tea and conversation on a regular basis. She did her best to avoid speaking about the future.

The last days of the month ticked away, distancing her from the past, but bringing the inevitable sorrow closer. In the space of a scant few weeks, her world had tipped off its axis, and the peace she had thought would come with Claes's passing had not yet obliged her.

~

She moved from the house on Thuynstraat that she had so briefly shared with Claes, bringing Angela and eventually Rosa with her. The Thuynhuis, as it had been named, was a single-storeyed pavilion for visiting dignitaries located in the Company garden. The reception rooms to the right and left of the hall and the backroom beyond were furnished with beautiful chairs and tables from the East. There were Oriental rugs on the floor, ornate objects on tables, maps on walls, and exquisite tableware of New World silver arranged in polished wood cabinets.

A book open on her lap, Floriane gazed at the pink oleanders in the garden, then let her head drop. She steadied her forehead in her hands. The wall-mounted clock ticked loudly, pushing the day forward. Floriane tapped the chair with her knuckles, got up and eased the knots in her spine. A line of large, pincer-jawed black ants surged forward in single file across the polished floor in the direction of the kitchen. She turned towards the door. 'Ants, Angela, in the *voorkamer*.'

Angela appeared at the doorway carrying a cup of sour Cape wine. 'Where?'

'Speeding towards your kitchen.'

She dumped the contents of her cup on the floor and massaged it in with her foot. 'I get more wine and go around house. They're bad at this time.'

'Good idea.' Floriane stamped her feet on the ground and flapped the skirt of her dress to dissuade any adventurous mountaineers. 'Is Rosa busy or can she rustle up some *pampoen koekies*? The secunde has said he will drop by at teatime, and those pumpkin fritters are his absolute favourites.'

'I'll tell Rosa to start cooking. You need air. It's been days since you've gone out and had any exercise.'

'You're right. Can you find me my *kiepersol*? I'll walk up to the old house and back.'

Shaded by her parasol, Floriane turned right past the cemetery, and walked on towards the Gentlemen's Canal. The water was high, as brown as beer, and raced down the brick-lined canal. Despite the commander's repeated call that household soil be cast into the sea and rubbish carted to the beach, a slave girl came out of a house and threw a pail full of slops into the *gracht*.

Floriane marvelled at how the town had started to spread. Nine months after she had first walked in Good Hope, the streets were still unpaved, rutted and uneven, but more white gabled burgher houses now flanked their sides, handsome with their high stoeps, framed windows and shutters.

Without paying much heed to her route, she followed the road towards the sea. She paused for a while in the shade of a high myrtle hedge and watched silver sparkles of light dance on the bay's deep sapphire water. The beach lay beyond the sand dunes like a blinding white ribbon, swathed in feathery brown seaweed, the tang of salt sharp on the air. She felt her purpose drift.

Changing direction, Floriane found herself on the wide pillared stoep of a house on Zeestraat, staring at a heavy brass doorhandle. She lifted it and let it drop. The knock was too loud, too firm, unnerving. She almost turned away.

The door opened and a curly dark head peered out.

'Is either Johanna or Malliet at home?'

The maid stood to one side. 'Johanna is in the backroom drawing. If you go and join her, I'll bring tea.'

Floriane did as instructed, and found her leaning through the back shutters, her elbows on the wide oak sill.

'What are you drawing?'

Johanna turned and squinted as her eyes adjusted to the light. 'There's a gull on some driftwood by the beach. I'm trying to do it justice with my charcoal.'

'Don't let me stop you. I just popped by on a whim to see how you are getting on lodging with Malliet.'

'We're no different than we were at the Castle, except that we now have our own beds. The freedom to do what I want and where, though – well, that is something quite novel!'

From the edge of the room the maid asked if she might bring in their tea things. Johanna ran forward and took the tray, setting it down on top of a tapestry-draped table, and poured Floriane a cup.

She studied the contents. 'How is Frans?'

'Still horrified it was his sword that ran through Mijnheer van Loon, but the minister in Stellenbosch has helped him realise that it was not his fault.'

Floriane nodded encouragingly. 'I cannot imagine how complicated his feelings must be. I am pleased he is being helped in that regard.'

Johanna picked up her cup, now filled, and blew on the liquid. 'Do you miss the house in Thuynstraat?'

'That's come out of nowhere.'

'I thought to make some sketches of it for you, in case you did.'

Floriane was touched by her thoughtfulness. 'I was tempted just now to stroll past, but I changed my mind because I have a favour to ask of Malliet.'

'She's gone out with Pieter.'

'They seem to have grown close.'

A smile bloomed on Johanna's face. 'I think they will get married when her mourning period is over. Malliet says that she is in no great rush, but I suspect otherwise.'

'Has the commander agreed to an earlier date for your marriage, now all danger is past?'

'In principle, but Frans is caught up with work in Stellenbosch he has to complete first. What did you want to ask of Malliet, if it is not a private matter?'

Floriane grew serious. 'I have learned that the folk Claes purchased for the homestead in the country are now my responsibility to either sell on or set free.'

'You can't sell them,' Johanna said, springing from her chair.

'They might end up somewhere awful, with someone who whips them.'

She inclined her head. 'I agree. That's why I wanted to ask Malliet if she would buy them from me, let them learn a trade, and then grant them their freedom. She is the only person I know well enough to ask who has the money to do so.'

Johanna stared at the window. 'That's what they are doing today, for me. Pieter and Malliet have gone to the Orphan Chamber to lodge freedom papers for Olumjimi.'

'You are such a loyal friend, Johanna. It is no wonder people are drawn to you. Frans, Malliet, Olumjimi—' she broke off, fearing a tremble in her voice.

'As you have drawn in Merkel.'

The lump in her throat gave way to tears. 'No, I haven't.'

In an instant Johanna was by her side. She knelt down, took her hand and kissed her fingers. 'What on earth has happened?'

The grief came in fits and starts. 'I have to go back to Amsterdam,' Floriane sobbed. 'I only came to the Cape because I promised Erick de Witt. The jewels are now recovered, and I am ruined here. There is nowhere else for me to go but home. Merkel will not want the taint of an association with me.'

'Of course he will. I may be young, but I'm not blind. You can tell from the way he looks at you that he adores you, Floriane.'

A sick, hollow ache took hold of her stomach. 'He has been offered the position of Cape commander when Arent Speelman sails to Batavia. It is an enormous step up for him and he's not likely to turn it down.'

'I think he would rather have you as his wife than the vlek as his command.'

'But he hasn't asked me, Johanna, and I don't think he ever will.'

Floriane dawdled on the way back to the garden house, and by the time she got home the afternoon had all but slipped away.

She sat in her chair and tried to read but the light was so poor it made her eyes burn. After dropping the book on a cushion, she wandered into the kitchen.

Rosa was singing to herself as she worked, her voice a rich, velvet alto.

'That smells good. What are you cooking?'

The woman kept her eyes down. 'Milk tart.'

'Another treat for the secunde?'

'No. He's been by and gone. He drank some wine and ate five koekies, then said he couldn't wait anymore.'

Floriane felt a wash of guilt spread over her at her fearful evasion of him. With a huge effort, she asked, 'Did he leave a message?'

Rosa moved her hand to acknowledge the question, making light movements with her fingers as if the tips were touching each word. 'He said the watch on Signal Hill have seen the Texel fleet out at sea. The ships will drop anchor tomorrow, and the commander will be gone in a few days.'

Floriane felt her knees begin to shake. She picked up a bunch of summer radishes from a basket by the hearth and sank down on a stool.

Rosa must have heard the scrape of wood on stone, for she turned around to look. 'Are you not well?'

'I'm fine,' she lied. 'Pass me the vegetable brush and I'll clean the radishes for you.'

Rosa handed her a stiff-bristled brush from the sink. 'He asked if he could tempt you to meet him on the jetty at midday tomorrow. At the place where the passengers get off.'

Hour after hour, Floriane had been torturing herself asking why Merkel had asked to see her. When morning finally dawned, she stood in front of her clothes chest, wondering what to put on. *He won't notice what I'm wearing,* she thought, but still found herself dressing with more than her usual care. By the time twelve o'clock struck, she had donned a short yellow smock over a pale grey skirt she knew suited her well, and was waiting among a crowd of several hundred colonists at the head of which stood the commander, dressed in spectacular style.

The vlek reverberated to the crash of cannons, and flags flew from many gables. The news of the arrival of the fleet had run through the little town like fire in dry grass. Burghers and their families clustered on the waterfront in tight little knots to view the newcomers as they set foot on firm land.

From the end of the pier she watched the sloops row over from the nine great ships. Although the clear blue water was bright in the blistering summer sunshine, Floriane felt cold with dread as Merkel moved along the jetty, touching his hat in greeting as he wove his way towards her. She made herself walk towards him on unwilling legs, feeling as though she herself had stepped off a swaying ship, or had drunk too much wine. From beneath her peaked mourning cap she looked up into the honest brown eyes of her beloved German.

'You came,' he said.

Her chest was tight. 'Rosa is not forgetful. She gave me your message.'

For a moment they stood together by the water's edge, saying nothing, staring out across the bay. The rattling of a windlass rasped at her nerves.

Merkel was in good humour. 'What a great day. It's wonderful to see everyone out and about!'

She slowed her breathing. 'Is it?'

'Have you heard from your family recently?'

How could I have? 'Not since the last fleet dropped anchor.'

'It makes me very happy to have you by my side.'

'Does it?' Her eyes flicked anxiously to him and away again.

Merkel studied her. 'You seem a little tense this morning.'

Perhaps because I know what is coming. 'My nerves are a little strained, I admit. I was fitful last night. Was there something particular that you wished to say to me today on this precise spot?'

'The Cape of Good Hope – where two oceans meet – reminds me of us. It will always be our Cape. Our good hope. Where we first met.'

I will not cry, Floriane thought. 'The colonists also call it the Cape of Storms, because storms destroy all in their path.'

'I didn't know the weather had given that name to the vlek,' he said.

Floriane took a step away. 'We seem to be ill at ease with each other this morning, and our talk is of nothing. The unbearable heat has made my head ache. If you have something to say, please say it, that I may go home and lie down in the cool.'

She watched his lips move and forced herself to register each word.

'I've long suspected I would end up a lifelong bachelor.'

Her last hopes withered and were gone.

'But I feel my truest self when I'm with you. I had intended to time matters better today and make my announcement at the moment the new Cape commander stepped off the sloop but, if you'll pardon the pun, I fear I have missed the boat.'

Her heart was beating too fast. 'Is the new commander not to be you?'

'No, it is not. I turned down the position shortly after Arent asked me. Today I planned to reveal my greatest surprise.'

'You're talking like a nincompoop, Merkel. What's the matter with you?'

His eyes were serious, questioning. 'I love you, Floriane, and believe I can make you happy. I am asking, in my clumsy German way, if you might accept to become my wife.'

Her eyes flooded with tears. 'But I am going back to Amsterdam.'

He dipped to one knee. 'I am proposing we travel together, if you'll have me.'

Floriane held out a hand to pull him up. 'With all my heart I'll have you, you silly German fool.'

⮢ CHAPTER 45 ⮣

AT HALF PAST ELEVEN in the morning on the last day of the year, beneath an already-blazing sun, the wedding party ambled towards the tower of the church that rose up above the tiled rooftops.

Hilletje was enormously pregnant now in a soft muslin dress. 'You look gorgeous,' she told Johanna. She had embroidered Johanna's gold bridal dress with green-and-red stitching, and edged the sleeves with deep cuffs of lace. 'I'm so glad I got the dress finished in time.'

Malliet let out a sigh. 'A torch-lit procession would have been more spectacular, if you'd been agreeable to an evening wedding. There's more romance in a lighted lamp than in blinding daylight through a window, however stained and gaudy the glass is.'

Johanna smiled at them both. 'You've all spent quite enough money on my wedding as it is, and it wasn't worth the additional fees required. A midday wedding is perfect, and anyway, I don't think I could have sat still all day waiting till the sun went down to finally marry Frans.'

She walked into the church on Pieter's arm along a paper trail of golden confetti. A sword swung out from his belt as he walked, his hair long and freshly washed. It seemed to Johanna that he had become a man in the months since she'd known him, and not for the first time, she regretted how badly she'd used him. That he was now wearing her wedding ribbons on his sleeve and walking her to church so that she could marry Frans made her take pause.

'Tell me you don't think too badly of me, Pieter.'

She felt his eyes on her face. 'That's all forgotten. In my heart I knew that you would never be mine, but look at me now. In only a few months I shall be married to Malliet and there is no happier man alive than me. Truly, you were the agent of providence.'

'Frans might disagree with you today,' she said, laughing, as they entered a side door at the church.

Shortly after midday, on a signal from an official, the wedding party moved through to the room where the registration would take place.

'This is a bit different from the day we all got married,' Elke said. 'Half the colony was present.'

Johanna nodded. 'I'm glad we kept the wedding small. I didn't want the whole vlek to attend – only the people who are important in my life.'

The minister took up his book and read out the marriage proclamation. At the end of it, he asked, 'Frans de Jong, do you promise?'

Frans pushed his mother's ring onto the second finger of Johanna's right hand and, eyes locked on hers, took her face between his palms. 'Yes, I do,' he said, and kissed her.

'Johanna Timmerman, do you promise?'

382

'Yes, I do.' Johanna stole a look at the minister, but whatever he was thinking about the absence of her giving a ring, his face bore no expression. Frans had declined it on the basis that it would not be safe to wear in the course of his work, but she suspected it was because he knew she had no money to buy it.

She'd imagined this moment so often during Divine Service in Amsterdam, staring at him during drawn-out sermons across the nave. She could hardly believe the day was real. In truth, it hardly *seemed* real. When they were instructed to kneel, the church itself felt as if it were floating around them, and they were the only two people in the entire world.

As man and wife they rose from their knees, and walked together into the churchyard under a tide of flowers.

Beaming with delight, Frans raised his beribboned hat to the guests. 'Thank you, my friends, for your generosity today. My *wife* and I—' he gave her a long, adoring look '—have no adequate words with which to repay you.' He paused and took Johanna's hand, turning it over to kiss her palm. 'Thank you for making me the happiest man in Good Hope.'

She felt as if her heart might burst. 'I love you, Frans de Jong. Thank you for making me the happiest girl in the world.'

Malliet had decided that it was her responsibility to provide a feast after the ceremony. 'In the Netherlands, weddings are held from the house where the bride lives,' she'd insisted. 'As you have been in my house these past weeks, we are having it here.' She'd only told Johanna at the last minute that Floriane had asked Rosa and Angela to assist, and that they had been cooking in secret for days.

After the cool darkness of the church, the backroom of Malliet's house felt hot and bright. A long yellowwood table ran its full length, with wreaths made up of evergreen from the

Company garden, and *Zevenjaars* flowers from Malliet's own. 'Obviously they won't last seven years, and I know the stems are a bit bristly,' she said. 'But I thought the white flowers looked a bit like tiny white tulips. I know your mother grew them, so I thought it might be a way of her sharing in your day.'

The thoughtfulness was too much for Johanna, and her eyes began to mist. 'You've been such a good friend to me. You're going to make me cry.'

'If you want something that will really force tears from you, wait for the terrible verses Pieter has penned to herald the delights of each course as it appears on the table!'

Once everyone was seated, Merkel chimed his spoon against his glass and rose from his seat. 'Ladies and gentlemen – dear guests. I ask you to be upstanding and join me in a toast to the happy couple.'

Everyone leapt to their feet. Karin clinked glasses with Brigitta and clapped her hands. 'We would like to give you our gift.' She went to a side table and unveiled their surprise. 'It's a detailed replica of a windmill, in honour of Frans. We copied it from the wheat mill behind the Devil's Peak. The brick is fashioned in nougat, the wings and mill shaft are chocolate, and the canvas sails are marzipan.'

A collective 'ooh' went around the table in appreciation at the splendour of the cake. Frans looked it over, nodding his approval.

'It's exquisite,' Johanna told them. 'It's so thoughtful of you both.'

'I hope it's as delicious as it appears,' Brigitta said, looking pleased.

Excitedly, Elke stood up and said, 'And now Lisje, Lotte and I would like to give you our present. But you must step over to the window to see.'

Frans smiled into Johanna's eyes. 'Let's go and take a look.' He helped her to her feet and led her to the window. They pressed their foreheads against the glass.

'See there?' Lisje pointed to the side of the road, where a small carriage and two fine grey horses stood. It had been decked with ribbons and flowers. 'You'll need transport to reach your new home. The others helped with the costs as well, but we three did the festooning.'

It struck Johanna just then that it would not be long before she and Frans would set off on their own. She leaned in close to him and continued to hold on to his hand. 'We would never have been able to afford this ourselves, which makes the gift so thoughtful and so typical of the wonderful friends you are.' She lifted her face to her new husband. 'To us both.'

When at last it was time for the dancing to begin, Frans slipped an arm around Johanna's waist, aware that a roomful of watching eyes were waiting for them to start. 'I confess not to know a single step.'

'Nor me.' She giggled. 'Dancing was not on our curriculum at the huis. But we must jig a bit, and no one will care one way or the other if we are out of time with the music.' Sure enough, the music played, and it was not long before the floor was crowded with shuffling bodies, few with more idea about rhythm than the happy couple.

'Remember to recharge your glasses,' Pieter called. 'We must be cheerful company!'

Towards dawn – when the remains of the wedding banquet had been cleared away, all the speeches had come to an end, and the musicians had finally been shooed from the door – Floriane approached the table where the eight orphan girls were sitting.

'Merkel and I need to borrow you all for a little while – if you could spare us five minutes in the voorkamer before everyone calls it a night?'

⁓

Johanna dabbed at her face with her handkerchief. 'What is it you need to tell us?'

Floriane crossed to the window and leaned her back against the sill. 'When Commissioner de Witt was here on his inspection, he brought me letters from Mevrouw Speelman, and paperwork from the Burgerweeshuis.'

Malliet sat with her hands folded in her lap. 'Your face is very serious, Floriane. Were there more papers we should have signed?'

'No, those are all in order, but you should all have been made aware of the opportunity to pay the uytkoop.'

Johanna chased after a memory. 'Mevrouw Visser told me to pay the payment when she was close to her death. I had no idea what she meant. I thought that her mind had gone.'

'The uytkoop is a prearranged fee that allows you to name your own heirs if you should have children. If you do not exercise that option, any money you inherited from your parents' estate reverts to the orphanage account on your deaths.'

Hilletje waved a cautious hand. 'I'm about to give birth but my parents were not wealthy, so what does it matter?'

'Clara Speelman discovered that none of you – boys or girls – had been given the option of paying it under Mijnheer van Loon's management at the huis in Amsterdam. She has done so on the behalf of you eight girls, out of her own funds. Claes systematically declined to make you all aware. He skimmed off untold unclaimed funds into his own account.'

Johanna studied Floriane's face. 'Is Erick de Witt involved in this somehow?'

Floriane narrowed her eyes. 'Why do you ask that?'

With a little shake of her head, Johanna said, 'I don't know. Something that happened at the hearing.'

'Ah,' Floriane said. 'Was it when you looked over at me?'

Johanna found herself nodding. 'Yes, there was that as well. But I was thinking of when the commissioner mentioned jewels reported stolen to him in Amsterdam and no one even blinked. Except you. It just made me wonder.'

Floriane did not answer straight away. 'Let me just say that I would not be surprised to learn that those jewels did not find their way back to where Erick de Witt said they were destined to go.'

Merkel and Floriane exchanged a look and then he said, 'We intend to ask the VOC in Amsterdam to investigate De Witt's involvement.'

Hearing murmurs from her friends, Johanna glanced around at them.

Floriane gave them a moment. 'We know it's late, but we don't know when you will next be at the vlek so this has to be done now. We must ask you each to take your turn with us, so you might be read the record of what is due you with all suitable discretion. We will begin with Johanna, and ask her afterwards to send the next of you in.'

Merkel asked Floriane and Johanna to sit side by side on a woven leather bench and seated himself on a curved teak chair. While the seven others withdrew and closed the door behind them, he waited, taking long pulls on his pipe.

'Are you curious about your inheritance, Johanna?' he asked.

Perplexed, she gave a small shake of the head. 'Not really. I am grateful to Mevrouw Speelman that any children I might have in the future will receive what they are due from the Orphan Chamber, but it will amount to very little. My mother was not wealthy, and I have no memory of my father.'

Merkel fingered his stiffly waxed moustache tips. 'There has been no little mystery over your affairs in Amsterdam, but it seems Clara Speelman is a fine investigator. The one piece of missing evidence, she says, that separates you from the money left in trust to you by your parents is your family Bible. She said if that were to be found, what she had discovered would be corroborated beyond any other claim.'

Johanna rubbed the end of her nose with the flat of her palm. 'I remember when I was admitted to the orphanage as a child there being a huge to-do that our family Bible was included in my mother's estate. The regentesses were excessively agitated that it could not be found.'

Merkel finished his pipe and knocked out the ashes. 'Floriane says that you have had it all along.'

Johanna turned to Floriane. 'I entrusted it to Floriane's safe keeping. She has it still.'

Floriane's eyes were discreetly lowered. 'I have shown it to Merkel, if you will forgive our nosing into your personal affairs.'

He glanced in the direction of the door and lowered his voice. 'Your Bible is proof positive of your parentage. Your father drew his own portrait at the back of the book, alongside the image he made of your mother. He signed them both. It was he who arranged for your admission to the Burgerweeshuis, should you be left without parents. In his papers, he also acknowledged you as his child. This was unprecedented at the time in his circles, so establishing your relationship beyond question has been important.'

'Who was he?' She did not know what she expected to hear and braced herself, swallowing hard.

It was a shock when it came. 'His name was Rupert Roth. He was German, an aristocrat from an impoverished family. We don't know for certain where he met your mother, but it was probably while he was in Haarlem studying portraiture under the tutelage of Frans Hals.'

'Rupert Red-hair. So that's where I got it from. Do you know anything else about him?'

Merkel let his long, lean fingers fall between his knees. 'He was a professional soldier. Later on, he joined the Navy – possibly as a privateer.'

Elbows propped on her knees, Johanna stared at him, incredulous. 'I always used to joke he was a pirate!'

'He amassed some money, that is certain. He left it all to you.'

'How much?' She felt a frantic fluttering in her chest.

Merkel stretched his arms as wide as he could. 'About this much.'

She fell back into her chair. 'Will it be enough to repay Malliet for Olumjimi's freedom?'

'More than enough,' he said emphatically.

'Does Frans know about this?'

Merkel chewed his lip. 'No. When Commander Speelman and Commissioner de Witt agreed to let the two of you marry, they made it a condition that neither you nor Frans be told of it prior to the ceremony.'

She huffed. 'Did he really think that Frans was only marrying me because of the money?'

'He believes in caution,' Merkel said, a note of apology in his voice.

Johanna's eyes flooded as she looked at the capable hand Floriane laid on her arm. 'This is all because of you.'

'Since we became friends on the ship, you have become as dear to me as any sister I might have had. Seeing you married has been the greatest achievement of my life.'

Johanna threw her arms around her and sobbed. 'What am I going to do when you have gone?'

'You have Frans now, who loves you every bit as much as I do. I couldn't go home unless I knew you were happy.'

⇐ CHAPTER 46 ⇒

TWO DAYS AFTER HER wedding, as a warm wind smelling of fish and salt blew in from the sea, Johanna shaded her eyes against the sunshine with the flat of her hand and pressed her lips tight. From the quayside she looked down on a turquoise sea white capped and wrinkled by the breeze. On the beach, a dog pawed and barked at something in the fine white sand.

A weather-beaten East Indiaman rocked at anchor in the bay, and a barge was on its way across from the quay, sailors thrashing at the water with their oars.

Johanna stood beside her husband, consumed by the moment. The lump in her throat gave way to tears that ran down her cheeks unchecked. Twice she had tried to speak, and twice the words died on her lips.

Floriane put her arms about her and held her tight against her bosom. 'I know. I know.'

They stood for a long time, Floriane's cheek pressed against Johanna's shoulder, and let their tears come.

Eventually, Floriane took a step away, drew herself up and set her shoulders back. She coughed to clear the catch in her throat. 'This is not *adieu*. Our letters going back and forth will keep us in touch. We'll say *au revoir* for the time being, and one day we will meet again.'

Johanna clutched at her hand. 'I will never stop thinking about you. Not for a minute. I've known you for barely more than a year, but you have given me a lifetime of love.'

Across the water, they heard a shout.

Merkel touched Floriane's arm. 'The barge is here. It is time.' He nodded his head, but Johanna could see this was not easy for him either.

Floriane caught at her sleeve. 'One more thing. We are going to make a petition to the Honourable Company at East India House on your behalf. As you are now married in the Cape with the uytkoop paid, I shall ask them to release your inheritance before the due date, so that you may benefit from it as soon as possible. I know that Clara Speelman will lend her support when I ask her.'

Johanna's chin quivered. 'I owe you such a debt. Rosa, Angela and Olumjimi too.'

Floriane turned towards the sea. 'They are beyond delighted to be on board a ship as passengers. Soon they will be in a country where no slavery exists. I am so grateful to Malliet for paying their passage, given my current financial embarrassment. That dear young woman has also given me contracts to sponsor Femke, so that she will be free to make choices of her own and, if she wants to, come to Good Hope to join you all without obligation to the Dutch East India.'

Johanna rubbed her swollen eyelids. 'It was such a joy to watch them climb into the barge, on the way to their freedom. Malliet has been so generous to everyone.'

'As you sow, so you shall reap. There will be time enough in the future for you to repay her.' Floriane pulled a package from her bag and held it out. 'I almost forgot. I still have your Bible.'

As Johanna took it from her hands, behind them the Castle's cannon fired a warning shot.

'We really have to go,' Merkel said. 'Before the tide turns.'

There was anguish in Floriane's grey eyes as she stepped into the barge. 'You chased a dream, and hung on to it, and made it real. You are a true sister of Good Hope, and forever in my heart. Be happy, darling girl,' she said, and was gone.

Johanna stood on the quay watching her friend's departure. Floriane had given up her mourning clothes, thrown away her face paints, and abandoned all pretence. The sun glistened on the pearls in the back of her hair, as she sat next to the man she loved.

Johanna watched for a while before Frans took her hand and turned her away.

⁓

With a flick of Frans's long whip, the newlyweds set out in their new carriage, which they shared with a small pile of possessions and some hampers of food.

The day was hot, the air heavy with scent. For the first time, it seemed to Johanna that heat was a visible thing. The landscape quivered around her, like a horse twitching itself free from a fly.

Parting from Floriane was almost more than she could bear. 'I feel that my heart has been uprooted. If it stopped beating it wouldn't hurt so much.'

Frans nodded. 'You have a huge heart, and love everyone who touches your life. It wouldn't surprise me if that even included Claes van Loon.'

Johanna leaned close, pushed back his shock of thick, golden hair and kissed his cheek.

'I didn't love him, but I think I understood him.'

'Really?' If Frans had doubts, he did not voice them.

She slid a hand under his arm. 'He loved Floriane. Remember I saw him nearly every day on the ship and his eyes lit up every time he saw her. I think in his tangled way he was trying to give her the best life he could, but his judgement was poor, and he made too many mistakes.'

'What about the womanising? Even you can't excuse that.'

She saw his fingers tighten on the reins, and with a small shiver, she pressed in closer. 'He thought Floriane was dying, and it scared him. I think the women were a distraction because he was lonely. At the end of the day, no one wants to be on their own.'

They covered the next few miles at a trot, Frans talking alternately to Johanna and to the horses. Every so often she put out a hand and touched his cheek, delighting in the close contact that had for so long been forbidden.

'Frans,' she said at last, 'we've not talked properly about the parrot shoot. Everything happened so fast after Mijnheer van Loon impaled himself on your sword.'

Frans pulled on the reins, slowing the horses to a stop. 'It's interesting you should use those words, because as I've struggled to come to terms with what happened, I've developed the suspicion that's exactly what he did.'

'Do you really think so?' Johanna forced herself to relive the scene. She could see how Frans might be right. 'He wanted you to kill him because he knew there was no way out for him?'

He gave her a resigned smile. 'Yes. I think he did what the Romans did when they saw the game was up. I think he was goading me into running him through, and what happened in the end was exactly what he'd planned.'

She studied her hands where they lay in her lap. 'Can I tell you something else? After the wedding, Floriane and Merkel told me that they planned to have Erick de Witt investigated for his involvement. Apparently, Floriane has reason to suspect the jewels the commissioner was so eager to get hold of will not end up where they were intended to go.' She thought for a moment of Claes's reaction at the hearing when Erick de Witt had mentioned the jewels. He'd been trying to say something, but the commissioner hadn't let him go on.

Frans went quiet for a while. Finally, he said, 'So we may never know all that really happened.'

'Which is why you mustn't blame yourself, my love.' Johanna leaned in to kiss his cheek.

⁓

Their journey to Stellenbosch took a long time. Frans had taken a modest rectangular house in the shelter of a mountain when he was working on his mill. Oak trees lined the handful of intersecting streets, earning it the nickname of Eikestad. He let the reins fall onto the horses' backs as they arrived. 'Welcome to our house in Oak City,' he said, as they lurched to a halt.

Frans hopped down and ambled to the back, where he busied himself unlashing the backboard. 'I'll unload before we lose the light.'

Johanna hitched up her skirt in one hand and clambered down on fatigue-wobbly legs, using the spokes in the wheel as a step. 'I'll sort out something to eat from the hampers Floriane gave me.'

He bent low over her hand and raised it to his lips, then led her into the long narrow voorkamer with a bedroom on either side. 'The kitchen is behind this room, and there's a ladder up to the attic where we can store food and anything else you've a mind to put there. I'm just sorry I've so little to give to you other than a few sticks of furniture.'

She was startled by the disappointment in his voice. 'I dreamed of this moment when we both had nothing. I thought I'd lost you, that you had died and by some miracle you came back to me. That finally you are my husband is more than riches enough.'

He led her into the first of the bedrooms. 'Had Olumjimi not gone back to Amsterdam, it was my intention to put him here.'

'But it has no furniture.'

'When Floriane said that he would go back to the Netherlands, it seemed pointless to waste money furnishing it. I spent what little I had on the room that we are to share. Come.' He led her across the voorkamer towards the second door, which stood wide open. 'This is where we will sleep.'

Twirling on her toes, she looked around. It was a low-ceilinged room, with very little in it beyond a table by the window that bore the tools of his trade, a wooden chest and a lone chair that stood to the side. The bed was pushed against the far wall, its curtains drawn wide, a pewter chamber pot and a pair of slippers tucked neatly underneath.

Trying to appear calmer than she felt, she threw him a provocative smile. 'Shall we try out the mattress?'

He looked straight into her eyes – a long searching look – and took her hand in his. 'Are you certain?'

She spoke softly, looking down at the strong fingers that covered hers, feeling suddenly shy of her feelings. 'We've barely had a moment alone since the wedding. I don't want to waste another second.' She pulled him towards the bed, sank down on the covers and kicked off her shoes. 'I want you to know me truly as your wife.'

He stood there smiling into her eyes then he too dropped down onto the bed, slid an arm under her waist and drew her closer to him, resting his warm cheek against her own.

Her heart nearly burst when he gathered her close. 'I nearly lost you,' she murmured, running her hand up inside his shirt until her fingers found the raised flesh of his scar where the knife had done its work.

'But you didn't.' He swept her hair behind her shoulder, his lips trailing kisses along the nape of her neck. He pressed himself closer. 'I could drown in the smell of you, Johanna.'

She knew he was waiting for a sign from her that she was happy for him to go on. With a deep sigh of contentment, she yielded to the invitation of his body and turned over to face him.

Hours later, her hand caressing the back of his head, she said simply, 'I hope now you know that truly I am yours.'

⸻

The day after they arrived, with the breakfast plates already cleared away, Johanna and Frans dawdled over steaming cups of coffee. She sat with one leg curled under her. Her husband – how she lingered over that word in her mind – stretched out his long legs in front of him.

'It's customary for a husband to give his wife a wedding gift,' he said.

Johanna played with her spoon. 'Until my inheritance is released, we must draw on our huis frugality. We can only spend money on essentials.'

'And then we must pay Malliet back every penny that she's given us.'

She sighed. 'She'll never accept it and at some point, Pieter will inherit from his uncle, and then they will not know what to do with all the gold. We will have to find sneaky ways to repay her. It will be a challenge, but one we can do together.'

Frans eyed her calmly and poured more coffee into his cup.

'Don't you need to be off to work?' she asked.

'I have negotiated a rest day, because there is somewhere particular I want to take you.' Frans got up from the table. 'But getting there might be a trial for your Castle-dweller's feet.'

Johanna looked at the soft leather *veldskoen* on her feet and pushed back her stool. 'There's only one way to test out these new walking shoes.'

Outside, the spicy scent of crushed wild sage rose from the bushes as they climbed the narrow, gravelled track.

Johanna chuckled softly to herself, thinking back about the past days.

'Are you laughing?' Frans lifted an eyebrow.

'I was just remembering Olumjimi and Angela and Rosa getting into the barge. Wearing shoes.' She smiled broadly at him.

The path dipped, rose again then levelled out, like a ribbon of white silk on a rumpled green cloth. On both sides, golden bush flowers swayed in the breeze, and dense spikes of coral-red flowers grew tall out of sharp-toothed leaves.

Frans held down a springy branch for Johanna to step over. 'Olumjimi looked a trifle uncomfortable, I thought.'

'I suspect he will soon become accustomed to freedom again.' When he nodded, she asked, 'Where are we going?'

'Let's rest here,' he said, settling her on a ledge of stone. 'We have been given a wedding present, but I can't bring it to you, so we have to go to it.'

'Something else from Malliet?'

'No, from Merkel. When he was teaching me to fight, he told me he had owned a parcel of land for a long time, the grant of a visiting commissioner. Its title deed is surveyed and registered in the Company's strong book. It was always Merkel's intention to farm and set up trade when he stepped away from administration at the vlek.'

'Why didn't he sell it?'

His green eyes sought hers. 'He wanted us to have it. At the parrot shoot, he told me he had transferred the title, so the land is now ours.'

She covered her mouth and fell back a step. 'How did we come to have such wonderful friends?'

'I told you before, you touch people's lives.'

'Is it much land?'

'Eight hundred and ninety-one morgen.'

Johanna widened her eyes, her incomprehension undisguised. 'I don't know how big that is.'

'About two thousand acres.'

Flabbergasted, she leaned against the stone. 'That's . . . vast.'

He hopped up and stretched out his hand, which she took. 'It is. Let's carry on, and you can see for yourself where one day we will build a house.'

The sound of cicadas was shrill on the air when, some while later, they stood in silence, awed by the beauty of the land. The hillside fell away in front of them to a plain, its wide slopes green with young vines in neat, ordered rows.

Frans spread his coat over the grass, and they lay on their backs staring up at the wispy clouds. Johanna took his hand and laid it across her cheek. 'When I used to dream of you at the orphanage, I imagined us living on my mother's farm.'

A little frown of concentration appeared between his eyes. 'I remember.'

'I told you on the ship that I wanted to find a place where birds could come to feed.'

'You did, and when you have had enough of the sky, I have something else to show you.'

She sat up, the sun blazing down on her head. 'Where?' She mopped her face with her sleeve.

He angled his head towards the hill. 'A little further on.'

By now she was on her feet. 'Let's go. I can't wait to see what it is.'

They continued walking for a while. Her dress stuck to her back, rivulets of perspiration sliding down her spine as the two of them climbed up the rise. At the top, a beautiful lake came into view.

'Oh, my goodness,' she cried, running down to the water's edge and dragging Frans behind her.

Up to its knees in the water stood a marabou stork, its unfeathered head hunched into its shoulders. Beyond, on the far bank, a disturbed blacksmith plover hammered out its alarm call, *tink, tink, tink*. From the reeds and rushes that lined the dam, weaverbird nests hung down almost to the surface of the water.

Frans stood still a moment, a smile cracking his face. 'Olumjimi told me that the weaverbirds make their nests from woven bits of grass, but the entrance is at the bottom, which makes them vulnerable to snakes.'

'We will have to tell our children to be careful when they come and play here.' She felt herself glow at the vivid memories of the intimate night she and Frans had shared.

He turned her away from the water and pointed.

Rooted to the spot, she was stunned. 'You built a windmill,' she breathed, eyeing the wooden tower and its wheel at the far end of the dam.

'It's actually a wind-powered water pump that draws water up from an underground spring to the dam, so the lake will never dry up. Not only have we water if we decide to breed cattle or irrigate our crops, we also have a wonderful habitat for birds when you want to come up here and draw.'

A thought struck her. 'How did you manage all this in so little time?'

He thrust his hands into his pockets. 'I had help.'

'Malliet?'

'Indirectly. She asked her manumitted folk, and those with the skills came. I made the design, but they built it. That's why I couldn't get to the vlek till the end of the year, because I wanted it finished when we got married.'

She looked up at him, a flare of concern rising in her chest. 'But—'

'Never fear.' He smiled down at her. 'They were paid for their work.'

'You know me so well,' she murmured.

Frans rubbed at his face with his sleeve. 'The air's very heavy. I think we're going to get caught in the rain. We should run for cover.'

They dashed for an overhang of rock. From beneath it, Johanna watched gusts of wind fling dust around in whorls, and clouds flick across the darkening sky. As she shifted her gaze to a line of leadwood trees, lightning cleaved the horizon and the first fat drops of rain plopped onto the earth. Within seconds, the thunderstorm was smashing its anger on the thirsty ground. Despite their shelter, the rain blew in and soaked them. Then it was over as suddenly as it had come.

She put her arms behind her head and closed her eyes. 'I love weather,' she said, as Frans began to stroke her hair. His hand moved to her face, his lips soft against hers, his arm around her waist.

After a moment, she pulled away slightly. 'I'm so sorry you had to suffer so much. I never meant to cause—'

He put his lips on hers again and for a time they were quiet, clinging to each other in their sodden clothes.

Taking a breath, he whispered, 'Never doubt for an instant that I chose you, Johanna de Jong.'

She gazed up into his beloved face and threw her hands around his neck. 'We are wet through,' she said, with a smile on her lips. 'Do you think we should take off our clothes and spread them in the sun?'

'How long will they take to dry?' He spoke in his most serious voice.

She screwed up her face, pretending to think. 'Hours and hours, I'd imagine.'

⇐ AUTHOR'S NOTE ⇒

THE IDEA FOR THIS story came in two parts. On holiday in South Africa I had dinner in the lovely restaurant Catharina's, which forms part of the Steenberg wine estate in Constantia, Cape Town. The restaurant is named after Catharina Ras, the first owner of the estate. In an era when women had no legal rights, Catharina pioneered land ownership in South Africa. Her fascinating story is printed on the back of the menu and as I read it, I saw the earliest outline for the story of my character Johanna.

Born in Lübeck, Germany, Catharina Ustings was to become one of the most controversial and daring figures ever to settle at the Cape. Newly widowed at just twenty-two years old, it is said she stowed away on board a ship dressed as a man, and sailed into the Cape just ten years after the first Cape commander, Jan van Riebeeck, landed there in 1657.

The Cape was a fierce, wild place with laws to match, and no place for a young widow on her own. Catharina did not have to wait long for husband number two as the Cape was predominantly populated by men.

Hans Ras, a soldier and freeburgher, survived a knifing incident on his and Catharina's wedding day but was killed by a lion a few years later.

By the time she buried husband number four, a Swede named Laurens Cornelissen, Catharina had learned that marriage could not be relied on as a source of security and set her sights on owning land herself. (It is unclear why she chose to retain the name of her first husband at the Cape.) In 1682 she approached Simon van der Stel, the Cape's first governor, and requested twenty-five morgen of land at the foot of the Steenberg mountain. It is rumoured that they were romantically involved, but whether they were or not, he granted her request, and presented the land to her as a gift. She called the estate *Swaaneweide*, 'The Feeding Place of Swans', which I used as the working title for my book.

Catharina later approached the Dutch commissioner on his annual visit of inspection for a legal title deed for her land, which he granted in 1688. The title deed, which today is displayed in the original manor house of the Steenberg Hotel, granted her a mandate 'to cultivate, to plough, to sow and also to possess the farm below the stone mountain'.

Catharina's story gave me the bare bones of a book, but I needed more to flesh out my novel. I decided to look into the administration of the Cape of Good Hope at this time in history. My research took me to Amsterdam, from where the Dutch East India Company – also known as the VOC, the most powerful trading company of the era – administered the Cape in the seventeenth and eighteenth centuries, until British forces landed in 1795 and claimed it for King George III.

While researching the VOC at the Amsterdam City Archives, I came across a ledger of orphans who had worked for the Company. The register formed part of the records of the Burgerweeshuis – the Citizens' Orphanage – which only accepted orphaned children of Amsterdam citizens, who either had sufficient funds held in trust or a sponsor to pay for their board and lodging. The original building still stands and now houses the Amsterdam Museum, a section of which is dedicated to the former use of the building.

The male orphans were apprenticed to a guild to learn a trade such as cooping (barrel-making) or carpentry, and were then able to find employment with the VOC. It is still possible to see the glass-fronted lockers where the boys kept the tools of their trade, and I have used these lockers as the backdrop to a scene in the Amsterdam section of the book.

The female orphans were trained in skills that would eventually equip them to seek self-supporting employment, more often than not as domestic maids. Whether or not they ever scrubbed the aforementioned lockers is purely invention on my part. At the time my story is set, Van der Stel, who was then the Cape commander, had written repeatedly to the Lords Seventeen in Holland, asking for marriage maids to be found from the orphanages in Amsterdam and Rotterdam. Of the forty-eight girls requested, only eight agreed to make the voyage to marry freeburghers at the Cape.

It is true that the Dutch East India Company was in constant need of cheap labour to populate its sailing fleets that facilitated trade with the East. It is also possible to link the Burgerweeshuis orphanage with the Company through a journal – which still exists – entitled *Book of Orphans Who Went to the East Indies.* Within its pages of scrupulously kept records, it is possible to see the name of each boy, the ship he sailed on, the job he was employed to do and his fate. Any money he was owed in back payment was brought into the orphanage's account. A random entry, by way of illustration:

> Pieter Mathijsz Sparmont from Amsterdam went to the East Indies on de *Ridderschap* in 1686 as a ship's boy. Missing since the end of August 1692 in Batavia [now Jakarta, Indonesia]. 1701 still missing. In January 1705 still missing, but his estate worth 131 guilders 4 stuivers and 15 pennies brought into the orphanage's account.

It didn't take much further inspection to see that children who sailed to the East Indies often died in the service of the Company, but their unclaimed wages were returned to the Burgerweeshuis in Amsterdam. While this is not conclusive proof that the Company and the orphanage were involved in a mutually profitable arrangement, there were enough similar entries to suggest a plotline for my novel.

A final note about some other characters who are based on real people of the period, but whose timelines I have massaged in the interests of a more compelling read, and whose names, motivations and behaviour are entirely my own invention:

Erick de Witt is very loosely based on Jan van Riebeeck, the first commander at the Cape. I have borrowed some descriptions of De Witt's past from Van Riebeeck's time in Tonkin, in modern-day Vietnam, where he was dismissed for 'trading on his own account'. Whether he was trading jewels or not is my own conjecture, but that he was sent home is fact. Somehow, he managed to convince the Lords Seventeen to give him another go, and he was sent to plant the Dutch flag on the tip of southern Africa in 1657 and establish the colony on the site of what is now Cape Town.

The idea of the assault on Frans de Jong came from an incident on board *Batavia*, the flagship of the VOC before the ship wrecked in 1629 on the Houtman Abrolhos Islands eighty kilometres off the Western Australian coast. Twenty-seven-year-old Lucretia Jansz, wife of Boudewijn van der Mijlen, was on her way to the city of Batavia to join her husband. She was reported to be a beauty, and had caught the eye of the ship's captain, Adrian Jacobsz. She spurned his advances but he was not a man to turn the other cheek. One night Lucretia was assaulted in the dark by a group of men but was never able to identify the culprits.

The idea of burying Claes van Loon twice came from reading O. F. Mentzel's *The Biography of Rudolf Siegfried Allemann*. Written in 1784, the book describes the funeral arrangements of Governor Pieter Gijsbert van Noodt in 1728. Hugely unpopular with the colonists, Van Noodt was said to be cruel, obnoxious and corrupt. The real burial took place at night in secret, the corpse taken by slaves to a spot in the bush. A second official ceremony took place a day or so later, the coffin ornate but empty. The exact location of Governor van Noodt's remains is unknown, to this day.

Commander Speelman is modelled on Commander Simon van der Stel. His wife, Johanna Jacoba Six – a wealthy Dutch socialite – did not accompany him to the Cape; I found conflicting opinions as to why, so I have made up my own explanation for why her equivalent character in my novel, Clara, does not. Johanna Six's sister, Cornelia, did sail with Simon to take care of his brood of children. Johanna and Simon became estranged; after his departure from Amsterdam in 1679, they never met again.

⌒ GLOSSARY OF TERMS ⌒

In the Netherlands

VOC (Vereenigde Oostindische Compagnie) aka the Dutch
East India Company, also referred to as the Honourable Company,
or even John Company (although not in this book), was founded
in the Netherlands in 1602. It soon became the most powerful
trading company in the world, sending ships to East Asia to buy
Indian fabrics, Chinese tea, Javanese coffee, pepper, cinnamon
and other spices and trade them on European markets.

The chief departure point was **Texel**, a small island to the
north of Amsterdam – to which crews and passengers were
ferried by barge. It was a deep-water port and the fossil water,
rich in iron from Texel wells, did not spoil in the barrels as
quickly as regular water. December and January were the chief
departure times.

The **Lords Seventeen**, a council of seventeen directors,
representing the main ports or chambers in the Netherlands,
administered the VOC from East India House in Amsterdam.
Each of the directors served for a term of office of three years.
There were eight representatives from Amsterdam. Zeeland

had four; Enkhuizen, Hoorn, Delft and Rotterdam each had one. The seventeenth was nominated by the other members of the United Netherlands' independent states and was generally not from Amsterdam.

The VOC established the European colony at the Cape of Good Hope as a refreshment outpost between the Netherlands and the East so that ships could put in and take on fresh water, vegetables (grown locally in the Company garden) and fresh meat, which was obtained by trading with the local Khoisan tribes.

The Lords Seventeen ruled the nascent colony at Good Hope from the Netherlands. No member of this body of august men ever stepped foot in South Africa.

At the Cape

An equivalent council, the **Council of Policy**, was set up at the colony. It consisted of the functionaries who were responsible for running and ruling the settlement, among whom, in order of seniority, comprised:

The Commander – In charge at the Cape of Good Hope but reporting to the Lords Seventeen in Amsterdam

The Secunde – Second in command and often responsible for financial matters

The Independent Fiscal – Official in charge of law and order at the Cape

The Landdrost – Official involved in local government

Freeburghers – Former employees of the Dutch East India Company who had been freed from its control; any white male who was not a Company official.

For clarity, a **Free Black** was a person of colour not bound in slavery – usually, one released from servitude – before slavery was abolished at the Cape in 1834.

The Orphan Chamber

The establishment of the Orphan Chamber at the Cape of Good Hope arose out of the need to undertake the administration of the property of persons who died intestate and left heirs who were absent from the colony or who were minors. The property of persons who died on the voyage to and from Europe and found on board ship was also subject to the jurisdiction of the Orphan Chamber.

Author's note:

In history, the Orphan Chamber was managed by eight personnel but for the purposes of this book I have taken liberties with the structure, making the Independent Fiscal in overall charge assisted only by an orphan chamber clerk. I have also slimmed down the following functions and duties of the Orphan Chamber:

- the administration of the estates of persons dying intestate in the colony or on the voyage and leaving absent or minor heirs, as well as estates of those who had not specifically excluded the Orphan Master in their will, or had specifically appointed them even where their heirs were majors and resident here
- the registration of wills of deceased persons
- receiving and paying to present and absent claimants the portions or legacies due to them
- keeping a death register of persons who died at the Cape.

Glossary of Dutch words

Burgerweeshuis; the huis – the citizens' orphanage in Amsterdam

gracht – canal

haste je! – make haste!

kerstvloot – the Christmas fleet that set sail from Texel to the East, usually in December or January

kiepersol – parasol

kraal – animal enclosure

legger – Dutch term for a large barrel of wine, equivalent to 105 imperial gallons or 477 litres

mejuffrow – Miss

mevrouw/mevrouwen – woman/women/madam/madams

mijnheer/mijnheeren – sir/sirs

Moeder – 'Mother'; affectionate name for the housemother by the orphan children

morgen – a measurement of land, equivalent to 2.2 acres

Nieuwe Kerk – a fifteenth-century church in Amsterdam located at Dam Square

pampeon koekies – pumpkin fritters

papegaai – parrot

Papegaaiberg – Parrot Mountain

predikant – a minister in the Dutch Reformed Church

proost! – cheers!

regent – director (m.)

regentess – director (f.)

schoft, schoften (pl.) – literally 'section'. The orphanage day was divided up into four schoften.

stoep – wide doorstep or porch, equivalent to a veranda. Usually made of stone.

uytkoop – payment an orphan had to make to the orphanage, to name his/her own heirs. Otherwise any inheritance due would default to the orphanage.

veldskoen – South African walking shoe made from soft tanned leather

vlek – literally 'spot', but widely used for town or hamlet

voorkamer – front room

zevenjaars – seven years

zoetekoekies – sweet cookies

⮜ ACKNOWLEDGEMENTS ⮞

IN THE WRITING OF *The Orphan of Good Hope* very many people have helped along the way.

Five years of working with my brilliant editors Salomé Jones and Tim Dedopulos has made me so much better a writer, and I am beyond grateful to them both. With every book, I feel like we hold hands and climb a mountain till we get to the top and can breathe. Bring on the next!

Huge thanks also to my agent, Hattie Grunewald, whose calm, wise counsel kept me on track in those many moments of self-doubt. I'd have given up on this book so many times if you hadn't had my back.

I must thank my publisher Beverley Cousins at Penguin Random House in Australia for making so many helpful comments on the first draft of the book and my editor Tom Langshaw, who has taken such good care of the rewrite. Thank you also to the fantastic team at PRH – too many to mention by name – who 'got the buzz going'.

More thanks than I can put into words to my husband Harry, for his encouragement and good humour through the many drafts of this book.

I'd like to thank Malliet Pattrick and Marianne Boon for their help with the Dutch and inaccessible (to me) seventeenth-century documents. Particular thanks also to Malliet for allowing me the use of her name.

Thank you, Rolf Proske and Sandra Commerford at *Historical Publications Southern Africa*, for putting me on to the Mentzel Journals. Without your generous assistance, this story would have lacked so much historical strength. Every writer needs folk such as you both, and I am hugely in your debt.

Finally, thank you to Catharina Ras, whose life story I read on the back of a menu. You threw your knickers in the air, challenged the rules and provided the spark that inspired this book.

⪜ ABOUT THE AUTHOR ⪜

ROXANE DHAND WAS BORN in Kent and entertained her sisters with imaginative stories from a young age. She studied English and French at London University, and in 1978 she moved to Switzerland, where she began her professional career in public relations. Back in England and many years later on, she taught French in both the maintained and private sectors. Now retired, she is finally able to indulge her passion for storytelling. This is her second novel, after *The Pearler's Wife*.

THE PEARLER'S WIFE
Roxane Dhand

A distant land. A dangerous husband. A forbidden love.

It is 1912, and Maisie Porter stands on the deck of the SS *Oceanic* as England fades from view. Her destination is Buccaneer Bay in Australia's far north-west. Her purpose: marriage to her cousin Maitland, a wealthy pearling magnate – and a man she has never met.

Also on board is William Cooper, the Royal Navy's top man. Following a directive from the Australian government, he and eleven other 'white' divers have been hired to replace the predominantly Asian pearling crews. However, Maitland and his fellow merchants have no intention of employing the costly Englishmen for long . . .

Maisie arrives in her new country to a surprisingly cool reception. Already confused by her hastily arranged marriage, she is shocked at Maitland's callous behaviour towards her – while finding herself increasingly drawn to the intriguing Cooper.

But Maisie's new husband is harbouring secrets – deadly secrets. And when Cooper and the divers sail out to harvest the pearl shell, they are in great danger – and not just from the unpredictable and perilous ocean . . .

From the high seas to the deep seabed, from the latticed verandahs of Buccaneer Bay to the gambling dens in Asia Place, *The Pearler's Wife* is a stunning debut, inspired by a small yet pivotal moment in Australian history.

READ ON FOR AN EXTRACT

⤳ CHAPTER 1 ⤳

Fᴿᴏᴹ ᴛʜᴇ ᴅᴇᴄᴋ ᴏꜰ the SS *Oceanic*, Maisie Porter looked down on the wharf. The bugle sounded, signalling that all guests should curtail their farewells and go ashore. Her father had already averted his face and was walking away.

This is it, then, she thought. As she watched him vanish in the distance she could not say if he would miss her. She hoped so but in her heart she doubted it. Over the week before setting sail, Maisie had felt she was being edged towards a precipice, that her days with her family were counting down like the number of nights until Christmas Day. And now here she was, off to Australia. The bugle sounded again, and the ship slid into the stream.

Her mother hadn't bothered to see her off. Up until the last moment she had wondered if her mother might have made the effort, if only for the pleasure of seeing her go, to give the final shove that propelled her over the cliff edge, permanently out of view.

A few weeks ago, Maisie hadn't even known her cousin Maitland existed. Now she was on her way to marry him.

She hefted the leather bag at her feet and stood staring at the dot that was her father in the distance, traces of panic rising inside her again. Her heart began to pump hard against her ribcage, like a fist.

When she was a child, Maisie had thought her father was like one of the old leather reference books that lined his library shelves – something to touch only when allowed and to consult on rare and weighty matters – but like the books, he was solid and dependable. Although he was never a man to show his affection, she felt his loss like an engulfing wave.

A steward, tall and portly in his dark uniform, appeared at her elbow, startling her. He looked at her closely, in a way that made her feel exposed, like a curiosity at the circus. She became instantly conscious of her unfashionable travelling clothes, the heavy shoes that rubbed against her heels, the felt hat that couldn't quite contain her disobedient hair.

Then he blinked and smiled: a tight smile that turned his eyes to slits. 'May I be of assistance, Miss?'

His grim reproval washed over her. She knew that her face telegraphed her discomfort. She felt colour flood her cheeks, like the sting of the face slap her mother had given her when Maisie tried to protest the arrangement. She swallowed the lump in her throat. 'Might you show me to my cabin? I am travelling without my family but am to share with a Mrs Wallace.'

He consulted his list and squinted in the gloom. 'Miss Porter?'

Maisie nodded.

'Mrs Wallace is already in the cabin. I'll walk you there.'

He took her bag and pushed open the door, leading her down a flight of carpeted stairs towards the first-class staterooms.

She held on to the handrail, thinking the ceiling was too low, that her feet hurt, that she wanted to run away. The steward steered her along a narrow corridor, until he stopped with a crisp click of polished heels at a sturdy door.

Somewhere within the ship, a woman began to scream.

The ship had started to roll, its sides creaking, the roar of the engine a deep unfamiliar resonance. For a moment, Maisie braced herself against the wall and clung to the handrail. 'The lady sounds very distressed. Do you think she might require a doctor?'

'Hysteria would be my diagnosis,' the steward said, matter-of-factly. 'Happens every voyage as soon as we set sail.'

'But aren't you going to check – just to be sure nothing is seriously wrong?'

He doled out his opinion. 'Not much point. There's no pill that can cure her of this ailment. When she realises she's not going to drown, she'll stop. Simple as that. Now, here you are, Miss.' He took a step forward and knocked on the door, his touch surprisingly light.

Maisie mumbled her thanks and tried to ignore the persistent screaming.

The door opened inwards and a stout, big-jawed woman with a helmet of crinkly platinum hair appeared in the doorway.

The woman raised her eyebrows over steel-rimmed spectacles as the steward loitered. 'No need to stand there, steward,' she said, her clipped English poorly disguising her Australian vowels. 'You have already received your tip.'

The man sniffed but held her gaze for a fraction longer than was strictly polite before stepping away.

Maisie's shock at his boldness shrank her voice to a croak. 'Mrs Wallace?'

'Pompous little pipsqueak,' Mrs Wallace said, loud enough for him to overhear. 'Put an ordinary man in a uniform and he thinks he commands an army.'

She stepped to one side and gestured Maisie in. 'Come on, dear. We may as well get acquainted. We are to be roommates for the next couple of months, after all.'

Mrs Wallace was, Maisie understood, related to a friend of her mother. She had a tone of address which might easily have rivalled that of a major general. Though the older woman had been paid handsomely for her chaperoning services, her connection to home was of some comfort to Maisie, and she very much hoped they would get along.

Maisie looked round the tiny cabin. The room was spare and had a strong, clean smell, like pine trees. She took in the white rivet-studded walls, the little handbasin and tap concealed in a coffin-like upright stand in one corner, and the crisp linen sheets folded flat on the bunk beds, which were separated by a short ladder hooked over the foot rail.

'What's the matter, dear?' Mrs Wallace asked. 'You don't look very happy.'

Maisie tried to rearrange her expression into a smile. 'It's just . . . Well, this is not quite what I was expecting.'

Mrs Wallace blinked several times. 'In what way exactly?'

'I've never shared sleeping quarters before. It seems a very small space for two people. Especially in first class.'

Mrs Wallace smiled. 'You can't buy something that is not for sale, Maisie. Not even your parents, for all their money and influence. There are very few single-berth cabins on this steamship and you were simply too late to secure one.'

'Oh dear.' Maisie faltered. 'And there is no window. How shall we get fresh air?'

Mrs Wallace wagged a finger. 'You'll be very pleased when the weather turns foul, just mark my words. You wouldn't want seawater sluicing you in the middle of the night. Now, buck up dear. You need to have a wash and change for dinner.'

Maisie froze as confusion overtook her. Was she supposed to undress there and then, in front of Mrs Wallace? Whom she'd only just met? Maisie stared at the floor, fingering the top button of her jacket, aware that her eyes had become slightly damp.

Mrs Wallace coughed two or three times, as if she understood the awkwardness of the situation. 'Would you like the cabin to yourself while you change your clothes?'

Maisie nodded, pulling out the sharp pearl-tipped pin from her hat and tossing it onto the bottom bunk. Almost before it had landed, Maisie snatched it back up again and glanced at Mrs Wallace.

'Put it on the chair, dear,' Mrs Wallace instructed. 'We are going to have to learn to dance round each other, aren't we?' the older woman quipped brightly. 'There isn't enough room to unpack everything, so you will have to use your trunk as a sort of auxiliary chest of drawers. It is already under the bed. I am afraid that I have filled up the wardrobe with my own frocks, so you will have to fold your things carefully.'

Maisie felt a flicker of annoyance as she watched Mrs Wallace pat her hair into place and then squeeze past to open the cabin door. 'I shall go up to the drawing room for half an hour or so and see if I can rustle you up a cup of tea. How does that sound? And don't worry about the sheets. They've already half made up my bed and they're going to do yours while we are having our dinner.'

When she left the cabin, Maisie stood looking at the back of the door for a moment. As soon as the heavy footsteps died away, she began to unbutton her jacket.

She pulled her trunk out from under the bed and ran a shaky hand across its pitted surface. Bound with brown, wooden ribs and fastened with two brass locks, it wasn't new. She traced a finger over the initials stamped in gold on the scuffed black lid. 'Maisie Porter,' she said aloud. *What on earth are you doing here?*

Discover a
new favourite

Visit **penguin.com.au/readmore**